SHE AWAKENS BOOK 4

CAITLIN DENMAN

Copyright © 2023 by Caitlin Denman

First paperback edition January 2023

Cover Design by Dark Wish Designs
Edited by Belle Manuel

ISBN 979-8-218-10923-3 (paperback)

Allister's Map of Arealea
Shadow Mountain
Eastern Fae
Salhay
Brimes
Hugo
Rawu
Daruk
Fedum
Jerik
N
E
W
S

Contents

Prologue

Allister stops pacing and slips forward until he's right behind me, his nervous presence leaching into me. "Attina's waited an *extremely* long time for this. After every single thing she's been through, because of you and your father, this is the least you can give her. I know you're scared, but there's no hiding from this. Come out of the shadows, and say hello to your daughter, Titania."

No.

This can't be.

Titania's dead.

She died with my father and Oak months ago.

Slowly, a female figure pours out of the inky darkness of her cell. Her head's lowered, and the only thing visible—besides her lithe frame—is her hair. It's been tangled for so long it's now a tangled mop reaching down to her waist. A dark shell of what was once my mother.

My jaw drops to the floor as she creeps toward us. Allister stops his pacing and strides up behind me. His warm, reassuring hand is firm on my hip. I take a step back into his solid chest. His hand snakes around my middle, holding me tightly.

Ned moves from my side to angle himself between Titania and me. Both men protecting me, like always. We all know she can't reach me through the cell bars, but it's still comforting seeing how protective they are.

I notice her clothes are in tatters. Huge chunks of skin poke out here and there. She's still covered in dirt, but now blood splotches dot her body. Her shoulder, where I launched the wood spike through her, is covered in blood. My eyes roam the rest of her body, where blood and dirt mingle. The iron and earthy smell coming off of her coats my nostrils.

Not her blood.

My father's.

She finally lifts her head when she reaches the cell bars, and her sad, bright red eyes lock on mine. Sad because she knows what she did to Raven, Father, Oak—and me. The first night I met her flashes through my mind. Her crazed expression, the lifelessness behind her eyes—which is now gone.

The fire falling all around me. Oak's lifeless body under a broken tree.

And Father holding onto her as he said goodbye to me for the last time.

I drop my head and bring my hands up to push on it, trying to physically force the memories out of my mind. *"NO!"*

I tug on my powers. Instantly, a fireball forms in my hand, but before I know it, Allister's standing in front of me.

"No, Attina."

I make a move to get around him, but he grabs me and pulls me to him. I feel Ned slide behind me, placing his hands on my shoulder, encasing me in their body heat. Normally, I would be frightened by this, but right now all I feel is comfort and safety.

I drop the hand with the fireball on Allister, knowing it won't burn him, as I croak out, "She killed them."

Allister rubs my back. "I know. Shh, I know."

I shake my head into his chest as tears start to form. I want to be angry. I do, but with Ned and Allister here, all I feel is sorrow. She isn't my mother, just a vile Fae I want to kill. The stranger who stole my family from me.

From behind Allister, I hear, "I'm sorry, sweetheart. There's so much I missed out on, and I walk back into your life just to steal your father and Oak from us."

I almost hit Ned in the face as I swing backwards out of Allister's arms. *"Us?* You took them from *us*?"

She nervously nods, realizing she's said the wrong words.

She really thinks she was ever a part of our lives? She was gone. I don't care if it wasn't by choice anymore. I might have forgiven her prior to the night of my Awakening, but now?

No way in Hell am I forgiving her transgressions.

The ground around us starts shaking as I scream at her. Rock bricks which make up the castle above us clank together as they shake. My voice cracks, but I don't care. "Where were you for the past two decades? *Us*? You were never part of us! I grew up without you, not knowing what I was, and I was perfectly happy being ignorant of everything! Then, I get a letter written from you, and my life goes to shit! You took my father and Oak from me forever! They don't get to miraculously pop back to life like you." I look her up and down as I sneer at her. "Father was my mother and father. Oak was my best friend. They were my whole world! You are *nothing* to me. You will always be nothing."

"Hey, Attina." Allister coos next to me.

I flick my gaze over at him and point. "This man right here is the *only* reason you're not a pile of ash right now." I drop my hand and throw my head back. "You can rot down here for the rest of your miserable life, smelling the decay and shit in here until your dying days."

I notice the shaking ground stills as I twist on my heel and run out of the dungeon.

Allister says to her, "I'll talk to her Titania."

But I don't care. Nothing he can say will change how I feel.

Running down the stone alley with cells on either side. I race toward commander Demarco and James, who is still in werewolf form, whimpering.

"Aww, poor baby."

I throw my hand backwards me, calling to the liquid I hear in his cell.

"Urgh," sounds behind me as whatever liquid was there splashes in his face.

Sprinting out of the light of the lamps, Allister and Ned hold, I lift my hand above my head, tugging at the fire inside me, breathing it to life. The fire in my hand lights my way as I pass the torture room and cell which holds Henrik's hawk, Talon. The limestone brick walls of the castle suddenly feel suffocating.

I don't stop until I make it to the one being in this whole place who will understand what I'm going through.

Part One

Chapter One

Attina

When I make it back to the wooden barn, Raven's still on the ground in the middle of the alleyway in bedding in front of her stall. Her entourage has left, probably for more exciting things, all except Mylo. The sight of her blood red body and striking jet black mane and tail instantly soothe me. I breathe in the smell of pine shavings and take in the first calming breath I've had since I walked down to that gods-forsaken dungeon.

"Raven? Can we talk?" I meekly call over to her.

Mylo swings toward me and moves his head down to hers protectively. Raven's ears perk up, but I'm walking up behind her, and with her injury, she can't twist around and look at me.

"Always, kid," she answers.

I make my way to her and kneel on the ground, gently dragging my hand down her silky soft back, letting her know I'm there.

I quietly whisper, "Did you know?"

"Know what?" I hear the confusion and concern in her voice, and it's all I need to know Raven had no clue Titania was still alive.

Jumping up, I almost smack Mylo in the head—not realizing he'd moved so closely into us. Hurrying around Raven and plopping myself between her legs. Tears stream down my face in relief in the fact I wasn't the only one who didn't know she was here. I throw my arms around her neck and sob into her mane.

Raven pulls back a little, but there's not far for her to go since she can't get up. She won't be able to move on her own for awhile since that werewolf took a hunk out of her rump. "Hey! What's happening?"

"She's alive, Raven! Titania's alive!" I blubber.

Raven's breath huffs out in a rush as she panics and jerks away, like she's forgotten she can't physically get up. I lean back, push down on her, and try to soothe her by calmly shushing at her. I notice her eyes are dilated and opened wide, like a rabbit cornered by a snake. Mylo helps me by placing his head on top of hers. It seems to do the job and relaxes Raven back down to the ground.

She takes in big heavy gasps. "Where is she?" She rolls her head frantically back and forth. Mylo even lifts his head and mimics her movements, on the lookout for any threat to his mate.

I coo, "It's okay, Raven. I should have told you right off the bat; she's locked up underground in the dungeons. She can't reach us."

She finally settles into herself completely and lets out a hefty sigh. "Kid, you scared me half to death! I thought she was here in the barn with us!"

I quickly explain to her how Ned and Allister brought me to the dungeon to talk to Talon, and then urged me to see the other prisoners. How I found out James is actually a werewolf, and how I sort of attacked Commander Demarco. They then forced me to check out the last prisoner—who turned out to be Titania. And how she seemed to be lucid and normal now.

"Fuck! What is she doing here?"

I sit back, leaning on the middle of her belly between her front and rear legs. "I don't know. She tried to say she was sorry for taking Father and Oak away from us." I snottily scoff. "Like she was ever a part of *us*." I shake my head. "I screamed at her and told her I hope she rotted in that cell for the rest of her life and ran out of there. Then I came right to you."

Raven bops her head into me. "I love you, too, kid."

I wrap my arms around her and nuzzle her. "I hate that she's still alive. She doesn't deserve to breathe."

Raven pulls her head out of my grasp. "I agree."

A thought suddenly hits me and hope swells within me. "Hey, wait! A Fae's powers can't hurt them or their mate, right? Father was Titania's mate. Do you think he's still alive?"

But when I turn my head toward Raven, my hope is dashed and sorrow fills my heart again. "No, even if her power didn't kill him, everything in the area was decimated. The concussion from her devastating power would have easily killed both of our fathers."

I don't know what to say, so I simply answer, "Oh."

"Besides, she said they were dead. If she's lucid now like you say she is, then don't you think she would have figured out if her mate and companion were alive before she left them?"

I silently nod. Sometimes, I hate it when she uses logic. "So, what should we do?"

Raven pins her ears back, and a snarl lifts her lip. "I can't do much being lamed up like this, but I think you know what you have to do."

After I talk to Raven for a bit, her head starts to bob like she's about to fall asleep. It makes sense; the medicine Kalven gave her makes her ravenously hungry. Ned's constantly bringing her tons of food, and now, after she's finished her food, she's sleepy. It happens to the best of us.

Gently, I push myself up, careful not to bump into Raven. She doesn't notice my movement, and her head finally droops down onto the ground, asleep. I turn to where Mylo dutifully watches her—flinging my arm around until I grab his attention. Does he realize he can't ignore everything around him, but Raven, and still effectively protect her? I point two of my fingers to my eyes and then at Raven, then point to everywhere else around us. When he bobs his head up and down and peers around the barn, I can tell he understands I need him to keep an eye on her, and their surroundings.

I'm surprised Allister and Ned didn't chase after me when I ran out of the dungeon like a crazy person. I'm sure Ned understands I need time. He always seems to understand me in his own way. But Allister, on the other hand; either Ned talked him into giving me time, or he wanted to take care of Titania after what I said to her. I hope it's the former rather than the latter.

I feel a knot of jealousy forming in my gut at the thought of him choosing to take care of her instead of me. I know he sees her as a mother, but honestly, I don't care right now. She needs to answer for what she did.

Walking out of the barn, I decide to meander about the grounds for a while, trying to get my bearings within the court-yard blocked in by a stone wall. I make my way to the other side of the vine-covered castle, past the stone stairs into the face of the castle and I stop in my tracks along its far side.

In front of me, sits a fighting pit. Fae spar in the open space. Even having been with Allister as long as I have, I'm still shocked with how normal Fae appear. The only difference between these Fae and the humans back at sanctuary are the beautifully elongated ears these people are blessed with and some stunningly colored eyes. I reach up and run my hand over my rounded ears and make sure to drag my long brown hair over them, concealing them. I'm already bound to get some stares from these people since I'm an outsider. I don't want anyone mistaking me for a human. I'm not sure how these Fae feel about humans, and I really don't want to find out the hard way.

In front of me are two large circular dirt pits. One where Fae practice hand to hand combat, and one where two Fae are fighting with wooden swords. The first fighting pit has one muscled out male Fae facing four opponents. His cropped brown hair somehow stands up in spikes. His green piercing eyes glare at the four people circling him. His angular features, including a nose which is more beak-like reminds me of a predatory bird. Each movement he makes as he stalks in a circle is calculated and smooth, like he's in complete control of every muscle in his body.

The second fighting pit has two racks of weapons on either side. The racks are filled with swords, daggers, axes, some strange weapon which has what appears to be a metal spiked ball on a chain attached to a handle, and everything in between.

Past the two fighting pits is a long firing range where a few Fae stand, shooting arrows into hay which has been clumped and tied to appear like a real opponent. I instantly know what will make me feel better.

I make my way over to the firing range. If I shoot a few arrows, I know I'll feel more grounded, even if it's fleeting.

I'm halfway past the first ring when I hear a loud, "Hey, you!"

I spin on my heel toward the middle of the ring. In an instant, I'm faced with the man from the sparring ring. He towers over me enough that I have to lean back to lock eyes with him.

I place my hand to my chest. "Me?"

He crosses his arms and cocks his head. Do all Fae males know how to cock their heads and make it seem intimidating, or is it only the ones I've run into?

His nostrils flare and he snarls down at me, "What are you doing here?"

I shuffle back to get a better glimpse at him; craning my neck is already beginning to ache. By now, all the Fae surrounding both sparring rings are staring at our exchange.

I point to the firing range. "I just wanted to shoot some arrows and let off a little steam." I'm surprised at how meek my voice wheezes out.

Yes, he's terrifying, but I shouldn't act this frightened of anyone. I'm powerful, more powerful than any Fae here, and I need to remember that fact. I steel my back and raise my chin.

As I move, a smirk crosses his features like he's gazing down on an annoying growling puppy trying to defend its bowl of food. "This training area is for residents only. You don't belong here."

I place a hand on my hip as I jut it out. "And who are you to tell me I can't train like everyone else? Being new doesn't mean I'm not staying."

He leans his head back and laughs. "I hate to break it to you, Princess, but you are *not* staying here. The king told me as much already." His wording surprises me. Does he truly know who I am?

I narrow my eyes. "Still doesn't tell me who you are."

The man stands a little straighter, lip lifting into a snarl. "Oberon. I'm the Captain of the Eastern Fae army."

"Whatever," I say as I flip my hair behind me, trying to show how insignificant this Fae is as I turn and stalk away from him.

To my side, I hear gasps slip from the Fae watching our inte
raction. *"Human!"*

Shit! I forgot I was hiding my ears.

When I flipped my hair, it must have exposed them. I'm wrenched backwards and thrown up against the side of the castle. Vines poke into my back, and my breath is ripped away from me as Oberon's massive forearm is thrust under my chin. He jerks me off my feet until I'm choking in his hand.

Oberon growls, "What is a *human* doing here?"

Well, that answers my previous question. He obviously has no idea who I am.

Panic starts to set in as I claw at his arm and realize my fingers are just gliding off, the sweat from him sparing earlier preventing me from grabbing a hold of anything. I gasp for air like a mouse being constricted by a boa, but no air fills my lungs.

"I said, what are you doing here!" Oberon pushes me harder against the stone wall of the castle.

I raise my hand to call to my powers, but then, Oberon's eyes glaze over, and his arm releases me. I slide down the wall and bend over, gulping and coughing for air. Oberon's arms go limp at his side. From the ground, I see Allister swaggering around the corner of the castle.

He bends down by my side and begins rubbing circles on my back. He lifts his head and glares at Oberon. I do the same and notice Oberon stomps back, shaking his head like he's trying to shake a bug out of his hair.

A snarl rips from Allister. "Apologize to my mate, or I will end you."

It's strange the voice emitting from him doesn't sound like the Allister I know and love. It sounds like someone cold and deadly. I wonder if this is the voice he uses under Shadow Mountain.

Oberon's jaw hangs wide, and he takes a couple steps back. "You're—you're—"

Allister interrupts him. "Yes, now apologize to my mate, or I will crush your mind."

Oberon's eyes flick to mine, and I can see the fire and hatred plain in them as he grinds out, "I'm sorry, human. It won't happen again."

I open my mouth to correct him, but decide better of it. Sometimes being underestimated is better than being overestimated.

Next to me, Allister growls, "If you ever touch my mate again, you will cease to exist. Understood?"

Oberon nods as he turns around. He throws his arms above his head and stalks away from us. "Everyone, back to work before I run a sword through you!"

"I could have handled him, you know," I croak. I want to yell and scream at him about Titania, but after he saved me, I find the raging fire in me caused by that situation is completely doused.

A soft smile tugs at Allister's mouth. "What did I say about you not having to do everything on your own?"

I don't really have myself put back together when Kalven strides around the corner. Even with his white, milky eyes he notices us. He pinches his brows in confusion as he takes in Allister and me huddled on the ground.

He shakes his head. "I don't even want to know what weird mate thing you two are doing right now." His off-white robes sigh around him, and his long gray hair sways on the slight breeze in the air. He crouches down and latches his hand around Allister's forearm, urging him up. "You're both being summoned by the king."

"Ugh, great, what does he want now? We were just in there," Allister says more to himself than anyone else. He then gets up and bends over me. "Are you okay to stand?"

I silently nod. Allister shoots his hand out for me to grab on to, but I push him away. It's not like I don't need the help. Help would be great right now, but I don't need these Fae thinking I'm weaker than they already do, especially if they're to be our people someday.

When I rise, I release a big sigh and physically shake myself. I peer over at Kalven. "So, what does Gerald want?" I purposely call him by his first name. He's not the rightful king, and I will not acknowledge him as one. He doesn't deserve the title.

"He's going to tell you what he's decided about the two of you. He's calling a meeting in front of the entire Eastern Fae court."

Chapter Two

Attina

"Wonderful," Allister spits sarcastically.

I place my hand on his arm, drawing his attention to me. "Hey, at least we're already getting things in motion. Soon you'll be on the throne where you belong."

Allister turns, grabs my hand, and brings it to his lips. "With you by my side, my queen."

My cheeks heat, and warmth spreads in my belly.

Kalven clears his throat. "I thought I would let you know and give you some time to run up to your room and get the smell of the dungeon off of you."

I turn my head and smell my shoulder. Where there was once the smell of lavender and roses is now the smell of death. No wonder Kalven told us we needed a bath.

"Thank you, Kalven. I would hug you, but I'm sure you don't want to smell like me." I chuckle.

I walk past him, but notice Kalven grabs Allister up short, placing his hands on Allister's shoulders. "You can do this, little cub. You *are* the rightful heir to the throne. He can't throw anything at you that you can't overcome."

Allister locks eyes with him and pulls him into a hug. "I know I stink, but thank you."

Kalven jokingly coughs. "Get yourselves into a bath! That's thanks enough."

I shake my head and snicker at them. They act like such old friends. Who would have known they were separated for over a century?

Allister pulls away and wraps his arm over my shoulders, dragging me into him tightly. We begin making our way to the front of the castle, but Kalven shouts after us. "There's still time before you're called in front of the court to start working on an heir you two!"

Allister and I stop dead in our tracks. Our heads whirl toward each other, and I notice his face is as red as mine must be. I watch as redness spreads from his cheeks to his ears.

We're both silent as we walk into the castle. When we make it to our room, the tension is heavy between us. I move through the room Gerald decided to stick us in. It's vast.

The white stone walls, like the rest of the castle, are swathed in vines. In the middle of the room is a huge bed covered in blue silk sheets. My cheeks start to heat all over again thinking of what we did in those sheets a few hours ago.

I stride over to my right, over to the claw-foot bath tub. I run my hand along the long length of it, noticing it's big enough to fit two. The porcelain of it cools my heated skin. I nervously giggle and try to brush off what Kalven said. "Kalven wasn't being serious, was he?"

All of a sudden, Allister's body is up against mine. Spinning me and pressing me up against the edge of the tub. He wraps his solid arms around my middle, his body pushed against my back, heating it.

In my ear, he whispers, "He may have been. And it's important for the king to have an heir, but having children is rare within the Fae. You being half human might be different. Humans are as fertile as rabbits. But I don't want to push you into anything you don't want."

I quickly twist in his arms. "It's not that I don't want it!" I lay my head on his chest and wrap my arms around him. "It's just—we barely found each other, and we still have to take on Henrik. I couldn't imagine fighting him while I'm with child."

Allister lays his head on top of mine. "I understand. I don't want you storming into battle with our child inside you. It's hard enough thinking of you stepping into battle on your own, let alone with our child in your belly." He turns his head and takes in a deep breath, running his nose from my shoulder to my neck, devouring my scent. He clears his throat. "Would you like to take a bath?"

My chest tightens at his words. Of course, I want to bathe with this stunning man. Even with everything we've done together, I'm still nervous for this level of intimacy. I tilt my head up and lock eyes with his purple ones. I swear the blues and reds of them are swirling faster than usual. His long black hair eats up the light around it as it brushes my nose. Suddenly, I feel embarrassed, like his eyes are bearing into my soul somehow.

I drop my head back onto his chest, into his long dark hair and nod. "Yes, I'd like that."

A beaming smile crosses Allister's face. He bends down and hikes my tunic from my body, leaving me bare. I instinctively wrap my arms around my body, covering myself as much as possible. He swaggers back, his eyes pinch in a predatory stare as he hovers above me. He slowly reaches his hand out, like he's trying to not spook me. His calloused hand touches my arm covering my chest and gently pulls it away from my body.

His eyes turn dark as he takes in my full form. His hands land on either side of my shoulders and he guides me over to the bed, sitting me down. In a flash, he's kneeling down in front of me. He pulls on one of my boots, gently tugging it off and works on the next. As my boot slides off; my dagger, the one which matches my sword, clatters to the ground.

Allister's shoulders shake, and when his head jerks up to me, I see him chuckling. "I forgot you put a dagger in your boot even when we're perfectly safe and secure in my family's castle."

I place my hand gently on his chiseled jaw, "It's not our castle yet, love. It's Gerald's, and I've managed to piss him off by simply existing, so I'd rather be safe than sorry."

He grunts in affirmation, stands, and moves back to the tub. He lays his hand on the edge of the tub then turns back to me. "You want to heat this for us while I get undressed?"

I furrow my brow in confusion, stand, and with more confidence than I feel, pad over to the tub. Where there was an empty tub moments ago there is now a tub full to the brim with fresh, clear water. I whirl around, "How do other people—" But my words fall short when I see Allister. His tunic is off and his pants hang low on his hips. His abs glisten in the sunlight, vying down into his pants. My cheeks heat as my mind goes straight to what I know is under them.

Allister chuckles, and I swear he tenses his muscles more than really necessary as he gestures with his hand in circles in front of him. "How do other people?"

I shake my head and twist around; I can't concentrate around him like this. It's completely infuriating. "Um—ah—I meant to say, how do other people fill the bath tubs here if they don't have water magic like you?"

"I would assume they either know someone with water powers or they bucket the water into their rooms themselves. Although, depending on where their room is, that might be a huge undertaking."

I dip my hand into the water, feeling the pull in my gut and a fireball forms in my hand, but it instantly goes out. Hmm, I'll have to try something else. I imagine the fireball coming back into my arm, becoming one with me. I watch as the skin on my hand turns red like I'm embarrassed or in a heated moment, but this time I am able to control it. Soon, the heat from my hand warms the water in the tub.

I ease myself down into the water, sighing as the hot water hits aches and pains I hadn't even realized I had. I lean my head against the edge of the tub and close my eyes, relaxing into the feeling. Allister, as always, is silent as a mouse. The only way I realize he's next to me is by the lapping of the water as he puts his foot in. When his legs intermingle with mine, I lift my head and open my eyes.

His sculpted chest sits above the water, and he lazily hangs his arms on the sides of the tub. His face is soft as he stares at me. "Your shoulders are almost touching your ears. You must be hurting. Why don't you scoot over here? I'll rub your shoulders."

I tilt my head and narrow my eyes at him. "I'm relaxing. I don't feel like being fondled at the moment."

He puts his hands up, and his jaw drops in an innocent gesture, like he's shocked I would imply such a thing. "I only want to take care of my mate. I won't turn it into anything more than a massage. No funny business, I promise."

I can't remember the last time anyone massaged my shoulders. Hell, I can't remember if I've *ever* had my shoulders massaged, and it does sound like it would be relaxing. I guess one massage couldn't hurt.

So I shift until I'm sitting in front of Allister, but far enough away from him he can only touch me with his hands, and nothing else.

Allister's warm hands land on my shoulders, and by the gods, I didn't know how amazing a simple massage could be. A moan escapes my lips. Everywhere he touches melts as his deft hands roam over my body. He moves from my shoulders down my spine, making me lean forward, slumping to give him better access to my back.

He moves his expert hands back up to my shoulders. I hadn't noticed how tight they'd become. I didn't realize it at the time, but he was right; they were up next to my ears. I didn't know I could purr, but apparently, I can.

As he works his way across my back, my hardened muscles turn to butter, everything in me relaxes. My feet, which I've pushed into the edge of the tub, push back. I sigh as I scoot into Allister's tightly molded body. I lie against him and liquefy until he's the only thing holding me upright.

I adjust myself, and all of a sudden, I feel Allister's hardened length against my back. I shoot up into a sitting position, the water sloshing around us with my movement.

I twist around. "Hey! I thought you said no funny business!" The words come out as more of a whined shriek though, not like I'm actually being serious.

If I'm being honest with myself, after the massage, I really wouldn't mind a little funny business. Surprisingly, him taking such good care of me makes me want to take care of him.

He chuckles, and his eyes sparkle with delight. "Hey, I didn't do anything. I can't help how my body reacts to my gorgeous mate leaning against me, moaning."

I narrow my eyes at him. "I didn't moan—much."

Allister wraps his arms around me. I let out a yip as he pulls me back into him. "It was enough," he says as he leaves quick, soft kisses along my neck, making me purr.

He pulls me tighter, but I quickly lean forward, making water spill out onto the ground around the tub. I flip and prowl on top of Allister. With more confidence than I feel I climb in his lap.

My voice comes out husky, almost seductive. "You know how wonderful you make me feel, physically and emotionally?"

Allister doesn't say a word; he only silently shakes his head, his face becoming sweet and innocently wide eyed.

"Let me show you," I say and move forward.

I plant my lips on his, and it feels like a bolt of lightning shoots through me, pulling me into him. I can almost feel his need for me in the way he devours my lips, and his need is my undoing.

Chapter Three

Attina

After Allister and I are done consuming each other, and half the bath water is on the ground from our vigorous love making, he pulls out a bathing kit I hadn't noticed under the tub earlier. He soaps up a rag and rubs me down until I'm sparkling clean, and I do the same for him.

I enjoy this. He doesn't suffocate me by acting like I can't take care of myself—its satisfying.

This man knows I am perfectly capable of defending myself, even if he did step in today with me and Oberon. He knows I can take care of myself, and yet he's always trying to take care of me. Taking some of the load on his shoulders. It wasn't like this with James; he was perpetually overprotective which was one of our biggest issues. He never thought me capable of doing anything on my own. We were never equals.

Allister and I are equals; he has my back, and I have his.

When we're both clean we crawl out of the tub, Allister pads over to the side of the room where I notice a doorknob hidden among the vines. He pulls on it and opens up a closet big enough to walk into. Up on a shelf, he brings down two towels. He quickly wraps one around himself, covering his tight butt from my sight. Then he walks over and begins drying me off.

My voice comes out snarky as I say, "I can do that, ya know. You're making me feel like a child."

He stills, and his face almost appears sad as his lips droop and he stares down at his hands. "But I enjoy taking care of my mate."

I roll my eyes. I seriously cannot say no to this man. I've tried over and over, but fail every time. I cross my arms over my chest and jut out my hip. "All right, fine, but just this one time, deal?"

"Deal!" He excitedly spits out, and by the way he says it, I know this won't be the last time he dries me off. I scoff at the thought; although, I must admit, him rubbing me down does feel nicer than I thought it would.

As soon as we finish getting redressed, there's a knock on the door.

"You ready?" Allister asks.

"I will be in one second." I pick my dagger up off of the floor and carefully shove it into my boot. I straighten, twist toward him, and raise my hand to indicate the door, "All right, you can open it now."

Allister lifts his chin and confidently stalks over to our door. He swings it open wide to reveal Kalven. The graying man smiles at his old friend and peeks around him. "The beds made, I guess you guys didn't work on giving us an heir."

I'm surprised at the tone of his voice; it sounds dejected. But then, Allister whispers something under his breath, and the two men are chuckling.

Heat rises to my cheeks. I'm not sure why I'm embarrassed, but I am. I shouldn't be. I mean, Allister is my mate, we're in love and doing things people in love do. I steel my back and raise my chin, faking the confidence I lack once again. I'm not sure where my confidence has run off to today, but it needs to come back.

I stomp over to them. "Okay, you two are worse than gossiping girls. Let's head down to the throne room."

When we make it to the huge throne room doors they're already thrown open, and I can hear chattering inside. I gaze up at the doors as we pass. The ornate cougars carved on them giving me pause again, someone took an excessive amount of time and care creating these.

We march into a full room.

Children crawl up the vines snaking up the walls. Even in such a big room, their laughter drowns out all the other conversation. We make our way down the same black rug leading up to the dais in front of us. As soon as our feet touch the rug, it's like everyone in the room notices us. Suddenly, a loud room full of chatter turns into a room you could hear a pin drop in.

The first person I recognize is Ned who's standing at the back of the room among other Fae who couldn't fit on the long wooden tables packed into the room. He rubs the back of his neck nervously. I wonder how he's allowed to show up to this meeting. He's an outsider, too, right?

He dips his head at me, and I return the gesture. Allister brushes up next to me and whispers, "Hold your chin up high."

I'm sure some of these Fae heard what he said, but I'm still glad he said something; I'd almost forgotten to haul my tough facade back in place. I tilt my head up and steel my back.

As we pass by tables full of Fae, everyone's eyes lock on us. We're obviously today's entertainment.

I hear hushed voices around us saying things like, "It's that girl" and "Wow, who's the handsome Fae?"

I slice my gaze over in the direction the sound came from and a growl crawls out of my throat. A cute Fae with shoulder length blonde hair jumps in her seat, like she's realized I'm an uncaged animal with the taste for blood, and in all fairness—I might be. Allister chuckles and shakes his head, but doesn't comment on the interaction.

We make it to the foot of the massive stepped dais, and all three of us kneel in front of it. Allister and Kalven raise a fisted hand to their chests, but I refuse. I refuse to ever show this man any fake reverence.

Kalven is the first one to say anything. "Sire, I brought Allister and Attina to you."

Gerald's voice booms from above, a contrast to how he sounded the first time we met him. I wonder if this is all a show for him. "Thank you for bringing the outsiders here, Kalven. You've always proved to be a faithful servant to the throne."

Gerald then stands, his purple sparkling tunic swaying around his ankles, and makes his way down the three gigantic stairs holding up his throne. When I climbed those stairs, I literally had to crawl up them. Now, Gerald makes walking down them seem effortless. I wonder how he does it. He's not much bigger than I am; he really shouldn't be able to be this graceful.

He begins speaking as he makes his way down to us. "As most of you know, there was quite a commotion last week."

The room erupts in chatter. I want to swing around and see what all the noise is about, but I don't. I keep my eyes on the threat in front of me, just as Ned taught me, which is honestly hard with how grotesque his face is. I again understand how this face gave Allister nightmares as a child. His bloated face is so puffy it almost appears to be covered in bumps. As he makes it down to the floor where we're kneeling, he brings his head up and his hooked nose sticks high into the air.

He stops in front of me, and I let my arm hang, allowing my hand to inch back by my boot, where my dagger is stashed. Everything inside me says kill this man now, get it over with before he can do something to harm us, but I know we would immediately be killed for murdering him. Instead, I sit there, at the ready, waiting for an attack.

His dry, cracked lips open as he tilts his hand. "One of the men by the open doors was an outsider. His name is Ned, and he has requested asylum from the Western Fae." He unfurls his arms to encompass the room. "We as a people have never turned a Fae in need away. So, I would like everyone to welcome him and assist him in any way he needs."

Why does this make me feel like Ned has betrayed us? Like he's chosen Gerald over us?

He lets his hands fall and glares down at Allister and me. "Whereas these two come with a different story. The male Fae who I've been told is named Allister."

This angers me to my core. He disrespects the rightful king like this? Disrespects my mate like this? I feel a heat rising within me. I quickly peek down and notice my skin turning pink, drawing a smile to my face.

Gerald glances at my pinkened skin then tugs his head back. The motion is small and quick enough to make me doubt anyone in the throne room noticed it, but I did.

He lifts his head to the room and continues, "Allister claims to be the late king's heir. But we know the heir to the throne was turned into a mindless killer for Henrik. So, either this Fae is lying, or he's a spy."

Before I realize what I'm doing, I jump up and shout, "Bullshit!"

The room behind me takes in an audible gasp. I wheel around, turning my back to my threat. It takes everything I have to do it, but I know Allister will protect me. From the back of the room, I see Ned violently shaking his head at me, but I couldn't care less at the moment.

Below me, Allister growls, "Attina—"

I lock eyes with as many Fae in the room as possible as I continue, "I know some of you remember him. He spent his childhood in this castle." I angle my hand down, indicating Allister. "He played soldier with some of you as a child. He never forgot you. His mother, *your queen*, was taken against her will. You can't fault him for caring about the woman who brought him into this world." I search the Fae; some of them turn and talk to each other. "He became a merciless killer for Henrik to keep his mother and his people alive. He got his reputation killing Fae who would pick on weaker Fae in Shadow Mountain. His motive is, and has always been to protect. If you would give him a chance, then you'd see the amazing Fae he truly is."

From my left, I hear, "Sweet words coming from his *human* mate."

The words are filled with such roaring venom, I'm taken aback. More mutterings soar toward us as Oberon stalks out of the shadows by the dais. His thick, rope-like arms are crossed in front of him, and he lifts his lip in a snarl as his green eyes glare down at me.

Allister leaps forward, and a snarl rips from his throat. I've never heard such a guttural and primal noise rip out of him, and it shocks me. I barely notice Kalven stand up behind me and step alongside Allister. He tries to make it seem like a natural movement, like he's trying to see what the commotion is about, but I can feel the tension radiating off of him.

"Enough!" booms Gerald beside us, making me twist toward him. "We have a test for Allister to prove his worthiness. Don't you worry your pretty little head." He smiles down at me as he says the words. But instead of bringing comfort to me, his words and smile make me feel dirty, like I have a layer of grime coating my body. His eyes glisten as he notices the disgust I must have crossing my features.

He seizes the opportunity to capitalize on the moment. He slides forward, moving between Allister and me, and wraps his arm around my shoulders. He pulls me into him a little too tightly. His breath is hot against my head, and my stomach rolls at his sickeningly rancid breath.

I push back against him, but he doesn't let up. I decide I can either fight him here and make more of a scene, *or* I can play along and act like he doesn't bother me. I decide on the latter option, and I wrap my arm around his back. He turns his head and a sickeningly sweetly grin cracks his face.

His voice booms again as he playfully shakes me. "This gorgeous creature is Attina."

"*Human,*" Oberon hisses out. He obviously hates humans, and I'm suddenly hit with a thought. I wonder if all the Eastern Fae hate humans or just Oberon. Kalven doesn't seem to hate humans, but maybe he's the exception.

Surprisingly, Gerald backs away. "Silence!"

I notice out of the corner of my eye, Oberon jumps back and bows his head in submission to his king.

Gerald releases me and cuts in front of us; he turns and points to me. "She is the granddaughter of Henrik."

A few people scream, and a great commotion breaks out.

One Fae shouts, "Kill her."

Then another questions, "Henrik has a granddaughter?"

Gerald brings his hands up and down in what must be a quieting gesture, because at his movement, the whole room becomes silent. He places his hands behind his back and laces his fingers together as he turns and quietly stalks back and forth in front of us.

He drops his head and he shakes it, "I have had to keep some things from you all, and for that, I'm sorry."

I see the faces of the Fae in the room soften; a few women even bring their hands to their chests like he's a sweet baby bringing them a freshly picked flower. My mouth drops open in shock. Do they see who they are looking at? He might as well be a monster, and here everyone is gaping at him like he's some adorable newborn baby.

Gerald gazes pointedly at me. "Attina and I have talked. She is not here to harm us or overtake my throne."

"Then what is she here for?" some male voice shouts in the back of the room.

Gerald stops in front of me and whirls with his hand out, giving me the floor. "Well, she didn't seem to have a problem interrupting things earlier. So, I think before I finish telling you all I have to tell you, we should allow Attina to tell you herself why she's here."

Chapter Four

Attina

My breath catches as I slip forward. I know I already addressed all these people, but it was in defense of someone else. When I'm defending myself, I find I'm much less confident.

I hear in my head, *You can do this*. I jerk my head around and lock eyes with Allister as he smiles at me encouragingly. He said to be careful what we say when we speak through our minds since other people here could have the power to listen in, but he must figure saying that doesn't give away any secrets. It's simply him reassuring his nervous mate.

I smirk at him, but when I turn back around to the large room of people in front of me, my stomach drops. I clear my throat and quickly decide to fake this until I make it through.

"Hello, everyone, my name is Attina." I stand there awkward-ly waiting for a second too long. I quickly realize I'm not sure what I was waiting for. Was I waiting for these people to answer me back?

I silently admonish myself and begin pacing, hoping the movement will calm my nerves a little. "I am not a human nor am I a Fae. I am a mixture of the two." I bring my gaze to Oberon and send a withering smirk his way, letting him know he underestimated me. He simply lifts his lip and huffs, obviously not seeing me for the threat I am. I spin on my heel and stalk the other way, giving Oberon my back. I hope the movement shows him I *do not* consider him a threat.

People gasp and chatter again. I swear this is the chattiest group of people I have ever met in my life. It's much different from the town I grew up in, and in Sanctuary, you'd be lucky to get anyone to have a conversation with you.

I push on, "My mother was Henrik's daughter, Titania." I bring up my finger and stop, turning to the Eastern Fae people. "I think you would like to know, one of the things Gerald failed to inform you is the fact that Henrik's hawk is actually in your dungeons below us at this very moment."

A solitary shriek fills the air, and everyone in the room goes deathly still.

Gerald jumps in front of me. "Everyone, everyone, be calm! I *will* explain. You know you can trust me." His words seem to placate them.

He takes a step back, giving me the floor once more, but not before he shoots me a withering glare.

I smile sweetly at him. I'm surprised he's allowing to speak to his people again. But I guess if he didn't, he would run the risk of seeming like he can't control one little helpless, in their minds, girl.

I stride forward and begin walking between the tables, locking eyes with Fae as I go. "Yes, my mother is Henrik's daughter, but I was raised by my human father. I didn't even know I was half-Fae until recently. Henrik used his magic to turn my mother into a crazed beast, and then sent her to kill me." I lower my head. "She then killed my father—" My voice cracks. "—and her companion animal while her mind was not her own. Henrik took them from me."

I place my hands behind my back as I pace. "Shortly after, I was lucky enough to find my mate." I stop and swivel to Allister. This part of the story may just sway their thinking of Henrik's mindless killer. "Henrik sent him on a mission to exterminate me." I smile and walk over to him. I lace my fingers through his. "But as you can see, he didn't blindly follow Henrik's orders. He's not Henrik's dog. He is the heir to your throne. We *both* yearn for a better world. A world where Fae and humans can live side by side." I hear only a couple of groans at the thought, which gives me hope. I stand up straighter. "A world without Henrik."

I hear a scoff next to us. "And who'll defeat him? You, little half-breed?"

I pivot and point my index finger at Oberon. "You know what's funny about the term half-breed?"

"What?" he spits out, like I'm the dumbest thing in all of Arealea.

"My enemies, including Henrik, are the only ones who've ever called me by that name."

I hear gasps erupt around me; I whirl so my back is to the room and wink at Oberon. I swear I can see fire flickering in his eyes. By the time I turn to the room again, I've schooled my face into a solemn expression as I stare down at my hands, like his words offended me terribly.

I make sure to sound mysterious as I say my next words. "But, my mother did find something deep down in the archives of Shadow Mountain."

Everyone is silent around me, all sit facing me, enraptured by my every word. This is going better than I ever could have dreamed. "She found a prophecy saying the child born of the evil king's people and his enemy can defeat him by joining the broken clans and shedding blood together."

"And you think you're the one to do this?" Oberon snarls out. "Why should we take your word for it anyway?"

Surprisingly, Gerald cuts in, his voice high and excited. "*I* might know a way to decide if she has a chance at taking on Henrik."

I whirl around to where Gerald stands behind me. "It should be easy for the prophesized killer of Henrik to beat our army's captain, right Oberon?"

I pivot back to Oberon in time to see his green eyes darken and a sinister sneer cross his face. He straightens. "Personally, I wouldn't have a problem with it."

Ned's in the back waving his arms about trying to get my attention. I briefly lock eyes with him and see him mouth something I can't make out at me. I drift my gaze over to Allister who gives me one quick, curt nod. I copy Oberon's movement and straighten up as high as my short frame will bring me.

"Fine by me," I announce to the room.

Gerald gestures to the front of the castle. "To the sparring rings!"

Everyone jumps out of their seats and rushes for the throne room doors. People push and shove, trying to get to the sparring rings as fast as possible. I guess these people are at least a little blood thirsty. Oberon turns around and walks behind the dais, probably out some back door.

Suddenly, Allister's arms are around my middle and he's whispering in my ear, "You got this. I know you want to demolish him, but I need you to leave him with some honor."

I rip out of his embrace and swing around. "Why! He's been nothing but nasty to me. He needs to be taught a lesson." I furrow my brow and glare at him. I can't believe he would ask this of me. I want a little revenge, since when is that a bad thing?

Allister pinches the bridge of his nose before crossing his arms in front of his chest and tapping his foot in annoyance. "You do realize even after I take the throne he will still be captain of the Eastern Fae army, don't you?"

I take a stumble back. "Why would you allow him to keep his position?"

"He's a good man, Attina. I've known him since I was a child. He cares about this kingdom. He's trying to protect his people from someone he perceives as a threat."

Out of the corner of my eye, I notice Ned fighting his way through the throng of Fae still pushing to get through the throne room door.

Rather than answering Allister my eyes drift to Gerald. He sidles up next to Kalven who's now standing at Allister's back, gazing out into the room. I absentmindedly wonder if he's searching for a threat.

Gerald snarls, "I didn't realize you'd become close to this batch of misfits, Kalven."

Kalven barely peeks at him then returns to his scouting. "I'm simply making sure they don't try to sneak away, sire, nothing more."

Gerald clicks his tongue. "I hope what you say is true, because if it's not, we may have to reevaluate your loyalties and position in this court."

Kalven quickly bows to Gerald as he darts past us, behind the dais, to where Oberon snuck off to.

Ned finally makes it over to us, huffing like he's been trying to struggle up a fast moving river and finally made it to safety. I guess, in a way, he has. He rasps out, "You have no idea how much these people want to see you fail, Attina."

I shift my withering gaze to him. I know Ned didn't do anything, but I'm infuriated with Allister right now, and I can't help but let my anger bleed into this conversation.

I motion toward the door. "I already know. I saw them pushing and fighting to get outside first."

Ned adds on, "Yeah, and the more excited ones want to see Oberon smash you like a bug. Another hopes Oberon drags it out until you plead for your life."

My mouth drops open, and I throw my hands in the air, gesturing at Allister. "And you want to keep this man as captain after you become king!" I hold up one finger. "He obviously despises humans." Then a second. "He won't follow a half-human queen." And a third. "And he's openly undermined me."

Allister is calm when he answers, but I see his body tensing, giving him away. I know I'm frustrating him, but by the gods is he frustrating me in return! "Weren't you the one to point out how annoying counting off your arguments was?" Then he leans into me and whispers, "You're so hot when you're angry. If we didn't have somewhere to be right now, I would take you up against one of these walls until you yield to me."

My body responds to his words more than I want. My breath catches, and my belly gets warm and tingly. My cheeks heat, and my voice is hoarse when I turn my mouth to his ear. "Never."

He swaggers forward until I'm forced to lift my head to stare into his eyes. The wonderful smell of a forest right after a rainstorm permeates my nose, making me almost groan.

He drops his head so our noses almost touch, "You forget, you're my mate. I know ways to please you no one else in the world can."

Ned sighs next to us. "Seriously, you two! Can we not right now?"

I break eye contact first. Honestly, I can't take his intense stare, like I'm his favorite meal and he can't wait to get me alone so he can gobble me up.

Ned throws his arm out behind him. "Everyone is out there waiting for us. We need to hurry up, you two, not sit here and angry flirt."

Allister grabs my chin and forces my eyes back to him. "Beat Oberon, but leave him with some honor. Make it seem like a challenging fight. He has worked his whole life to be in the position he's in now. He's misguided by Gerald. He will see the error in his ways. I understand you wanting to demolish him, but please do this for me."

My scowl fades, and my eyes drift down to his chest. I feel my lashes brush against my cheeks as I gaze under my brow at him. "That's not fair. You know I can't deny you."

He places his hand behind my head as he pulls me into a kiss. His lips crash onto mine, his tongue staking its claim. Then, as fast as it came, the kiss ends. He pulls away. "Thank you."

From behind us, Kalven says, "All right, now everything's settled, let's get out there before they start to think you two ran away from a fight."

When we approach the sparring rings, there are Fae *everywhere*. Fae circle the fighting pit but they have also climbed up the vines on the sides of the castle and wall bordering it. But with how many Fae hang from the vines, I'm surprised they can hold all their weight.

I search the area and am glad to see none of the children from the throne room have made it out here. Children don't need to see this.

Fae chant and throw their fists into the air. "Oberon, Oberon."

I clear my throat behind the first Fae I make it to. He pivots and his brown eyes fly open wide. He hits the man in front of him and they both move to the side. In a few seconds I have a clear path to the sparring ring. In the middle of it I see Oberon. His shirt is nowhere to be seen, leaving his dark, rock hard muscles on display. He paces in the ring. I'm shocked to see him slap his face and scream a couple of times. Gerald stands in the center of the ring, scanning the faces surrounding it, probably searching for me.

Allister leans in over my shoulder as we walk. "Some warriors slap themselves to amp themselves up for a fight."

I furrow my brow, I wonder if he's actually taking this seriously. He has no reason to think he can't beat me.

When we make it to the center of the ring next to Gerald, the chanting ceases. I notice Kalven and Ned stayed at the edge of the ring; it's only Allister and me now. Oberon stops his pacing and makes his way over to us.

Gerald's voice bounces off the walls around us. "Today, Attina will fight against our captain, Oberon. If she can defeat him, we will believe her claim to being the chosen one. Magic is off limits. Does everyone here today agree?"

A thunderous, "Aye!" comes from the Fae surrounding us.

Allister leans down and pecks me on the cheek. I feel electricity arc between his lips and my skin. Then he moves away to stand between Ned and Kalven on the edge of the ring, letting me fight my own fight.

My heart swells at the thought. Him believing in me like he does means more to me than he knows.

Gerald lifts his hand in the air. "Unless there are any more questions, when I drop my hand you may begin. Ready?"

I get in my fighting stance with one leg in front of the other and my hands raised. "Ready," I answer.

Oberon throws his hand in the air. "Wait!" He points over at Allister. "He told me if I ever touched his mate again he would crush my mind."

A few people around us gasp. I have to keep myself from rolling my eyes. This is dramatic.

Oberon continues, "Do you allow me to fight your mate without repercussions from you? Even if I beat her?"

Allister's eyes narrow, and his body tenses. I can feel the anger radiating off of him even from where I stand. He just crosses his arms and gives Oberon a curt nod.

Oberon then faces me and lifts his lip in a snarl. "Okay, try not to die, little half-breed."

I growl at him as Gerald drops his hand. "Fight!"

Chapter Five

James

I pace my cell, my jaw clenched in frustration. I'm too big for this tiny cage, so all I can really do is march back and forth on my front paws. I hate this werewolf hair. It's maddeningly itchy. Why was I cursed to become a werewolf during the week of the full moon?

As a child in my tribe, being a werewolf was celebrated. We were a strong people and could take on anything with our brute force—until the Fae. The Fae, with their greed and their magic, stole everything and everyone I cared about.

Now, Allister has taken Attina. I'm imprisoned in this Fae dungeon, and the worst part is Attina isn't coming to my aid. I understand she's mad. But after everything I've done to be with her, the *least* she could do is visit me in my time of need. Doesn't she understand I need her right now? I'm sure I must disgust her in my new form, but I understood about her magic and loved her even after she hurt me with it.

My head droops, and a whine comes out of me. This isn't fair.

If I could only get out of here—maybe I could get to Allister. I'd love to rip his throat and watch as he choked on his own blood. I'd revel in Attina's screams, she'd finally learn I'm the only man for her.

Suddenly I hear grinding in the cell in front of me. It almost sounds like rocks moving against each other. I narrow my eyes, but the back of the stall is too dark, even with my sharpened werewolf vision I can't see what's happening.

"What the hell is that racket?" Commander Demarco shouts.

I roll my eyes. Even if I could answer him, I wouldn't. I figured he'd be upset when he found out I turn into a werewolf, but I honestly didn't realize how vicious he would be about it.

A ray of light enters the darkness of the dungeon. The grinding noise gets louder now, with each grind it gets brighter and brighter. Then like a damn breaking, half of the cell's back wall falls down to the ground.

In crawls a dark head, a growl releases from my lungs, and my hair stands up on end.

What fresh hell is this?

A woman stands where a wall once was. Her iridescently brown eyes lock on me, and hers widen as her jaw hangs open. Then a high pitched shriek leaves her mouth. *"James? Is that you?"*

Chapter Six

Attina

Gerald races to the edge of the arena while Oberon and I circle each other. We slowly circle each other counter-clockwise, taking in the other's actions. I can already tell he's a seasoned warrior. His anger is radiating off of him, but he's not letting it get to his head and rushing me.

He's calculating his next attack.

I don't want to be the one to move first. Allister taught me you can learn a lot from an opponent in their first strike. Considering he hasn't attacked yet, I bet he knows the same thing.

I can wait him out though.

It only takes about three more rotations until I see a crack in his resolve. His eyes flicker out into the crowd, in Gerald's direction. I bet Gerald wants this over quick. Oberon growls and fakes a lunge then pulls back. He huffs when I don't throw myself away from his feigned attack. I shoot him a shit-eating grin, and it's what cracks him.

He bellows, and this time, he hurls himself at me. His bulky muscles tighten as he dives for me. I stand there like a deer who heard a twig snap in the forest for almost too long—almost. Oberon is too big and running too fast to maneuver quickly. He's assuming I'm some dainty little thing who never needed to fight, needed to scrape, needed to survive. I counted on him thinking this way.

I didn't immediately demolish him earlier; Allister saved me, and I didn't correct him when he called me a human. I couldn't have planned this any better

At the last second, I sidestep, only leaving my leg where I was standing. He sees me move a second too late, his legs slamming into mine. The impact pounds like I had a board broke over my shin, but it's worth it.

His bulky body goes down.

Right before his face hits the ground, he throws his hands out and catches himself. He immediately whirls his head toward me and glares.

I raise my hands and shrug. "Maybe you should watch your feet a little better. Wouldn't want you hurting yourself." I take a few steps away from him. The crowd gasps, and laughter breaks out around us.

I hear Allister in my mind. *This is not the plan.*

Yes, I get this is not the plan, but I won't have someone serve me who doesn't respect me. Doesn't Allister see the only way to get Oberon to respect me is to beat him on his terms?

Oberon hits the ground with his fist, knocking up the dirt under him then jumps to his feet. His back to me, he shoves his fist under his chin and cracks his head both ways as he turns to me.

This time, he takes measured stride toward me, each footfall a planned move. As soon as he closes the distance though, he hurls a punch at me. I feel his hand fly on the air, and I block his boulder-like fist with both my arms.

But I don't realize until it's too late; it was a move to open up my side. His knee comes up and plows me in the chest, and I'm thrown sideways, the air knocked out of my lungs.

I don't care how many times my father or Ned knocked the wind out of me, I never get used to it. I gasp for air like a fish out of water.

Before I really know what's happening, Oberon has me knocked to the ground and has crawled on top of me. He has his hands locked onto my wrists, his nails dig into my skin, pushing down with all his force. I grunt from the weight of him.

You got this, love. We practiced this. And with Allister's words, I remember our training sessions back at our camp under the tree.

Oberon leans forward, taking some of the pressure off my body and whispers into my ear, "I told you to be careful, little half-breed."

When he pulls back, he grabs onto my wrists so hard, I can almost hear the bones starting to crack. I know at any second they'll snap in two.

I roar and move the way Allister taught me. I use every ounce of power I can muster to move my hands next to each other. Oberon laughs above me. "What are you doing, little mouse? Trying to get free? It's useless."

I don't expend the energy it would take to answer him. Instead, I take in deep, huffing breaths. He's a big, heavy Fae, and although I have created the advantage I need by taking away his leverage over me, getting him off of me won't be an easy feat.

I throw my hips up. The movement pitches Oberon forward just enough to knock him off balance. I quickly flip my hips, throwing him off of me. He doesn't release my wrists and drags me over with him until I'm straddling him.

I twist my wrists and jerk them out of his hands. He immediately grasps for anything to regain his hold on me. I yank one of his arms to my chest and spin my body, throwing his arm between my legs as I roll. With my legs draped across his chest, like Allister taught me, I elevate my hips. He immediately screams out in pain.

Sweat drips down my face into my eyes, making me close them. But I don't dare release my grip on Oberon. I push harder and harder with my hips into his elbow.

Good job, love. Perfect, I hear in my mind.

Right when I think Oberon's about to give up, I'm slammed by something solid from behind, and the wind is, again, knocked out of me. I let out a wail as I whirl around and see a mound of earth that wasn't there when we started. Oberon is up and grabbing at me quicker than I can figure out what's happening.

He grabs me by my long hair, right up against my scalp and heaves me up off the ground. He pulls until my head can't move back any further. I grunt from the pain. I've had my hair pulled on in the past—when I brushed my hair and I hit a knot or a branch rips out a stray hair as I raced by, but this? This feels like someone's stabbing hundreds of needles into my scalp. I bite my tongue to keep my scream down. I won't give him the satisfaction of hearing me in pain.

He wants to play dirty?

We can play dirty.

Oberon bends down. I feel his hot breath on my cheek as he snarls, "Looks like the little mouse got in over her head. You never had a chance." His breath smells sweet like he just finished eating a cake, and sweat drips from his brow on to mine.

I chuckle and watch as a fire in his eyes flares to life. I wipe his sweat from my brow. "Could you keep your sweat to yourself, please?"

He yanks my head back and forth. "Anything else to say before I end you?"

I hear murmuring around us, then Allister is in my head, *What are you doing?*

I ignore it all.

"Yes. I didn't realize we were using our powers."

Redness crawls up his cheeks into his hairline. He opens his mouth to say something. I feel the pull in my gut and will my fire to my hand. Reaching behind my head, I wrap my hand around the back of his.

He shrieks—releasing my hair, and jerks away from me, cradling his hand to his chest. I notice the bloody red flesh has already bubbled and popped. Gasps escape everyone around us, and the people closest to us take a few quick strides back.

Away from me.

Away from the threat.

I cock my head. "Wow, I haven't burned someone quite like that yet."

Oberon lifts his gaze from his hand to my face as he sways and huffs through the pain.

I straighten up, raising my chin a fraction.

I immediately hear Allister again. *Careful, you're scaring people.* He's seriously starting to get on my nerves.

I don't need his constant commentary. I can handle this.

"I tried to be friendly." I gesture to the people around us. "I wanted to become one of you. I wanted to take care of you all."

Oberon peeks between me and Gerald, not taking his eyes off of me for more than a second, like he's trying to come to some sort of conclusion. Out of the corner of my eye, I notice Gerald's brow is creased, and he's shaking his head. Oberon doesn't make a move to strike, so I march forward.

More to the crowd than to him, I say, "Oberon, hated me from the start. You made it your mission to attack me at each turn, both physically and emotionally. Then we get a chance to fight it out and put all of this behind us." I drop and shake my head. "But no, you cheat and used your powers. Little did you know how much of an advantage I have with mine. I'm assuming you only wield the power to control earth?"

I tilt my gaze back to him, but he quietly stands there in defeat, white as a ghost, gripping his injured hand against his chest.

I feel for my powers and wrap them around me as I speak. Fire, earth, water, and air dance around me haphazardly. "As you can see, *all* the elements bend to my will." I give my back to Oberon and face the crowd again. I shout so all can hear, "You said if I could beat Oberon, you would follow me. I believe I have fulfilled said requirement." I turn back and pointedly peer at Oberon, who solemnly nods. "Have I proved myself? Will you follow me?"

"Aye!" the crowd yells as one collective voice.

Gerald walks forward from the edge of the crowd. "And how exactly do you plan on overthrowing Henrik? No matter how willing my people are to follow you into battle, I will not allow them to fight without a solid plan."

I don't bother answering him; instead, I answer the surrounding Fae. "I do not have a plan yet. Gaining your support was the first key to bringing us closer to killing Henrik. Asking me to already have a plan is unrealistic." I twist my head and glare at Gerald's bumpy face. "But I *will* have a plan. I will save the humans and Fae from Henrik's destruction. And my plan will be approved by all *before* we make any moves against him." I throw my head back and shout, "We *will* be free of that monster!"

Everyone around me throws their heads back and cheer. They scream into the sky above them. I notice when some drop their heads back down, tears mist their eyes. The Fae around me raise their fisted hands to their chest, and nod before returning to the castle. Conversations abound as the Fae make the walk back to their homes.

I confidently stride over to where Ned and Kalven have made their way over to Allister. I wink at the men. "Well? Is that more or less what you were thinking?"

Allister crosses his arms and snickers. "Don't get too cocky now."

Someone clears their voice behind me. I wheel on my heel to empty air. I gaze down and see the top of Oberon's head. My eyes travel down him and see he also has a fisted hand over his chest.

"I will be forever in your debt."

I take a stumble back. "Why?"

"You could have killed me out there. I wouldn't have hesitated to kill you. But you didn't. My hand will heal. I will live to fight another day because you showed me kindness and respect today. Traits of a warrior, which I refused to give you."

I open my mouth to say something, but he pushes on.

"My sword and my life are yours until my dying day."

He lifts his head and cocks a brow, which leaves an expectant expression on his face. His admission makes me feel awkward, so I bow my head and simply answer, "Thank you."

Kalven then walks over to Oberon and places his hand on his shoulder, "Hey, how about we get you fixed up." Oberon clumsily stands up, he must be in much more pain than he's showing, and bows his head to me one last time as he follows Kalven to the infirmary.

I notice Gerald behind Oberon across the sparring ring, staring at our exchange, his head lowered. The shadow from his brow making his glaring eyes almost appear black.

Chapter Seven

James

Commander Demarco calls to the woman, "Hey, you! Get over here and let me out!"

The woman's brown eyes stay on me for far too long. Then the woman bounds down the pile of rock she created. Her hips sway, and she peers at the commander under her long lashes.

When she makes it to his cell, her voice comes out husky as she says, "Come over here, and I'll let you out, big boy." Her hand moves up and down the bar suggestively as Demarco makes his way over to her. She puts her other hand through the bars and pulls him close to her.

In a split second, she snaps and her features turn dark. She lifts her lip showing her canines and snarls, "Men are amazingly predictable."

She wraps her hand around his head. Then she slams his head into the cell bars in front of him with so much speed, there's no way the commander could have done anything about it. He falls to the ground in a loud thud, and I can smell the tang of blood.

Then the woman turns and races over to me. With my wolf sense, I can detect her smell is familiar to me, but for the life of me, I can't remember how I know this woman.

She grabs the thick metal cell bars in front of me, then takes one of her hands and places it on her chest. "James, it's me, Tala."

I jerk back and whimper. Tala was the name of my older sister who died when the Fae slaughtered our tribe. She was only a couple years older than me, so we were best friends. As kids usually do, we were completely oblivious to adult things and what was happening between the Fae and our tribe. We were playing when the Fae attacked us.

I remember a big hulking man picking her up from behind. She was kicking, scratching, and screaming, but the man still dragged her away from me. I ran after them, but out of nowhere, our mother picked me up and hauled me from the fray. She stashed me away and ran after my sister—neither of them returned.

The woman who calls herself Tala, lifts both of her hands in a calming gesture. "Shh, it's all right, JJ. It's really me. You still clench your jaw like when we were kids?"

I tilt my head and perk my ears up. I kick a tentative paw forward.

JJ was the nickname my sister gave me as a kid. She wasn't very skilled at talking yet and she couldn't figure out how to say

James correctly, so instead she called me JJ. I never told anyone about my sister, let alone her nickname for me.

How would this woman know to call me JJ?

But if she's my sister, why isn't she in wolf form? She should be in wolf form with me for two more days.

I cock my head and snarl at her.

"Wait! James, the Fae took me back with them to Shadow Mountain. One of the Fae took me in as his own. His own daughter had died, and I'm the spitting image of her. I've lived with them ever since—but I never forgot about you."

Nervously, I shift back and forth on my paws, could this be true? It sounds too good to be true.

"I thought you'd died that day. I never thought you could have gotten away from so much carnage. Hell, I was older than you, and there was no way I could have snuck away from those Fae. How did you get away? Where did you go?" Tala stands there and stares at me expectantly, like she thinks I can answer her in wolf form.

Here, answer me here, I hear in my head.

I shake my head and search around for whatever could've caused this intrusion into my mind.

James, it's me. Remember, wolves can talk to each other mentally.

I peer back at Tala. *Tala? You can hear me?*

Yes, James.

If you're Tala, why aren't you a wolf?

Tala answers out loud, "Henrik used his magic to help me with my pesky forced transformation. Now I can transform whenever I want. I just have to give him some vials of my blood whenever he asks for it." She points her nose into the air and grins, like she's proud of this. "Not a bad trade if you ask me."

Could he help me, too? I can't believe I'm asking this. Asking the man who slaughtered my tribe for a favor. But what choice do I actually have if I'm to get Attina back? By her reaction earlier, there's no way she'll want me knowing I turn into a werewolf. But if I could control when I transform, maybe she could handle that. Maybe it wouldn't be too overwhelming for her.

Tala nods excitedly. "Definitely! I'm on a secret mission for him. As long as I succeed with his mission I should be able to get him to help you. He's scary and vicious, but he will see what an advantage having you with us will be.

I war within myself about whether I should tell her about Attina. I'm sure Attina won't appreciate me running to her grandfather for help, but she'll understand when she sees my control over this monster inside me.

Maybe she'll even be happy for me.

I decide not to tell Tala about Attina yet. *How can I help?*

Tala lowers her head and glowers. "These ungrateful Fae have Talon somewhere. Do you know where they're holding him? I figured he was in the dungeons, so prior to leaving Shadow Mountain, I searched through our archives to figure out the Eastern Fae castle's layout and decide where would be best to tunnel in."

She tunneled in? I figured it was some Fae using their powers to get in, but werewolves don't have magical powers. Only brute strength. We're always stronger than normal humans, but during a shift, we could knock down mountains with our strength. I wonder if she can also tap into that strength whenever she pleases.

I hear some squawking from the other side of the room. I almost tilt my head, but decide better of it. Instead, I say into my mind, *I can show you if you get me out of here.*

She crosses her arms and juts her hip out, her short black hair sways against her chin, "Get on with it, JJ. You're just as strong as me in werewolf form. Let yourself out. I honestly don't know why you haven't already."

But then Attina... I think to myself. Then stop as I suddenly remember she can hear my thoughts.

She stands up straight, and her eyes widen as a look of recognition spreads across her features. "Are you staying in there for some girl?" She throws her hands in the air, "You're fucking kidding me right?" She paces back and forth—taking deep calming breaths, bringing her hands up and down as she goes. "You shouldn't stay locked in a cage for any woman. I don't care how amazing you think she is in bed; wolves are not meant to be caged like this. She's not worth it."

I growl and snap at her as I jump on my front end and place my paws on the bar. I lean my weight into them, and they creak against my body mass. Jumping up, I slam my paws into them. The whole front of the cell breaks off. Tala barely dives out of the way in time to keep her from being squished.

This way, I tell her as I lead her to where I heard Attina and some bird squawking. Tala trails behind me with my long strides. When we make it to the stairs leading to the dungeon, I catch Attina's scent from when she was last in here.

Attina's up there somewhere.

My body takes over, and I almost start up the stairs but stop at the base of them and shake my head. Turning around I see a bird locked in a cage in a cell. Seems overkill for a bird if you ask me.

I point my snout to the cell. *Is that what you're searching for?*

Tala finally makes her way over to where I stand. I never noticed how slow people on two legs are until now. How do they get anything done? She shrieks, and I start.

"Yes! That's him."

I ask, *Aren't you worried about all the noise we're making?*

"No, all the Fae are out in the sparring ring watching some cute little brunette fight some tree trunk of a Fae. With all the cheering and hooping, there's no way anyone can hear us."

Some cute little brunette? My stomach drops, and I forget to censor myself as I think, *Attina.*

Tala says, "So, *she's* the one you're stuck down here for." She shrugs a shoulder. "She seemed pretty tough, and she's holding her own against the Fae. I wouldn't be too worried about her." She twists around and winks at me. "If you want we can come back here later and steal her away, too."

I nod furiously; nothing would make me happier than to whisk her away from this place.

Then Tala turns back to the bird, bends over at the waist, and waves her hand at it. "Hi, Talon. It's me, Tala. I'm here to release you."

The bird snarls out, "I don't care who you are, just get me out of here."

My eyes shoot open wide, and I suck in a breath. *It—it—it talked! Did it really just talk?* I remember Raven talking, but there are more creatures out there who can talk? Seriously?

Tala throws her head back and howls as she strides over to the bird's cell. "Have you been living under a rock since the last time I saw you?"

I feel like she's scolding me, so I meekly answer, *No.*

Her canines are on display as she chuckles and places her hand on Talon's cage. "Apparently you have *a lot* to learn, little JJ." She opens the cage, and the hawk flies out, quickly finding its way out of the dungeon. "Well, are you ready to head home?"

Her words hit me. Daruk was my home for my whole life, but now it's gone. Then I was in Sanctuary, but that place didn't feel like mine. It would be nice to have a real home again. I've missed the feeling.

She walks over to me and rubs the fur on my shoulder. The one small gesture makes me feel more loved than I've felt in a *long* time. She grins at me over her shoulder as she heads down the hallway to where she broke a hole in the dungeon wall.

I follow the one person who's shown me any sort of affection for months. I hadn't realized how much I've needed kindness in my life. Attina has changed for the worse since she met that evil Fae Allister. She used to fulfill my every need. She used to be sweet and kind, now she's mean and vicious.

Now, here I am following a stranger because she's shown me a crumb of kindness. Attina and I seriously need to have a heart-to-heart. I will get this monster of mine under control, we will come back and whisk Attina away from this place, and then we can be together forever.

Chapter Eight

Attina

We leave Ned at the castle steps; he wants to check on Raven and Mylo. I told him I tasked Mylo with letting me know if there were any changes in Raven, but Ned doesn't listen to me.

"I would feel better if I could see how they're doing myself."

I shrug. "Suit yourself."

Ned peers at Allister, then back to me and awkwardly rubs the back of his neck. "Besides, I think you two need some alone time. I'm sure he was beside himself during your fight. I know I was."

"Aww, Ned!" I jump forward and wrap my arms around his neck.

He whispers into my ear, "I'm glad you're all right, but please don't worry me like that ever again. I can't take much more of it. I'm an old man, remember."

I move away from him and snicker. "I'll try not to worry you again." I raise a finger. "But no promises."

Ned shakes his head as his gaze travels to Allister. "Don't ever let her do something this stupid or reckless again. You got it?"

I turn to Allister, who bows his head. "Got it," he answers, and I'm shocked. Since when does Allister take orders from Ned? My head swivels between the two men, what is happening here?

Ned turns around and stalks off toward the barn, waving behind him.

I'm standing there stuck in shock when Allister wraps his arm around my shoulder. He twirls me around toward the castle entrance. "Why don't we take a nap? It's been a long day."

By how husky his voice is, I don't think he actually means go to sleep when he says take a nap.

"I could use a nap." I beam up at him.

As we walk up the stone stairs to our room, I interrupt the comfortable silence blanketing us. "Remember how you said you wanted to teach me how to block my thoughts?"

"Yeeess?" He drags out his words, urging me on as we make it to our room.

I start nervously picking at my thumb nail. I don't want him to take this the wrong way, but I can't have him in my head all the time. I have to be able to block him out when I want to. He was too distracting during my fight. I know he was trying to help, but I didn't need his voice in my head while I was trying to focus. We pass through our room door.

As I grasp at my rose necklace, I ask, "Will I be able to block out other people's thoughts?"

He closes the door behind me. Suddenly, he's got his arm blocking my advance and is pushing me back against the door. My head lands on a well-placed hand cradling me against the door.

In an instant, his face is right up against mine, so close our noses touch. His hands frame my face, and he leans down to me. I gaze up into his darkened gaze. His eyes mixed with the sharp scowl should terrify me, but it does the opposite. A heat rises in my belly at being this close to this infuriating man, being under such close scrutiny, and stealing his full and undivided attention.

"You don't want me in your mind?" he growls.

I stand up straighter. I won't budge on this, no matter how much I love this man. "I don't always want you in my head. Sometimes, I want my mind to be my own. You must understand."

He leans into me further.

I catch my breath.

His lips move against the shell of my ear. "But what if I want to always be inside you?"

I press on his chest, and he relents an inch. Only enough to allow him to stare into my eyes, his dark hair frames his face, making him look like an angered god. I half-heartedly push myself off the door, like I'm about to walk away, but Allister doesn't move.

"Are you trying to run away from me, little kitten?"

I don't answer him; I just glare. He hasn't flat out told me if he'll teach me how to block his thoughts or not. I don't want to argue about this. I would rather do other things to this man.

He continues, "Cause I enjoy the chase." He runs his hand up from my chest to my throat, grabbing me, forcing my head up to his—placing a rough kiss on my lips. I part my lips in a moan, allowing his tongue access to mine. I melt into his kiss. His other hand reaches around my back and pulls me into his body. I feel his excitement and moan again.

He breaks our kiss. "Do you know how beautiful you looked making Oberon bow to you?" He trails kisses down my neck as he wraps his other hand around me. "With one fight, you turned the Eastern Fae to our cause. You will be the greatest queen and wife of our time, my love."

"Wife?" I squeak out.

He pulls back, and his feral eyes search mine as he repeats, "Wife." His hand roves upward to my breast, and he crushes me back against the door. With a loud growl, his lips are back on mine. His hand travels under my tunic, his cooling touch hitting my stomach.

I groan and wrap my arms around his neck. His hands immediately slide under my butt and pick me up against the door. I wrap my legs around his waist right before there's a knock on the door behind me.

I jump and throw myself forward into Allister.

"What!" he angrily growls. "This *better* be important!"

Kalven's apologetic voice carries into our room. "I'm sorry, cub. Gerald has called another meeting. Your presence is requested."

Allister doesn't drop me. He leans down and places kisses along my shoulder. In between kisses, he answers. "Well, tell him his request is denied. We're busy."

Behind me, Kalven chuckles, and I realize he knows what we're doing. My cheeks heat, and I place a hand over my face. "I'll buy you ten minutes to get yourself together, but it's not a request."

"Fine, fifteen minutes," Allister snaps, but his eyes are soft when he gazes into mine.

"See you two in the throne room in fifteen minutes." I imagine Kalven sniggering as he turns and shakes his head.

I wrap my arm around Allister again and stare into his beautiful purple eyes. "You better put me down. We need to head downstairs."

But instead, he crashes his lips on mine, carries me away from the door, and walks me over to our bed. The silk sheets sigh as he plops me down on it.

"What are you doing?"

He stares down at me like I'm his salvation. So much love and pride fills his eyes, it makes me melt. I would do anything for this man. His voice is husky when he answers, "If you're okay with it, I don't want that asshole ruining our moment." He slowly crawls over me, allowing me the time to say no if I want, which makes my heart swell, it's always my choice. "I'd like to take hours worshiping your body, but we only have fifteen minutes. Is that all right with you?"

In answer, I rip my green tunic over my head, exposing myself to him. His mouth drops as he takes in my form. I reach up and grab his neck. I heft myself off of the bed and place my lips over his gaping mouth.

He growls and lays me back on the bed.

⋄

It ends up taking us twenty minutes to fully satiate each other. We just couldn't get enough of each other. We were both greedy, needing to touch each other, consume each other.

The throne room is packed; we're obviously the last ones here. The room gives off the smell of sweat and stale clothing you always get when people are packed together. Everyone stands when we walk in.

I think, *That's strange.*

Allister answers, *You're not used to this, but this is a sign of respect. You've earned their respect.*

A few Fae throughout the room nod, and I remind myself to be more careful with my thoughts.

I'm suddenly hit with a realization. With their heightened sense of hearing I wonder if the Fae around us could hear Allister and I make love. My cheeks flush at the thought. Kalven smiles at us knowingly when we make it over to him. I duck my head and glance away right after I see Allister grin.

Above us, Gerald shouts, "Two of our prisoners have escaped the dungeon."

The children in the room squeak. I'm not sure if they understand what Gerald is saying, or if his booming voice is what scared them. Whispers break out amongst everyone else.

"I've come to find out one of the prisoners was one of Attina's former lovers." He says it like I've had many of them. He holds his arm out toward Allister and me. "They came here and instigated a fight. Then, during said fight, two prisoners escaped! Can they really be trusted?"

My mouth gapes in disbelief. James is gone *and* he's trying to blame *me* for his disappearance?

I open my mouth to argue, but Kalven cuts me off. "Sire, you said *two* prisoners escaped. Who was the other prisoner?"

Gerald scowls down at Kalven with his vulgar brown eyes. "The Fae hawk, Talon."

Kalven twists to the room of Fae behind us. "Ah, so Henrik's Fae hawk which Attina and Allister captured and brought to us to extract information from." He takes a step forward and cradles his chin in his hand like he's thinking. He peers down at his feet as he paces in front of us. "Isn't it more plausible—" He quickly peeks up to Gerald and adds, "Sire, if I may."

Gerald curtly nods to him because what other option does he have? He wants the Fae people on his side and against us. If he doesn't allow Kalven, his right hand man, to speak it will seem like he's trying to hide something.

Kalven begins pacing again and restarts. "Isn't it more plausible Henrik sent someone here to retrieve his Fae companion animal? I mean anyone who's had a companion animal knows how intense the bond is between the Fae and their companion. Even if he's evil, he must feel something for the hawk. In the very least, he'd be furious Attina took something of his."

Oberon crawls out of the shadows. I had searched for him and couldn't tell he was there. How does he hide his hulking frame so well? "Also, when would they have had the time to steal it? Attina was fighting me, and Allister never left the ring side. I know they went up to their room afterwards and only left to head down to this meeting."

How he knows we didn't leave our room is a little disconcerting, but I'm delighted he's taking our side. Either he meant what he said after our fight or he's simply thinking through this logically.

Gerald sputters out, "Well, how do you explain her former lover escaping?"

Oberon turns up to his leader, lifts his lip and scoffs. "Come on, sire, even if she's slept with a thousand men—" He throws his arm out to Allister and me. "—she's found her mate. Why would she bother with leftovers? You haven't felt the mate pull, but let me assure you there's nothing in this world that could overpower it." He turns around and locks eyes with a stunning, busty blonde in one of the rows closest to where Oberon was standing moments ago.

I take the opportunity to grab Allister's hand and nod to him in encouragement. I've told him I love him, but I don't know if I've ever told him how I feel about the mate bond. And yes, Oberon is right, there is *nothing* in this world like it.

My eyes shift back and forth between Oberon, his mate, and Gerald. Even from here I can tell Gerald is fuming. His shoulders are heaving faster than they should with the harsh breaths he's taking. I have to admit I'm also shocked Oberon came to our aid. We didn't have to say one word for Gerald's accusations to be smashed to the ground.

Kalven picks up the conversation, "If this proves anything, it proves Attina is right. Henrik must be stopped. He has now sent one of his people into our lands." I hear angry chattering amongst the people. "He's broken into our home. And he's taken what was ours."

A few people scream, "He must be stopped! What's next? Will he steal our people? Our children?"

Allister entered the conversation, sliding away and dropping my hand. "I will not allow that!" He gestures between himself and me. "*We* will not permit it! We will fortify for the winter, we will draw our numbers, and together we will stop him!" He throws his fist in the air.

All the Fae in the room, even the little kids, throw their fists in the air and scream, "Aye!"

Behind us Gerald screams, "*Silence!*"

Everyone in the room jumps, including me.

Gerald stalks down the stairs, his eyes locked on Allister as he bounces a finger on his bumpy chin. "If memory serves me correctly, *I* am the King of the Eastern Fae, not you, Allister."

Allister snarls at Gerald before he turns his back to him. I quietly move between Allister's back and Gerald.

I stare down Gerald as I move, hoping he understands I don't trust him not to stab my mate in the back. When our backs touch, Allister says, *Thank you,* into my mind. I feel his fingers brush mine.

He then speaks to the Eastern Fae people. "I am the rightful heir to the Eastern Fae throne. Gerald told me I had to go through trials to prove it. I'm willing to do them to prove to my people I am their true king." Allister pivots toward Gerald. "I would now like to start the trials to prove this is *my* kingdom, not yours."

Gerald places his hands behind his back, rocking back and forth on his feet. A grin crosses his features, but there's something off about it, like he's holding something up his sleeve. He moves in front of us, facing the people of his kingdom. "Then we shall have him go through the Leon Quest."

The whole room goes silent.

Chapter Nine

James

*D*o *you think they'll blame Attina for our escape?* I think to Tala who sits on my back, her long black hair flowing behind her as I race through the forest, green every greens sliding through my vision. I didn't see a point in her running at my side when I could easily carry her lithe form.

With her hands wrapped in my fur, she pulls herself down closer to my ear and shouts, "Who cares? Your fur is like straw. She obviously wasn't taking care of you like she should have."

I clench my jaw and skid to a stop quicker than Tala can anticipate, and she goes flying over my head. She rolls along the ground and lets out a loud grunt as her back smacks into a tree trunk. She might be my sister, but she hasn't been in my life for decades—Attina has.

I stalk toward Tala. My anger floods through me. How could she say such a thing? I swat at her with my paw, knocking her to the ground. I snarl, *I care.*

Blood seeps out of Tala's mouth as sits up and coughs into her hand. She gazes down at her bloodied arm and my stomach drops. How could I?

I bring my head to her arm, the iron tang of blood filling my senses, and lick her arm, trying to fix the mess I just made.

She hisses in pain, her canines on full display and pushes my head away."I've had worse in Shadow Mountain. You're temper got away with you. It happens. Well, at least you didn't grow soft in your cushy human town." She chuckles.

I tilt my head. *Cushy?*

Tala stands up on shaky legs, and I instantly feel terrible. Maybe I overreacted.

She shakes her head like she's trying to clear it. Iron coats the air and blood droplets from her already healing face fling around from the motion, as she strides over to me. She stops in front of me, her brown eyes are hard as she growls, "Look, I know I wasn't there for you growing up. I honestly thought you were dead, and I was a child myself. It's not like I could go out on my own and search for you, JJ."

I hang my head; she's right.

"But, I'll always be honest with you. And right now I'm giving you a choice. Shadow Mountain is a kill or be killed world. If you leave with me, there's no turning back. I'll get Henrik to help you with his magic, but he'll want something in return."

What? I ask, and I can hear the worry in my head.

"Your loyalty. He'll want your unending loyalty, and if you double cross him, even to go back to Attina, he *will* kill you."

I audibly whimper. *So, I'll never see Attina again?*

Tala shakes her head and she lifts her hand to my snout. "We will come back and get her if she means this much to you. We will find a way."

I push my head into her tiny hand and close my eyes. *I'm sorry I hurt you. Attina's been there for me through everything. When I first showed up to her town, I wouldn't talk to anyone until I met her. Attina made me feel whole, like everything would be all right as long as I had her by my side. She's my world. She's the sun illuminating every dark day.*

"Why were you in the dungeon while she was up sparring with the Fae then?"

I crouch down and move my head to indicate she should climb back on my back.

Tala pulls her head back and narrows her eyes. "You won't throw me this time?"

I swear on Attina I won't throw you this time.

She climbs back on my back and we continue our journey.

I was in the dungeon because Attina has been brainwashed by some Fae. His name is Allister, and he's stolen Attina from me. He's convinced her she's his mate.

"Wait!" Tala shouts.

I stop, but not as abruptly this time. *Are you okay up there?*

"Attina as in Henrik's granddaughter?"

I hear the shock in her voice. I was hoping to keep this from her as long as possible. Will she still want to help me steal Attina away?

I wiggle under her as I reply. *Yes.*

"And he claims she and Allister are mates?"

Yes, I curtly respond, annoyed at her question.

I can hear the venom and malice plain in her voice as she answers, "Oh, this is going to be good. We will *definitely* steal Attina for you." She reaches down and pats my shoulder. "When we get Talon back to Henrik he'll make me his top slayer. Then, we'll steal back your beloved. You will marry Attina, and *you* will be the king of Arealea, brother."

Chapter Ten

Attina

After Gerald announced Allister would be performing the Leon Quest, he simply excused everyone, and they silently got up and left the room. Ned then made his way over to where me, Allister, Kalven, Gerald, and Oberon all stand in a circle.

"What's the Leon Quest?" I ask Gerald.

I'm sure Allister has the same question by his pinched brows, but I figure it will come off better if I'm the one who asks, instead of the one who's supposed to be the heir to the throne. You'd think an heir to the Eastern Fae throne would know something so obviously well known to all of the people here by their shocked and solemn reaction.

Gerald snickers. "Why don't you ask the heir to the Eastern Fae throne?" His eyes slice to Allister; he knows Allister doesn't know what it is either. "Being the—" He raises his fingers in air quotes. "—'heir to the throne,' he should know what it is."

I cross my arms over my chest and tap my foot on the floor in annoyance. "Because I'm asking *you*, Gerald. What is it."

He rolls his eyes, but surprisingly he answers, "The Leon Quest is the right of passage each heir to the Eastern Fae throne has to go on before they're allowed to take over the throne. It's named after the royal family line." I peek at Allister; I never asked him what his family name was. Leon is an interesting one.

"What must be done?" I press.

Kalven's eyes glide between Gerald and me as he cuts in. "The test is three part." He lifts his pointer finger. "First, we have a map he must unlock with a drop of his blood." Then, a second. "Then he must traverse an uncrossable river and make his way to the Cave of Kings." Then, a third. "There, he must prove himself worthy."

I throw my hands in the air. "Prove himself worthy? What the hell does that mean?"

Kalven places his hands behind his back and shrugs. "No one knows. All the past kings have kept it a secret. All we know is how to work the map. We don't know how to cross the river or what awaits him when he makes it to the Cave of Kings."

Gerald doesn't let me ask another question as he quickly snaps, "Oberon, go get the blood map." I can tell he's angry with the man by his tone, but Oberon doesn't seem to notice as he hurries behind the dais.

Instantly, a wave of awkwardness blankets the air. Gerald is almost fuming, and I don't blame him. His right-hand man *and* his captain stood against him and sided with the Fae trying to steal his throne. He just found out the two people he thought were most loyal to him had no real fidelity to him, it must be unnerving.

Thank goodness Oberon doesn't take long retrieving the map. He strides out behind the dais, and I'm struck by how the man exudes confidence. He exudes the confidence a king would have when he wore his crown. I wonder if that can be taught or if he's naturally confident in himself.

The rolled-up map Oberon hands the king is ancient; I can tell from here. Instead of parchment, it's made from some sort of hide. The age of the hide has made it dark, almost black. The map is tied shut by a fawn colored ribbon. On the ribbon is a blood red seal.

I squint and can barely make out a paw with claws embossed in the wax. This must be his family's seal. When Gerald unties and unfurls the map, the inside is much lighter, almost a bone white. Brown blobs dot all over the map itself.

I pinch my brow and narrow my eyes in confusion. "There's nothing special about your map." I point to Allister. "He showed me one identical to it not too long ago."

Gerald lets out an evil cackle, like I'm the stupidest being in all of Arealea. "It's called a *blood* map. Did you think this would be it?" He nods to the center of it. "What do you think all those stains are? Gravy?"

I take a glide forward with my mouth open, ready to rip him apart, but Ned's arm shoots out.

His arm slams into my chest, stopping me in my tracks. "Let's assume not everyone here has lived their whole lives in this castle. Some of us have had to scrape to stay alive. It didn't leave us much time for researching the ways of the people trying to wipe our species off the face of the planet."

Gerald growls, but Oberon smoothly answers, "From what we understand, the heir of the Eastern throne is the only person who can show what this map truly reveals. The heir needs to prick their finger and place it on the parchment."

I quickly lift my leg and whip out my dagger. Oberon's eyes follow my hand, and I watch as his face pales. I smile in satisfaction as I hand it to Allister, and he pricks his finger then hands the dagger back to me.

Oberon gestures to the map. "With a drop of the heir's blood the map will show the way to the Cave of Kings."

Allister brings his finger down to the hide and lets his blood spread out onto the page. When he pulls his finger away, nothing changes.

We wait.

And wait.

Gerald clears his throat. "Well, I think—"

Then it happens. Allister's blood touches one of the lines on the map and mixes with the ink. The ink wets. His blood quickly trails through the rest of the map and to the far east, almost off of the page, is a big squiggly line. Directly on the other side of it is a big circle, which must indicate where the Cave of Kings is located.

Everyone is left speechless.

Without a word, Oberon moves in front of Allister. I flinch to shield my mate, but suddenly Oberon is kneeling on the ground with his fisted hand to his chest. "My king."

My mouth hangs open. Out of everyone in this castle, I wouldn't think Oberon would be the first to kneel to Allister, but here he is calling Allister his king.

"Oberon!" Redness spreads from Gerald's cheeks all the way up to his forehead. He angrily huffs out, "It hasn't been proven he is the heir yet! This could all be a trick of some kind of magic!"

Oberon slowly rises and moves between Ned and Allister. I'm glad he chose to stand between them instead of Allister and me. It's a very telling movement and I appreciate it.

Oberon stares down Gerald. "We all know Henrik is the sole Fae who can perform blood magic. Besides, you aren't the only one in the castle who remembers King Leon's son. We both know Allister is the spitting image of King Leon." He points to the map in Gerald's hands. "This is the proof I needed to affirm he is our rightful king." He then turns to Allister. "You must still go through this rite of passage, but do so knowing—" His eyes dart to me for a split second. "—I am here to protect our queen from anyone who would do her harm." His eyes then flash to Gerald quickly enough that if I weren't staring, I would've missed it.

I guess he thinks I need protecting from Gerald. Interesting. I wouldn't have thought he would do any harm to me, even if

Allister weren't around, because he knows Allister would kill him. I need to be more careful around here. Allister and Ned are right. I've gotten too used to being around them and assuming all Fae are like them, but that's not the case.

Gerald's lip quirks up. "Oberon, as of this moment, you are relieved of your duties. I will find someone loyal to the throne to be the captain of *my* army."

Oberon bows at the waist. He turns to leave, but Allister puts his hand on Oberon's shoulder, stopping him. "Don't get too comfortable with your freedom. It will be short lived. When I get back, you will be captain of the army again."

Oberon quickly kneels in front of Allister once more. "Thank you, sire!"

He stands and leaves the throne room without another word.

A scowl is plastered on Gerald's face when the doors close behind Oberon. "I think we have handled everything which needed handling. If you'll excuse me, Kalven, I need to speak with you." Gerald shoves the map into Allister's hands before stalking off.

Kalven places his hands behind his back. "Yes, sire." He follows him as Gerald makes his way around the dais.

Just before Gerald gets to the side of the dais where he'll disappear from sight, Allister calls to him, "I will be leaving on my rite of passage at dawn. I expect nothing will happen to my mate while I'm gone. I don't need to explain to you what will happen when I return if I find one hair on her head out of place, do I?"

Gerald's back straightens as he whirls on his heel. He bellows, "Is that a threat? Are you threatening the king of the Eastern Fae?"

Allister lazily slips forward, cocking his head at Gerald like a predator staring at his next meal. "No, Gerald. It's a promise."

Gerald growls as he turns and exits the room, Kalven hot on his trail.

When they leave, I peek up at Allister, sadness suddenly overwhelming me. "I'm assuming I can't leave with you?"

Allister invades my space, forcing me to tilt my head up to meet his gaze. One of his hands goes to my cheek. "No, I'm sorry, kitten. I must do this one alone. But after this, I will be by your side for the rest of our lives." He drags me to him, placing a soft, sweet kiss on my lips. I feel my fire rising in me as his lips move with mine.

I sigh when he pulls away. I wish he didn't have to leave, but I know there's no other choice. I don't know how many days he'll be gone, but we need to do whatever it takes to get him on the Eastern Fae throne. "Well, are you ready to spend one more night together?"

He smirks. "Feisty little kitten, aren't we?"

I purr at him, "Always."

Following Ned, we get to the throne room doors, and Allister yanks one open, allowing me to walk through first. As I pass him, he smacks me on the butt, making me jump forward and squeak. I gaze behind me and playfully glare at him, then walk head first into Oberon's solid chest. I get knocked backward, ending up in Allister's awaiting arms. He's always there when I need him.

I open my mouth to apologize, but Oberon cuts me off. At first, I'm annoyed, but when I hear his words, my annoyance turns to warmth.

"I'm sorry, my queen." He bends his head. "I should have noticed you and moved out of your way, Your Grace."

I instantly feel uncomfortable. Not that he makes me uncomfortable, but he shouldn't be bowing to me. I still don't feel like I deserve that. I wasn't born into royalty, so I wonder if I will ever *feel* like royalty.

His gaze lifts to Allister. "My king, I just wanted to speak with you before you left on your journey. You and the queen—"

I wonder if he'll ever call me by my first name again, I went from *half-breed* to *my queen* in a matter of minutes.

"—have been placed in the room in the highest tower of the castle, if I'm not mistaken?"

Allister wraps his arm around my middle, tugging me back to him. "You are correct."

Oberon clears his throat. "With your permission, I would like to switch rooms with the Fae who lives closest to you. I would like to be by our queen's side while you're gone."

Allister releases my middle and weaves his fingers through mine, passing me and dragging me with him.

As we cruise by Oberon, Allister whispers, "Follow us to our room."

Not a question, a command from the king.

Chapter Eleven

Attina

Oberon shuts the door behind him when we get up to mine and Allister's room. "Did you not like my idea, my king?" Oberon asks the question, obviously hurt by Allister's reaction.

Allister walks past Oberon and leans on our door, crossing his arms. The smell of lavender and rose petals from our bath only hours before hits me as I walk way over to our bed and sit on it, leaving Oberon between us. He seems to realize this. His head starts swiveling back and forth between Allister and me, like he can't decide who to give his attention to.

Allister saves Oberon from making the wrong decision. "Oberon, I know you remember me. I appreciate you calling Gerald out on the fact that he's pretending he doesn't know who I am." He blows out a loud huff of air. "I know he knows me. He's probably said as much to you considering you were his captain and the person responsible for keeping this castle safe." Allister pauses.

It takes Oberon a second to grasp the fact that Allister's looking for an answer, but as soon as the realization hits him, he places his hand behind his neck and rubs it. "Yes, he did," is all he says. But it's enough.

"I figured as much." Allister closes his eyes and drops his head back against the door. He stands there for a second before he straightens and walks over to sit by my side. "In answer to your previous statement, I would love for you to take the room below ours." Allister grabs my knee. "You've made him see how tentative his hold on the throne truly is. I was hoping he wouldn't discern it until after I returned, but you bowing to me ruined my plan."

"Oh." Oberon drops his gaze to the floor, his voice is meek when he says, "I'm sorry. I already failed you, sire."

Allister stands and strides over to Oberon. He smacks his shoulder. "You can make it up to me by taking the room under ours and protecting my mate until I return."

Oberon's chest swells, and raises his fisted hand. "Aye, sire." His eyes travel to where I sit on the bed then return to his king. "She will be safe with me. You don't have to worry."

Allister tilts his head. "I better not have to." He points to Oberon's head. "Because you know what will happen if I return and something has happened to her."

Oberon's eyes shoot open. "Umm—ahh—uhh—yes. No worries, sire." His hands begin fidgeting at his tunic. "I will get the rooms switched right now." He turns to leave. Then, almost as an afterthought, he turns around and bows at the waist to Allister.

When the door closes behind Oberon, I scowl at Allister. "Why did you do that?"

Allister smiles a toothy grin, and his voice sickeningly sweet when he answers. "Do what?"

I roll my eyes and flop back on the bed, propping my arms up behind me. "You know what I mean. You scared him. He would have done what you asked without you having to scare him."

Allister bends his head down and slowly stalks toward me—like he hasn't eaten for days and he's about to pounce on his prey, and maybe he is. My belly goes loose and taut all at the same time, and a fire lights under my skin. "Fae follow power. But my father once told me they also have to be reminded of that power from time to time. If you don't remind them of your power, they start getting these crazy notions of taking your power from you."

"I doubt Oberon would be a Fae to try to take anything from you. He bowed to you immediately—even with Gerald standing right there."

Allister crawls up my body achingly slowly. He drags his nose from my belly button up my chest to my chin, taking in my smell the whole way. "Yes, but if he hadn't bowed to me, Gerald would have left you alone. Now, I'm not so sure."

I lie flat on my back and clear my throat—which has now gone dry. "What do you mean?"

Allister bends down and places a kiss on my cheek, then my forehead. "He wants to keep the throne for himself. If I go on this journey and return back as the rightful king, it takes the throne away from him."

"Yes, but what do I have to do with it?"

He jerks back and locks eyes with me, his gaze all business now. "Fae have gone crazy from losing their mate. If you die while I'm gone, it would drive me insane, and I'd no longer be fit for the throne."

All the air leaves my chest. "Oh."

Allister's eyes instantly become sultry as he crouches down and kisses the crook of my neck. "Now I have Oberon scared enough he will guard you with his life. He won't let anyone into this room without your permission. I told you he's a good man, he's just been led down the wrong path."

I scoff and roll my eyes, turning my head away from the ridiculous man above me. "Got it, you—"

But before I can finish Allister grabs my chin and draws my face back to his. His eyes are dark glazed over. He leans down—his lips devouring mine. A hand drifts down to cup my breast.

I let out a small moan, and his lips muffle the noise.

He pulls back and stares me straight in the eyes. "The biggest, strongest Fae in the Eastern Fae territory is already putty in your hands. You're going to be a better queen than we've had in centuries."

Icy coats my veins. I know this is what I've been working toward this whole time, but me? Queen? I don't know if I'll be as amazing as everyone seems to think I'll be. I wiggle out from under him and sit up, wrapping my arms around my legs.

Allister sits on the edge of the bed, his lip stuck out in a pout. "What's wrong? Did I do something you didn't like? From your reactions I—"

I cut him off, lay my head against my knees, and stare at the bed in front of me. "You didn't do anything wrong. I love the way you touch me, but it's—"

"It's what love?" Now his brows are furrowed in confusion.

I can understand his reaction. One minute we're all over each other and then the next I'm worming my way away from him and curled in a ball.

"Queen. I can't think of myself as a queen." I worry at my rose necklace. "Why would *anyone* listen to a queen who's different from them? I grew up as a human, not a Fae. Everyone outside around the sparring ring heard Oberon call me a half-breed and he's right I am a half-breed. I don't belong with the humans or the Fae. I belong nowhere."

As soon as my words leave my mouth, Allister shoots up and scoots over to my side. He sits down on the bed and drags me into his lap. "You belong with me." He places his forehead down on mine as he takes a deep breath. "You were born to be by my side. By my side means being my queen. You were born to be queen. Don't you see?"

I shake my head against his.

He chuckles. "Yes, you do. You're the smartest person I've ever met. I know you understand what I'm saying."

And he's right, I do understand. I hate admitting he's right, but this time he is. If we're mates, and he's the heir to the Eastern Fae throne, then whether I feel worthy or not, I was born to be his queen. If I don't feel worthy, then I need to work on myself until I do. I let out a long breath, calming myself. My shoulders sag as the tension releases from them.

Allister picks me up and lays me on the bed in one swift motion. My legs hang off the side of the bed and suddenly, he's kneeling in front of me and has my pants pulled off. Fire lights my cheeks.

"What are you doing?" I croak out.

A devilish smile crosses his face like he's privy to some secret I know nothing about. He says, "Kneeling before the future queen." Then his head shoots under my tunic, and I yip in surprise.

The silky sheets glide along my skin as I try to scramble back away from him on instinct alone, but he wraps his hands around my knees, holding me in place. As his tongue touches me, all thought of escaping leaves my mind. I lean back, a moan leaving my lips.

His tongue is magical. I'm not sure this isn't one of his powers. He knows exactly where to touch me to make my body catch fire.

"Allister," I moan.

He slips a finger inside me, making my back arch, and my breaths come in pants as I feel myself coming closer to an edge.

I roll my hips against him, pushing his finger deeper inside me. My panting ratchets up a notch, and just as I'm about to reach my release, Allister's head pops up out from under my tunic.

I groan. "Why'd you stop?"

His eyes roam over my body and turn dark. He must see the flush to my skin and the way I can't catch my breath. His voice is husky as he answers. "I'm not done with you yet. Being the future queen is an extremely demanding job. Are you up for the task?"

I eagerly nod.

Allister slowly undresses in front of me. Each article of clothing he takes off slower than the last, allowing me to take in his strong, sensual form. He has muscles in all the right places, and I swear he's flexing each and every one of them as he moves. His tunic comes off, and I almost drool at his rippling abs. Next are his pants. He ever-so-slowly unbuttons them and inches them off of him. His thick impressive length springs free of its confines.

My mouth goes dry, and I gulp as my body goes loose and warmth spreads between my legs. Allister predatorily crawls over me. "You know that power of yours always gives you away."

I knit my brow in confusion. As I open my mouth to ask him what he could possibly be talking about, my eyes drift down to my skin, and I see it's reddening. My cheeks heat, but with the color of my skin I doubt anyone could tell the difference.

Allister's lips crash onto mine. His tongue sweeps across my lips, asking to be invited in. I open my mouth and he claims me.

He breaks our kiss, leaving me breathless. His lips move to my cheeks, and in between landing soft kisses on my cheeks, he says, "I don't know how many times I have to tell you, you don't have to be embarrassed. It's the sexiest thing I've ever seen in my life."

I gasp, how could he have known I was embarrassed when my whole body is red, not just my cheeks. I lean back and stare into his eyes. "You mean it?"

He chuckles as he leans his face into my neck. He runs his nose up the length of my neck, taking in my scent. "Yes. And I'll keep reminding you how sexy you are until you realize it yourself."

As the words leave his lips, he runs his hand down my side, down to my butt, and grabs on. A sigh releases from me. His hand sweeps up and shoots under my tunic. He massages my breast. Pinching my nipple, forcing a grunt from me, and making my back arch again. His hand pushes up the side of my tunic. I know what he wants, so I grab the hem of the fabric, and in one swift motion, yank it up and over my head, leaving me bare under him.

His eyes travel down my body, and his eyes glaze over in lust. A growl escapes him as I feel his hardened length at my entrance. He stills, pulls back, and searches my eyes, asking for permission to continue.

I run my nails down his back a little harder than I normally would, and he lifts his head to the ceiling and bows his back against the sensation. "I want you, Allister. I will want you for the rest of our lives. You make me whole."

His gaze drops back to me. When my words hit his ears, his body tenses and his eyes soften. He pushes forward, sheathing himself inside of me.

I groan as my body accommodates his girth. He moves inside me over and over. I wrap my arms around his neck and crash my lips onto his. I bite onto his bottom lip as I fall apart around him, reaching my climax. I feel him smile against my lips then, in one motion, he flips us over so I'm straddling him. I'm surprised to realize, somehow he's still inside me.

He sits forward and props himself up with his hands behind him. Leaning forward, he whispers into my ear, "Now it's your turn to please your king."

I let out a low growl as I move on top of him. He takes one of his hands from behind him and places it on my hip, guiding me. Then his hand moves to my breast. He palms my breast as he throws his head back and groans in pleasure. His hand slides to my neck where he latches on and we lock eyes.

Spurred on by his moans of pleasure, I move faster. He wraps his arm around me and tugs me to his chest. Then he's pumping himself inside me. In and out until I think I can't handle how fast he's going.

Pressure builds inside me until all I am is sensation.

A scream rips from my throat as he pulses inside me, his seed spilling into me. I bring my forehead down to his as I pant on top of him. Allister wraps his arms around my middle, dragging me close to him. As he buries his face in my chest he tightens his grip on me like he's he hasn't drank water for days and I'm his own personal oasis. I glance behind him and see the sheets steaming, but they didn't catch on fire like the first time we had sex. Progress. I'm controlling my fire better already.

Allister moves his head and starts placing soft kisses all over my chest. He dips to my breast, sucking on my nipple. I buck in response and push him away. I glare down at him as I feel him chuckling against me.

"I love how I can make your body react so beautifully."

I pinch his chin and force his eyes up to mine. "You're the only one who's ever gotten that kind of reaction out of my body."

He whirls us around, throwing me on the bed beside him. I nestle my head into his shoulder. "You sure James never made you feel like that?"

I chuckle. "No, James *never* made me feel like you do. Not once."

He rolls over me, planting a swift kiss on my lips. His hand drags down my front, and I already feel the anticipation of having him again building. He must know how he affects me because his gaze travels down my body.

He cocks an eyebrow. "Want to take a bath?" Then he runs his hands between my legs. He grabs my thigh which makes the answer fall out of me.

"Yes."

I sit up, but before I can, Allister pushes me back down. "Oh, wait, I almost forgot." He leans forward down to the thigh closest to him. His lips lock onto my leg, and he starts sucking.

It hurts, but is also delightful at the same time. I arch my back, and a moan leaves my mouth as his sucking intensifies. When I feel like I can't take it anymore, he unlatches and shifts away, smiling down at his handiwork. I sit up and peek at my thigh only to see a round red splotch marring my skin.

My mouth drops. "You marked me!"

He stands up and faces me. He holds his head a little higher and his chest is puffed out as his answers, "Yes, I did. Now anyone who tries to steal you from me will know you're mine."

I stand up and walk over to the tub, throwing my hands up in the air as I move. "I think I'd have some say in any stealing happening."

Allister passes me with his nose pushed up into the air. "You never know. Better to be safe than sorry. You're rather delectable."

He places his hand on the edge of the porcelain tub, and it begins to fill on its own. I slowly swagger over to him, swaying my hips as much as I can when I'm this close to him. I push my bare chest forward a bit more as I say, "Fine, then I get to return the favor."

His chin immediately drops to his chest.

I giggle. "You're gawking."

"If you didn't want to be gawked at, you wouldn't stick them out like that." He brings his hand up to my shoulder and rubs his hand down my arm.

Everywhere he touches, I feel like lightening jump from his skin to mine. He leans forward, his lips touching my ear. "You want to mark me? Then get on your knees."

Chapter Twelve

Attina

The next morning, I find myself standing at the gate to the castle with Ned and Oberon on either side of me, waving goodbye to Allister and Mylo. He refused to take any of the horses here. He told the stable hand he didn't want to deprive anyone of their capable stead, but I know better.

I know he didn't trust any of the other Fae horses, and I don't blame him. Raven and Mylo have been with us through our whole adventure. He knows he can trust them. But with Raven still laid up with her injury, the only choice was to take Mylo. It took lots of pleading to get him to leave Raven's side. But then Ned promised to stay in the stables with Raven every night until they returned, which did the trick.

I wish I could have one more night with him, maybe go with him, but I know he has to do this alone. He must take back his throne and this is the only way to accomplish that, even if I already miss his intoxicating smell.

I'll miss you, I say to his mind.

I'll miss you more.

Take care of Mylo. Raven needs her mate.

He answers, *What about you?*

I flash him a picture of me punching him in the chest. *Of course, I need you. It goes without saying. Come back to me in one piece. Promise?*

I will always come back to you, he answers, and then everything goes quiet.

I turn around and notice all of the Fae who came out to watch their possible future king ride off, have disappeared. I sweep my eyes between Ned and Oberon. "Where'd they all go?"

Oberon is the one who bows his head and answers. "They hurried back to their prospective duties. You haven't been here long, madam, but everyone here has a role in contributing to the castle. Some cook, some hunt, some perform repairs when needed, and so on."

Ned rubs is neck and clears his throat. "Um, *madam—*" He emphasizes the word, and I can tell it's taking all his restraint not to laugh out loud. "I'm going to go sit with Raven in Mylo's stead. If you need me, just call." He points to his head before walking away.

"Will do," I curtly answer as I turn my full attention on Oberon. "Don't call me madam."

Oberon straightens his back. "You are to be queen, you deserve respect. I say madam in reverence."

I groan. "I'd rather you didn't." But then an idea hits me. "It's offensive to me."

Oberon hisses, "Offensive?"

I don't answer him. I simply turn on my heel and make my way over to the training pits. The smell of blood and dirt cloys at my nose. When I don't hear him following me, I call over my shoulder, "Aren't you coming?"

Then I hear his hurried footsteps as he races after me.

"Yes, I find the term offensive because you are to be our captain. A position which, unless I'm mistaken, is honored and sought after. I would never give the position to someone I didn't trust with my life. Someone I trust with my life is my friend."

Oberon sounds shocked when he says, "You think of me as your friend? Even after I tried to kill you and called you a half-breed?"

We make it to the edge of the sparring rings, and I stop, taking in my surroundings as I wait for him to catch up. The area is alive with fighting Fae again. A different Fae takes up Oberon's old position in the first ring, taking on multiple opponents. Everyone else is spread out. Most stand and wait their turn around the sparring rings, and only a handful are practicing at the archery range.

I don't take my eyes off of the scene in front of me as I tuck my hands behind my back. "It's true, you didn't make the greatest first impression."

He grunts at my side, but I continue.

"But, you know what my mate will do to you if I'm harmed while he's gone." I turn my face up to his and beam at him. "For now, that means we're friends. We can see how things go after Allister returns. Until then, you can call me Attina."

His face slackens in shock. "Um, okay. Thank you." He adds, "Attina," to the end as an afterthought.

I turn back to the fighting in front of us and lift my hand toward the archers, "Now, I'd like to practice if you don't mind. Unless I'm still not allowed?" I cock my eyebrow up at him.

His shoulders heave up and down as he chuckles and shakes his head, "You're allowed anywhere in the castle as long as you are by my side."

I leave Oberon behind me as I pass the sparring rings, make my way to the archers. "Only *if* I'm by your side?"

His voice flits to my ears. "Yes, because I don't want you going anywhere without protection until the king returns."

I turn on my heel; his request shocks me. "You want to babysit me until he gets back? How long will it take for him to return home?"

Oberon shrugs, his face unyielding. "Hard to say. The last king did this journey before I was born. Each king is different so there's really no way of knowing. But king Allister entrusted your safety to me and the only way I can guarantee your safety is if you are by my side at all times."

I scoff and roll my eyes as I turn back around to the firing range in front of us. "You forget, I bested you. I think I can take care of my—"

But before I can finish, the tip of a blade is pushed against my side, and Oberon's breath is hot on my ear. "You may be excellent in a fair fight, but anyone who wishes to hurt you won't fight fair."

I feel a thrill run through me at Oberon's threat. I realize it's a false threat, but this could be fun. I pivot around, away from the blade, and grab his arm. Before he has a chance to stop me, I have him slammed up against the castle wall with his arm—and the knife—up to his own throat. His eyes widen and his breath comes in pants.

I growl at him, "I see your point. I guess babysitting isn't the worst idea." I huff at him as I push off of him, allowing the knife to dig into his throat enough to barely draw blood.

Oberon shoves off the castle wall and bends over as laughter comes roaring out of him.

I glare at his ridiculous position. "What's so funny?"

He has a hard time getting control of his faculties, but he eventually masters his laughter, standing up straight and wiping a tear from his eye. I notice a drop of blood slip down his neck from the cut I left, but in the next second the cut stitches itself together. "I'm glad we'll have such a fierce and fiery queen." He immediately grows solemn as he continues, "But don't let your fire get the best of you. I'm here to protect you from threats you might miss. You're not the lamb, you're the wolf."

A picture of James flits through my mind. The last time I thought of myself as a wolf it was about James acting like a shepherd protecting his unsuspecting lamb, not realizing I was the wolf. I wonder where he is.

Who took him from the castle? It must have something to do with Henrik since they took Talon with them, but why would Henrik want James? And why would James leave with one of Henrik's agents?

I make my way over to the side of the firing range where more bows are hung on pegs and quivers with arrows are held in a wooden barrel. Picking up a bow and quiver, I quickly inspect them.

I'm not impressed. The wood is flimsy and soft.

My gaze travels over the targets, and I'm amazed to find the few people practicing are somehow hitting the target dead on. They must practice day and night to become this accurate with such rudimentary tools.

I peek up at Oberon and growl, "This is embarrassing. Please remind me why Henrik is scared to attack our territory? We have no archers, and our bows are pathetic. We couldn't even begin to defend ourselves until he was nearly inside the castle."

Oberon walks over to one of the firing ranges, and I follow. "Gerald's never been one to see the advantage of long range weapons. He wasn't particularly effective with them himself, so I think he thinks if he can't do it, no one should. All compulsory training has been hand-to-hand combat."

I place the quiver over my shoulder as he throws his hand behind him.

"If you'll notice, our fighters don't even practice with their magic."

I turn and see what he's saying. I didn't notice it before, but he's right. No Fae welds magic as they land blows on their opponent.

I furrow my brows and face him. "You used your powers against me."

Oberon's hand goes to my shoulder, and he spins me back to the target. "Yes, but I learned to fight with my powers prior to Gerald becoming king. There are a few of us who did, but sadly, there aren't many left."

I tug an arrow out of the quiver, nocking it. I almost drop my bow when I draw back on it and feel the riser over bend to my pull. I draw on the bowstring a few times, trying to get the feel of it. When I finally release my arrow, it goes high and to the right. I hear a couple of chuckles around me, but the Fae never stop shooting. I want to head up to my room and grab my bow and arrows, show these Fae I'm not incompetent, but I feel like getting my bow would be cheating. If these Fae can hit the mark with these bows, then I can, too.

I shoot a few more times, getting better with each arrow flying from my fingers. Oberon covers my shoulder with his hand, and I'm pulled from zeroing my attention on the target in front of me. I notice the sun is setting, and everyone around me has left.

"Maybe this challenge is better taken on tomorrow," he quietly says, like he's afraid to offend me.

I quietly nod in answer. I'm frustrated it took me this long to get on target with these weapons. It shouldn't have taken me this long to get proficient, they're just *so* different from what I'm used to.

"Tomorrow I'd like to make some changes to training. No, not changes—additions," I state as I return the bow and quiver.

Oberon places his hands behind his back and takes up his position at my side. "I will go see what Gerald thinks about it. He will probably want to converse with you about it."

We walk in silence as we pass the entryway to the castle and make our way to the stables. I love the smell of bedding and horses, it's a smell unlike any other and always brings a smile to my face. I'd like to check in on Raven and Ned before turning in for the night. When we make it to Raven's stall I peek over the stall door. Raven has a fresh bandage on her stifle and is peacefully sleeping. Ned has brought down a cot and lamp and is reading in bed. I smile, but don't interrupt them. It does my heart good seeing them together. I truly appreciate him looking after and sleeping next to Raven.

I can tell him tomorrow. Let them get some rest tonight.

We turn back and head to the front of the castle. I'm surprised by the comfortable tranquility that falls over Oberon and me. He's a comforting presence. We ascend the stairs and Oberon walks past his room to my door. He opens it and walks in.

The shock is plain in my voice as I stop in the doorway. "Where are you going? You're not staying in here!"

He walks around the room like he's on a mission. It's not a big room, but he checks in the tub, under the bed, and opens the closet. He doesn't answer me until he's done.

"No, I won't be staying with you, but you can't be too safe. Let me check your room from now on." He makes his way toward me, and I move out of his way.

I grasp onto the door and begin closing it behind him. When he's out the door, he whirls around, drops into a bow."I will be here when you wake up in the morning. If I'm not here, do not leave the room until I am."

I close the door. There didn't seem to be much to say to his declaration. I sigh and lean against the door. I hope Allister will be back soon. I really don't want the oppressive Oberon following me around like a shadow for any longer than absolutely necessary.

Chapter Thirteen

Allister

The smell of pine rushes past me as Mylo runs beneath me. I lean down, pat him, and wonder how Attina and Oberon are getting along. They're both stubborn and strong-willed. It'll be interesting to see if they will be great friends or sworn enemies when I get back.

It's getting late; I should check on Attina. *Hi, love, how are you?*

I can hear the excitement in her voice when she answers. *Hey! I forgot you said you could hear me anywhere in the world. How are things going? Are you on your way back yet?*

I chuckle softly. *No, not even close.*

I can almost feel her disappointment through our bond.

I'll come back as soon as possible kitten. How are you getting along with Oberon?

He's insufferable. He insists on following me around everywhere. We're not doing this again if you ever have to leave in the future.

We'll discuss it when the time comes.

Nothing but air answers me.

Oberon knows the consequence if anything happens to you. He won't let you get too far from him. Can you deal with it until I get back? I just need you safe until I return, and this is the best way to do so.

I imagine her lips out in a pout as she answers, *I guess.* Then there's a long pause before she continues. *But get back soon. My patience is not unlimited.*

Yes, my queen, I answer, cutting the connection.

It's only been half a day, but I already miss her more than I'd like to admit. If I talk to her much longer, I'll turn right around and choose to stay in bed naked with my mate for the rest of time and let Henrik do whatever he wants with this world. As long as I have her next to me, I wouldn't mind allowing this world to burn.

But I know she would.

She would never stay while Fae and humans suffered around her.

I don't deserve her.

We didn't get much sleep last night. After we were done worshiping each other's bodies I taught her about shielding her thoughts. In all honesty, I would've been completely happy if we just cuddled all night. But I couldn't imagine leaving her here with other people who could read her mind.

Our type of power is rare, but there's always been more Fae with this power in the Eastern territory than in Shadow Mountain. It was exhausting, but it had to be done. There's no one size fits all approach to blocking thoughts. My other power is water so I imagine a dense protective wall of water around my mind. Someone with earth powers would imagine a wall of earth. But for Attina, with all her different powers, we had to do some experimenting.

She was a trooper though. She didn't give up. She kept trying until she figured out what worked best for her. Then once she figured it out she lifted and dropped her shields until it was as easy as breathing for her.

The interesting thing we found out though, was while we block our thoughts the other person can't feel where their mate is. I tried to poke and prod to find her, but no matter what I did she was lost to me.

It was a horrible feeling.

I know cutting the connection now will be hard on both of us, but I *have* to concentrate.

I need to do this for us and our future.

Chapter Fourteen

Attina

Opening my eyes, I notice the moonlight streaming in from the one window in the room. I wonder what woke me. I sit up and peer around. The moonlight pouring in is enough to scan the room, searching for any threat, but I don't find one.

I was having a dreamless sleep for once. I didn't realize it before I laid my head down, but I wore myself out yesterday. My arms feel like liquid fire from fighting the bowstring on those flimsy bows half the day. I flop back in bed and turn on my side. Maybe I heard an animal outside or something.

My body relaxes.

I feel the darkness closing in.

The blankets around me are tight and comforting. Tighter than I remember them being when I went to bed. It feels like how Father would tuck me in as a child. The memory warms my heart, and I dig my head further into the pillow. I smile at the memory washing over me. How he would sit in my bed next to me and dig his fingers under me, making sure I was safe and secure.

Then the blankets yank down on top of me, pushing me further into the bed than should be physically possible.

I knew somebody would test me while Allister was gone.

I quickly let out a calculated half scream then take a gasp of air and hold it. I know I won't be able to take another for a few seconds.

I throw my eyes open in shock, pretending I'm scared and vulnerable.

It's all a ploy though.

I could easily get out of these constricting blankets, but I want to see who's doing this. I have an inkling, but I need confirmation of a few things. So, I lie in wait.

It doesn't take more than a few seconds for me to hear the footsteps coming up from the bottom of the bed where my attacker must have been hiding when I woke up.

"Tsk tsk tsk, half-breed. You should have closed your window." My heart stops for a second. Oberon?

My fears aren't realized though as Gerald bends at the hip to push his face right up against mine. I realize I'm relieved to see his disgusting face. I discover I truly want Oberon to be as good as Allister says he is. It would disappoint me greatly if he betrayed us and turned out to be as evil as Gerald.

I open my mouth to say something to Gerald, but at the last second, I remember I'm supposed to be scared, in shock, and having trouble breathing. Instead, I open and close my mouth like I'm gasping for air.

Gerald's rotten breath is hot on my face when he snarls, "Having trouble breathing there, little half-breed? This is my power. I can control inanimate objects such as blankets. Sounds like a stupid power, until it's wielded the right way."

I think to myself, *Sounds like a chicken shit power perfect for a snake like you*. But instead of saying anything, I quickly nod at him and try to plead with him to release me with my eyes.

"You shouldn't have come here. You or your mate." He stands up straight and places his hands behind his back. "No matter. I will kill you tonight, and when your mate returns, he will go mad with despair. He won't be a problem anymore. I will keep my throne, and Henrik will leave us alone as soon as he finds out I killed his granddaughter for him. The rest of the world can burn in his fires, for all I care, as long as I have my kingdom."

The blankets squeeze down on me harder, forcing me to release the breath I'd been holding in a big huff. I tug at my fire power, and with half a thought, I have fire rolling off of half my body, burning the blanket covering me.

I really need to stop burning my bedding; people will start talking.

Gerald's eyes fling open in shock, his hand flying to his open mouth, and he slowly backs away from me. He obviously wasn't paying attention during my fight with Oberon. How he ever thought he could threaten me shows how pig-headed and unfit this false king is. Fae follow power, but strength doesn't equal smarts. As the blanket melts from my body, so does Gerald's hopes of ever staying in power. I cut off my flames before it can burn my nightgown and sit up, staring him down.

"Did you get all that?" I call out.

Oberon slams open my door, his lip lifted in a vicious snarl, and prowls inside, aiming for Gerald. "I did, my queen."

Gerald jumps back into the corner of the room, his head cutting between Oberon and me. He makes his decision. His eyes narrow, and he dives at me with his hands out like he's about to throttle me.

It takes everything in me, but I don't move to stop him. I wait to see what Oberon will do. Whose side he's truly on. Overpowering Gerald is not my greatest concern right now; I can overpower him if I must.

Then a brick is yanked out of the wall behind him, and I barely have enough time to watch it fly through the air and slam into the back of Gerald's head. His mouth goes slack, and his eyes glaze over as he falls to the ground in a heap.

"Is that enough to prove my loyalty?" Oberon calls across the room.

I'm surprised he realized what I was doing.

I tear my gaze from Gerald and peer at Oberon. "Am I really so transparent?"

He trudges over to Gerald's prostrate form. I slide my legs onto the bed, trying to get as far out of his way as possible. He bends over and pauses to answer. "You could have demolished him with one thought. You have extreme amounts of power streaming through you. He wasn't a threat to you. You're much more calculating than I could have guessed though. You surprise me."

I wrap my hands around my ankles. "Caught onto that, too?"

He chuckles as he hefts Gerald's limp body into his arms, cradling him like a baby. "You screamed just loud enough for me to hear. Then lay there and waited for Gerald to spill his plans. You didn't panic or free yourself—you let him think he had the upper hand. Why he would attack you after your show of power today is beyond me." He shakes his head as he marches toward my door. "Then you sat there while he attacked. You could have stopped him, but you wanted to see what side I was on, if I would attack him for you or stand there and watch things unfold."

I stand up and follow him out of my room, my gray night-gown sighing around my knees. "Where are you taking him?"

His footsteps are noiseless, like he walks on clouds, as he makes his way down the stairs. I absentmindedly think he could make an incredible spy. "I'm taking him to the dungeon. He attempted to murder you. Murder is still against our law. It's one of the few laws he didn't change from the past king."

I feel a drop in my gut. The dungeons—where my mother is.

"What will we tell the other citizens?"

He stops and turns around. "You need to have Kalven call them to the throne room and you will inform them you are the queen until your mate returns."

"But you're the one who technically defeated him. Doesn't that make you king?" I question, remembering the story as to how Gerald ended up occupying the throne.

Oberon's eyes glitter as the realization hits him, he could be king. His green eyes turn dark for a split second before he shakes his head, clearing them. "No. I would not be a great king. I am much more suited to serve. You are our queen. Whether you seize the position now or when your mate returns matters not."

I place my hand on his shoulder. He could have taken the throne, and I would have waited until Allister returned. I know he wouldn't harm me. His actions tonight proved his loyalty and if he did try to enact Gerald's plan of killing me and driving Allister insane, he must know Allister would still kill him for his transgressions. No, he wouldn't have harmed me, but he could have made things inconvenient for me.

"Thank you, Oberon. Your loyalty will be rewarded."

He nods once as he turns and makes his way back to the dungeons. I grab a hanging lamp, the last one with a candle lit inside of it, as we descend the stairs leading to the dungeon. When we walk down those final set of stairs, the stench of body odor and waste hits me square in the face. I feel the smell coating my skin.

The first thing I notice when I take in the scene around me is the cell Talon was in the last time I was down here. The cell door is open, and his cage is wrenched apart like something with claws ripped it free. We walk to the back of the alley toward where my mother's cell is. The air down the alley is fresher, the stench less pungent. I wonder why?

I realize I might just be annoyed enough by tonight's turn of events to deal with her.

Oberon, with Gerald in his arms, makes his way past James's old cell. The front of the cell is still lying on the ground, and I notice the cell across from his has its back wall ripped out. It appears someone has built a temporary wall by taking the old stones and stacking them up, but there is still enough space to allow some air to flow through. No wonder it smells better back here.

I follow Oberon to the stall facing my mother's. As I stand there and watch him unceremoniously chuck Gerald into the back of the stall my mother peeks out of the darkness of hers. Surprisingly, Gerald doesn't move after being thrown so hard to the ground.

I watch Oberon grab the empty water vase out of the corner of the cell and walk it out. Then I notice the blood streaming down his arm and immediately realize why Gerald didn't wake up. Oberon hit him a lot harder in the back of his head than I thought. I wonder if he'll ever wake up, but find the thought of him not waking up doesn't really bother me.

"Attina—" I hear my mother's meek voice behind me.

I ignore her.

Oberon moves to walk past me, but I clasp onto his forearm. It's like wrapping my arms around a coiled snake about to strike its next meal. His strength shouldn't surprise me after I fought him, but it does. "Let me take care of it. You've done enough for the night."

He peers at me and for a minute. I think he's about to argue with me, but then he bows his head and hands me the vase. I take it from his hands and he watches as water fills it from nowhere.

His voice is even, nonchalant as he says, "I keep forgetting you can control all of them."

"Seems like Gerald forgot, too." I wink over at him and walk the vase back into the cell. I walk over to where Gerald still lies and place my fingers on his neck, checking for a pulse. A strong thump pulses under my pressure.

Letting out an audible huff, I curse my bad luck. As I leave the cell I'm surprised the commotion of us walking around and throwing Gerald in his cell didn't wake Commander Demarco.

Titania's timid voice flits to my ears, sending my nerves on edge and fire to the surface of my skin. "Attina, I need—"

I turn back and prowl over to her cell. The first thing I notice is she's no longer in rags. She's wearing one of her tunics I brought from her room in the tree. Allister must have brought it to her.

Anger floods my system. I know they're her clothes, and she's like a mother to him, but my feelings are still hurt—whether it's rational or not. Her hand wraps around the cell bar, and I reach to place my hand on hers. Titania's face softens as she realizes I want to touch her, until my hand actually makes contact and sears her.

Her shrill screams fill my ears, and she jerks back, trying to get away from the pain, but I clamp down, holding her in place.

"This is a fraction of what you did to Father and Oak. You deserve to burn. Mark my words, you *will* burn. Your needs mean nothing to me. *You* mean nothing to me."

Her cries of pain bolstering me, making me push a little more heat into my hands before releasing her. As I meander away, I can see the off white of her bones. A sinister smile cross my lips, as I turn and walk down the aisle. Straightening my back, I peer into Demarco's cell to see him cowering in the back. It does my heart good to see him quivering.

Behind me, I hear her shocked and saddened voice. "You're no better than *him*!"

I throw my hand up in the air and keep walking toward Oberon who's already making his way out of the dungeon, apparently unphased by my actions. I could get used to being around him; there's no judgment when my evil side slips out, just acceptance.

"It's all thanks to you!" I yell back at her.

Chapter Fifteen

Attina

After leaving the dungeon, I make my way to Kalven's examination room with Oberon in tow. I fling open the door to the room where he examined me when I woke up after being knocked out for a week. The room still looks the same. One big table in the middle with high shelves on either side packed top to bottom with containers filled with magical potions. This time the medicinal stench doesn't assault my nose as badly.

I stride over to the left side of the room and knock on the door which Kalven told me was the way to his room. I hear grumbling on the other side of the wooden door before it's swung open.

Kalven snaps, "Wha—"

But he doesn't finish whatever he was about to say when he sees my face. His head swivels to where I know Oberon stands behind me, his brow furrowing.

"Attina? Is everything all right?"

"I need you to call everyone to the throne room in the morning. I thought I'd give you a heads up."

He sighs, his white nightgown—in contrast to Oberon's black one—crinkles as he turns to slump on the edge of his small bed. I can see the exhaustion consuming him. I feel bad for waking him this early, but it needed to be done.

I follow him in, stopping in front of him. "Has Gerald approved this? You know I can't do anything without his permission."

His gaze shifts to where Oberon's leaning against his door frame. He lifts his hand toward him. "And what is he doing here? Since when did you two become best friends?" He cocks an eyebrow. "Does Allister know?"

Anger courses through me at his allegation. He doesn't know me, but he obviously has zero faith in me. My palms itch. I don't have to peer down at my hands to know they are turning pink from the fire craving to crawl to the surface and teach him a lesson. I take a deep breath and calm myself before I say something I'll regret.

"Allister told him to watch over me while he was gone."

Kalven's long white hair hangs down his arm as he leans around me to check with Oberon who nods in agreement.

I dive to the left, cutting off his line of sight to Oberon, forcing his gaze on me. "I know you don't know me well, but I'm Allister's mate. I could never do anything to harm him."

Kalven peers down at his hands. "I'm sorry. I know you wouldn't. I could immediately see how much you love him. I've always thought of him as the son I never had, so I'm a bit overprotective."

I glide forward, placing my hand, which has now gone back to my normal skin color with my calming temper, on his shoulder and duck my head to meet his gaze. "I'm glad he has you in his life. He's wanted a family forever, it's nice to see him around someone from his past who loves him."

I see tears form in his eyes at my words. He wipes away a tear as it fights to fall down his cheek. "Now then, does Gerald know you want to call everyone to the throne room?"

I release his shoulder and decide to take a seat next to him. My eyes drift to Oberon who stands there like an old pine tree forgotten by time, solid and unchanging. I give him a second. Give him a chance to butt in and take the throne which should, at the moment, rightfully be his. Oberon drops his gaze and shakes his head, so I turn to Kalven and answer. "Gerald is no longer king. I am now the Queen of the Eastern Fae."

Kalven's mouth drops, but not for long as questions spill from his mouth. I'm completely honest with him. I tell him what happened, how he tried to kill me in the middle of the night, how Oberon heard it all and stopped him. Kalven covers his mouth and a snigger escapes his lips, "You're a feisty little minx aren't you? I get why you're Allister's mate." He elbows me playfully as his head slices to Oberon, "And you don't want the throne? I'm surprised."

Oberon stands up straight and holds his hand out to me, "Take the throne? Just in time for her mate to return and seize the throne from me? I'm better at being the Eastern Fae captain anyway. I'm built for battle, not a throne."

Kalven clicks his tongue, "Hmm, I'm impressed." He turns in his seat toward me, his left leg lifting up to the bed between us. His white eyes harden and his brow pinches as he says, "Okay, so you're the queen now. We can't tell the others Oberon defeated Gerald, it must be you." His gaze slices to Oberon, "Are you all right with that?"

Oberon nods once—crossing his arms over his chest and leaning back against the doorframe.

"All right, as soon as the sun rises I will gather everyone. You may want to freshen up beforehand." He leans in and sniffs my shoulder. "You smell like you've been in the dungeons."

I chuckle and shake my head. "I will freshen up and meet you in the throne room then." I stand and turn toward Kalven, standing over him. "Thank you for this."

He stands so close to me his body ends up almost pushed against mine. It's a more intimate distance than I'm really ready for with this man, but I stand my ground.

Then his arms fly around me. "Thank you for being the change this world needs, and thank you for taking such great care of Allister. I haven't seen him in many years, but I can tell the happiness I see is new for him." He pulls me back from him, allowing him to look me into my eyes. His white eyes stare back at me, and I'm again surprised he can see with such clouded eyes. "It will be nice having a daughter for a change." He winks at me and then drops his hand and makes his way over to Oberon. He places his hand on Oberon's shoulder before walking out of the room. "You're a good man."

After I've bathed and changed into a fresh green tunic and pants, I make my way down to the throne room. When I open my door, Oberon is already standing there waiting. I smile up at him. I'm glad Allister left him with me. It's funny how my outlook on him changed in twenty-four hours. I thought it would be terrible having him shadowing me, but it's been surprisingly comforting having him around.

Oberon opens the throne room doors for me, and I pace over to where the throne sits on huge stairs. My hand cups my chin in thought. Should I climb up to the top and sit in the throne? I mean, royalty sits in thrones, but I hate how high the throne is. It's too far away from my people.

I jump when Oberon's voice fills my ears. "Would you like help up there? I know it's a bit of a climb." He would make an amazing spy.

I turn around, placing my hand on the lowest stair and push my butt up on it. "No, thank you. I won't lord over these people. I'm their queen, but I would also like them to think of me as their friend."

Oberon peers down at me with one brow cocked. He's obviously skeptical of my idea. The phrase Fae follow power flits through my mind again. I've heard it enough times for it to be cemented there. But my gut tells me this will work.

It doesn't take long for people to start flocking inside. I notice Ned. He turns to take up his spot by the back of the room, awkwardly rubbing his neck again, but I manage to catch his eye and wave him over. He glances back and forth between me and where he was heading, obviously trying to decide if he should listen to me or not, but he eventually makes his way over.

"What's up?" he whispers when he gets to my side. His gaze shifts to Oberon nervously.

I place my hand on his forearm, trying to comfort him. "He's my guard. You can talk freely in front of him, Ned."

His brows furrow. "Your guard? Why do you have a guard?"

"Allister," is all I have to say to watch as realization washes over him.

Ned takes a slides away from me and says a little louder, "What's happening? Do you know why we're here?"

I swing my legs back and forth. "You could say that."

Ned cocks his head at me in question. But before I can answer, Kalven walks over. "Everyone who could make it is here. There are some elderly I told to stay in their rooms. There's no reason for them to exert themselves walking down all those flights of stairs."

I jerk my head back, surprised. "Why are they upstairs if they can't make their way up and down them?"

Kalven stares at the ground. "The royal quarters are on the ground level. All other quarters are upstairs. There was no choice."

I growl. "That will change today. I want them moved to the ground floor, to whatever room they need. You will also have to live on the ground floor. Unless you have patients in your care by your room, I want you there for them in case they should need anything. Oberon, if we must, I want you to carry them down the stairs. The royal quarters will be my current quarters until further notice."

Oberon nods, and his chest puffs out, like he's suddenly proud of something. "It would be an honor, my queen."

Ned's head snakes back and forth between the three of us. His face drains of color as he takes in Oberon's words.

I ignore him for the moment and climb up on the stair I was just sitting on. The men around me pivot to face the now filled room. Most of the Fae in the room sit at tables, but some lean against walls. I can hear children squeaking in laughter. Some Fae face forward and see me waiting on the dais, but then immediately go back to their conversations.

"Excuse me!" I shout, but no one stops talking. I yell again, but nothing.

Kalven turns and asks, "Would you like me to get their attention?"

I gaze down on him and think for a second. While it would be easier, but it doesn't really set the stage for these people to respect me. No, I need to do this one on my own, so I shake my head at him. I open my hand, and a fireball appears from nowhere. Kalven's eyes widen as he quickly twists forward.

I raise my hand and shoot my fireball up to the ceiling in the middle of the room. It hits the rock ceiling with a loud thump. Screams fill my ears, and I hear the scraping of chairs as Fae jump from their seats. The fire crawls along the top of the ceiling, finding something up there to burn, probably spider webs, then dissipates.

Everyone in the room silently gazes me. "Thank you for your attention. I have some things I would like to speak with you all, my people, about."

Someone from the back—I can't make out the person since they hide behind others, probably in fear of me burning them alive—shouts, "We are not your people! Gerald is our king."

I lower my head and scoff. "Oh, how wrong you are. Gerald is in the dungeons."

Everyone in the room gasps, but I push on.

"He tried to assassinate me in my sleep last night. I was able to foil his plan and defeat him."

"You lie!" the man from earlier screams, striding forward into my line of sight.

He's a smaller man; his figure is lithe, but his face is full. His pinkened cheeks give away how angry he is.

On my right, Oberon hisses, "That's Darob. He's Gerald's lover."

I'm surprised, but don't let it show as I shift my gaze back to Darob. "It is true." My hand goes out to where Oberon stands. "You may ask Oberon if you don't believe me. He was your captain, and he's been one of your people his entire life." My eyes scan the rest of the Fae in the room. "I'm sure you all can trust his word. Oberon?"

Oberon takes my cue and stomps forward. He fiddles with the truth a little, saying he happened to be passing by my door when I knocked Gerald out. But other than that, he sticks with the truth. As he speaks, I see faces fall and hear gasps tumble from lips.

Oberon finishes and takes a step back, sliding his arms behind him.

I pick up where he left off, my voice booming across the wide expanse of the room. "As you can see, *I* am your queen now."

Murmurs break out as Fae talk amongst themselves about this turn of events. I'm sure there's much for them to talk about. I'm an unknown to them. I came here battered and broken. I have fought against their king since the moment I opened my eyes. I am the granddaughter of the Fae who took their king and queen from them. I'm sure these people don't know what to think; maybe they're even scared.

"I will have some immediate changes I would like to see implemented today. First, I have spoken with Oberon and Kalven about getting the elderly to the first floor. Anyone who can help please see either of them after this meeting. Secondly, I will be tearing down this throne." I gesture to the huge set of stairs behind me. "I do not want to lord over you. I want to be someone you can go to with your problems."

I notice the Fae closest to me fling their eyes open in shock.

I press on. "Then, I would like every able body above fifteen to meet me in the sparring ring after lunch. Finally—" I lock eyes on the man who had been so vocal about his dislike of me. "Darob, please see me after everyone leaves."

I peer out into the crowd and shove all the sincerity I can into my voice as I say, "I would like to do right by you all. I want this to be a place everyone is proud to live in. I don't want you to follow me simply because I am the most powerful. I want you to follow me because I have earned your loyalty."

You could hear a pin drop by the time I finish my speech. Slowly, one by one, Fae around the room begin nodding; some even smile.

I let out a big huff of air before announcing, "You are dismissed."

Everyone gets up, but to my surprise, about twenty Fae come forward to help move the elderly to the ground floor.

With their help, it wasn't long until everyone was situated in their new rooms. The rooms for the Fae royalty were astounding. They were caverns instead of rooms. Lush rugs covered the floors, hulking wooden dressers were filled with silk clothes, and the beds were down-filled monstrosities which could hold six people easily.

Each of the families we moved thanked me profusely over and over. I took their thanks in stride, but I couldn't understand how this wasn't already done. A king should take care of his people in any way possible.

While getting everyone settled, I'd forgotten I'd asked Darob to come see me until I heard someone clearing their throat behind me.

I whirl around to see his lithe figure. His eyes are a dark green, almost black, like the color of a forest before the sun rises and after the last star winks out. His nose is thin and hooked over his tight lips. His voice squeaks as he says, "You asked for me?"

I hand off the last bundle of clothes to be brought to this particular room to an older Fae. His eyes crinkle as he takes them from me and smiles.

Then I turn back to Darob. "Yes, I feel like we're going to have a problem."

Darob lowers his head. "No, my queen."

"I know you were Gerald's lover." I watch and wait for his cheeks to heat, but they never do.

This is all new to me. Men in Daruk were never lovers. I'm not sure what would have happened if they had been. There weren't enough humans in the world as is and two men can't produce offspring, maybe that's why it wasn't done?

Personally, I couldn't care less what two adults did behind closed doors. "I need to know where your loyalties stand." I feel Oberon's hulking presence stalk up behind me. I didn't want Darob to be intimidated by him, but I also appreciate the backup.

Darob's eyes narrow at me. "What are you going to do with Gerald?"

I lift my chin and straighten my back. "I haven't decided."

His eyes rake over my body. Not in a hungry way, in more of an assessing way. "Will you kill him?" His voice is strong like he's confident and sure of himself, but I notice his hand nervously pulling at a string on the edge of his sparkling blue tunic.

I let out a loud huff and walk over to where an elaborately carved chair sits against a wall. Darob's gaze follows me as I perch on the edge of it and lean my elbows against my knees as I cradle my chin on my thumbs and my fingers rest against my lips.

I shake my head slowly. "No. He may have tried to kill me, but honestly, I'm used to being hunted. I can't hold it against him. And I may not agree with how he ruled, but he kept everyone here clothed and fed, which is more than I can say for my grandfather. But as soon as my mate returns and is found to be the rightful heir, I can't guarantee he'll feel the same way."

I hear a small snort in front of me, and I raise my eyes to see Darob's shoulders shudder. I cock my head and pinch my eyebrows at the strange sight. I imprisoned his lover and here he stands laughing in front of me? He walks forward and crouches on his knees in front of me. I lean away from him, ready to jump away from him if need be.

"Gerald is an asshole." His words shock me, and I drop my mouth open. "You can act shocked all you want, but you know it's true just as well as I do. He was a powerful man. I loved him for his power, not for him."

I'm at a loss for words, my mouth continues to hang open.

Darob reaches out and pats my knee as he stands. "Do what you wish with him. I don't really care. I was simply giving you a run for your money back there." He points his thumb over his shoulder, back to where the throne room is located. He twists around to walk off, but seems to remember something as he stops himself and pivots back to me. "Oh, and if your mate doesn't return my bed is always open to you my queen." He bows to me. When he stands up straight he throws me a wink before leaving the room.

I roll my head to Oberon who strides over to me and reaches his hand out for me to grab onto. His shoulders quake as he laughs, and I realize my mouth is still hanging open.

I use his hand to rise while he says, "I should have told you how Darob is. He loves himself. His affections change with the wind based on who can give him what he wants in the moment."

I'm still in shock over our little conversation all I can manage to say is, "Fae follow power."

I'm pleasantly surprised when every Fae within the age range I stated at the meeting are at the sparring rings after lunch. I slip into the middle of the first ring, dirt lifting into the air with each step, and everyone files into a circle around me. I peer at the Fae around me, and a smile cracking my face. Everyone surrounding me has a pleased expression plastered on their face, their eyes alight with happiness. I wonder why though? What happened? What did I miss?

An older Fae in front, with long blond hair and a red tunic, one of the men who helped move the elderly Fae to the ground floor, calls out. "We wanted to thank you for allowing our families to stay in your rooms."

I'm taken aback by his statement. "They're not my rooms. My room is up there," I say as I point to the tower leading up the front of the castle.

He shakes his head. "Those rooms are rightfully yours. You put our needs ahead of your own. Don't think each and every one of us didn't notice. It has been a *very* long time since we had a ruler who put our needs first."

I don't want to offend him by arguing the point, but I really didn't do much. I simply treated these people the way I would like to be treated. I keep my mouth shut and bow my head at him. He waddles forward and places his hand over his chest the way Allister did to Gerald when we got here. In turn, everyone around him follows his lead.

A loud hoot from behind me cracks the silence.

I spin my head to see Hazel perched high in a tree on the other side of the wall surrounding the castle. I glare up at her, and turn my back to her. Where the hell has she been all this time? She better have a good excuse for being gone this long.

I scan the Fae in front of me and I shout, "War is coming."

Gasps fill the air and everyone's hands drop from their chests.

"You will need to be prepared to fight. I have been watching everyone practice the past few days and those who've been sparring are doing great, but I notice not everyone trains, you have no archers, no real weapons training, and no training with your magic. That will change today."

Chapter Sixteen

Attina

"First off, do we have any blacksmiths here with us?" I call out. I can barely make out two Fae raising their hands in the back. "Please move to the castle wall and wait for me, you will be making weapons instead of fighting."

My gaze travels over the rest of my people. Then it hits me, these are *my* people. Their lives are in my hands. There will be a war, and I have to make them as prepared as possible. I have to give them the best chance at surviving what's to come.

Between Oberon and me, we were able to get trained soldiers teaching the new recruits. I found the few archers I saw practicing yesterday and put them in charge of a group of soldiers, teaching them how to shoot an arrow. While they practiced, I was able to get the blacksmiths moving on making more weapons for everyone. We needed swords, war hammers, and everything in between.

I'm leaning against the rough castle wall when Oberon stalks over to me. His muscled arms swinging by his side and an image of Allister, with his tense corded arms caging me, flashes through my mind. My heart drops. He only left yesterday, and I already miss him so much. I try to call him through his mind, but my words hit a hard wall. He must be blocking everyone out.

I frown as Oberon stops in front of me. "Everyone is training—"

I push off of the wall and cut him off, "I need to speak to you, Kalven, and Ned." My eyes drift to where Ned stands trying to pull back a wobbly bow and I snicker. I need to get these people some real bows.

Oberon moves in front of me, blocking my view of Ned. "I have some people I'd like to introduce you to if you don't mind?"

His eyes are hard so I decide his needs are more urgent, and I quietly follow him behind the castle. I haven't been back here yet, and I'm surprised to find nothing here. It seems like a waste of space. Behind the castle stands five Fae. Each of them are huge, they remind me of mountains. Except for the small willowy girl standing in the middle.

"These are our Mori Niko. Henrik has his slayers, we have Mori Nikos." He slides forward and places his hand on the shoulder of the man farthest to the right of me. The man has short shorn blonde, almost white hair and his golden eyes shimmer in the sun. "This is Liam. Our brain and brawn."

Liam's lips quirk up and he bows his head to me. I can already tell he's gonna be a troublemaker just by his smile. That smile could bring any female to her knees, I even feel my own wobble.

Oberon moves to the next man in line. "This is Hudson, our secrets and intelligence man."

The man's sour expression never falters as I look him up and down—surprised he could be anything close to a spy. He's built like a solid brick castle and his flaming red hair and silver eyes definitely make him stand out.

Oberon then moves to the woman. "Then this is Hudson's mate, Ava."

Out of nowhere, the girl races forward. I stiffen and jump back, ready for a fight. But she shocks me by jumping on me and throwing her arms around my neck. She grabs my shoulders and pulls me back, her long perfect blonde hair makes her emerald green eyes stand out in shocking contrast.

She throws her thumb over her shoulder. "I saw you fight that lug the other day. Thank you for finally handing his ass to him. I've been trying to do it for years. I know we'll be great friends." Then she quickly lands a kiss on my cheek before trotting off to stand next to her mate.

My eyes shoot open, and I bring my hand to my cheek. I've never had a girl friend. James was my only friend growing up. Is this what having a girl for a friend is like?

Oberon glares at Ava as she makes her way back to her spot. "Sorry about her, Attina. She's a little touchy feely."

"It's fine," I answer as I nod to him, the cue for him to continue.

He places his hand on the next man in line. "This is Lincoln."

The man shifts nervously and bows to me at the waist and his long gray hair falls around his face. When he stands back up, I'm shocked at how much he seems like a bigger version of Kalven. He even has his gray eyes, they're not clouded over like Kalven's, but they're definitely the same. It's strange; Kalven told us he didn't have a son.

Lincoln clears his throat. "I think you've already met my uncle."

Ah. That explains it.

I nod once to him and turn my gaze on the last man is a man with rich umber skin and black shining hair. "This is Derek. He's the muscle of the operation." I can see why. He's the biggest of the men, and I don't know how his tensed muscles aren't ripping out of his skin.

My eyes pointedly land on each of them for a second, sizing them up. "I want to fight each of you. I've already assessed Oberon's skills, now I'd like to assess you five. Powers and all."

Each of their eyes widen except for Liam. He stands there like he saw this one coming. Brawn and brain indeed.

I gesture to the empty area around us. "We can use the area here if you'd like. This way we can stay away from prying eyes?"

Before I get an answer Derek's hulking frame is bounding toward me. I throw up a wall of earth. He dips down and throws his shoulder into it, shattering it just as easily as the werewolf did.

I hear someone whistle behind him. "Damn, Derek."

He barrels at me, and I steel my nerves. I inch my way back to the castle wall, pretending to be nervous. He's big, but he doesn't seem to see what a disadvantage such bulk can be. He must get through every fight based on his muscle alone.

Right before he slams into me I use my Fae speed and turn away from him. He notices at the last possible second and tries to slam on the breaks. I have long enough to see his eyes open wide as he slams his shoulder into the white castle wall covered in hard unforgiving vines with a loud crack. A grunt leaves his lips as he hits and he slides down the wall. Then I see the huge indent his massive body left in the castle wall and my mouth goes dry. No wonder he's relied on his muscles for so long. I would've been dead if he'd hit me with that much force.

I turn to him and place my hand on his shoulder. "Muscle won't get you through every fight." He shrugs me off and plops on his butt. Leaning against the wall he rubs his shoulder, moving it up and down like he's trying to get feeling back.

I turn back to the Oberon and the four Fae left behind him. Ava, whose face is now bright red, bursts out in laughter. She jumps up and down on the balls of her feet and screeches, "That was *amazing*!"

Oberon rubs the back of his neck nervously. "Maybe we should just fight each other. It might be an easier way to see our skills. See our powers."

A thought hits me, and I whirl back to Derek who stares at the ground with tensed arms like he wants to kill it, "What are your powers? You didn't even think to use them."

He glares up at me, and I can almost see the fire rising in his eyes as he growls out, "Water."

Hmm interesting someone who's this sizable and strong would have such a delicate power. I turn back to Oberon. "No, I think this is the best way to assess everyone."

Ava jumps up and down behind him, flailing her hand in the air she shouts, "I'll go! I'll go!"

I chuckle and gesture to her to come forward.

She moves around Oberon. She tilts her head to her shoulder, and I hear it crack. She does the same to the other side, then begins cracking her knuckles one by one. She lowers her head and gazes at me under her brow as she says, "I hope you won't take it easy on me just because we're friends."

I shake my head and bring my hands up in a fighting stance as I say, "Wouldn't dream of it."

All of a sudden wind picks up out of nowhere. Where there was a slight, cooling breeze, now there's a whirlwind of dirt and leaves. I take my eyes off Ava for a split second and when I look back she's gone, the only thing left is dust and air. I notice her mate, Hudson, smirking but with his sour expression it comes off forced.

I take the air around me and wrap it tightly around my body until I'm locked in my own little cocoon. The wind stops swirling around me. Above me I hear, "What a neat little trick, you'll have to teach it to me sometime."

I search around me, but before I can find Ava, she's crashed through my barrier, throwing me forward into the ground, and landing on top of me. I grind my teeth, annoyed she surprised me. She grabs onto my arm and tries to wrench it behind my back, but I call to the earth under me. The earth pushes me sideways, knocking Ava off my back and throwing me on my butt.

Ava jumps up and back, quick as a cat. She's strong, much stronger than I originally guessed. She's learned how to overcome her size and be a threat by mixing her smarts and her abilities. I'm impressed. I notice the leaves surrounding us keep flying behind Ava's back, like the wind is physically coming from her.

I wonder if she has nerves of steel. I tug on the dropping feeling in my gut and let fire roll over my skin. I push myself into my fire, letting it grow and swirl with the wind around it. As we stand there Ava drops her hands and takes a curls her body back, away from the fire inching closer to her, almost singing her skin.

I hear a voice behind me, I'm guessing it's Hudson, scream, "Ava, Stop!"

Ava locks eyes with him as she releases her hold on her power, like she's his puppet and he's controlling her body with strings. The wind immediately stops, and my fire rushes back to me. When it mixes with the fire still around me the flame brightens and flares up, almost reaching above the castle wall.

Ava drops her head and whispers barely loud enough for me to hear. "I submit." Her face is drawn, disappointed, like she failed somehow.

I let my fire extinguish and stride over to her. I place my arm across her shoulder and mumble to her, "You did great. I'm impressed. You'll have to show me how you disappeared. Now *that* could come in handy."

Her face perks up as she glances at me with sparkling eyes. "Really?"

I nod and lean in. "You even did better than Derek."

She jumps up and down and claps her hands. When we make it over to Hudson she excitedly wraps her arms around his thick neck. "Hudsy, she squealed I did better than Derek! Can you believe it?" He leans forward and plants a soft kiss on her cheek.

It's not an overly sensual kiss, but I still feel like I should be averting my eyes. I glance at the ground and hear him say, "I told you, you were good, babe."

Behind us I hear Derek growl, "Well, if you don't need me anymore I'm going to see if Kalven can't give me something for my shoulder." I turn to see his tensed hulking body leave and round the corner of the castle.

I glance with furrowed brows to Oberon. "Did I do something wrong?"

He shakes his head and crosses his arms, glaring to where Derek took off to. "No, he's a terrible loser. He just needs some time to cool off."

I shrug and move in front of the last three men. "Well, how about we get this over with, and I'll fight you three at once." I grin at the men.

Everyone seems taken aback, but Hudson takes my words in stride and answers me. "You're that confident? I know you trained with Allister, but he's one man."

I lower my head and snarl, "One man is all it takes." It annoys me more than I thought it would to have someone doubt my mate's abilities. He's my equal. If they can't defeat me, they sure as hell wouldn't have a chance against him.

I glide back and take a calming breath. Don't fight mad, he's only trying to rile you up. Then an idea strikes me, and I growl as I allow my fire to roll under my skin, turning my skin pink once again. I want them to think I'm angry. Angry people are sloppy in a fight.

Hudson, Liam, and Lincoln stalk forward. They advance until they surround me, forming a triangle around me. I raise my hands, but they stand there, like they're a wolf pack waiting for the alpha to signal them.

Then to my left I hear Oberon shout, "Fight!"

Chaper Seventeen

Allister

I can finally see the rushing river Kalven was talking about in front of me. He was right; it's more massive than any river I've seen in my life. It's as wide as two Eastern Fae castles lying top to bottom. The white peaks of waves jump and crash over hidden rocks. I can barely see the other bank over the raging rapids.

I gaze down at Mylo before jumping off his back. I pat him on the neck as I say, "Well, I guess this is where we part. Will you wait for me?"

He nods in answer. I wish he could talk. It would have made this journey a lot less boring. I could have talked to Attina through our minds during the trip, but I chose to block her from my mind instead. She needs to keep her wits about her.

She's in a den of vipers, and I don't want her to be distracted around those deadly Fae.

I take a deep breath, letting it out as I make my way over to the river. This is going to suck. It's almost winter. That water will be freezing. I wish Attina was here to warm me up. The thought of her body against mine, her mouth trailing down my chest brings a smirk to my face and makes my body harden. I shake my head, it's only been a few days, and I already ache for her.

I need to get this over with and get back to my mate. I have plenty of torturous things I'd like to do to her.

Chapter Eighteen

James

My wolf form strides into the poorly lit throne room behind Tala. We pass two stoic guards swathed in gold from head to toe. I've never seen this much gold in my life. If one could smell sadness, that's what the room would smell like. My eyes land on the two massive thrones on a dais in front of me. The one to the right, the smaller one, holds a malnourished woman, her head droops and her dark hair hangs in her lap as she stares down at her hands.

On the throne to the left, the black throne which appears to be made out of charred bones, sits a bulky man. The first thing I notice is his red eyes. They're so striking they're almost scary. His aquiline flared nose points down to his broad chest. My breath catches as I feel the massive power radiating off of him.

This must be Henrik.

The man who took everything from me, but who I must play nice with to get my Attina back. I clench my jaw.

Tala stops at the bottom of his throne and takes a knee. I bow my head, it's the best I can do in this form.

Henrik's voice booms off the walls of the room. "You both may stand." He stalks down his dais and places his hand on Tala's shoulder.

My back goes stiff. I don't like the man who murdered our whole village touching my sister. I swallow a growl.

"You did wonderfully, Tala, my top slayer. You brought Talon back to me." As if on cue Talon flies up and perches on the back of Henrik's throne.

Tala bows her head. "It was my pleasure, sire."

Henrik's hand leaves her shoulder and my body physically relaxes. "And you've brought your brother?" he asks, like he's confirming the sun is still in the sky.

She places her hands behind her back. "Yes, sire. The Eastern Fae was holding him in the same dungeon I found Talon in.

Then I hear Tala in my head, *Bow.*

I do as she commands and when I peek back up, Henrik is standing in front of me. He gazes over to Tala. "Does he wish for me to give him control over his wolf form?"

Tala cuts her head in a nod and a sinister smile crosses Henrik's face. "You know this means you will have to serve me for the rest of your life?"

I whimper, but nod. Yes, I understand the cost. His head slices back to Tala, "Why would he be willing to submit to me like this? You were a child, I understood why you would, we trained you correctly—" He points at me. "—but why would he be willing to do this? It's not like wolves to submit, even to someone more powerful than them."

I turn my gaze to see Tala's toothy grin stretch from ear to ear, "This is the best part of my journey. My brother has a claim on Attina."

When the words leave her lips Henrik's head slices back to me, his eyes almost sparkle—no not sparkle, flame in delight. "Perfect." Before I really have time to process the meaning of his words he pulls a knife out from behind him. A grin flashes across his face as he says, "This will hurt." He slices the blade of the knife down my shoulder.

Chapter Nineteen

Attina

All three massive males run at me simultaneously, dust flying up from their speed. And like the fight with Derek, I wait until the last second and dive between them. These men aren't as hulking as Derek though, and they manage to stop in time to barely keep themselves from slamming into each other.

I whirl around, but I'm met with Liam's quirked up lips like he knows something I don't. Then he raises his hand to my face, a blinding light leaving it. I reach up to block my eyes as someone hits me from the side. A loud yip escapes my lips as I slam into the ground. I can barely see Hudson's hulking body holding me down. How's that possible? He was standing on the other side of the courtyard a second ago.

I call to the earth and slam a wall of dirt into his side. I hear a loud huff escape him as all the air is knocked from his body. Standing up, I face my other two attackers. Hudson huffs against the wall behind me, trying to get air back into his lungs. I smirk, knowing he didn't expect my attack.

Liam and Lincoln face me, both in a fighting stance, but I'm not stupid enough to think these men will fight me with fists. Liam's golden eyes sparkle, and I instantly know what he's about to do. I throw up a wall of earth just as he turns his whole body into a freaking beacon of light. I shove the wall of earth forward with all my might, slamming it against him with enough force to throw him back into the castle wall.

I barely have time to notice Liam's limp body sliding down the wall before I feel something shooting through the air at me. Without really thinking, I throw up a wall of air and instantly an arrow sticks into it. My gaze flicks to Lincoln whose long gray hair is draped over half his face, a sinister smirk crawling up his face, but no bow in sight. I twist my head around, searching for whoever could have taken then shot. Lincoln lifts his hand, twitching his finger as another arrow flies deeper into my shield. I feel my shield crack and drop. The arrows dropping with it.

I glance up to the top of the castle, but see no one. This time, I watch Lincoln as he twitches his hand again. He must be controlling them somehow. I feel the arrow flitting through the air toward me, trying to take me down. I'm almost hurt by the fact he's seriously trying to take me down. I fought all the others and they fought with all they had, but they didn't show such murderous intent.

I see Kalven and Lincoln, and I almost forgot they're two different people. They've each had their own life experiences which made them who they are today. Their night and day differences are glaringly obvious at this moment. Where Kalven wants to heal, Lincoln wants to kill. I wonder what happened to this Fae to make him this bloodthirsty.

I can hear the arrow whiz toward me.

I take a half a stride back and grab the arrow midair in front of my face. I hear Ava shout something to my left, but I ignore her. I snarl at Lincoln who takes a step back himself, his eyes widen a fraction as he throws up both his hands and waves them in my direction. I throw up my shield of air and barrel over at him as fast as my Fae speed will take me.

I grunt as I feel a few dozen arrows hit my shield, but I move fast enough to miss most of them before my shield shatters. I jump at Lincoln, throwing my hands around his neck. I use my momentum to flip over him and chuck him over my shoulder. He flies through the air and lands with a thud on his face. I hear all the air leaving his lungs in a loud grunt.

I don't let him recuperate.

I jump on his back, grab a hold of his long, shimmering gray hair and yank his head back. At the same time, I grab my dagger from my boot and shove the blade under his neck. Everyone races forward at where I have Lincoln pinned and freezes. The rose pommel of my dagger, the one which matches my mother's sword, bites into the palm of my hand.

Then, barely out of the corner of my eye, I see him flick his wrist one last time. In an instant I feel another arrow, one from where I dropped my air shield racing back at me. There's not enough time for me to throw up a shield so I lean back out of the way, but I don't lean back fast enough. I hiss as the head of the arrow slices along my cheek, the sensation of fire burning my skin hits me, right before it imbeds itself into the castle wall next to Lincoln's head. Wet blood trails down my cheek.

I slam down my foot onto his hand, hearing it crunch beneath me. Leaning down, I jerk the dagger tighter, and growl into his ear, "Do it again, and I'll kill you." I feel wetness under my fingers as blood trickles down his neck.

Ava jumps forward and bends down in front of Lincoln, "What the hell Lincoln! Why would you do that? You weren't supposed to try to kill her!"

I wrench my face around him so I can see his reaction. He shrugs and tries to turn his gaze toward me. "I had to be sure you were the princess."

I snarl, drag my dagger away from his neck, and slam his head forward. It smacks into the dirt hard as I crawl off of him. "That's already been established. I am the future queen to the Western Fae throne."

Ava backs away into Hudson's awaiting arms. Lincoln grunts as he gets to his own feet. I notice the slice along his neck is already almost healed, only a dark pink line remains. I bring my hand to my cheek and notice my own scratch is healed; only a trail of caked blood remains.

Lincoln spins up and holds his head like I slammed him harder than I actually did. "Yes, and you're the queen on the Eastern

Fae throne as well. Which means, in essence, you will be the queen of all of Arealea. I had to know you were worthy."

I stand there in shock. "So what, you're the dramatic one of the bunch?"

He crosses his arms in front of his chest and chuckles. "Yes, I suppose you could say that."

Then I hear someone clapping behind me. I swivel on my heel and lift my dagger before I notice who it is. Ned stands there leaning against the wall clapping. A smile, reminiscent of the smiles Father would give me when he was proud of me, plastered on his face. "Good job, girl. I guess all the training you've been doing finally paid off."

I huff and shove my dagger back in my boot. "What are you doing here? You're supposed to be training with the rest of them."

He pushes himself off the wall and looks into the tree across from him. I follow his gaze to see Hazel perched there. "Some birdie told me I should come watch the show."

I roll my eyes, but walk over to him and throw my hands around his neck, pulling him tightly to me. "I'll deal with you two later. Why don't you go practice? I'll get you when I'm done." He turns and walks off without question.

I smile at his back and spin around, locking eyes with Oberon. "I need to speak with you and Kalven privately."

Oberon walks off in the direction Ned left, and I'm left standing in front of the rest of the Mori Nikos. All of them hang their heads, like they've failed somehow. Well, all of them *except* Lincoln, who stands there with a mysterious twinkle in his eye.

"You all fought well. I would like to speak to all of you after dinner, if you don't mind? We have some things I would like to discuss. Until then, I would like you to work with the other Fae. Help them learn to fight in a real battle." I pointedly stare down Lincoln. "Help them learn to fight with their magic."

Ava lifts her head and runs over to me, throwing her arms around my neck with such force I'm almost thrown backward. "I thought you were about to tell us we weren't good enough! So we get to be friends?"

I reach my hand around her and awkwardly pat her back, "Yes, we can be friends."

She releases me, and I follow Oberon. As I wave my hand over my shoulder I shout, "And don't get anyone killed okay?"

My blood runs cold when Lincoln shouts back, "No promises, Princess." But when I turn to look at him, he winks at me, calming my anxiety.

Oberon walks back into the castle, to Kalven's examination room, where he's standing inspecting some potions on one of his shelves. Oberon strides in ahead of me and clears his throat, grabbing Kalven's attention. I wave at him. "Hey, can we talk?"

"What can I do for you?" he says as he turns and leans his back against the shelves, crossing his arms. I now notice how skeptical he is of me. How did I miss this? I thought his opinion of me changed when I became queen, but I guess I was wrong.

I walk over and jump on the examining table in front of him, leaving Oberon by the door. I wave my hand in front of his body. "So, is it all Fae or just something about your line which exudes distrust?"

He cocks his head; not really an answer.

"I met Lincoln today. He tried to murder me in a friendly sparring match."

He drops his head and chuckles under his breath. "He's always been feisty."

I jump off the table and walk around it. Putting it between us. "Feisty? I tell you your nephew tried to kill me and all I get is he's feisty? You were warm and inviting when Allister was here, and now you're acting completely different. What the hell is happening?"

Kalven turns his back to me and fire burns in my belly at the blatant disrespect. "I've known Allister since he was a babe. *You* on the other hand, I met less than a week ago and you've already overthrown our king and managed to somehow get his captain to become your lapdog."

I growl and jump over the table, wrenching Kalven's shoulder to face me. I snarl, "You will at least face me when you're being insolent."

He gives me a knowing smile and leans down. "How did you get Oberon to bow to you?" Then he rakes his eyes up and down my body. Even with his clouded eyes the movement is obscene.

Oberon marches to my side before I have a chance to open my mouth. "You can stop with the act. She's obviously not breaking. Her temper is under control. I've yet to see her lose her temper like Henrik, even when Gerald tried to kill her. She rightfully could have killed him and she didn't."

Kalven winks at me. "Sorry, I had to be sure you weren't secretly like your grandfather."

I throw my hands up in the air aggravated by this waste of time. I pinch the bridge of my nose. "You know what? I'm going to just act like none of this ever happened. Your entire line is insane, it's a blessing you never had children. Let's start over."

Kalven throws his arm over my shoulder in a friendly manner, like he didn't act like I could be evil seconds ago, and snorts. "It is a *very* good thing I didn't have children. Now, what can I do for you?"

I slide back on the table and Kalven drags a chair in front of me while Oberon leans against one of the shelves. "Allister said Henrik hasn't attacked the Eastern Fae because your numbers were too massive." I glance out the door for a second, remembering all the people out there sparring.

"This is true," Oberon answers.

"Where are those people? The people here can't be who he was talking about." Even I can hear the confusion plain in my voice.

"They live in the mass of our territory. They're mostly farmers. They help supply the castle. The Fae outside the castle barter with others, or use the little gold they have, for anything they need; food, leathers, animals, and everything in between. They mostly govern themselves. Allister's father, Rufus, convinced Henrik they were all soldiers. Most of them haven't ever been to the castle or held a sword.

I lean back and splay my hands out behind me. "Well, I think since it's about winter time and they won't be able to grow food we should make good on Rufus's words."

Chapter Twenty

Allister

Crawling out of the river on the other side of the bank, I'm drenched in freezing cold water. Using my water magic to calm the waters and make a protective shield around me was futile. This water must have some sort of magic of its own to prevent anyone from using their magic to tame it, uncrossable water indeed.

Glancing back to the other side of the river, I wave to Mylo. He probably doesn't cares if I live or die, but now at least he'll know he has to wait for me to get back. Hopefully, he does.

My body starts shivering uncontrollably, and I'm getting drowsy already. I need to get a fire roaring as fast as possible. I can't pass out and have hypothermia set in. The mouth of what I'm hoping will be the Cave of Kings is not too far off. I can make it. As I walk I pick up sticks, carrying them in the crook of my arm. The sticks smack loudly against each other as my body shakes. I almost drop them twice before I make it to the cave.

I sit down.

My vision blurs in and out.

One minute I'm stacking sticks, the next the world is spinning. I can't physically hold myself up anymore. I shakily grab the flint I have in my pocket, haul it out and strike it. But it's soaking wet and isn't giving off a spark.

My vision goes dark.

This is bad.

Chapter Twenty-One

Attina

Oberon props himself on the table next to me. His massive chest stretching the fabric of his dark blue tunic. "And how exactly do you think you'll get *all* those Fae here? Besides, what are you going to do with them when they get here?"

I lean over to him and place my hand over his. "Thankfully I have my right –" I raise my hand to indicate Kalven. "—and left-hand men to figure that out for me. I don't know this territory, or its people, so I'm delegating this to the both of you. We can make a temporary housing area outside the castle walls. There are enough Fae here, we could get it done before the snow comes. But when it comes to how to get them here, I'm leaving that for you two to decide." I jump off of the table and squeeze my way between Oberon and Kalven. "I'm going to go check on Raven and talk to Ned and Hazel. If you need me, I'll be in the barn. We can talk about it after dinner with the Mori Nikos. You also have them at your disposal."

I make a detour over to the sparring ring and find Ned, sweat rolling down his face, in the middle of it taking on two Fae I hadn't seen practice yet. I shouldn't be surprised at how adept a fighter he is, but I am. I know he taught me how to fight, but he's really pushing himself now. Dirt clings to the sweat dripping down his face and his breath is falling out in huffs.

A Fae lunges at him and he moves with more agility than I thought possible, vaulting out of the way. The man trips and falls on his face. His other opponent, a woman with short brown hair, jumps on Ned's back, but Ned flings himself up. The momentum throws her backwards and she goes rolling out of the ring.

I glide into the ring. Everyone around it freezes and Ned's opponents instantly bow. I meet their eyes when they stand up. "Can I steal Ned from you?"

The woman is the one who answers. She fidgets nervously with her hands, picking at her nails. "He already beat everyone here. Maybe if you take him, someone else can win for a change."

A smile quirks up my lips and my eyes slice to Ned, who holds his head high. "You both looked like you were improving. Keep up the good work, and I'm sure it won't be long until you're the ones knocking him to the ground."

They both stand straighter and push their chests out like I gave them a sense of pride. I wink at them as I hold my hand out to Ned. He walks over to me, and I lace my arm around his. We've never been this touchy feely, but it's about time we were. He's been like a father figure to me since I showed up at Sanctuary, it's time I start treating him like one.

As we leave the ring he asks, "You sure you wanna be touching me with all this gross sweat coating me?"

I place my head down on his shoulder in emphasis. "Yes, I've missed you. Being around you calm me."

He reaches his hand out and pats my hand. "I'm glad."

We walk in silence until the barn comes into view.

"You know, the last time I was at Sanctuary, I ran into Nathan."

I slice my head to him. "You did? Were you used to be friends?"

He shakes his head. "No, I didn't even know who he was really. I'd seen him around, he worked for me, but we'd never had a conversation. He was worried about you, and said you were like a daughter to him."

"I've known him my whole life," I answer.

"From one father figure to another, he wanted me to tell you he's proud of you and he misses you."

My heart swells. I miss Nathan, too. He used to annoy me back in Daruk. He constantly took my father's attention away with town business, and I blamed Nathan for his absence. Now that I'm older, I understand that wasn't the case.

As we make it to the barn doors I stop and tug Ned to a stop next to me. "You know you've filled the hole my father dying left right? I consider you a father as well."

Ned pulls me in for a hug. His face buries in my hair. "You're the daughter I never had. I will never replace your father, but I'm glad I can help ease the pain of his passing a little."

When he pulls back, I notice tears lining his eyes which instantly brings tears to mine. I quickly wipe them away. Ned does the same.

"Let's go check on my girl."

We walk through the barn to where Raven usually sits, but today she's standing! I race over to her and throw my arms over her neck. "Hey, girl! I can't believe you're up! How are you already standing?"

She looks down on me and now I notice how stiff her body truly is. Her voice is tight as she says, "This is the first time I've been able to stand on my own."

I squeak, "Don't you think you should have waited until Kalven could be here?"

"Yeah, probably." Then she gingerly makes her way to her knees. I race forward and help push on her shoulder to give her a balancing point as she lies back down. As soon as she's on the ground, she starts heaving out heavy breaths.

I sit on the ground next to her and stroke her neck. "I know you want to be up and moving, but you can't yet. At least wait for Kalven to be here before you try to stand again."

She hangs her head and gasps out, "My legs hurt so much. I need to move them. It's not natural for horses to lie on the ground for days on end."

I shush her, "It's all right. I'll talk to Kalven today. It seems like you're pretty tired after standing on your own. I'll come over with Kalven tomorrow and we can figure out something to get you a little relief. He's coming by later to check on you right? He better check on you every day."

She scoffs. "Yes, he's like a hen fretting after her sick chick. He pops in all the time."

"He better be." I sit there and lean my head against her. Just taking in her smell, the smell of home, of family. My eyelids start feeling heavy, her scent and warm body calming me.

I hear a loud hoot and dive up and away from Raven. I scan the area for where the noise could have come from until my eyes land on Raven's stall. Perched on the edge sits Hazel. I instantly relax when I see her, but annoyance quickly sets in. I lean back down on Raven and cuddle back into her side. "Why are you here?"

Hazel ruffles her feathers. "That's all you have to say to me? Even after I left you again?"

I don't even give her an answer. What's the point? All she does is leave without a word. How can I trust someone who doesn't stick around?

She cracks into my thoughts. "I know where James is."

I shoot up into a sitting position. I can feel my face pale as the blood leaves my face. "Whaaat? How?"

"I followed him, Talon, and his sister."

I furrow my brow. "His sister? James doesn't have a sister."

"The werewolf who broke him out."

I throw my hands up in the air like I'm trying to physically clear my thoughts. "Hang on. I don't get it. A werewolf broke him out? But there were no claw marks on the dungeon wall. How could a werewolf get in here without leaving a trace?"

Hazel glides down to stand in front of me. With the way I'm sitting she towers over me, which is a little unnerving. Then she goes off into a speech about how she knew we couldn't leave Raven so, instead of sitting around doing nothing, she made herself useful. She scouted all the tiny towns in the Eastern Fae territory and returned in time to see a woman breaking into the dungeon. After a while, she saw Talon fly out along with a woman, and a werewolf.

I cut in, "You couldn't have known the werewolf was James."

She goes on to explain how she followed the three of them, but even with all her years of experience, Talon still caught sight of her. He pulled back away from his companions and flew to her. He explained the situation and told her he wants to help us as a double agent.

This shocks me. "He does? Why?"

She shrugs her wings. "He says he's tired of Henrik controlling him. He wants to be free."

I ask the question which has been burning on my mind since she started talking. "So, why did James's sister come to break him out?"

"That's the most kismet part. She came to break out Talon and just happened to stumble upon him."

I bring my hand to my chin in thought. "But if she's his sister shouldn't she have been a werewolf, too? You said she was a woman, like not in wolf form."

Hazel throws her wings out, the movement startles me, making me jump. "I asked Talon about it. He said Henrik used his blood magic to allow her the ability to control her wolf. She can use her wolf's strength and speed while choosing when she shifts. She's not forced to shift based off of the moon cycle like other werewolves. It's where Henrik got the idea for the werewolves he's been sending to attack you. Those aren't true werewolves, they're his experiments."

I nod. Yes, Father told me about his experiments. I lean my back against Raven. Thoughts flooding my mind. I peer over my shoulder at Ned. "Could you go get Kalven and Oberon? They're supposed to be figuring out how to get all of the Fae in the territory here, but this is more urgent."

Ned silently nods once then turns and leaves us.

"Well, do you believe Talon is on our side? I can't imagine him standing against Henrik unless things were truly terrible with him."

She fidgets back and forth on her claws. "I'm not sure, but he was rather forthcoming. He said he would get away as often as he could to bring us information on Henrik."

I stand up. Needing to move my legs I pace in a circle around Raven and Hazel. "But if he's not bringing us the correct information and we use his intel to attack Henrik, then we could be walking into a trap."

I'm still pondering this when Ned walks into the barn and clears his throat. Kalven quickly spits out, "We haven't figured out how to get the Fae here. Neither of us have been out to the towns in quite some time. We're having logistics issues."

I happen to stop in front of Hazel so I move over, allowing the men a clear line to her. "I have a solution to your problem then." I point at the owl. "Hazel has recently flown over the Eastern Fae territory. She can be trusted. Oberon, I would like you to work with her to figure out a reasonable solution." I pin him to the spot with my stare.

Oberon simply turns around and gestures for Hazel to follow him. He calls over his shoulder, "All right, bird, let's get going."

Hazel glances up to me, suddenly unsure of herself for the first time since I've known her. I furrow my brow at her and point out the barn. "Go on, go help him."

She ruffles her feathers and shakes her whole body before taking off after Oberon. That was strange. I wonder why she acted like she was flustered.

Kalven stares at me expectantly. I walk over to him and place a hand on his shoulder. "Well, it appears you're freed up for my next task. I hope you enjoy experiments."

Chapter Twenty-Two

James

When we walk out of the throne room, past the smoky quartz walls with small golden veins cracking throughout, I gaze down at my human arms in shock. I was supposed to turn back to human tomorrow, but here I am walking next to my sister as a human. I inspect my arm. "How do you control it?" I ask Tala, knowing she'll understand what I'm talking about.

She glances at my arm once before turning back forward. She scoffs and annoyance drips from her words and she lifts her lip exposing her teeth as she snarls in annoyance, "You think about it. Picture what your arm looks like when you're in wolf form."

I do as she says and instantly claws crawl out of my nails and thick brown hair sprouts along my arms. I gasp, but as soon as I think of my arms turning back to normal, they do. I let out a sigh. "And you can tap into your wolf power? What do I need to do to tap into mine?"

Tala throws her arms up. "You don't do anything! It just happens okay!"

I jerk back away from her and clench my jaw in irritation and shock. She was so nice and understanding the entire ride here. What changed? My voice doesn't hide my emotions when my words shake out of me. "Is—is everything all right? Did I do something wrong?"

Tala turns her hard gaze on me, but for a split second I see it falter. She grabs my arm and shoves me into a dark alcove. She pushes me against the wall and whispers in my ear, "Listen JJ, we can talk about it all later tonight. You don't understand how cutthroat the Fae are in this place. I grew up here. Trust me on this one. You don't want anyone here knowing anything but the bare minimum about you. Even the walls here have ears." Almost in emphasis her eyes move to the wall next to us. "So, let's just talk about this tonight okay?"

I push off the wall and drag her into a hug. She stiffens at my touch, but I don't care. When I jerk back, I whisper, "Fine, then what are we doing now?"

Her brown eyes almost gleam as she answers, "We're going to train."

⚜

After a day of Tala absolutely ruining me and slamming me into the ground repeatedly, I ate a dinner of onion soup and moldy bread then headed to bed. My bedroom isn't much, but it's more than some of the people here have. Walking through the mountain today I saw how impoverished the Fae living here are. The children don't have fitting clothes and the adults wear rags. Everyone here is underweight, even the soldiers, but the civilians are skin and bones.

It doesn't feel right.

But, if I'm to get Attina back, I have to act like I don't see what's happening around me and push forward.

My room door opens and light streams into my tiny room. I'm lying on the puny bed which fills most of the room. It's a thread bare, mildew smelling mattress without a pillow or a blanket. If this room wasn't in the middle of a mountain, I would be freezing.

Tala scoots between the wall and the bed. I move to my side, allowing her to crawl into bed with me. She lies next to me, and I wrap my arm around her shoulder. I remember doing this as kids except I was the one in her arms. "I'm sorry for today, JJ."

I shrug. "I won't become a better fighter without you being hard on me. I get it."

She shakes her head and her short black hair rubs against my forearm. "I mean how snippy I was with you today. Living here is hard. You have to be the best of the best just to survive."

"I've noticed. You won't be able to live like this forever. People are starving, Tala."

She turns in my arms and stares up at me. "I have nowhere else to go, JJ. I've lived here almost my entire life. This life is all I know."

I lean down and hug her, smashing my cheek into hers. "When I get Attina back, the three of us can leave together. We will figure it out. There are plenty of dead towns out there in the world we can make our own."

"You would do that for me?" she asks. Her voice is shaky like she's not certain I'm being serious.

I playfully shake her. "Yes! You're my family. Family sticks together no matter what."

Her body tenses. "Do we have to wait to get Attina? Couldn't you and I just leave together, JJ?"

Anger floods me again. Why would she say something like that? My ears heat as the breath leaves my lungs; I can't even smell the disgusting mattress beneath us as I'm consumed with rage.

I lung forward and snatch her throat. I squeeze until she's thrashing next to me and choking for air. "Now why would you go any say something so mindless? Why would I leave without *my* Attina?"

She gurgles out something, but I don't care enough to listen.

Instead, I ask, "Are you done? Do you promise to stop doing things to anger me? I really hate having to hurt you like this."

She nods her head, but with my hand grasping her throat, there isn't much room for her head to move. I release her. She gasps, tears flood her eyes, but she doesn't leave or even look at me like a betrayed her. She just lies there like she knew this was coming.

Did she anger me on purpose?

She turns over and curls into my chest. "Henrik wants to speak to you tomorrow. He wants information on Attina."

I lie back, snuggle into her hair and feel her physically relax. I want her to sleep so she'll stop saying stupid shit and quit pissing me off. "Great. Hopefully he'll have some sort of plan to get her back and then we can leave all this behind."

She whispers back, "I don't think it will be that simple." Then her breathing becomes steady and deep.

Chapter Twenty-Three

Allister

I know I'm dreaming because I'm running through an open field with Attina on Raven's back and me on a cougar's back. I left Attina at home and Raven was still too hurt to do anything but lie on the ground. Besides, I've never seen a live cougar in my life. Attina's laugh flits through the air filling my ears and making my heart skip a beat. Her smile, stunning as usual, knocks the air from my chest. Her lavender smell filling my nostrils.

I gaze down and run my fingers through the cougar's fur under me. Its strong muscles bunch and relax as it pounces through the air. I can tell my cougar is holding back, waiting for Raven to catch up. Its fawn colored fur sparkles in the daylight. It turns its head back to peek at me and a gasp escapes my lips.

The animal has my purple eyes.

How is that possible?

I groan as I stir awake. My body feels so heavy. I sit up, but my legs don't move. It almost feels like they're buzzing. The smell of wet fur assaults my senses. I rub my eyes and when I open them I see fawn fur.

What the—?

My eyes roam over a beastly body, this can't be real. My gaze locks on the long tail, the gigantic paws, and the dark tipped ears. Its side moves up and down and a purr escapes the creature which makes my legs vibrate. Is this the cougar I was dreaming about? No, it can't be.

I tentatively reach my hand out. This animal could turn around and maul me. There have been stories, passed down over the years, of rogue cougars dragging humans off into the forest.

When my hand makes contact with the cougar nothing happens, it just sleeps there, like I'm not here. I push on it a little harder, but there's no change, how is this thing sleeping this hard? I need to drag my legs out from under it and sneak out of here as quickly as possible.

I put both of my hands on the cougar and grunt as I push. Its side lifts off the ground a smidge, barely enough for me to move my legs. I wiggle them out from under the massive body and gently place the cougar back on its side. Almost as soon as the sleeping beast hits the ground, it stirs.

I quietly scramble closer to the mouth of the cave, but I'm slammed from the back, causing me to sprawl onto the ground.

A growl fills my ears.

Oh, shit! Not good!

The cougar's breath is hot on my ear. I try to move around, find my dagger, my flint rock, anything to hit the animal with. Maybe if I can hit it hard enough—

But my thought is broken off by a voice growling in my ear. "Where do you think you're heading off to? I didn't lie on you for two days just for you to take off while I'm resting."

Wait, this is a Fae animal? Then I realize its claws are retracted, it could drive them into my back or neck and render me helpless, but it hasn't.

Obviously, I'm a Fae animal. I'm only twice as big as a normal cougar.

Was his voice in my head? No, not possible. My blocks are up, there's no way it could get through them.

Yes, I can speak into your mind, even with those blocks up. Then I hear a voice outside of my mind. "Don't you know what I am?" The cougar slowly moves its weight off of me. I roll over and see it sitting down staring at me with its head cocked.

I shake my head. "I don't really know what you are, only what I've been told. You could have killed me, but didn't. Why?"

I gaze back over to where I'd tried to start a fire before I gave in to hypothermia. But where there should be nothing but ash from a lit fire, there are only the sticks I haphazardly stacked. I think back, but can't remember actually lighting the fire.

I peer back at the cougar. "Did you lie on top of me to keep me warm?"

It nods its head hard enough to make its ears flop slightly. "You were blue and shivering when I found you." The animal picks up its paws and extends its claws. "I could have cut your clothes off of you, but I didn't trust myself to not accidently cut you and with how close you were to dying I didn't know if your accelerated healing would work."

I look down at my clothes, glad I still have them and don't have to trek back to the Eastern Fae naked. I chuckle under my breath at the thought. "Okay, so who are you to me?"

The cougar drops its head and tentatively inches toward me. "I'm your Anima. You can call me Cedar."

I'm confused. "But your Anima is supposed to be within you. I already have one."

Cedar comes over and rubs his massive head against my shoulder, "Feel for your Anima. Is it still within you?"

It can't hurt to try. I'm not sure why, but I trust this animal. I mean it could have killed me by now, but it saved my life instead. I close my eyes and feel for my Anima, but come up blank. I frantically search within myself, but there's nothing there. "Wha—what—"

Cedar cuts me off, "It's because of your bloodline. All the kings and queens from the Leon family have their Anima outside their body. When you were born I was brought to life in this cave, but my subconscious lived inside you until you walked into the Cave of Kings. I've lived here waiting for you all these years. I've been waiting here for over a century. When a king or queen meets with their physical Anima the two mesh into one being. Why didn't you come find me sooner? Didn't your father tell you all of this?"

Cedar sits his butt right down next to me, and I lean against him, already feeling incredibly comfortable with him.

I take in a deep breath and sigh. "My father died when I was a kid." Then I remember the third part of this rite of passage. "I thought I had to prove myself worthy somehow? How am I supposed to prove myself?"

Cedar cocks his head and his tail twitches. "Prove yourself? I guess you losing your internal Anima is proving yourself. That wouldn't happen unless you were the true king." Then he nudges me. "Well, what about your mother? She would know about your Anima waiting for you." But the words sound sad, like he's realizing the answer on his own.

My voice is low and solemn. "She was taken by the King of the Western Fae. She might as well be dead."

Cedar's head drifts down to my shoulder and he rubs it against me. I see the white spots on the back of his ears. They make him appear like he literally has eyes on the back of his head. "Then you're all alone? That's why you never came to get me?"

I lay my head against Cedar's, his warmth calming me. "Until recently, yes, but I found my mate. You'll love her. She's smart, powerful, and beautiful. Her smile lights up my life and even with all she's been through she has the biggest heart of anyone I've ever met." I sigh at the tightness in my chest. I haven't been gone long, but I miss her so much already.

Cedar jumps up, his tail swings around back and forth. "She sounds amazing! Let's go meet her!"

I suck in air through my teeth as I get up. I hadn't realized how sore I was from shivering so hard and having a giant cougar lay on top of me for two days. I peer into Cedar's purple eyes, which now that we're both standing, are almost level with my own. "Did I seriously sleep for two days?"

He nods. "Yes, I thought you were gonna die. I had a little meltdown while you were sleeping."

My brows furrow. "Why?"

Cedar snakes his body around me and he gazes up and down my body, almost assessing me. "I'm like any other Anima, I'm just outside your body instead of within you. If you die, I die."

I turn around and make my way out of the cave. When I get outside, the sun is shining. It's up above us which means it must be about noon. I can't believe how long I slept. I wrap my arms around myself, trying to warm myself from the chill in the air. It has only been two days since I went for a swim, crossing the river in front of us, but the temperature is already sinking.

I nod toward the river. "I am not looking forward to crossing that again."

Cedar falls behind me, and I take a few deep breaths in and out, amping myself up for the freezing plunge when suddenly, I'm being thrown back. My arms fly out, trying to keep myself upright. I lean forward and grab onto fawn fur.

I screech, "What the—?"

I settle on Cedar's back as he trots over toward the river, he glances back and locks eyes with me. "You really think I'm letting you almost kill yourself again?"

I gaze between the immense river and Cedar. "And how ex-actly are you planning on getting us to the other side? We have to walk further down and find—" But before I can finish my sentence Cedar is running toward the river. I shout, "Cedar?"

He ignores me and picks up the pace.

I scream, "Cedar! Stop!"

When he doesn't, I lean down on his back so my chest is flush with his back and brace myself, and then we're flying through the air.

A scream tears from my lungs as we soar over the river. We land on the other side with a thump, and I feel Cedar chuckling underneath me. "Did you actually think I'd let you die? I'd die, too, remember?"

I glare down at the back of his head and dig my fingers down into his fur. "I'm glad you think this is funny. I'm riding a freaking gigantic cougar, who I met less than an hour ago, and he just sailed across a river. Forgive me for not believing in you." I let my voice lace with sarcasm as the words fall from my lips.

Cedar glances back at me again. "It's fine. Just don't let it happen again."

I growl at him as he makes his way away from the river. I hurriedly say, "Wait! I have to find Mylo."

Cedar's head moves back and forth as he searches the area around us. "Mylo? Who's that?" He pounces forward as he says, "Whoever it is probably left already, let's get going."

I bring my thumb and first finger to my lips and whistle. "Mylo! I'm back!"

Then, out of nowhere, a dark red mass comes barreling out of the trees. Mylo's eyes are wide when he sees me on top of a cougar. He throws his dished face up in the air and rears. A fearful cry ripping from his lungs.

I hop off of Cedar and move my hands up and down in front of me in a calming gesture. "Shh. Mylo, it's okay. He won't hurt you."

Mylo lands back on the ground, but his eyes are still wide, like he doesn't trust me.

"It's all right, Mylo. If he wanted to hurt you he would have by now." I reach my hand behind me and pet Cedar's side. "See, he's okay. He's a nice cougar."

Mylo snorts at me and throws his head in response, letting me know how upset he is about this turn of events. I step into him and run my hand down his face. "Thank you for staying here and waiting for me. You could have taken off, but you didn't. Why don't we head home to our mates?"

Mylo shakes his head up and down excitedly in response.

Chapter Twenty-Four

Attina

Hazel and Oberon have a solid plan on how to get all of the Eastern Fae to the castle faster than I thought possible. Oberon truly immersed himself in the project and took over everything for me. He says in a few weeks' time, we could have everyone in my territory back at the castle and a small town built to sustain everyone through the winter. I had some obvious questions about how we could sustain them, how we would feed them, but he told me to just leave it to him. So I did. He seems to enjoy being needed and in all honesty I have enough to deal with as a new queen.

I still have to figure out how to get into Shadow Mountain and once we are in, how can we defeat Henrik. I don't have many options for information about the castle. I had Allister, but he's gone, and I haven't been able to reach him in days. Hazel and Kalven have both been inside the castle, but it's been at least a century since either of them has been there. Kalven mentioned a tunnel, but who knows if it's still there. Talon is gone, and I'm not sure if he's coming back and Raven has no memories of living there. Which leaves me one option.

Titania.

My mother.

I want her dead, but when Talon escaped, all my inside information left with him. I stand up from the wooden table. I decided to have dinner with the citizens here. I want to reinforce the feeling that I'm approachable. I'm one of them. I can listen to their problems and help them out.

Everyone's rather wary of me which means I sit on my own for most of my meal until Oberon and his Mori Nikos took up seats beside me. I was grateful for their company. I couldn't keep up as they all joked and laughed at their past experiences.

I wish I could have friends like that. Ava seemed very interested in her mate, totally engrossed in every word Hudson uttered. She said she wanted to be friends, but I understand. Sometimes your mate can take up a large part of your world and there's nothing you can do about it. So, I quietly stand while Oberon talks to them of his plans for the upcoming weeks.

As I make my way out the double doors of the throne room, I hear my name. "Attina!"

I stop in my tracks and pivot around to see Ned racing over to me. "Whatcha doin?"

I can't hide my exasperation as a sigh escapes my lips. "I have to go see Titania. I have some questions for her about Shadow Mountain."

He eagerly inches into me. "Well, you shouldn't be going anywhere alone. Oberon is distracted so I'll go with you."

I shake my head and stare at the ground. If I look at him, I know I won't be able to tell him no. I don't want to see my mother alone, it's too hard being around her, and I can never keep my temper under control. No one should have to see me be that person.

"No, you should be with Raven. Remember you told Mylo you would watch over her in his stead? Do you think Mylo would ever leave her side?"

Even I could hear the uncertainty in my voice though, and as soon as Ned put his hand on my shoulder, I knew I wouldn't be leaving alone. "Do you really think Raven would ever forgive me if I let you head down there on your own?"

Reaching my hand up, I pinch the bridge of my nose. "Are you sure? I've never had an interaction go well with that woman. You weren't there the last time I saw her. It wasn't pretty."

His mouth hangs slightly and he stands there watching me for a second. "Yes, I want to come. I'll be your voice of reason." Then he surprises me by grabbing me by the shoulders and dragging me into a hug. "You're better than him. You're nothing like Henrik."

I dig my face into his shoulder as I feel the tears heat my face. "Sometimes, I'm not so sure about that." Then I draw back and wipe my face with the back of my hand. I let out a loud huff and steel my spine. Regaining my composure, I say, "Let's get this over with."

I hate coming down here. The dungeons have become my own personal trigger. I know there are worse things, I could be in a cell alongside Titania and Commander Demarco, but I'm never proud of myself when I leave this hell hole.

I pass the area the Fae use to torture their prisoners and wonder if I'll need to torture Titania to pry this information out of her. A little piece of me hopes I'll have to, but I shove that feeling down deep. Henrik would think like that. Not me.

The cold has seeped into the room enough for me to have to wrap my arms around myself. I gaze over to the hole James's sister created, the hole which was haphazardly repaired, but has already fallen apart, when she wrenched him and Talon from my grasp.

Anger instantly floods me. She stole Talon from me, and now I have to deal with my mother. I throw my hand up toward the dungeon wall and the bricks she toppled begin righting themselves. The bricks crash and grind as they move back to their original places. She must have waited for an opening where everyone would be distracted to take down this wall. If everyone weren't distracted with mine and Oberon's fight, maybe I wouldn't have lost my prisoners.

I rub the back of my neck, no I know that's not true. If we hadn't been such a distraction she would have created her own distraction, which could have meant her hurting some of the people here. I guess in some odd way I'm glad things happened the way they did.

Gerald stands in his cell with his hands wrapped around the bars, growling at me. I lift my head and act like he doesn't exist. Then, as I pass Commander Demarco's cell I notice he's peacefully sleeping in the back of it. How anyone could sleep peacefully here is beyond me.

Ned, who's quietly followed me this whole time, breaks off to stop at his cell. I hear quiet words and know he's trying to wake Demarco up. I know they've been friends for years, but I don't understand how Ned can keep trying for a friendship which is obviously dead.

I reach Titania's cell, but she must be in the back hiding again because she's nowhere to be found. "Titania, I need to speak with you. I have some questions."

No answer.

I try again. "Let's not act like children, come out and speak to your daughter."

Nothing.

My shoulders tighten as stress floods my body. Why can't anything ever be easy with this woman? Then all of a sudden the sight of the brick wall partially down flashes in my mind. What if she somehow escaped?

My blood runs cold. Another prisoner escaping on my watch is *not* what I need right now. No one will believe I can protect them if she escaped. Talon and James fled on Gerald's watch, but he blamed me for their escape. If my own mother gets loose everyone here will lose faith in me and they might even blame me for Talon and James's escape. I can't allow that to happen.

If she's gone I need to find her and hold her accountable for her actions in front of the Eastern Fae citizens.

I call to Ned, "Could you please get the cell door keys from Oberon?"

"Of course," he replies before I hear him race off. So much for protecting me at all times, I think as I giggle to myself and shake my head.

Ned's back in a flash holding out the keys and winking at my gaping maw. "I told you I was quick."

I gaze down at the cluster of keys in my hand; there must be fifty keys here. "Did he happen to tell you which ones unlocked which cells?"

I bring my gaze to him as he shakes his head and reaches out to my hand picking out three keys. "No, but he told me these were the only cells being used at the moment, so we only have these to search through instead of fifty."

I hear Commander Demarco groan in the cell behind us. "You better go try to talk to him. I know you still want him to be your friend still."

He rubs the back of his neck with his hand, embarrassed. "Thank you. I know it's stupid. I should just give up."

I walk over to him and wrap my arms around his neck, dragging him into a big hug, "It's not stupid. You have a big heart. You're a better person than me."

Then I hear a growl from the cell next to us. Well, I guess that answers if Titania escaped or not. I release Ned and notice his pursed lips, making his face appear to be filled with concern as he mumbles, "Are you sure you want to do this?"

I take a step back and stare at the ground. "I don't want to do this, but I have to."

Ned grabs my arm, the gesture drawing my gaze to him. His tone is serious as he says, "Yell if you need me. I'll be right over there." He points to Commander Demarco's cell, and I quietly nod to him.

Another growl escapes the darkness of my mother's cell as Ned walks off to the other cell. I turn to where my mother must be standing in the shadows. "Titania, get out here, be an adult about this." Again there's no answer. I snort, "Fine, it's not like you've ever made life easy for me."

I walk to the cell door and begin trying each key. True to my mother never making things easy for me, I don't get the door unlocked until I get to the last key. When I hear it click I decide to take the keys out of the door and fling them on the ground so neither one of us can reach them through the cell bars. I'm not taking any chances with this woman.

The door groans as I open it and enter. Now, with the dungeon wall partially fixed the urine and feces smell is already growing. I cough as I slip into the cell. I would have thought she'd rush for the door, trying to escape or attack me as soon as I walked in, but she didn't.

I throw my arms out to the side, leaving myself vulnerable. "Here I am, this is obviously what you wanted. Are you coming out or are you going to make me come in there and get you?" To show her how me coming in there and getting her would turn out, I summon fireballs in the palm of my hands, letting the fire slowly crawl over my body. "I won't ask again. You have five seconds before I come get you. One—two—three—"

Then out of nowhere, Titania throws herself on me. As her arms wrap tightly around my neck, I hear the hiss of her skin. Then the nauseatingly putrid smell that always accompanies flesh burning, tickles my nose. I try to wiggle away from her, but she doesn't relent. She holds on tighter with all of her considerable Fae strength.

I growl, "Let go or you'll burn yourself alive."

But she doesn't release me.

I'm torn. Either I can burn this woman alive and avenge Father and Oak, or I can extinguish my fire and get the information the people of Arealea need for me to defeat Henrik.

For a split second, I'm almost selfish enough to damn the world all for revenge. But then pictures of Ned, Mylo, Raven, and finally Allister flash through my mind. I would be damning them, the family I found along the way, along with the world, and I couldn't do that.

I release my fire, and Titania begins whimpering, barely able to keep herself standing. I bend down with her until she's sitting on the ground. I wrap my hands behind my neck and try to pry her arms from my neck, but her skin gives way, peeling from her arm.

I coo at her, trying to get her to listen to me. "You have to release me, Titania. As soon as your healing starts, your skin will be stuck to mine, and I'll have to burn you again to get you off."

She grunts as she pulls her arms from my neck. Then I can really see the damage. Her bones are stark white against the charred black of her skin.

I shake my head. "Why did you grab me? I was covered in fire. You knew you would get burned."

She gazes up at me with her piercing red eyes, and her voice comes out as a whimper. "I haven't been able to hold you since you were a baby. It was worth being burned alive to be able to hold you in my arms once more."

Her words almost break me.

Almost.

I feel tears forming behind my eyes, but I swallow hard to push them back. I sit on the ground next to her and put my face in my hands. I take a deep breath to calm myself.

This is the woman who killed the two most important people in my life. She took them from me.

I should hate her. I repeat these words over and over in my mind until I can bring back up the wall she's slowly, brick by brick, knocking down.

I exhale as I rub my hands down my face. I lock eyes with her still charred form and almost lose my resolve, but I push through. "I need some information. I planned to use Talon for this, but as you know, he's escaped."

She folds her hands in her lap. "Anything I can do to help you."

She's acting like this just another day, as if all children burn their parents. I don't understand. She's not upset. I've burned her not once, but twice, and now I need her help? I would be furious and refuse. I thought this would be much harder.

I cock my head and grumble, "I need to know the layout of Shadow Mountain."

Her voice wavers as she speaks. "What about Allister? He's been there recently hasn't he? I don't know when he left, but I'm assuming it was after your Awakening."

I glare at her. "His whereabouts are *none* of your business."

If she hadn't brought up my Awakening—when she killed my family—I probably would have told her where Allister is; but she brought it up, she can deal with the consequences.

She lowers her head to stare at the ground between us. "I thought he was your mate? He seemed like your mate by the way he held you so tenderly when he brought you down to see me. Is everything all right between you two? I know mates aren't guaranteed to be a good fit, but I knew him before, and I thought—"

I cut her off, "What you thought doesn't matter to me. We are not friends. We aren't even mother and daughter. As far as I'm concerned, my mother died when I was a child. I need information, and you will give it to me."

She leans back and cuts her gaze away from me. I can see the tears streaming down her cheeks and there's a hitch in her voice as she says, "Why should I help you if you won't even be civil with me?"

I snicker. "Because I will kill my grandfather. The man who took your mate, your daughter, and your life from you."

Chapter Twenty-Five

Attina

We talk for a while before I need a break. I repeat my mantra in my head, she killed Father and Oak. I hate her. But I find myself feeling more and more comfortable with her. The information doesn't get me far anyway; she only tells me the basics. There's one wooden door into the mountain with a spell carved into it which only allows beings who live within the mountain to enter unchecked. Well, it sounds like I can't enter through the front door.

Ned and Commander Demarco chat for a while, until their conversation gets heated, and I use their argument as an excuse to leave.

I'm turning the lock in the cell door when Titania wraps her now healed hands around the cell bars. They're so small and delicate. How could such compact hands cause such an upheaval in my life?

"You'll come back won't you?"

I break my gaze from her hands and glare into her red eyes. I remember those eyes staring down at me during the night of my Awakening. I quickly remind myself of the night she took everything from me.

"If I need more information I'll be back. Other than that? No."

Twisting on my heel I walk down the hallway where Ned's trying to calm down a screaming Demarco. Yanking on his forearm I twist him around, dragging him away from the fray.

But as we walk, of course, Demarco has to get in one last jab. He screams, "You disgust me."

And after the time with my mother I'm glad for the challenge. I release Ned and whirl around, stalking back to Demarco.

With my head down, I snarl, "I hope you were talking to me, because if you weren't, we're going to have a problem."

Ned comes up beside me and yanks on my arm, trying to drag me away. But I want this. I want to crush this little man, and damn the consequences.

Demarco sits down in the middle of his cell and crosses his arms. He clenches his jaw. "I was talking to both of you."

My fingers slowly curl around the bar in front of me. I open my mouth to say something when out of nowhere Allister's voice flits through my mind. *I'm on my way back, love.*

I whimper, and my knees instantly turn weak, but by the triumph on Commander Demarco's face, I know he thinks he was the cause of it.

I sigh. "Your life was just saved by a Fae. Remember that the next time you want to mouth off." I don't give him a chance to answer as I drag Ned out of the dungeon with me.

Ned squeaks, "Did you hear from Allister?"

I glance at him before turning back to the stairs in front of us. He sounds almost as excited I heard from Allister as I am. A smile cracks my features as I silently nod.

My thoughts turn to Allister, and questions spill from me. *You are? Are you okay? Did it go well? How's Mylo?*

I hear his throaty chuckle as he answers, *Missed me, did ya?*

I roll my eyes. *Answer my questions. I just visited Titania. My patience runs thin, even for my mate.*

You what? Really?

I click my tongue. *Allister!*

We're all fine. It shouldn't take us as long to get back. I have a big surprise for you when we get home.

My heart swells at his words. *When we get home.* I guess this is our home. I've never felt like I fit in anywhere, but here?

I nod to a passing Fae with short cut gray hair and piercing gray eyes. I feel like this is the first place I can truly call home.

I've already made some big changes here. Get home soon so I can show you what I've done while you were away.

I hear silence from Allister, but also something else? Frustration?

No, anger. Something I said angered him. I wait for his answer for a second.

Is everything all right?

He growls. *What did that bastard do to you? I will crush Gerald's mind if he laid a finger on you, and then I'll turn Oberon into a drooling mess for not protecting you.*

I fumble for the right words. Gerald didn't technically touch me, and Oberon let me handle the situation. I don't want to upset him until I'm in his arms and he can see for himself I'm unharmed. *I'm fine. No one touched me unless we were in a fight I asked for. Which, by the way, I won every fight.*

I push some pride into my inner voice because I'm very proud of myself for how far my fighting has come. It's been a long hard journey transforming from a girl who'd never thrown a punch to someone who can hold her own against the top Fae in all of Arealea.

I can almost instantly feel the anger from him dissipate. Then he chuckles in my. *That's my girl.*

Hearing him call me his girl has warmth pooling in my gut. I can't get enough of him claiming me as his. I want to hug myself and squeal like a girl, but Oberon cuts in front of me. My cheeks heat, and I'm not sure why. I feel like he's walking in on something intimate. Then Ned catches up to my side. I was so engrossed in my conversation with Allister I'd completely forgotten he was following me.

Oberon bows his head to me. "I have some plans I would like to talk over with you."

I nod back and bring up my hand, silently asking him to give me a second. *Oberon is in front of me with some things I need to handle. Be home soon?*

Always, kitten. Be safe my love and keep our bed warm for me.

A fire ignites in me. I feel it trailing over my skin like Allister's fingers would. My skin starts to turn pink as I gaze at Oberon. He looks me up and down before a wicked grin spreads across his face. "Did you hear from the king?"

My eyes widen, and I nod. How did he know I'd heard from Allister? Am I that transparent? "He's on his way home? How did you know?"

He chuckles and points to my pinkened skin. "You only ever turn pink when you're angry or it has to do with Allister, and you don't seem angry right now." Wow. I didn't even notice. But now I'm thinking about it, he's right. He's surprisingly observant. I'm glad he's working for us and not Henrik.

I place my hand on Ned's shoulder. "You should go check on Raven, I'm safe with Oberon." Ned gazes between Oberon and me, his stare almost assessing if I'm actually safe with this Fae. I encourage him to leave by saying, "Give her a hug from me."

My words seem to work because he scoffs and turns away. I wonder what that was about? Does he not trust Oberon?

"What can I help you with? I need to make my way to see how Kalven's doing with our project, so let's talk while we walk." I gesture to him to lead the way.

He wraps his hands behind his back, and I slide into line next to him. "I just have some things I would like to go over with you prior to executing my plan." I silently nod, allowing him the space to continue. "I would like to send some convoys out to retrieve these people. Bring everything they'd need, including food, for the winter. Now I have to tell you, if we need them past the winter and early spring I don't know how we'll feed them next year. They grow our food, they have to be back to plant in spring."

When I glance over to him, his hard eyes are pinned on me. "Okay, then that means we have to defeat Henrik by then or figure out a new plan."

He stops and turns to me with sparkling eyes. "Right. I would also like to send the Mori Nikos with Hazel to accomplish this mission."

I suck on the inside of my cheek. "You realize they're our best warriors. If Henrik decides to attack while they're gone we're fucked."

He drops his head to the ground. "In all honesty, whether they're here or not, we're screwed if Henrik attacks. We'll only have a chance against him once we get our people here and can get them trained."

I sigh, knowing he's right. "Okay, you can send them. But I require you to stay with me. If you leave, Allister will kill you. It won't matter if I sent you away or not, and I will not have your blood on my hands."

His gaze drifts back to mine, and I'm surprised to see his lips tug up in a grin, "I accept your terms." He bows, turning to continue our trek to Kalven's laboratory.

We talk about some small aspects of the mission until we reach Kalven's door. His examination room door is wide open so we pass between the table and wall of containers. Oberon knocks on the next door for me, the door to where he performs autopsies, and almost instantly Kalven flings open his door, like he was waiting for us.

When Kalven opens the door I'm knocked back by the overwhelmingly sour stench of death and decay. The lighting in the room is dim, but as soon as he gets close to us I can see the blood dripping off of him.

Oberon immediately pulls out his sword, throws his arm out in front of me, and barks. "What's the meaning of this?" Kalven shrinks back in answer.

I place my hand on Oberon's shoulder. "You can put it away, he's performing a top secret experiment for me."

Oberon whirls around, sword still raised, but he's obviously forgotten it's even there. He stumbles out, "What could you possibly—"

I pointedly stare at the sword and back at his face.

Shaking his head, he sheathes his sword.

"I need to show you this anyway. I should have shown you this as soon as the experiment started. I now realize how dangerous it could have been."I bow my head to Kalven, who turns and walks into the dimly lit room.

Oberon snarls, "Why can't we have some light in here?"

I raise my hand, lighting some of the candles I can barely make out dotting around the room.

But as soon as the room is illuminated a roar rips through the room. Oberon violently throws his arm into my chest, throwing me backwards. Saws and other dissecting tools clatter to the floor as my back slams hard into the wall behind me.

In front of us, a Solis thrashes against its restraints. Its head slices to us and its rotting teeth gnash in our direction, it tries to haul its body from the table, but the ropes covering its arms, torso, and legs keep it firmly in place. The man was young when he was turned. His brown skin is stretched loose over his scrawny, starving frame.

Oberon raises his sword again. He brings it up over the Solis like he means to kill it.

I throw out my hand. "Stop!"

He freezes with his sword mere inches from the monster's throat. I push myself off the wall as Kalven putters around, blowing out the candles I've just lit.

"The creature calms down considerably when the lights are low." And it's like the Solis understands him because as soon as the words leave his mouth, the man lies still.

Kalven comes to my side as Oberon stands there with his mouth open, probably in shock. It takes him a few solid minutes to say anything and Kalven, and I give him the time he needs to process this turn of events.

Oberon stiffly turns, his lip lifted in a menacing snarl, and his gaze moving down to my face. "Explain. I'm supposed to keep everyone here safe and you brought this thing in without my knowledge?"

I lean my back against the wall and Kalven decides this is the time to pick up every tool my body slamming against the wall knocked down. Not being any help at all. "When I first met Kalven he said something about the Solis not being truly dead. I couldn't get it out of my mind. I know the Solis are Henrik's creation and he used blood magic to breathe them into existence."

Oberon hisses, "How could you possibly know such a thing?"

In an attempt to alleviate the tension I wink at him. "Family secrets." I realize the room is dark and he probably can't see me.

He huffs, but doesn't say anything in return so I continue.

"Long story short, I wanted to see if Kalven could release them from whatever magic they're under using my blood. I'm Henrik's granddaughter, his blood runs through my veins." I shrug. "It could work. So we trapped one and brought it here to see if Kalven could break whatever hold they're under."

Oberon's hand goes to cover his face and he shakes his head, "I don't even want to know how you guys did that or how you got past me without my knowledge." Then he moves over to where Kalven is placing the fallen tools back on the wall. "And why are you covered in blood? The Solis seems unscathed."

Kalven turns back to him and happily squeaks, "I was cutting up a body."

Chapter Twenty-Six

Attina

Oberon growls and slams Kalven up against the wall behind him, the motion stirring up the iron smell of blood. The tools clatter to the ground again and Kalven sighs, almost more annoyed at the fact he'll have to pick those up again, than at the threat in front of him.

I shove my arm into Oberon's, forcing him to release Kalven. Kalven slumps down the wall behind me. Glaring up at Oberon, I snarl, "Why don't you look around the room before you attack your king's family." And, even with the dim lighting, I can tell Oberon's face pales at the realization of what he's doing. He knows how much Kalven means to Allister and if he were to find out how Oberon attacked him? Well. let's just say it wouldn't be pretty.

Oberon grunts and stalks over to the other side of the room, his shoulders visibly stiff. "What the hell!" he shouts.

I groan as I make my way over to Oberon's side, I didn't want to see this part. I was hoping Kalven would have it done by the time I came to check on his progress. I exaggeratedly exhale. "We trapped this Solis who was obviously starving. He needed to eat."

Oberon turns on me and towers over me. I can almost feel his hatred toward me radiating off of him. The ground underneath us shakes, his powers seeping out of him. Then he roars, "How could you!"

Great. He got the wrong idea. I seriously need to get better at communicating. I cock my head and smile up at him. I want to back away from him and cower, but I refuse to allow myself to appear weak in front of anyone ever again.

"You really have zero faith in me don't you? This is one of the Solis I killed the day we came here. They don't decompose, so they're all still scattered out there."

He immediately jerks back. His hand goes to the table next to him for support before remembering it's covered in blood, and he yanks his hand back, then drops his head in apparent shame. His voice comes out shaky as he says, "Oh."

I place my hand on his arm. "I know you haven't known me long, and you're used to dealing with a crappy leader, but I would never harm my people. You can trust me, Oberon. I *will* be a good queen. I can't guarantee I won't ever make a mistake, but I expect you to let me know when I'm fucking up."

His eyes finally rise to mine. I see something close to pride and determination in them as he curtly nods to me, then walks out of my touch and back over to Kalven. He stands in front of him and commands, "Explain."

Kalven moves over to the table, holding the Solis, and props on it by the creature's feet. "Well, through my limited studies of these creatures, I've discovered they're not technically dead like everyone's assumed. Their heart pumps and their blood moves. Except, it's in such a delayed way, any normal doctor would determine them dead. It's why they can be mortally injured and keep attacking their prey. Their injuries barely register with the creature because of their near stagnant bodily functions." He raises his hands in my direction. "As Attina stated, this was done by Henrik through blood magic. It stands to reason then that Attina's blood may reverse the spell."

Oberon's gaze shifts back and forth between Kalven and me. "You actually think this could work?"

Kalven opens his mouth to answer, but I cut him off. Oberon doesn't want to hear the medical interpretation of the odds of success, he wants a yes or no answer. I noncommittally shrug. "It's worth a shot."

Oberon leans against the table holding the Solis, staring down at it, "And if it doesn't? Will these humans turn back into themselves when Henrik's killed? Or will they be stuck like this forever?"

I let my head drop to the ground, which is answer enough for him. The theory is they will turn back when Henrik is dead, but so little is known about blood magic, we truly can't know what will happen. They might all simply perish when Henrik does. There's no way to tell.

Kalven takes the opportunity to chime in. "Well? Are you ready for me to draw your blood?"

I nod to him before I find a seat tucked away in a corner and bring it over to where Kalven stands. He quickly digs through a drawer and takes out a needle and some supplies. Oberon turns to leave the room, but I call to him, "Not so fast. I'll need you to help me to my room after this. He'll need a lot of blood for the test, and I want to get it done all at once."

Oberon clears his throat. "I'm not great with medical stuff. Needles freak me out. So, if you want me on the floor next to you, I'll stay. Otherwise I'll listen for you in the other room."

I snicker as he leaves the room. Such a big bad warrior and needles make him faint? I whisper to Kalven, "I wouldn't want to be his doctor."

Kalven's gaze flicks to the door where Oberon exited and then goes straight back to my arm and his work. "Ever since he was a kid, he's cried when I've had to give him a shot. Every damn time."

⚊⚊◆⚊⚊

I n the middle of the night, I hear him. *Attina? You awake?*

I shoot into a sitting position in bed, the covers sliding down my body. *Allister?*

I hear a laugh. *Who else would be talking to you in the middle of the night?* Then his voice holds a tinge of jealousy as he asks, *Have you been talking to anyone else in the middle of the night?*

I roll my eyes. *Shut up. Where are you?*

His answer is husky. *Why don't you come to the gates and greet your mate? I've missed you and our bed.*

Heat instantly pools in my core, and I throw the covers back, jumping out of bed. I throw on my boots and run out of the room, leaving the door swinging in my wake. I make it almost halfway down the stairs as a thought hits me.

I better get Oberon.

I race back to his room, slam my fist on his door. "Allister is here! You better get out here—"

Oberon swings the door open, and his shirtless form fills the empty space. My eyes trail down his tight form, moving from his sculpted chest to the V above his pants. He props against the door and chuckles at my reaction. "I'm glad your mate is here. Now, I don't have to deal with you anymore."

My gaze drifts up, and I'm surprised to find I'm not embarrassed by my actions. I stick my tongue out at him. "You better head out with me or he'll be pissed at you."

"All right, let me put a shirt on. I'll be right back." He closes the door a bit before grabbing a shirt from the end of his bed. He throws it over his head and makes his way to the head of the bed, leaning over and kissing his mate and patting his child's head. "I'll be back in a bit."

I hear a woman's voice mumble, and I turn away from the door. I shouldn't have peeked in; that was a private moment.

Embarrassment instantly washes over me for ogling Oberon. I'd want to rip me limb from limb if I was his mate.

Oberon walks out his door and slaps me on the back. "Let's go get our king."

I nod to him and trot down the stairs. Heat rises to my cheeks, but if he sees it, he doesn't comment on it.

We hurry out and stand by the one gate in the white bricked wall surrounding the castle to wait. The night air is cold. I hope we don't have to wait long. A couple minutes turn into ten. Ten turns to fifteen. When Allister spoke into my mind he felt like he was close, but then he broke the connection again and he was lost. Was I so wrong at how far away he was?

I peek over at Oberon who stands there shivering right alongside me. "Why don't you head back up to your warm bed. I'm sure your family misses you. I can wait alone. It's fine, I'll cover for you."

His gaze slices to me. "Do you want me dead? 'Cause that's what'll happen. There's no way in hell I'm allowing you to wait on your own. My family might miss me, but they'd miss me a lot more if Allister crushes my mind for leaving you alone."

It's only then I realize. "You're afraid of him."

Oberon brings his hands to his mouth to blow some warmth back into them. "Yes, I am. There aren't many Fae who can listen in on other people's thoughts. But out of those few Allister is the deadliest. His reputation is known throughout the Fae. He kills without reason."

"Then why aren't you afraid of me?" I taunt. "I'm his mate, his equal, shouldn't that alone terrify you?"

His shoulders shake as he softly snorts, and then drapes his arm across my shoulders. "You don't give the vibe of being a killer. That's why I underestimated you so badly when we first met. I know how powerful you are now, but no, I wouldn't consider you terrifying, more like sneaky scary."

I slap his hand, but as I do, I hear a guttural growl from the gates. I turn to see the most beautiful man I've ever seen sitting astride a humongous cougar. Heat instantly spreads throughout my body, and my knees go weak at the sight of him.

He jumps off the cougar, then stalks through the gate, and over to me. I forgot how well his black fighting leathers hug his body. His head tilts down and a knowing smirk crawls up his lips as his eyes rake up and down my body.

He opens his arms, and I take off at a run. Throwing myself into his arms, I hit his body with a thud, knocking the air from my lungs. When I gasp a breath in, I'm hit with the smell of a forest just after a rainstorm. I'll never get enough of his comforting scent.

I bury my head down into the crook of his neck, tears freely flow as he whirls me around. He gingerly places me on the ground before I notice him glare at Oberon. He roars, "I told you to protect her, not hit on her."

He strides forward and Oberon quickly moves away from him. "My king...I...I'm..."

I race in front of Allister and smack him in the chest. His furious stare transfers to me. "What?" he snaps.

"He did nothing wrong. He's been an absolute gentleman! We're friends."

"Friends?" His eyes drift back to Oberon who's frozen to the spot then land back on me, "Fae can't be friends. All they know is death and destruction."

He moves back toward Oberon, and I slam both my hands into his chest this time. I command, "Leave him alone."

I hear a deep voice purr behind Allister say, "I like her." But I ignore it, I have more important things to deal with right now.

His face is dark when he locks eyes with me and growls, "You're too close. You're *my* mate."

I bring my hand to his cheek. "I *am* yours, and *you* are *mine*."

Allister's eyes instantly soften at my touch, and he snakes his arm around my midsection, pulling me into a constricting hug. He buries his face in my hair and takes a deep breath of my scent.

He releases me, and I instantly want to be in his embrace again. My body aches to be in his arms. I pivot to his side. I'd like to go over to Oberon and make sure he isn't shaken too much, but with Allister's temper, it's probably better for everyone if I don't.

Oberon bends at the waist, his fisted hand drifting to his chest. "I'm sorry, my king. Our queen told me she wanted every-one to see her as someone they could go to with their problems, that we should see her as a friend. I was obeying her wishes. I tried to stay away, but we've become friends in your absence. As you can see, I haven't left her side." Then his voice waivers as he adds, "I accept any punishment you see fit to dole out."

Chapter Twenty-Seven

Attina

I peek up at Allister's face; his purple eyes are almost black in the moonlight, but a small smile quirks up his lips, "You may rise. Thank you for keeping my mate safe. As she pointed out, I overreacted. The first time I see my mate again and another man has his arm over her shoulder. You have a mate, I'm sure you understand."

Oberon rises and silently nods at Allister. "Yes, my king. It won't happen again—"

Allister stops him by raising his hand. "No, if Attina wants to be your friend, far be it for me to stand between you two. Just make sure you're *only* friends."

Oberon's gaze drifts to me. "Yes, I will." He coughs into his hand as he glances back behind us. "Um, are we just going to act like the *giant* cougar doesn't exist or—?"

Before I can turn around, I feel a furry head rubbing against my arm. I jump and spin around as the animal opens its mouth and speaks, "So this is our mate? I remember rubbing against her and tackling her. I like her. She's feisty." Then the cougar picks its head up to mine. Its tongue shoots out of its mouth and the hard prickly, dry surface scrapes up my face.

"Ugh!" I shout and jump away, wiping my face after the beast's assault. I glance between the animal and Allister. "Someone explain."

Allister's hand reaches out and softly pats the cougar's broad fawn head. "This is Cedar. He's my Anima."

My brows pinch, and I cock my head. "You already have an Anima. I felt it when you were teaching me to find mine remember?"

Cedar stalks toward me, and I shuffle back. I was taught from a young age to be afraid of cougars; they're well known to kill for fun and leave bodies uneaten. I know this cougar wouldn't hurt me since it's a part of Allister, but I can't get the picture of it standing over my mauled body out of my head.

Cedar twitches his tail. "It's a long story. Want to cuddle, and I'll tell you all about it?"

I gaze between Allister and Cedar with what I can only guess is terror in my eyes, because Allister drops his head, pinches the bridge of his nose. "Cedar leave her alone. She doesn't want to play."

His head slices back to Allister, and I take the opportunity to scurry behind him.

Allister wraps his arm behind himself to touch me knowing I could use a little reassurance. "See? Just give her until tomorrow. I promise I'll bring her to see you and you guys can get better acquainted then."

Cedar hangs his head, but acquiesces. "Fine."

I peek around Allister and point my finger toward where the barn is situated. With more confidence than I feel, my voice booms. "You can stay in the barn tonight. My horse, Raven, is injured though. If the blood is too much you can sleep outside the castle. If you hurt Raven you hurt me, so make your decision."

Cedar turns in the direction I point, then back to me. My breath catches at his focused stare. "I could never hurt you. I will sleep in the forest tonight. I doubt a cougar would be welcome there in the middle of the night." He turns back adding, "Until tomorrow, mate." Then he hops through the gates and into the darkness.

I let out a loud breath as my heartbeat slows down. Behind us, Oberon chuckles. "I guess I'll leave you two to it. You have *a lot* of catching up to do."

Allister and I whirl to face him. Allister wraps me in a hug as we go. I love how touchy feely he is right now. I lean back into him, letting the heat radiating off of him warm my back. I rub my hand up and down his arms.

Allister's solid voice fills the courtyard. "Thank you for watching over my mate. Your actions will be rewarded."

Oberon's eyes drift to mine, and he smiles. "She didn't need much supervision. Our queen can take care of herself."

Allister's arms tighten around me at Oberon's lingering stare. I clear my throat, which seems to bring Oberon out of his reverie, and my voice is tight when I say, "Thank you, friend."

He bows to us. "Goodnight, my queen and king."

I bounce on my feet. "Goodnight." I feel Allister's head bob against mine, nodding back to Oberon.

As Oberon leaves, I'm spun by Allister. He traps my chin in his fingers and tilts my gaze to his. "You have some explaining to do. You have our captain wrapped around your little finger. And he's calling you *queen*? He wasn't doing that when I left."

I try to glance away, but he holds me in place. I sigh and whisper out, "Well, I *am* queen."

Allister shakes his head and opens his mouth. But instead of saying anything, he bends down, wraps his arms under my ass, and picks me up off the ground, throwing me unceremoniously over his shoulder. His clothes smell fresh but feel stiff from being shoved in his saddle bag on his journey.

I squeal out, "Put me down! I can walk." But he just chuckles under me and slaps my butt. I have to throw my hand over my mouth to staunch a moan as it escapes my lips.

He growls out, "You will explain everything to me after I'm satisfied you're all mine."

I squirm on top of him. All the nerves along my skin burn at his touch.

He grabs onto my thigh as we enter the castle. "Stop wiggling or I might drop you."

But I know that's not true.

He'd never drop me.

He doesn't move his hand from my body though, he keeps moving his hand, massaging it. I run my nails up and down his back.

I smile when a groan hits my ear. "Oh, kitten wants to play, does she?" His hand moves down, caressing the apex of my thighs.

I moan loudly, the sound echoing off the castle walls.

I heft myself up and swing my legs forward, wrapping them around his midsection while he climbs the stairs. I'm glad he's the graceful one of the two of us, because if I was the one doing the walking, I would have already fallen backwards and probably hit every stair on the way down. His hands move under my butt, and I lace my arms over his shoulders. Crashing my lips on his. His tongue slides along my lips, asking for an invitation. I open my mouth and allow him access. A small whimper escapes my throat. I'm thrilled to have his touch on me again. I yearn to have his body over top of me once more.

He slams me up against the wooden door to our room. I let out a loud groan and jerk back from him, laying my head against the door. A knowing smile tugs up his lips, and I growl at him. One of his hands leaves my body, and the skin chills at its absence.

He opens the door behind me, and I lean forward into him. I grab onto his ear with my teeth and gently tug on it. His hand goes back to my ass, the sensation sending a thrill through me.

He walks to the backside of the door, before pressing my back into the door and closing it with my body. Where the icy wood touches my skin sends a pleasurable shock throughout my body.

I whisper into his ear, "Let me down for a second."

He groans, but does as I say, and I quickly shimmy out of my pants. I gaze back up at Allister, and his purple eyes sparkle as he watches me slowly yank my tunic over my head. While my hands are still trapped, he grabs the tunic above my head and roughly pushes me against the door.

He roars, "I've missed you."

I slide down the door until I'm on my knees in front of him. He finally releases the tunic, and I'm able to drag my hands out of it. I grab at his pants, unbuttoning them and yanking them down to his ankles. His thick hardened length springs out.

I lean forward and wrap my lips around it, showing him how much I missed him. Allister groans as he rocks back and forth. The velvety feel of him in my mouth heats my core.

It doesn't take long before Allister pulls away and leans down, grabbing me under the arms. He picks me up and pushes me back against the door. The chilled wood grain cools my hot skin as I lace my legs around his middle. His hard member rubs on me as his lips claim mine. He moves his hips and groans into my mouth.

Then he lets me slide down the door a bit, and he rubs himself against my entrance before sheathing himself inside me. I yell at the sudden fullness. Ugh, I've missed this. I've missed *him* so much.

Allister isn't soft and gentle like the other times we've made love. Now he's rough and claiming. I'm his, and he's trying to show every male within earshot I'm his, including Oberon. He pounds himself inside me over and over. My screams of pleasure just seem to egg him on.

He moves one of his hands from holding me to run up my body to grab my breast as he slams into me. He leans down and places his mouth around my nipple, sucking hard.

I throw my head back, hitting the door behind me, and scream as I tighten around him. My orgasm is his undoing as he spills into me.

When we're both spent, Allister lays his forehead on mine. "I love you so fucking much."

I place my hands on either side of his face and stare into his soul through his tired amethyst eyes. "I love you, too, Allister."

Then he picks me up and carries me over to our bed, yanking back the covers and placing me down gently. He covers me before crawling into bed behind me. I roll on my side and he wiggles up next to me, wraps his arm around my middle, and drags me in tightly against him.

Then he says into my ear, "Now kitten, time for you to explain what happened while I was gone."

I explain how Gerald tried to kill me, the way Oberon protected me, but let me claim the victory, my mother, Kalven's experiment, the plans for the future, and everything in between.

I wait for him to yell and scream about how I handled things, but he doesn't, instead he lifts himself onto his elbow. I turn around, but where I expect there to be anger in his eyes all I see is awe. "I left, and you not only took my throne back for me, but you have a plan in motion to take your own throne." His eyes sparkle in the moonlight, and I realize he's about to cry.

I graze his cheek with my hand. My heart breaks not knowing why he's upset. "Allister, what's wrong?"

He wipes the tears away. "I don't know how I got to be mated with such an amazing and strong woman." He leans down and wraps me in a tight hug, "You're everything I ever could have dreamed for and more."

⋯◦⋯

The next morning, Allister and I decide to head down to the dungeons and speak with my mother one last time.

The smell of old blood coats the air as we pass the cell holding Gerald, he races forward and slams into the cell bars. "Wait, Allister, please let me out. Your mate attacked me!"

Allister doesn't even turn to peek over at him. "No. You will be tried before the court and punished accordingly." Then he strides on by.

I'm almost bowled over by how calm and level headed he's being. I fully expected him to kill Gerald on the spot.

As we move past the cell, I question him. "I thought you'd kill him on sight. Why didn't you?"

His soft gaze searches my face. "Oh, he will die, don't worry. But his death will accomplish a lot more if it's done in front of the court. Each and every Fae in the castle will know what happens when you attack my mate." His voice is hard and filled with so much authority that even if I wanted to argue with him, I wouldn't.

We make it to my mother's cell, and I open the door with the keys I snagged from Oberon before he set everyone out to sparring practice this morning. He should be up top sending the Mori Nikos and Hazel on their mission. Then he said he'd train the rest of the Fae some more on how to wield their powers in a fight.

The door opens with a creak as I move away and allow Allister to enter, then follow behind him. I don't lock the door after us. I'm not worried about Titania attacking us and getting free now. This is where she wants to be, she told me so herself.

Titania races forward and throws her arms over Allister's neck. His hands snake around her waist, embracing her. I fight a growl before I hear a choked sob release from her throat.

She pulls away, and I can see tears streaming down her face. "Allister! I'm so glad you're home."

He holds onto her forearms and chuckles. "I wasn't gone long."

Her eyes turn worried as she gazes back to me and darts away. She drops her head and stumbles out, "Sorry—I—um didn't—"

Cutting her off, I get in one last jab. "I know your history. At least you could be a mother to someone."

Her shoulders sag, and she visibly folds in on herself. I almost regret what I said, but it was the truth, so I steel my back and haul an unaffected mask over my features. I find the more time I spend with her, the more I feel bad for her.

I shouldn't though. She deserves this for the pain she caused. For Father, for Oak.

Allister turns to me and his eyes narrow into a glare. I shrug at him because I'm not about to apologize. He places his hand on her shoulder and leans down, trying to grab her gaze. "We need to make a plan to get into the mountain, Titania. We need your help. You're the best strategist I know. If you help us, I can get you out of here."

She perks up.

Her eyes sweep up to meet Allister's gaze, then she peers over at me looking for reassurance. I silently nod. We talked about it this morning. Initially, I fought him on it, but he convinced me it was the best option.

When I originally came here I came in search of answers, but I got few of them. All she wanted to talk about was how Henrik turned her and how she didn't know what happened until she woke up to my father's dead body wrapped around hers. She hadn't even known she killed Oak until the day I met her. She was still hoping to find him whenever she was able to find me. She had left our campsite and took off in search of me, assuming I would travel to the Eastern Fae. But they hadn't heard of me and they took her prisoner, trapping her down here, unable to find me.

She races over to me and throws her arms around my neck.

I refuse to hug her back, and I give a pointed stare at Allister.

He comes up behind her and gently places his hands on her shoulders. "Attina isn't ready for that."

When she's pulled away, I spit out, "We've talked about this."

She drops her head again and twists into Allister's chest, covering her face. She whimpers out, "Yes, I'm sorry."

I huff and spin, moving over to the cell bars, leaning against them. Allister stares at me, but I don't even peek at him. I refuse to be made to feel bad for not wanting a relationship with her.

It's our relationship and my choice. Not his.

I bark, "Will you help us or not?"

She turns back to me, and I can see the tears flowing down her face in the dirt caked there. Clean rivers of skin poke out under the dirt now. She dips away from Allister and wraps her arms around her body protectively and pointedly stares at me. "I will on one condition."

I lace my hands behind my back. "What's your condition?"

"Attina gives me a chance to be a mother. I don't deserve her forgiveness, but at least give me the chance to start to mend things."

I take a deep calming breath instead of doing what I really feel like doing. I want to yell, I want to scream out no!

But I'm a queen now. I have to think of people beyond myself. This is my best chance at making a real plan to get to Henrik. Allister trusts her strategizing skills. He's been through more battles than I have, so I need to trust his experience and instinct.

I turn back to her and notice Allister's expectant face. "The best I can give you is we'll see. I'll try to put my hate and anger side." Her eyes light up with joy and I can't help myself but to say, "This isn't for you—" I dip my head toward Allister. "—or even for him. This is me putting my personal life to the side for the good of my people."

She sighs and her shoulders sag like she's disappointed. "The best option is for you to sneak into Shadow Mountain alone—"

Allister doesn't wait for her to finish. "Out of the question. No way in Hell is that happening."

I step forward, closer to her. "How?"

Allister starts to argue, but I hold my hand up, and surprisingly, he doesn't continue. He either decides to listen to me, or he doesn't want to stop me and Titania from talking.

She glances back and forth between me and Allister, assessing the situation. "The passage you spoke of earlier. It's filled in now. But I saw you can control earth. Dig it back out. Reveal to Henrik his weakness. Pledge yourself to him."

I laugh because it's so simple it might just work.

We might have a fighting chance at defeating the tyrant.

Chapter Twenty-Eight

James

I walk back into the throne room with Tala by my side. She snatched me from sparring against a snarky little Fae. Even after being here for a couple weeks I still hate the Fae. I've yet to meet one who's redeemed themselves. They're all nasty, power hungry assholes. I've been learning how to use my werewolf strength, and I'm shocked to find I'm able to actually keep up with these creatures using my improved speed and strength. I'd just landed a particularly satisfying uppercut when Tala cut between me and my opponent. The Fae in front of me immediately froze mid punch. Tala didn't bother to glance the Fae's way as she ordered me to follow her to the throne room.

I didn't realize how important Tala was when she first brought me here, but apparently, she is. Every Fae we walk by shows her some sort of reverence or glares daggers at her, there's no in-between. I also haven't seen her friendly with anyone here. She sticks to herself, like she's not really a part of the world around her.

The halls we walk are relatively empty, so I figure it's safe to ask, "Don't you have any friends here?"

Tala's short hair brushes against her chin as she turns her. "I'm not one of them. How could I be friends with them?"

I drop my head and stare at my feet. I feel bad for her. She's been here for so long—alone. "Weren't you lonely over the years?"

Out of my peripherals I see her face back forward. She shrugs, but I can almost hear the loneliness in her voice as she says, "I didn't need friends. I trained harder than all the others, day in and day out, since I got here. I trained to be the best and sometimes you have to squish the little people on your way to the top."

I shift my gaze to my sister and contemplate her. Maybe we aren't so different after all? I would squish anyone to get what I want, too. "Is that why everyone here stares at you the way they do?"

She proudly smiles and her teeth gleam in the low light. "Yep! I'm Henrik's top slayer. There is no one who outranks me besides Henrik himself. I take orders directly from the king and disperse the men under me accordingly." Something Attina and Allister told me in the forest pops into my head, and I stop moving. Tala turns around and crosses her arms in front of her chest and taps her foot impatiently. "What are you doing? Henrik doesn't wait for anyone."

I cock my head. "Attina told me Allister was Henrik's top slayer. Are there two of you or was she lying?" She's never lied to me in the past, and I'm not sure why she would lie now. Maybe the Fae brainwashed her into thinking he was more important than he is?

Tala's eyes drop along with her arms. She clenches her fists as defeat and anger radiate off her. "No, she didn't lie. Allister was the golden child. He could do no wrong." Her gaze lifts to mine, and I see so much hatred floating around her eyes. "Since I learned to fight I've always been the better warrior. But he was the favorite long before I was ever brought here. His mother is Henrik's wife—"

I cut her off, "He's Henrik's son?"

So if Attina is Henrik's granddaughter, and Allister is Henrik's son, that would make Allister Attina's uncle... and Attina and Allister are together...this is too weird.

She waves the air in front of her. "No, no. His father was the Eastern Fae king. It's a long story, I'll explain it all tonight, but no, your Attina is not mated to her own uncle."

Her words knock the air from my lungs. "Then, they *are* mates?"

Wrapping her arms around my neck, she squeezes me too tightly, forcing me to gasp for air. "Henrik told me they were. Allister left on a mission to kill her, discovered they were mates, and switched sides. He came back not too long ago and convinced Henrik he was a double agent, but now it's obvious he was lying."

I jerk away from her. "So, what do I do? Attina is mine and now you're telling me this *Fae* has some sort of claim to her?"

Tala reaches down, intertwines her fingers in mine, and tugs me down the hall. I unclench my jaw when I hear her words, "Henrik can fix it."

When we make it to the throne room doors Tala inclines her head to the guards. "He's expecting us, Agar." The guards bow their heads in return, then open the thick black doors

When we walk in, Henrik is sitting on his throne, but the throne next to him is vacant. I wonder what happened to that poor woman. She seemed so sickly and frail, hopefully she's resting somewhere.

Tala and I stride to the base of the dais, she kneels and places a fisted hand on her chest as she deeply bows. I copy her actions. Then I hear Henrik's voice boom throughout the room, "You may rise." We both do as he says and place our hands behind our backs. Henrik's red, menacing stare lands on me. "I haven't been able to talk to you much since the first day you came here. I hope you're settling in well?"

I try to put confidence in my voice, but it still waivers as I answer, "Yes, sire, thank you."

He cocks his head, the motion making him look like a hawk who just cornered a rabbit. "You're afraid of me. Good, you should be. But remember I'm the one who can give you my granddaughter."

I bow and say, "Yes, I will remember that."

"You have become a puzzle piece I didn't see coming. I will be honest with you boy. I was planning to kill my granddaughter."

Without thinking, I gaze up at him and growl. Tala hits me in the back causing me to stumble forward. I immediately fall to my knees, put my forehead on the floor, and beg for my life."I'm so sorry, sire! I reacted without thinking. I love your granddaughter more than anything. Please don't kill her. Take my life instead."

Henrik doesn't answer though. Instead, he stands and walks down the dais. Standing in front of me, his voice is cold as he says, "You may stand."

I sit back up and crawl to my feet with my head still bowed. I'm not brave enough to look this man in the eye now.

Henrik continues, "You really do love her. The only reason for someone to react so stupidly would be love. Does she love you back as ardently?"

I sigh. "She used to. Prior to Allister turning her against me."

Fire forms in his hands. My body instantly starts shaking. He's about to use those fireballs on me. I just know it. The world around me comes in and out of my vision as I wait to be burned alive.

Then Henrik closes his hands into fists and the fireballs disappear. He places his hand on my shoulder. I jerk at the contact, but my action only makes him laugh. "You don't have to worry, grandson. I won't be hurting you anytime soon."

My eyes widen, and I gaze up at him in awe. "Grandson?"

Henrik smiles, actually smiles. He doesn't come off as a man who ever smiles, but he's doing it now.

"Attina is the heir to my throne. I want her back and away from people who would corrupt her against me further. She has one side to the story. She has yet to hear my side. I would like to give her the chance to decide for herself after she's been told *everything*."

I silently nod and nervously pick at a loose thread of my pants. I'm afraid to say or do anything wrong at this point, so I figure silence is best.

Henrik drops his hand from my shoulder and paces back and forth in front of Tala and me. "Talon has told me much since he's returned to me." He stops in front of Tala and bows his head to her. "Thank you again for getting him back." She nods and he continues pacing. "I've determined the only way to part those two is to kill one of them. I want Allister dead. He is a traitor and a liar."

Tala uncertainly squeaks out. "It would give me no greater pleasure than to eliminate Allister, sire. Please allow me the honor of disposing of him for you."

He makes his way back up to his throne. "I would like you to train your brother through the winter and then *both* of you will dispose of him. It's important your brother go with you and bring Attina back to me."

"Why do we have to wait until winter?" I ask without thinking.

He cocks his head and his nostrils flare. I think he's going to say something, but instead he throws his hands out. A fireball shoots at me. I dive away, but I'm not quick enough. At first the fire feels cold, but then I scream as pain shots up my arm like someone shoved a needle from my fingers to my shoulder.

I drop on the ground and focus on not vomiting as I cradle my arm.

"Maybe that will teach you to not second guess me mutt." I peek back at Henrik and can almost see the fire dancing in his eyes, a sick smile cracks his face. He enjoyed that. "That was a warning, Next time I'll kill you."

Tala slams her chest with her fisted hand and I stand and do the same with my good arm. She didn't even react when he burnt me. We'll have to have a talk about this later. I'm angry now and she knows what happens when I get angry. We bow, turn around, and exit the room.

"Oh, and grandson?" I stop and twist around. "I have plans for you and my granddaughter. Big plans. See to it she makes it back home safely?"

I nod and bow at the waist. "Of course, sire."

Part 2

Chapter Twenty-Nine

Attina

It's a few weeks before the Mori, Noki, and Hazel return to the castle with the rest of our denizens. By the time the massive party arrives at the castle, snow already sticks to the grounds. Oberon has become such a huge asset. He's taken on the day to day guidance for the Fae in the castle. Half the Fae build for the incoming citizens and the other half train to fight, then after lunch everyone switches.

When they all arrived there was enough basic housing so everyone had somewhere to sleep for the night. Construction will have to continue, but it won't be long until everyone's comfortable.

Allister wanted to wait until everyone got here to officially claim his throne. Today we are to have the ceremony marking him as the official king and afterward, we're holding Gerald's trial.

"It'll be good for the people to see how those who break our rules will be punished under our reign," Allister says from where he paces in the middle of the throne room. He always says 'our reign', it's never his; it's us, as a team.

I stand from my throne, my hands running over the coarse roses in bloom adorning the ends of the armrests. I dismantled the massive stairs so now instead of lording over our people; Allister and I can be equal to them. We even destroyed the old throne and made two of our own. Both are made out of oak wood from outside our castle's walls. I requested it instead of the traditional Larche wood in homage to Raven's father, and my first companion horse, Oak. It makes me feel like he is still here in some significant way.

I walk behind Allister's throne, clumsily smacking my arm into the cougar paws decking the tops of it as I make my way over to where Allister still paces, his chin in his fingers as he stares at the floor. He passes me without really seeing me, and I wrap my arms around his middle from behind. His broad strong back flexes against me until I lay my head down on the back of his shoulder.

"Everything is going to be okay. We'll get through it together." I feel him exhale as the saying we've come to always use, through any hardship, settles on him.

He twists in my arms and cups my cheek. "Thank you, love. I couldn't do this without you."

I stare at his perfectly angular face and chuckle. "You were born for this. You could do this blindfolded."

He leans down and places a soft kiss against my cheek. His breath is hot on my ear when he leans down. "I wouldn't have the drive to do any of this without you. Until I met you, I was simply surviving. I didn't care about a better world until I met you." Would he really never have taken back his throne without me? I draw back and stare into his piercing eyes, realizing what he says is true.

As we stand there mere inches apart from each other his eyes darken. His hand reaches in front of me, going to my stomach. He pushes me backwards until I'm pushed against one of the throne room walls. Vines shove into my back, and I take a sharp breath of air right before Allister's lips crash down on mine. Heat sparks between us and a groan escapes my lips. My groan breaks whatever thread of self-control Allister had left. He wraps one hand under my butt, lifting my thigh around him and the other runs up my tunic.

I break the kiss and move to his neck, kissing and sucking on it, his long black hair hiding my face from the world around us. His hand snakes down from under my tunic to inside my pants, my skin heats and my body shakes in anticipation. I feel his lips on my neck lift as he smiles. His hand travels to the apex of my thighs and he growls when he finds wetness there. He curls his fingers, and I suck in a bated breath.

Then a cough from behind us breaks through the room, and we both freeze. I drop my leg, and Allister checks to make sure all my clothes are in place before he turns. "What?"

I move to his side and see Kalven's lithe frame filling the doorway, a shit-eating grin covering his face. He locks his white eyes with each of us and bows his head. "I'm sorry to interrupt you two, but it's almost time for the ceremony to begin. I'll be bringing everyone here shortly. But until then, I wanted to show you something, cub."

Allister runs his hand through his hair, then holds it out for me to take. His voice turns short and harsh. "Fine."

He pulls me over to where Kalven still stands. I cock my head at him. "So, where are we going?"

He smiles down at me. "To his parent's secret quarters."

I open my mouth to ask another question, but Kalven ignores me, turning around and walking off. I peek up at Allister who shrugs and follows him out of the castle.

We walk in silence.

When we make it down the castle stairs Kalven makes a left, skirting around the livestock barn. I break away for a second and sneak into the barn. I'm happy to see Raven is up and tentatively walking around. Cedar, Mylo, and Hazel all stand around watching her. Mylo's face is pinched in worry, Hazel appears to be falling asleep, and Cedar is cheering her on. "You can do it! One more step!"

A grin cracks my face. Cedar really has been the best addition to our family. He's so positive and wants everyone around him to succeed. He's become everyone's cheerleader, not just Raven's. None of the Fae animals are scared by him anymore, but all of the normal animals are. We tried having him sleep in the barn one night and it was a disaster, so now he sleeps near the end of our bed. Well, after our alone time.

I turn back to Allister and Kalven. I notice they've both stopped walking and are staring at me. I hurry over to where they're waiting and whisper, "Sorry, I just wanted to check on everyone real quick."

Kalven crosses his arms. "Is Raven exercising as I instructed?"

Allister strides over and wraps his arm over my shoulder as we continue trailing Kalven.

I answer, "She is. Mylo looks like he's going to worry himself into an early death and Hazel is about to fall asleep." Then I turn my face up to Allister's. "And Cedar is cheering her on."

Allister leans down and kisses me on the top of the head. "Good. He's doing his job."

I quirk my eyebrow up at him. "His job?"

Allister squeezes me once. "Protecting you is his job. Raven is a part of you."

Tears threaten to well in my eyes.

But before I let my feelings get the better of me, Kalven stops. "We're here!"

My brows knit as I turn around. We're back behind the castle where I fought the Mori Noki. But there's still nothing back here, just an empty alley.

Kalven walks to the portion of the wall I knocked Derek into. There's still indentations from his massive body hitting the wall. I smile at the memory. He still doesn't want to chat with me; he just shoots me daggers every time he sees me. The man can hold a grudge, that's for sure.

Kalven winds his hand through the vines crawling up the castle wall. It takes him a couple tries, poking his hand in and out of them before he finds what he's searching for. He yanks on something underneath and a door pulls away. You'd think the vines would prevent the hidden door from opening, but they magically melt away around the edges of the door.

Kalven stands back and holds it open for us. He bows and points his hand into the door while he says, "After you, my king and queen."

Allister's stiff, and his face is pale next to me. All I can do is try to understand what he's going through. He obviously never knew this room existed, and now he's walking into a room possibly filled with his parents' most prized possessions. It must be daunting.

I tug on Allister's hand. Dipping my head toward the door I ask, "You ready?"

My words drag him out of his reverie and he walks forward. I wait for him to go first before I follow him in. He squeezes my hand, and I return the gesture. I know he needs my strength right now, and I'll give it all to him.

Kalven follows me inside and closes the door behind us. As the door closes darkness engulfs the room for a split second until candlelight flickers on. Allister turns to me. "Did you do that?"

I shake my head. "The room must possess some kind of magic."

I take in a sharp breath, the smell of dust making me sneeze as I digest the room around me. It's a treasure trove in here. Everything from necklaces to gem encrusted swords line the walls and floors. Everything is haphazardly strewn about in piles like someone tried to organize it, but got overwhelmed and gave up. In the middle of the room is a massive four post bed.

I walk over to it and hear Allister behind me ask Kalven, "Can anyone come in here?"

I drag my hand down the red silk bedding. Fancy golden stitching weaves throughout the blanket. Cougar paws, a theme I've become familiar with, dot the blanket. It's so soft and plush. I wonder what such a big bed is doing here and who used it. I wipe my hands down the blanket to brush the dust away.

I turn back to where Allister and Kalven are talking. "The only people who can come in here are the Leon bloodline, their mates, and anyone trusted enough by the family to be added to the ward. To anyone else, the door handle will be hidden. It disappears unless someone allowed in the room is standing in front of it."

"Who used to sleep here?" I shout over to him.

Kalven's eyes dart over to me as he walks over to the bed and sits on the edge of it, a cloud of dust flying about. "The king and queen used to live here." His eyes dart over to Allister, "You don't remember sleeping in here with them as a child?"

Allister's eyes widen, and he turns, searching the room like he's looking for something. "I *might* remember something about this room?" Kalven and I are quiet as he walks around the room. His hand lands on a few things before he stops on the other side of the bed from us. He gently places his hand on the blanket and runs it back and forth in his fingers. "I don't remember anything in this room except for this." He stares down at the cougar paws with a smile on his face. His eyes are soft as he recalls, "I remember mother tucking me in under this comforter. I'm not sure how old I was, but I remember her soft voice as she put me to bed and read me a story."

Kalven stands and walks to the end of the bed where a wooden chest sits. As he opens the lid, I notice the latches are made of gold. He leaves the chest open and waves his hand over to Allister, "Come here. This is what I wanted to show you."

Allister and I move simultaneously. When we make it to the chest, Allister takes in a sharp intake of air. His hand reaches up to grasp his chest, and he stumbles away from the trunk. I peer down into the trunk and see shining armor inside. I'm almost taken aback by how similar it is to my mother's armor. But where hers has roses in bloom on the shoulder, this one has cougar paws curving over the shoulders.

I reach down and pull out the chest piece. I'm surprised to find it's as lightweight as my own armor. Allister's eyes are still wide as he stands there, his eyes glued onto the armor in my hands.

I pointedly ask Allister, "Whose was this?"

Kalven opens his mouth to answer, but I slice my gaze over to him and almost imperceptibly shake my head. I don't want him to tell me; I want Allister to answer me. I stand still and wait for him to collect himself. Eventually, his eyes leave the armor and make their way to my face. "It was my father's. I thought he took it to Shadow Mountain and it was lost forever." He grabs the armor from me, then pulls it over his head.

Kalven wraps his hands behind his back. "I thought you could wear it tonight when you announce yourself as king."

Allister peers over to him and nods. He leans over and checks out the rest of his armor before standing and turning toward the door we entered through. "We should get back and start the meeting."

Kalven and I silently follow him out. No one says a word until the door closes and the vines wind back together making the door invisible once more. A heaviness started radiating off of Allister as soon as he pulled his father's armor over his head. I think the weight of him taking over his family's throne finally settled on him in that moment.

I wrap my arm through his. "Are you okay?"

He silently nods, and we make our way back around the castle.

Chapter Thirty

Attina

Kalven ushers us back through the hidden door Gerald always used to enter the throne room when he was king. I'm a little uneasy because the hidden passage starts in one of the rooms I gave to the elderly, so we have to walk through someone's bedroom to use the passage.

Luckily, the room is empty.

I gasp when the door swings back, and I take in the filled throne room. Even with Gerald's gargantuan stairs dismantled and our thrones pushed back, the room is bursting with life. I notice people are even hovering outside by the open doors.

"This room was never built for so many people, only for people living within the castle," Kalven says over his shoulder in front of me.

When he strides through the door all of the Fae who were sitting at tables in the room stand in unison. Kalven moves to the side and when the room takes in my form they all bow. I raise my chin and make my way to stand in front of my throne. Allister follows behind me, standing in front of his own.

I wait for him to say something, but he just angles his head down at me, waiting for me to start, always allowing me to lead.

I turn my attention to the room in front of me and clear my throat. I bellow so everyone, even those in the back, can hear. "Thank you for being here. I would like to introduce myself to those of you who have recently traveled to the castle. My name is Attina. I am half Fae, and Henrik is my grandfather."

I hear gasps from the newcomers, but the people who have lived here just smile and nod. I notice some even whispering to the new arrivals.

"I beat your former king to take over this throne, but it was merely a temporary solution to take down a terrible king." I sidestep and place my hand on Allister's back. "This is your rightful king by birth, and my mate. He has done his rite of passage and is back to claim his throne."

I glide back and sit on my throne while Allister takes the floor. "I'm sorry to everyone here for how long it took me to come back and take the throne which is rightfully mine. I should never have left you under Gerald's rule. For those who don't know, my father was taken by Henrik and my mother was forced to be his bride. I grew up under Shadow Mountain for most of my life and had given up on a better life. But—" He gazes over his shoulder at me, and all I can see in his eyes is pure adoration.

"Finding my mate showed me how wrong I was." He turns back to his people. "There can be a better life for all Fae and *we* will construct it. All of us together."

Someone by the doors shouts, "How can you prove you are our king?"

Allister places his hands behind his back and grins, like he was expecting this question. He lifts his index finger and begins nervously pacing. "I'm glad you ask. I'm sure all of you know our past rulers had cougars as their Anima. In my absence, I had forgotten something vital. All our royalties Anima live outside their body." He stops mid stride and gestures his hand to the throne room door. "I would like for everyone to meet my Anima, Cedar."

A loud roar followed by some high pitched screaming echoes. Then the flood of people by the throne room door splits in two and Cedar comes striding in like he's the star of the show and it's his time to take center stage. His head is held high like he's the royalty here, but I guess in a way he kinda is. He roars again as sidles up next to Allister. Allister rubs his hand through the fur on his back before giving him a pointed glance. Cedar nods once, wraps his body around Allister, and makes his way to my side.

When he plops down next to me, I rub his shoulder. "Hey, boy, you have a good day?"

He turns his head to me. "Hi, mate. It's been okay."

The people in the room *ooh* and *ahh* at the sight. It's not every day, even when you're a Fae, you get to see a talking cougar.

Allister scans the room in front of him. "Now, if that's set-tled?" No one answers him, so he continues. "I would like to deal with your previous king. If you'll come in, Oberon."

I hear more murmuring as Oberon shoves Gerald through the throng of people at the doors. At the sight of him some Fae shrink back. His clothes hang a little looser than they did the night he attacked me, and his cheekbones are a little hollower.

We didn't starve him. I ordered him to be fed along with the other prisoners, but I discovered as my people found out how nice a leader could be, they became bitter toward him and began regularly "forgetting" to feed him. None of the other prisoners suffered except him. When I discovered this, I scolded the Fae responsible, but I couldn't find it in myself to be mad at them. I understand their bitterness toward him. As Oberon pushes him to the front of the room, boos erupt from the Fae around us.

I immediately stand up, my throne feet scraping against the floor. "There will be no booing. No matter what this Fae has done, he will have dignity." The room instantly goes silent, and a palpable tension hangs in the air.

I sit back down and continue rubbing Cedar's shoulder. His body begins vibrating under my touch. Fae whisper, and I no-tice a few point my direction, but I don't care. I will not budge on this.

Gerald's sad eyes lock on Darob's, searching for a friendly face, but he gets none. His lover turns his head and hikes his nose in the air away from him. The realization that he doesn't have a friend in the world must hit him as he slumps forward and hangs his head, ready for his sentencing.

I don't have long to feel sorry for him though, because as he's walking, he locks eyes with me. His eyes narrow, and out of nowhere he picks up his leg and kicks backward into Oberon's gut.

Oberon falls to the ground, releasing Gerald. He rushes at me, a roar ripping from his lips.

He must not have noticed the giant cougar by my side.

He doesn't get far before Cedar races from my side and pounces on Gerald, knocking him to the ground and wrapping his gaping maw around Gerald's head. Blood trickles down his head and settles in the eye not being smashed into the ground.

Allister strides over to Cedar and skims his hand over his raised hackles. With his boots mere inches from Gerald's face, he announces, "This was your king. He tried to murder my mate while she slept." Gasps fill the room. "I'm sure I don't have to explain the anguish it would have caused me, all but cementing his place on the throne. But my mate defeated him. She took back the throne before I had a chance to take it on my own. She brought my people together from all across this great territory. Now, she wishes for *you*, her people, to decide what to do with this worthless hunk of flesh."

Gerald wriggles under Cedar. But all he accomplishes is to force Cedar to dig his teeth in deeper to hold onto his head tighter. A whimper escapes Gerald's lips as blood trickles down his face. The noise serves to bolster Allister's words, reinforcing his worthlessness.

Fae would never follow someone so weak.

Out of the corner of my eye I notice Ned skirting the room. He makes his way to fill the space Cedar left at my side. I reach up and grab his hand for strength. I knew this was coming, but I didn't realize how hard it would be on me to allow someone to be sentenced to death.

Someone I could save.

But if I saved him now, the Fae would never follow me. They would see me as weak as the man we're killing today.

Allister's voice booms as he says, "What say you? Shall we exile him, allow him to run off to Henrik and betray us? Or shall we end him here?"

I hear a resounding cheer of, "End him!"

From where Gerald lies, his eyes lock onto mine, and all the hatred he has for me seeps out of them. My stomach bottoms out.

I want to stand and shout, exile him, but I know I can't. This is the way things are done with the Fae. I've always heard how bloodthirsty the Fae are, but this will be my first time seeing it with my own eyes. I clutch onto Ned's hand for strength while training an impassive look on my face.

Allister turns around to face me. "Do you have any objection, my queen?" The question is short, but holds so much meaning. He's showing our people he defers to me. My opinion matters. I'm not just his mate, but his partner on the throne.

My eyes travel over our people. They all wait with bated breath for the death they know is coming. I now notice the lack of children around. In all the other meetings, they ran around and played, allowing the adults to make the decisions. Now, they solemnly sit by their parents. The ones I can see seem to be holding their children in place, forcing them to watch the scene unfolding. I didn't grow up in this world. I'm shocked parents would want their babies to watch death.

I gulp."No, my king. You may proceed."

Again, using words which hold weight. *Allowing* their king to do his job through my words. I'm surprised how strong and steady my words come out with how shaky I feel.

Allister nods, and I hear him inside my head say, *You're doing great, love. I know this is hard on you. You can't save everyone.* He then turns to Cedar and pointedly stares at him. I know he's telling him in his mind to kill him.

I move to turn away, but Ned barely yanks on my hand, pulling me back to the moment. We talked about this. I can't look away. It would show weakness. I have to watch the demise of the man who took Allister's throne and tried to murder me.

Cedar doesn't hesitate to snap down on Gerald's head. A resounding crack echoes throughout the room. I watch as Gerald's head and face crunch together. Blood pours on the ground as his face and brain are smashed beneath Cedar's powerful jaws. His eyes, which are still somehow focused on me, go blank as his life drains from him.

My stomach lurches. Cedar's bloody maw releases Gerald's head and trots over to Allister as the Fae around us break into cheers. How can these people be so happy for death? He was a terrible man, there's no denying it, but is death really ever justified?

I break out in a cold sweat. All I want to do is race from this room. I'm barely holding it together, and the people in front of me are happier than I've ever seen them. I'm to lead this world of death and destruction? How much more of this will I be forced to endure to prove I'm worthy of being followed?

My eyes land on Ava, she sits with the other Mori Noki members in the front of the crowd, her long blonde hair swings as she nods at me like my mind is a book splayed open on the a table before her.

In the short time she's been home, she's quickly become one of my best friends and closest confidants. She instinctively knows me, sometimes better than I know myself. I squeeze Ned's hand once before I shoot out of my seat. I can change this for the future—and I will. Damn the consequences.

I stride forward to Allister's side. "I will be frank with all of you. I did not enjoy his death." The room goes silent. Allister clears his throat next to me, but I ignore him. "I was not raised with death and violence in the human world. I allowed what happened today to go on because I was told if I didn't, no one would respect or follow me."

Allister pushes through my thoughts, *What are you doing, kitten?*

I immediately block him from my mind. I gesture to encompass the room."But I think they're wrong. You are *my* people." Then I drop my hand to where Gerald's dead body lies, "These are the old ways. We are going to be fighting for a new life. One where humans and Fae can live in harmony. I'll give my last drop of blood for each and every one of you in pursuit of a better tomorrow. But it will be a world of peace, a world without violence for violence's sake."

The room erupts into cheers. Fae pump their hands in the air and slap each other on the back, and honestly, I'm shocked. I never would have thought these people would follow me. I thought they would be stuck in their ways, incapable of, or not wanting to change. But I guess I was wrong. I guess all these people really wanted was a leader to lead them into happier times.

Allister slides closer to me and wraps his arm over my shoulder. I peek up at him and see him beaming down at me. He turns to the room. "The gods blessed us with the queen we needed, didn't they?" The room blows up into hoots and hollers and Allister has to screech over them. His hand goes out to where Oberon stands. "Our captain will give you all orders to where you should be. We will be fighting a war soon. So, until then, we need you all battle ready."

Oberon raises his hand, turns, and exits the room. Everyone in front of us scrambles to follow him to the front of the castle.

Allister pulls me into his chest, his lips hot on my ear. "You beautiful, frightening thing."

Chills run down my spine as he places a kiss on my neck under my ear.

Chapter Thirty-One

Attina

Allister trails kisses down my jaw. Every place his lips land sparks with electricity. My toes almost curl with thoughts of what I would do to him if we were alone. I peek over Allister's shoulder at our people quickly filing out of the room. I bring my hand to his cheek, intending on dragging his lips to mine, when I notice my mother stalking over to us.

I roll my eyes and let out a groan of annoyance which Allister mistakes for pleasure.

"Eager to be alone are we?" he asks.

I place my hands on his chest and push him around so he can see who's approaching.

He clears his throat. "Titania! How are you feeling? Is your room suitable?"

She beams up at him as she strides to my side. "It's wonderful, thank you, Allister. I just wanted to say how proud I am of my children."

I snap, "You should be out training with the others."

She turns to me, and I feel her hand stutter at her side; she stopped herself before reaching her hand out to me. The movement is so infinitesimal that anyone else would have missed it. I'm not sure why, but I'm almost disappointed she stopped. I've basically trained her to not touch me without my permission. So why am I feeling like this?

Her head swivels back and forth. "I didn't think I needed to train with the others."

I narrow my eyes and open my mouth, but Allister cuts me off, "Everyone should be training. We could use you out there teaching the beginners how to keep from dying." Then he places his hand on her shoulder. His eyes turn soft as he continues, "I'd never be the fighter I am today without you."

Titania unabashedly wraps her arms around his neck. I stifle a growl as she pulls back. "So you two will be out there? It didn't look like you were going to join everyone."

Her knowing grin brings a heat to my cheeks, but Allister just chuckles. He slides over to me, wraps his arm over my shoulders. "We'll be out there in a minute, I promise."

Titania shrugs. "Whatever Your Majesties desire. You are the rulers now. An heir will be expected sooner rather than later." Then she winks and pivots on her heel. She struts away from us, and I notice Ned, who must have waited quietly by my throne making his way over to her rubbing the back of his neck. She pauses long enough for him to catch up. They both make their way out of the throne room, quietly chatting the entire way.

I narrow my eyes at their backs. Since when did they become so friendly?

Allister squeezes my shoulders, dragging my attention to him. "Ready to go out there?"

I turn into him and dig my fingers in his soft gray tunic. I tug his face down to mine and crash my lips on his. Wrapping my arms around his neck, I break the kiss.

I lean up and press my lips to his ear. "You heard her. Our people expect an heir. Even if we don't want one now, we should at least practice."

Allister growls, and his hand cups the back of my head before he grabs a handful of my hair, yanking my head back. "You're playing with fire kitten."

I smirk and tug on the pull in my gut, allowing my fire to dance along my skin. "Then let's burn."

The fire dances in Allister's eyes, and I can see the wheels moving in his head. It barely takes him a second. "Ned! Close and lock the doors."

I hear some chuckling at the room entrance just as the sound of the massive doors closing hits my ears.

Allister leans down and growls, "Now you have me all to yourself."

I extinguish the fire on my arms. While I couldn't hurt him with my fire since we're mates, I don't want to get lost in the moment and scorch my clothing. I wrap a hand around his neck and drag it down to my lips, trailing kisses down his neck, to his collarbone where I stop and suck on the soft skin. I reach my hand down into his pants and find him already hard for me. He drops his head back and groans as my hand wraps around him and moves up and down his velvety length. His breathing turns into pants before he steps away.

I release him as he grabs me by the forearm and drags me to the side of my throne. He pushes me forward so I'm bent over it, the roses on the arms digging into my stomach. Electricity shoots down my back as he runs his hand down my spine.

"I don't know what got into you today, but I love it." He yanks my pants down to my ankles.

In the next moment, I hear the fabric of his clothes shifting. His hand moves to my now slickened entrance. His voice is husky as he says, "You're all ready for me. Good, kitten."

Then, without warning, he's thrusting into me. There's a small pinch as I stretch to take in his sizable girth.

He pounds into me over and over, faster than he ever has, like I awakened something in him.

I groan with pleasure. His hands snake their way around my body and up to my breasts to rub my hardened nipples.

He pinches them, and the sensation makes me scream in pleasure, not caring who can hear me. I whimper as he continues his relentless pounding and releases my nipple. His hand moves into my hair, and he pulls my head back by my hair.

I cry out again, and he snarls, "Yes, let them hear you. Let them hear you're mine."

"Allister, please," I beg.

I don't really know what I'm begging for, but Allister must, because he starts pounding me harder than I thought possible. His hand reaches down between my legs, and he rubs the spot at the apex of my thighs.

My legs start to shake from the pressure building between them. I'm glad I'm against my throne or I would probably fall. I reach my hand to the other armrest and grab on to it, digging my nails into it. With his other hand Allister reaches around and pinches my other nipple.

It's my undoing.

The ground shakes under us as I screech, finding my release.

I pant and gasp for air, but Allister doesn't wait for me to catch my breath before he's dragging me backwards and to my knees in front of him. I grab onto his hard length, wet with my juices and shove it into my mouth. He groans as I move my mouth around him. His hand wraps over the top of my head, and he guides my head back and forth.

His breathing comes in short fast gasps as he cries out, "Fuck, Attina! Don't stop."

I move my mouth faster and dig my nails into the backs of his thighs, shoving him deeper into me. His hand tightens against my head, and he thrusts once deep into the back of my throat as he comes inside my mouth. When he tugs himself out of me, I swallow and smile up at him.

His jaw drops open, and he kneels on the ground with me. He brings his forehead to mine and closes his eyes. "Fuck, you're amazing. I'm the luckiest Fae alive."

I snort, ready to blow it off as post-coital craziness when his hands go around my head and pulls my eyes to his. They're hard and serious, like he knew I wasn't taking him seriously.

"I'm not just saying that. You're the most precious thing in the whole world to me. I hope you know that."

All words escape me, and all I can do is nod in answer.

He cups my cheek and presses my lips to his. When he moves away he says, "Good. Now we should really get out to the training pits." We stand and right our clothing before heading out the doors. Allister chuckles next to me, and I cock my head up at him. He gazes down at me, and his purple eyes almost sparkle in happiness. "Did I really just make you cause an earthquake from pleasure?"

I stop and whirl toward him, crossing my arms in front of my chest. "I think I caused the earthquake. You had nothing to do with it.

He leans back, and a cackle bursts from his chest. He laughs for much longer than I think really necessary before he pulls himself together and wipes tears from his eyes. I glare up at him.

Then he leans forward and places a soft kiss on my forehead. "Whatever you say, love."

I humph, turn and stomp out into the courtyard.

I'm shocked to find my mother in one of the sparring rings fighting Ava. Didn't we tell her to come out here and help train the beginners? Ava's definitely *not* a beginner.

Ned cheers from the sidelines. "Get her, Titania!" My mouth drops open.

Okay, seriously, when did they become so close? I'm not sure if I like this turn of events.

I move to break up this pointless match, but all of a sudden Allister's arm is around my stomach yanking me back to him. He bends his head down. "Let's just see what they do. You might have beat Ava, but your mother hasn't fought in who knows how long. She's probably rusty."

I think, *I know the last time she fought. It was against an inexperienced girl and her mate who refused to fight her to save himself. It wasn't much of a challenge.*

Allister drags me flush against him tighter. *I'm sorry I brought up that memory love.*

I lean my head back against him. *It's okay.*

Hudson's cheer draws my attention back to the fight. Fists fly almost too fast to see. Both of them land blows, but none connect hard enough to do much damage. The women back away and the crowd around us erupts. No matter Allister's uncertainty in the fight, I know what will happen. I know their powers and Ava is no match.

The wind picks up and Ava disappears. When she reappears, she's behind Titania. Her fist connects with the back of Titania's head and she lurches forward from the impact. Ava retreats, which is her biggest mistake. To think this woman needs a second to regroup is dangerous. She should have continued her assault until Titania surrendered.

Titania stands up straight and her red eyes almost glow as a feral smile cracks her lips. She slowly turns around. "My turn."

Her hand shoots to the sky and a bolt of lightning shoots to the ground next to Ava. The bolt doesn't hit her, but the impact of it crashing to the ground throws her backwards. My stomach drops as Ava flies through the air. She flips around and a screech leaves my lips.

I throw my hand out, wishing I could stop her momentum. I can see the direction she's flying and if she doesn't crack her skull I'll be surprised. Fae heal quickly but a crushed skull is beyond what a Fae is capable of healing.

Then out of nowhere, Ava freezes upside down midair.

Chapter Thirty-Two

Attina

Loud gasps fill the air from all the Fae around us. I stand with my arm out, frozen. Did I just—?

I jump as Allister whispers in my ear, "Why don't you let her down, you beautiful, frightening thing."

I slowly lower my hand, and Ava's body gently lands on the ground. Her mouth opens and shuts wordlessly. Her eyes are wide in shock, and she stares at me with something close to fear plastered across her features.

I pinch my brows and turn my head to Allister. My words come out broken. "How—? What just—?"

Allister leans down and places a soft kiss on my forehead. "Remember how you could move things when your powers first appeared? Seems like your powers are still growing, kitten."

Then the shock of the moment wears off, and my head slices to where Ava now has her head cradled in her hands. I race over to her and hit my knees hard on the ground in front of her.

She shrinks away from me, her eyes fly open wide like a bird who's just had its wings clipped and is staring down a rabid dog.

I coo. "Hey, it's me, are you okay?" Then I reach for her shoulder. She doesn't shrink away this time. Instead, she jumps forward and throws her arms around my neck.

Behind me, cheers erupt.

Ava says into my ear, "I'm fine. Thank you."

I draw back and stare into sparkling green eyes. "Are you sure?"

She throws her arms around me again. "I'm fine, Attina. I would've been fine, but it would've really hurt."

Then above us a deep voice says, "Hey."

Ava squeals before she releases me, and I'm thrown back from her jumping to her feet. "Babe! Did you see that? It was so fun!"

I chuckle and stand as Hudson wraps his mate, his typical sour expression gone for once, in his arms and walks her to the edge of the ring.

Before Ava and Hudson disappear, she twists around and waves at me, yelling, "Thank you, sweetheart. I'll see you tonight."

Waving awkwardly back, I open my mouth to reply, but Titania fidgets, drawing my attention. Turning, I point my finger at her. My voice booms as I shout, "You and me right here, right now."

Titania pleads with her hands, shaking them as she backs away. "Please, no. I don't want to fight you. It was an accident. I would never hurt anyone here." Her eyes leave me and drift to my mate. "Allister, please tell her I wouldn't have hurt the girl on purpose."

I growl at her, then I hear Allister's voice in my head, but I block his voice out. I don't need him trying to convince me not to do this. This is happening whether he approves or not. We need to resolve things for her to ever be a part of my kingdom. I refuse to allow her to stay unless we do this.

I lower my head and snarl, "We fight or I banish you. It's your choice."

Her gaze travels between Allister and me. Her eyes begging him to help her, but I know he won't. I'm his mate. Even though Titania is like a mother to him, he will choose me. I lead these people at his side, not her.

He doesn't say a word and her shoulders slump as the realization of what she must do falls over her. Her voice is meek as she wheezes out, "Fine. You win."

I hear my people around me whispering. I can't make out what they're saying, but I can only imagine. Everyone knows this is my mother. They must be confused as to why I'm furious. It's not like sparing isn't inherently dangerous. Accidents happen. But seeing Ava soar through the air reminded me of when she sent Oak flying through the air. Unlike Ava, I couldn't save him, he never recovered.

I take up my fighting stance and order. "No powers. It gives me too much of an advantage, and I want you to feel this." She falls into a fighting stance and we begin circling each other, but she rushes at me without thought. She must want this fight over with already. Her hand flies at my face, and I duck under it before throwing an uppercut into her chin. Feeling her bones crush under my fist is satisfying.

I yell, "I'm not so helpless this time around."

Her eyes go wide before she charges again. Throwing myself to the ground, I kick my leg out while I spin. Driving my boot into her legs she topples to the ground on her back—the air heaves out of her lungs in a rush. Gratification washes over me, tugging a smile up my face as I stand up and stride over to where she lies sprawled on the ground.

Suddenly I'm on my back on the ground along with her—my cockiness made me forget a rule Ned taught me—always make sure your enemy is completely incapacitated.

She throws herself over me, and I see the tears streaming down her face. She wraps her hands around my neck and squeezes. "I'm sorry! I killed your father and Oak, and you should never forgive me for it. You're right, I should die for it. I killed my mate and the only friend I ever had. I deserve death."

My eyes widen, and she releases my neck and climbs off of me. I lie there waiting for her to attack again, but she doesn't. She simply backs away. Her shoulders wrack as she lifts and throws out her arms. I barely understand her over her sobs.

"You deserved better. I left when you needed me, and I took away the men who were there for you when I couldn't be. Avenge them."

My stomach leaps into my throat, and a cold sweat spreads over me. This is what I've wanted since I found out she was alive. Since my Awakening, I've craved her death.

But now?

With her in front of me begging for death?

She screeches as she cries, the pain she feels leaking out through her voice. She's been so stoic this whole time. Like Father and Oak's death didn't affect her like it affected me. Like her world didn't end the day she murdered them.

But now I see that's not true.

Her world did end when Father and Oak died. She was just trying to salvage whatever was left without them, and what was left was me. She got captured searching for me. She kept trying, no matter how I treated her. I yelled and screamed and ran away, but she still tried. I burned her, but she still came back for more. Hell, she even burned herself trying to hug me.

And I've done nothing but make her life hell.

Henrik killed my father and Oak. Not the woman in front of me. He tortured her and changed her into a mindless monster. My father wouldn't want this. He wouldn't want his mate to beg for death from her daughter. He would want us to be a family, and I'm surprised to find I want that, too.

I slowly rise to my feet.

I walk over to the woman who gave birth to me, the woman who left everything she knew to have the family she always wanted. The woman who has endured so much and never stopped trying.

To my mother.

When I get to her, I see her whole body tense. She squeaks out, "Do it, baby." So I do.

I throw my arms around her middle and unbidden tears rip from my face. My back wracks as I cry into her shoulder. It takes her a second to realize what's going on.

Her hands stay raised for an extra beat before I feel her head move down to mine. Then, almost as fast as the lightning she attacked Ava with, her arms clamp down over my back, and her chest heaves as she cries into my hair.

We stand there holding each other, crying until Allister comes over and wraps his arms around us. He dips his head down between us. "I'm so happy you two *finally* got through this, but other people need to spar. There's still a war coming. These people need to train. I'm not saying stop, I'm just saying let's take this somewhere a little more private."

I nod into my mother's chest, and then lift my chin high. I might be an emotional mess, but these are still my people. I want them to see I'm still their strong leader even if I'm a crying wreck. I lift my hand and wipe the tears away as I lace my other arm through my mothers. I know my face and eyes are beet red from crying, but I don't care.

When we walk through the throng of people who were watching our exchange around the sparring ring, some smile at us while others glare. I don't care though. Let one of these Fae think I'm weak and think they can take me or Allister to steal the throne from us. I'd welcome it at this point.

On the other side of everyone, I freeze.

Raven stands with her bandaged hip and her mouth dropped open. Milo hovers next to her and so does Cedar.

Cedar, oblivious to the tension around him, trots over to me. "Hi, mate!" He rubs his head against my hand and purrs. Sometimes this creature acts so much like Allister, it's creepy.

I rest my hand on his head without breaking eye contact with Raven. I can see the hurt in her gray eyes. I know she's thinking how could I forgive the woman who took everything from us. We both talked about how we would make her pay one day. I had the chance to avenge both of our father's deaths, and all I did was hug my mother.

She leaps her front end off of the ground and pivots to the side. I know she wants to run away, but she physically can't yet. She's finally walking, but slowly. I race over to her. "Raven, please. Hear me out."

I see the pain in her eyes even though she holds her head up high and turns her face away from me.

"Please," I beg again, but she ignores me.

Milo follows her slowly, hanging his head. His eyes lock on mine, and by the sadness I see in them, I know he hates what's going on right now.

I stop in my tracks and let her limp away from me and into the barn. Cedar trots over and wraps his body around my legs just as Allister's arm comes around my shoulders and pulls me into him. "She'll get over it."

Rubbing my face into his chest the fabric of his tunic scratches my skin as I shake my head, weeping again. When the tears start there's no plug big enough to damn them. I don't think she will."

He places his lips on top of my head. "Yes, she will. She will understand. Just give her some time." He squeezes me, and I feel like he's trying to squish all the pieces of my heart back together.

Then from behind, us I hear a man clear his throat. When I turn on my heel, I see a man I've never noticed before. He's almost as big as Oberon, but he's much wider.

His hazel eyes sparkle. "I'd like to challenge you for the throne."

He yells so loudly, everyone in the courtyard whirls toward us. I rub the tears from my eyes and the snot from my nose. I slip out of Allister's embrace to accept his challenge when Allister's silky voice rings out from behind me.

"I accept your challenge."

Chapter Thirty-Three

Attina

The challenger pushes through the throng of people circling around one of the sparring rings where Liam and Lincoln demonstrate how to use their powers to their advantage in a fight. Allister, on the other hand, merely stands at the back and waits.

I clear my throat. "Wha—"

Everyone in front of us turns and bows, making room for us to follow. My jaw drops.

I hear Allister's husky voice in my head as I follow him. *You always seem to forget I can crack into people's minds. I politely asked everyone to make way for us to reenter the ring.*

My eyes flick to the back of his head, his black hair sparkles in the sun. *I don't think I'll ever get used to you talking to people without words.*

His voice is cold when he answers. *You might not. But after today you'll never forget it.*

I want to say more. Ask him what he means, but we make it to the sparring ring as his words leave my mind.

The man who challenged us is pacing back and forth on the opposite side of the ring. His mouth's moving, but no words leave his lips, like he's trying to psych himself up for what's to come. Allister confidently strides into the center of the ring, and I follow suit with my head held high, like the queen he deserves, not the mushy mess I've been acting like.

Allister gives his back to our challenger, places his hands behind his back, and addresses our audience. "Today there has been a dispute to our throne. The ways of our people are clear. Any one of you may challenge the reigning monarchs and, *if won*, claim the throne for your own. My family has reigned for centuries upon centuries, but at one time, this is how we achieved that throne."

Allister faces our competitor. The man stops pacing and meets Allister's gaze. "What's your name, Fae?"

The man's eyes crinkle. "Rayne."

Allister nods once, then ignores him once again. He places his arm over my shoulder. "Rayne has challenged us. He wishes to claim the throne for himself, and as we have done for centuries, we will fight to determine who's worthier. I will fight. And like so many challenges before us, this will be a fight to the death."

A fight to the death? What?

My stomach hollows out and my breathing comes in short gasps. What if he loses? I should fight. He challenged us because of my vulnerability, not Allister's. He's shown nothing but strength whereas I've shown nothing but weakness.

Father's words from so long ago ring through my head, *Fae follow power*, and I have shown them anything but. I try to maneuver out from under Allister's arm, but he holds me in place.

I shriek into his mind, *You don't have to do this! Let me fight. I'm the reason he's challenging us, not you.*

Allister drops his head to meet my gaze, and for a split second, I feel like we're the only two people on a raft in the open ocean. His eyes pin me to the spot as his words fill my head. *You should have more faith in me, kitten. Top slayer, remember.*

But—I reply, but I'm instantly cut off.

Suddenly, a scene of the top of his head between my legs flashes in my mind. *After this, I'll show you what exquisite power I'm capable of having over you.*

Between my legs slicks with anticipation for what he might have planned for us later, and I jab him in the side with my elbow. He plays like it hurts and exaggeratedly moves away from me before wrapping his arm around me once more. He leans down and places a gentle kiss on the top of my head. "Your queen has shown kindness, forgiveness, and strength."

I turn back to our people, and my cheeks heat. I can't believe he let them see our exchange. I completely forgot they were there, but I know Allister didn't. He's so smart and calculating, but he shows his playful side in front of our people? Since when?

Allister must have overheard me. *Since someone showed me there's another way. We can lead from a place of love instead of a place of power.*

Allister's voice rings out again. "Those traits do not show weakness, they show wisdom beyond her years. Your queen grew up amongst humans, not Fae. To some, it would be a shortcoming. But I say it's an asset. She learned understanding and how to listen to her feelings with the humans. She learned how to be fair and just, how to understand and overcome, how to never take a life for granted and to give second chances."

I have an eerie feeling the *give second chances* part is him talking about him and my mother. My mother murdered my family in her madness but I somehow found it in myself to forgive her. Then there's how he and I first met. How he was meant to kill me, almost *did* kill me, but here I am by his side. We wouldn't be here today if I hadn't pushed past our first encounter.

Allister pivots around. "My mate would be upset if I didn't ask you one last time. So Rayne, are you sure you'd like to continue?"

Rayne glares at us under his brow and grits his teeth. Then snarls, "Aye!"

Pivoting away from the crowd, Allister turns to me and lifts his hand to place it behind my head, then pulls my face up to his. His lips claim mine. The spark created by their meeting makes me jump, but Allister just pulls me to him tighter. I snake my arms around his neck and moan into his mouth. My body melts against his. I reach up, drag my fingers through his long hair, and drag his forehead to mine, "Come back to me."

He smiles and his words sound heavy as he whispers, "Always. Even in death I would find my way back to you."

Cheers break out around us, and Allister's chest shakes as he chuckles. He cups my cheek. *I'm always so in awe of how much our people love you.* Then he leans down and places a soft kiss on my brow. *Let me handle this, kitten.*

I take a step back. There's many things I will fight him on, but I can't fight him on this. He's protecting his family, his throne, and his people. No matter how much I want to fix this and fight for him, I can't. I need to let him do this.

We are a team, and I need to start acting like it. I pick up his hand and kiss the back of it, like he's done with me so many times before.

I give him one last look, letting my eyes travel over the gleaming silver armor he still wears. He stands straighter as I take in his chiseled jaw, and his purple eyes almost sparkle as he watches me stare.

I turn and make my way to where my mother and Ned stand on the edge of the ring. Ned places his hand on my shoulder. "He's going to be fine. You'll see."

Allister pivots back to face Rayne just as I feel someone's hand wrap through mine. I turn my head and Ava smiles at me. I lean my head on her shoulder as a silent thank you for being here, giving me support. My mother even rubs my back. I don't flinch from her touch now though. Something changed between us. I see her touch and affection for what it is now, love.

In front of us, Allister instructs, "This will be a fight to claim the Eastern Fae throne, winner takes all. This will be a fight to the death. Magic is allowed, surrender is not. I will ask you one last time, do you wish to continue, Rayne?"

Rayne bounces on the balls of his feet and shakes out his arms, limbering himself up. His voice is stiff as he shouts, "I do! Now quit yammering, and let's get on with this thing!"

Allister bows his head. "As you wish."

Then Rayne is running at him. He tries to throw his fist into Allister's face, but Allister simply sidesteps out of his reach. Rayne then twists around, his closed fist flying through the air. Allister barely ducks out of his way; the fist comes so close to his face, I'm not sure how it didn't connect.

I hear screeches behind me, and the next thing I know, Cedar's vibrating body is purring in front of me. He growls, "Why is he playing with him? He should just end it."

I don't get a chance to answer, though, because my attention is brought back to the ring in front of me. The vines growing along the castle wall start shaking behind Allister's back. I suck in air through my teeth to stifle the shout trying to escape my lips.

I can't interfere; Allister needs to do this on his own.

A vine shoots out and wraps around Allister's ankle. It rips him back, but only manages to bring him to one knee. A smile quirks up the corner of his mouth. "Nice try."

Then, seemingly from nowhere, Allister pulls out a sky blue dagger. It takes a few seconds for me to realize it's not a regular dagger, but one made out of ice.

Wow, he's seriously talented.

Allister cuts the vine from his leg and stands back up. Then vines zip out from the wall fast as lightning. Allister brings his hand up the dagger, and the blade elongates into a sword. He begins slashing at the vines around him, but the assault takes all his attention, and he loses sight of Rayne.

Rayne pulls a dagger from his boot just as he makes it seemingly unnoticed to Allister's back. He lifts the dagger, and I throw my hand over my mouth, a scream ripping from my lungs. Then, out of nowhere Rayne is thrown to the ground by an invisible force.

He drops the dagger and screams in apparent anguish. The vines flop to the ground at Allister's feet, and he twists around to face the man who tried to stab him in the back. Allister's ice sword melts into water and saturates the ground under him.

Allister crouches down by Rayne's face. "You grew up in the country, so I'm sure you haven't heard the rumors. I was Henrik's top slayer. I have a reputation of killing anyone who crosses me on the spot. My powers are water and mind control. You never had a chance."

Rayne rocks back and forth on the ground writhing in pain. His hands push into his head like he's trying to hold it from exploding. "Please, have mercy," he shouts between wails.

"Gladly," Allister says as he stands.

Instantly Rayne's body goes limp. His hands fall from his head, blood trickles out of his nose, and his chest stops rising. I saw this once before, when Allister's men tried to kill us, he crushed one of his men's minds. Now he's done it again. He killed this man without even having to lay a finger on him.

I hear a woman's scream from somewhere in the back. Probably his mate watching as he dies by the hands of her king. I feel an instant sorrow for her loss.

His eyes travel over our people. "I allowed this to happen to show everyone here what happens when you cross me or my mate. This is *our* kingdom, and I will not allow anyone to seize it from us. My mate showing emotion does not equal weakness. I will not show such mercy to the next Fae who dares to cross us."

Cedar walks over to Allister and wraps his body around him before sitting down next to him. Allister's eyes land on me, and my heart skips a beat as I take in his darkened eyes.

His voice is sharp, not its usual silky smooth tone as he points to the body in front of him. "You have been warned."

Chapter Thirty-Four

James

As the days drag on, I'm exceedingly anxious for our trip to snatch Attina. I can't wait to have her back. She'll be mad at first I'm sure, but she'll get over it eventually.

It's been nice having my sister back. I finally have someone who loves me no matter what again. I lost that with Attina as soon as Allister came into the picture, but maybe we could restore that.

Once a week, Tala and I go to Henrik's throne room, and he drains our blood. It seems to me like he takes much more blood than he could possibly use from us, but what do I know about blood magic?

Today is my day for draining.

I stride into the throne room where Henrik has the usual set up waiting. A chair, a knife, and a table with a dozen empty vials waiting to be filled. The smell of lavender incense wafts to my nose. He always lights that disgusting smell when he bleeds me. I think he's trying to mask the stench of blood, but nothing really covers that smell.

I clamp my jaw when his grating voice reaches my ears. "Hello, grandson." Henrik's voice is chipper today; he's always in a good mood on draining days. I think he gets some sort of sick pleasure out of it.

Wordlessly, I drag my feet over to the chair before taking off my shirt and sitting in it. I don't even want to know if he makes my sister take her shirt off. Maybe he gets some sick pleasure from it.

"Let's get this over with," I snap. Normally, the man scares the ever loving shit out of me, but on days like today he gives me more privileges and I don't have the energy to be afraid.

He buries his knife in my arm. Blood pours out of me with a gurgle as he finds my vein and slices up to my elbow, the smell nauseating me. For a normal human this would be a death blow, for me it's just pain.

I hiss as he takes vile after vile of blood until my body begins to heal of its own accord. I can already see my skin beginning to pale and I'm starting to feel lightheaded but I know were not done yet.

"We're almost done." Henrik almost sounds giddy as his nostrils flare in anticipation.

The tip of his blade is freezing against my now cooling skin. He drags it along my throat, playing rather than cutting. I swear he enjoys this more than one man should. Then, without warning he stabs the tip of the dagger under the base of my chin and cuts down to my shoulder. I hear his intake of air like the sight of my blood gives him pleasure.

He fills the rest of the vials, holding up and staring at the last one like it was his child.

"Agar!" His loud shout pierces my ears making my head throb and my stomach roll.

The throne room doors open and one of his golden guards strides in and abruptly yanks me up off of the chair. We stand there and wobble while Agar waits for Henrik's orders—like we always do.

Henrik waves us away. "Bring him to his quarters."

We turn around and my feet all but drag hang behind me as Agar carries me toward the door.

Before we make it out of the room though Henrik calls to us, "Oh, and Agar, remember he's prone to vomiting after these sessions." I almost miss the, "Worthless beasts," he tacks on at the end.

Agar gets me to my room and I manage to not puke up my moldy lunch. He hurriedly chucks me on the hard bed making me groan. As she shuts the door he growls, "Mangy mutt."

Thank the gods I won't have to have my blood let for another week.

It's still worth not dealing with the forced change being a werewolf brings.

I lie in bed and stare up at the dark rock ceiling under my moth-eaten sheet. It's so cold in here without Tala. She's outside sparring while I recover from this week's draining.

She doesn't trust anyone here so we figured it wouldn't be safe for both of us to be drained, weakened, and incapable of protecting ourselves.

So one day, Henrik drains me, and two days later, he drains Tala. This way, one of us is always at full strength and capable of protecting the other. Luckily, along with keeping our strength, we haven't lost our ability to talk through our minds. I can rest peacefully knowing if anyone tried to attack me, I could call to her.

But lying here alone, I can't control my thoughts. I keep thinking of that night in the woods when Attina gave herself to me. How her body felt, the noises she made, how our bodies fit so perfectly together. I run my hand down my body, imagining it's hers again. I can't wait to have her back. This room, hell this whole mountain, will be so much warmer and brighter with her in it.

I only have to wait a few more weeks.

Then she'll be mine once more.

And if she tries to leave me ever again, anger me like this again, I'll be sure to show her how terrible like can be without me in it.

Chapter Thirty-Five

Attina

The next day, Allister and I head to the courtyard to help with training. Grunts of people already sparing fills the air. We've decided we'll spend all day training which gives Oberon a chance to really work on the finishing touches for the new arrival's houses.

As we take the last step down from the castle, Allister turns to me. "I would like you to train with the Mori Noki today."

I stop, glare at him, and cock my head. "What? I thought we were going to teach the new Fae some fighting techniques? I've already beat all the Mori Noki in a fight. I doubt they could teach me anything."

Allister points his finger in the air and leans into me. "And *that* is exactly why you should train with them. You can *always* learn something. No one is so perfect they can't learn something new. You even just found a new aspect of your powers yesterday. If you insist on listening to Titania and going behind enemy lines, I insist you train with them today."

I cross my hands over my chest and roll my eyes. I can hear the annoyance plain in my voice when I say, "I could be more help as a teacher." I know I'm being pigheaded about this, but I really feel like I'm right.

Allister crosses his arms behind his back and bends down so his face is mere inches from mine. It's a little nippy out today, and it takes everything in me to not curl into the heat radiating off of him. "Please stop being so stubborn for once in your life and humor me."

I raise my hand and flip my hair around my back, smacking him in the face with it as I stomp off. "And what do I get out of this if I listen?"

Allister doesn't move to follow me. I'm about to twist around when a picture flashes before my eyes. The images flashing through my mind are of us in his family's secret room. Allister's behind me pulling my hair as I fall apart around him.

Now, I whirl to him and scowl. "You promised something similar yesterday and never ponied up the goods. How do I know you'll do as you say?"

Allister growls as he glides forward into my space. His hand shoots up and curls around my throat. He puts pressure on my neck, but not enough to hurt by any means. He drops his head so his mouth skirts over the shell of my ear. "Kitten, your mouth is running away with you."

Behind me, I hear someone tentatively clear their voice. Allister releases me and slides back, straightening his black tunic. Disappointment floods over me; things were just getting good.

Anger seeps out of me as I snap, "What do you want?"

But when I pivot on my heel, I'm surprised to see Ava. She glowers at me. Anyone else would have probably cowed at my tone, but not Ava.

"Get your little ass over here and spar with us." Her eyes drift to Allister for a second. "Oberon told us about your little plan, and you need all the practice you can get."

Narrowing my eyes at Allister my words come out in a groan, "How many people know about this *secret* plan?"

Ava jumps into my line of sight, her long blonde hair swaying behind her. "Only your family and the Mori Noki know. We're the only one's who'd have a chance at saving you if you need saving from that hell hole. We needed to know."

Frustration wells in my belly but she doesn't give me a chance to be angry with her. She throws her arms around my neck and giggles. "So just shut it, and come hang out with me today. Is that so bad?"

When she pulls away, I can see actual hurt in her eyes, like she really thinks I don't want to hang out with her. Shaking my head, I throw my arm over her shoulders. "No, not bad at all."

A beaming smile breaks my face as I peer up at Allister. "Fine. You win."

He mouths *thank you* to Ava before he moves in and kisses my forehead. "I'll be helping your mother with training the troops today."

Releasing Ava, my eyes flick between them. "Gotta go smooth things over with Raven first."

I move toward the barn, but Allister glides in front of me. "Give her some more time. Kalven gave her something which is supposed to knock her out for a day or so, but then she'll be completely healed. You can take her on your journey and talk to her then."

My brows pinch and I cautiously say, "Oookay? That doesn't sound completely fishy or anything."

Allister shrugs. "Or you can go wake her. You know how pleasant she is when she wakes up from a deep sleep."

Almost as if on cue, Cedar comes trotting up behind Allister. "Hey! I want to watch our mate fight today!"

A cackle rips from me as I reach my hand out to him. His head comes up to my shoulder, but he ducks down to rub his head against my hand.

He purrs as I scruff the top of his head. "Fine, let's get going." Twirling on my heel I give my back to Allister, not angry with him, just confused.

⸻ ◆ ⸻

The rest of the day goes by smoothly. I thought I would be fighting the Mori Noki one by one, but obviously they all had a different idea. We learned from each other today. I taught Ava how to form a wall of wind. Derek put his muscles to the side today and showed me how to make a dagger of ice like Allister did yesterday. Oberon even took a break from building and advised me on how to build a stronger wall of earth; one Derek couldn't smash through as easily.

Hudson and Liam's powers are very different from my own, but they still have a lot to teach me. Liam is brutal. He shows me how blinding an opponent even momentarily can give you a huge advantage in a life and death situation. I'd never really thought about it, but he's right. I remember during our fight how thrown off guard I felt after he blinded me with his light.

Hudson on the other hand is an amazing strategist. I guess you would have to be as the spy of the group. He walks me over to the shooting range. He's so tall he has to duck his head down to look me in the eyes. "I hear you're an amazing shot."

I shrug. Anyone who is any good at anything can tell you, you don't want to toot your own horn.

Hudson chuckles and grabs one of the newly commissioned bows. I had Oberon test them for me and he said they were exceptional. I've seen our people learning to use all kinds of weapons, but I haven't actually been able to wrap my hands around any of them.

I pick up the bow, and I'm instantly in awe. The craftsmanship is so superior to what I thought it would be. The quality is almost on par with my own bow. I heft it up and down, weighing it in my hand, and I'm surprised to find it's much lighter than I thought they would end up being. The weight of a bow can be a very tricky thing and can greatly affect how accurate it is. A bow is a balance between strength and accuracy, creating a deadly weapon unlike any other.

I grab up a quiver and throw it over my shoulder as I walk to a shooting lane. In front of me again is the straw target made to look like a man. I draw out an arrow, nock it, aim, and in quick succession fire it and two more. The arrows land one in each eye and one in the middle of the forehead.

Beside me Hudson whistles then his face settles back into its usual tartness says, "Not too shabby, but why haven't you used your fire powers?"

I've never thought of that. "I've only ever used my power through my body. I've never transferred it to another object. Do you think I could do that?"

Hudson shrugs and Liam walks up, his lips quirk up, and chimes in, "No harm in trying."

I turn back to the target in front of me and take a deep breath. I tug on my fire. I think of it going to my hands and transferring from my hands to the head of the arrow. I push my fire from me like I would when I make a fireball.

Suddenly, the entire arrow bursts into flame. The fire is so intense and so instantaneous the arrow crumbles in my hand. Then the fire begins traveling up the shaft of the bow. I call water up from the light snow around us, but I'm too late. The damage is already done. The string snaps in my hand, and I slump my shoulders. Great, I just ruined a good bow.

I jump when a hand lands on my shoulder. I turn and am surprised to see the quietest of the bunch standing next to me. Lincoln's piercing gray eyes stare into mine and he shirts on his feet. "Hey, it's okay. I bet if you have an accelerant on the head of the arrow you could light it with your hand." His eyes dart over my shoulder at where I know Hudson and Liam are both standing and growls, "*Someone* should have thought this through better." But his eyes are soft when they land back on me. He gently takes the bow from my hands and chucks it behind me to the men standing there. He then spins me around to face where the swords and other weapons are stored. "I have an idea."

I stand in the middle of a sparring ring holding a sword. I'm facing Derek who also stands with a sword in his hand, muscles tensed by the weight of his weapon. I grumble, "I already ruined a bow, I don't want to melt a sword, too."

Lincoln stands in the middle of us. I hear him scoff as he drops his head, his gray hair falls around his face, shielding it from sight. When he lifts his head, his eyes sparkle in amusement. "Your friend Ned helped make those. Apparently his father was some master blacksmith? I'm guessing you'll have to try really hard to melt that sword."

I gaze down at the sword in my hands. Ned helped make these weapons? How did I not know this? He said his father taught him a little of the craft, but by the sword I'm holding in my hand, it looks like he taught him more than just a little. I pull on my fire as I run my hand up and down the sword. This time the sword lights instantly. My jaw drops open in shock.

Then out of nowhere Derek's sword is coming down toward my head. I scream and throw mine up to block him, the fire instantly disappearing. He lands blow after blow. I thought this would be a friendly match, but I should have known better, seeing as I'm fighting Derek. He snarls out, "You better learn to light your sword while you're being attacked. Not everyone will wait for you to be ready, queeny. It's not a nice world out there. Time for payback."

Fire lights inside me. Who does this Fae think he is? Does he think I've had some sheltered life? I've been through hell and here he is acting like I've been raised in a palace my whole life. I swing my sword hard into his and our swords grind against each other. He holds his ground and pushes all his weight into me, but with how angry I am, I hold my ground.

"You think I had some sheltered life in a castle? No, *you* had a sheltered castle life. You might be skilled in battle, but I'm skilled in *survival*."

I stomp back from him and lift my sword. The whole thing catches fire instantly, my powers feeding off my anger. "You want payback? Come and get it."

Derek drops his sword and lifts his hands in the air. "I was just fuckin with you. You kicked my ass fair and square last time."

I huff and drop my sword. The fire instantly going out. What the hell? Is he for real? I silently glare at him and wait for him to elaborate.

Derek bends at the waist in a deep bow. He then straightens. "I'll be the first to admit I was a little upset when you beat me."

"A little?" Liam scoffs from the sidelines.

Derek shoots him a glare then his eyes are back on me, "You are my queen. I respect you. I wanted you to see what you're capable of. I've noticed heightened emotions bring out the best in you and your powers. The only way for me to show you that is to piss you off. I hope you can forgive me." He bows his head and waits for my answer.

I take a few steps toward him and wrap my arms around his shoulder. "You're a good guy Derek. I'm glad to call you—" I trot back and pointedly stare at each of the Mori Noki around me. "—and all of you, my friends."

Everyone runs up and throws their arms around me, wrapping me in a group hug. I laugh so hard they end up holding me up to keep me from falling to the ground from laughing so hard. I've never had such a community of family and friends. It's so nice having so many people around me who I feel like I can count on, it's making me giddy.

When I get myself together everyone takes a step back, except Ava, who leaves her arm around my waist. I lean into her and place my head on her shoulder. Then in a flash Lincoln's face is right up in mine. He points at Ava, his finger pushed almost against her face as he excitedly asks, "How did you keep this one from being thrown into the wall yesterday? Your power is different from mine, you shouldn't have been able to do that."

I draw my face away from him then explain to him how my powers first started and my journey since then.

Having friends is nice.

Chapter Thirty-Six

Attina

After all of our people head to bed, Allister and I stand in our throne room at the head of one of the tables. At the table sits all the Mori Noki, Oberon, my mother, Ned, and Kalven. Cedar sleeps in a purring ball at my feet.

Allister's arm is draped over me, holding me close to him, like he's trying to keep me from running away. Like I would *ever* run away from this man. He gazes over our friends and family and begins the meeting, "We're here today to talk about what the future holds. Our queen will be leaving us to infiltrate Shadow Mountain. Titania and Kalven know of a secret passage into the mountain. It's blocked by rubble, but with her powers, clearing it should be a breeze for our queen."

Allister rocks me back and forth, and I use the break in his speech to cut in and ask my own question. I pointedly stare at Kalven, his clouded eyes lock on mine as I ask, "Kalven, have you gotten anywhere with our secret project?"

He drops his head. "No, my queen. I have some answers, but not enough to change any plans."

I shrug and huff. "Well, it was worth a shot."

Kalven sounds disappointed in himself as he whispers, "I'll keep trying."

He sits closest to me so I place my hand on his shoulder. "You're doing wonderfully. There's only so much you can do. I understand that."

He bows his head. "Thank you, my queen."

When I glance back at the group, I notice all the confused looks around us, but I'm not sure I really want to share with everyone what we were talking about. I saw Oberon's reaction and Allister's wasn't much better when he found out, so I don't want to go through that again.

Allister notices me hesitate and picks up the conversation. "I'm sure you all can understand my hesitance to allow my mate to go into enemy territory. When she points out the weakness in Shadow Mountains fortifications Henrik will rectify his mistake immediately. Without the tunnel, if anything happens to her while she's inside there's not a whole lot we can do about it."

Oberon, who sits next to Allister, lifts his lip and cuts in, "I've said it before, and I'll say it again. I don't like this. It's too big a risk."

I understand what he means. Fae have been known to go mad from losing their mate. If Allister lost me, he wouldn't be fit to lead our people which would leave them vulnerable for Henrik to seize this territory.

From down at the last seat, my mother chimes in, "My daughter can do this. She is strong. She is the future of Arealea. Trust the prophecy."

I pin my gaze on Ned who, of course, sits next to her, nervously rubbing the back of his neck. "What about Commander Demarco? Where are we on that front?" Ned and I had talked about the human aspect of the prophecy. How we would need Demarco to fulfill that part of it. We need to bring human and Fae together to have a chance at defeating Henrik.

Ned takes a deep breath and stares at his hands. I expect him to have bad news so I'm surprised when he says, "Commander Demarco is amenable to the plan, but he would like to speak with you personally, Attina. He said he'll talk to the half-breed, but not that Fae bastard." Ned lifts his hands and quickly adds, "His words not mine."

I glance up at Allister and he nods. I love how much he trusts me to take care of myself. Honestly, his trust makes me feel more capable.

Then Allister turns back to the people in front of us. "I would like for everyone here, Kalven excluded, to follow her to Shadow Mountain."

Hudson shouts, "Henrik has his damn hawk back! He'll spot us in a second."

A conspiratorial smile creeps up Allister's face. "Haven't you noticed Hazel's been gone? She's with Talon. He's agreed to be on our side, so don't worry your pretty little head about Henrik's hawk."

⬥○⬥

After the meeting, Ned and I are walking down the stairs to the dungeon, our steps reverberating odd the stone walls around us, when I finally get the courage to ask Ned, "What's going on between you and my mother?"

In front of me, I see his shoulders instantly tense. "I don't know what you're talking about."

I scoff; apparently, I have to spell it out for him. "You're always standing by her, you're constantly searching for her when you're not with her, and I see the way you look at her."

Ned makes it to the bottom of the stairs, lifting the lamp in his hands up to my face. With the light I can see worry plain in his eyes. "Would it be a problem if I had feelings for her?"

I cross my arms over my chest and stick my hip out, "It depends. Would you look at me differently for how I treated her?"

Then, fast as a snake striking, Ned wraps his arm around my waist and jerks me down to him. He leans his head into my shoulder and huffs out a tense breath before pulling away and steadying me on my own two feet. He places his hand on my shoulder. "You're like a daughter to me. She is your mother and you two had a relationship *way* before me. I would never get between you guys. And no matter what happens between

Titania and me, *if* anything happens, you will always be my daughter."

My eyes fill with tears, and I shoot back into his arms, slamming my face into his chest. "You're my dad, too. Thank you. I approve."

Ned chuckles, but I can hear the knot in his throat as he says, "Good. Now, I only have to deal with your mother."

I push him in the shoulder playfully. "Just ask. I see the way she looks at you, too." Ned's eyes are wide as I push past him and head down to Commander Demarco's cell.

Every cell down here is now empty except Demarco's. I run my hands along the cold cell bars as I pass. The thrumming of my hand hitting them and my feet on the stone floor are the only sounds breaking the heavy silence. I reach the commander's cell with Ned following closely. The commander sits with his back facing me. His head lulls against the cell bars.

Ned clears his throat. "John, I brought Attina for you to speak with."

Demarco pivots so he can face him. "I don't see her."

I growl. Are we seriously going to be this petty today? I move over next to Ned where Demarco can see me. "Hello, Commander."

His eyes widen in feigned shock at my sudden appearance. "Attina! Good to see you again. How are things?"

I cross my arms and tilt my head. "I don't have time for your games Commander." I dip my head toward my friend, "Ned here, said you wanted to speak with me."

The commander shoots up onto his feet faster than I thought possible with a man his size. While my guards were keeping food away from Gerald, it obviously isn't the case with the commander. While he's lost some of his muscle mass since he's been here, he doesn't seem to have lost one ounce of weight. His green eyes also lost zero of their fierceness in his time here as he pins me to the spot with his glare.

He snarls out, "Isn't that what this has been for you this whole time—a game? You played innocent and naive. You played helpless. You even played that boy."

I won't engage with him. I've already taken things too far with him. Engaging now wouldn't help my case.

I sigh. "What would you like to speak to me about, Demarco?"

His eyes flash to Ned, and then slice back to me. "Ned said you wished to make me a proposition."

I cross my arms over my chest and glance to Ned. "Oh is that right? He said that?" I, of course, authorized him to offer Demarco a proposition, but with our history, it's probably better if I act like I had no idea.

I sit on the ground and cross my legs. It leaves Demarco towering far above me, in a position of power. But in my eyes giving up my position is a bigger show of power. I can sit on the ground in front of him *knowing* I could kill him at any second.

The corner of Demarco's lips tug up into a sinister smile at the sight of me beneath him. "Do you have something you'd like to speak with me about?"

I lean back on my hands so I can meet his gaze. I nod. "Yes, I would. I would like to speak to you about eliminating Henrik."

Demarco throws his head back and a bellowing laugh releases from his mouth. He lifts his hand to his chest as his belly jiggles. "And how do you plan on pulling something like that off?"

I shrug and say, "It's really quite simple. I need your people and my people to distract him while I attack from within."

His sharp jaw drops, and he stumbles back. "You're serious."

I sit forward with my elbows on my knees. "I am."

He grabs the bars caging him and wiggles his way down to sit on the ground with me. He sits so his face is almost pressed against the bars, "Let's just say I'm willing to do this. I'm not saying I am, because its suicide, and I won't lead my people to their death, but let's play your game. What would I get out of the deal?"

I grab the bar to the right of his face and bring mine close to his. I emphasize, "*Besides,* being the reason humans can come out of hiding? When I become Queen of Arealea I will want you to be the general of my armies. You will have full control of humans and Fae. No one will be above your rule besides me." And Allister, but I don't need to mention that, he hates Allister.

He leans away from the bars. He seems to mull over what I just offered, "My people don't stand a chance against Fae."

I drop my head, anger washing over me. He threatened me with his people coming to retrieve him, and now they wouldn't stand a chance? I told him they wouldn't, but to save his own hide he was willing to throw his soldiers to the wolves. Now, when we have a real chance at defeating Henrik he doesn't want to use them.

I hold back a groan and push, "Your people wouldn't be alone. My people would be at your side. Fae can only be killed by weapons made by Fae, so I would need your people to fight the Solis Henrik is sure to bring to the fight. My Fae will fight the other Fae."

He throws his hands in the air, obviously frustrated, "And how do I know this isn't some huge ploy to get all the humans in one spot to kill us off once and for all? How do I know this isn't some game?"

I shoot to my feet and glare at him. With his size I have to tilt my chin up so I'm not sure how frightening I look, but I don't care. "You don't. And there's nothing I can give you to prove to you I won't double cross you. Only my word and Ned."

"And Ned?" Ned and the commander question simultaneously.

I lay my arm over Ned's shoulder. "Ned is like a father to me. I will send him with you as leverage. If I double cross you, you have my permission to kill him."

Demarco turns his head back and forth between Ned and me, taking us both in, sizing us up, trying to figure out if I'm telling the truth or not.

Then I add, "And if you do this, you get to rule the entire Arealean army."

He lifts his hand to his chin, pauses, and then slowly nods. "I'll do it."

Almost dismissively, I answer, "Ned will have all the information for you. Get some rest. You two will be leaving at dawn."

I shoot my hand between the bars, Demarco jerks back from it before pulling himself together and taking my hand, shaking it.

As Ned and I make our way back up the stairs from the dungeon, Ned whispers to me, "How do you know he'll keep up his end of the bargain?"

I stop and turn around and stare down at him, "Ned, I know you will get what needs to be done, done. You know the inner workings of Sanctuary better than anyone. The people there trust you." I point with my chin back to the dungeons. "Do you seriously think they trust him? I expect either he will do the job or you will be the new leader of Sanctuary."

Chapter Thirty-Seven

Attina

I bid goodnight to Ned before heading up to bed. I'm surprised to see my mother leaning against our tub while Allister sits on our bed. I walk in and gently close the door behind me, leaning against it.

My eyes travel from my mate to my mother. "Heeeyy. What's going on here? Are you both ambushing me?"

Allister chuckles as he stands and strides over to me. His movement is confident, strong, somehow sexy even. I stand up a little straighter when he makes it over to me.

He leans down and places a kiss on my head. "No, love. Just discussing you leaving tomorrow."

My stomach flips, and I squeak, "Tomorrow? Already?"

My mother pushes off the tub and turns toward me as Allister wraps his arm around my hips, pulling me tightly into his side. "I know it's sooner than you thought, but every day you're here brings a bigger possibility of trouble."

I parrot, "Trouble?"

She walks over to me and Allister moves away, giving us our space. She laces her arm over my shoulders. "Allister told me about James. What he did to you." She pulls me into a tight hug. It takes me a second before I respond and wrap my arms back around her. "I'm sorry I wasn't there to protect you. I should have been."

I jerk back away and shake my head, but the movement makes me realize I have tears forming in my eyes. I was like this with Father, too. I could be tough and strong around everyone, but him. I've never had my mother in my life, but here I am, still breaking down in front of her at the mention of her protecting me. I'm hit with the smell of apples as she drags me back into her arms and shakes me violently as I fall apart.

I hiccup as I pry away from her into Allister's awaiting arms. "He'll be there. I haven't allowed myself to think about it, but he'll be there, I'll be trapped in the mountain with him." The last time I saw James he was behind bars and prior to that I had Ned and Allister by my side. He didn't pose much of a threat then, but if we're alone?

Allister twists me toward my mother and wraps his arms tightly around me from behind. My mother grabs my hand and affirms, "You can do this. You are stronger than you know. You will be the one to kill Henrik. You're not going to let one boy get in the way of your destiny are you?"

I screw up my face and shake my head. She's right. I can do this. It feels silly to be more worried about one human boy than I am of Henrik. Henrik could kill me in an instant. With my power now, James doesn't pose much of a threat. I know my concern is irrational, but I can't help it. Something about him just makes my blood run cold.

I can't just turn it off.

It's not that simple.

We all move to the bed and sit to talk. Apparently, Kalven and my mother sat down after the meeting and tried to figure out where they remembered the tunnel to be. "Honestly, all either of us remember is it's on the east side of the mountain."

I bend over and place my head in my hands, "That's it? That's all you've got? How am I supposed to find this place?" All of a sudden this plan seems unachievable.

Mother places her hand on my shoulder. "You'll find it. Don't worry. There's a creek that runs behind the mountain. You follow it and you'll find a cave. The entrance is in that cave."

This all sounds extremely broad. How long is the river? Am I going to have to spend days searching for this damn thing? "What about all of the dangerous animals surrounding the mountain?"

Allister and my mother both cock their heads at me. "What?

"As a kid, I was always told of the animals who made their home around Shadow Mountain. Deadly creatures which couldn't be found anywhere else in the world. They were the things of my childhood nightmares."

Allister and my mother both shake their heads, and Allister says, "Maybe that's something humans tell their children to keep them from wandering around Shadow Mountain?"

I huff and slump my shoulders. "It always sounded real, and I never thought Father would lie to me."

My mother places her hand on my knee and sweetly answers, "Silas would have done anything to protect you. If telling you a white lie could protect you, he would have done it in a heartbeat."

I know she's right.

I change the subject. "So, once I get into the mountain, what's the layout like?"

Allister and my mother go off into their memories of Shadow Mountain. Obviously, Allister's information is more recent than mother's, but she was privy to areas in the mountain Allister was not. Apparently, he wasn't even allowed in the royal quarters because he wasn't Henrik's son, simply an offspring of the enemy.

It's well into the night before my mother stands to take her leave. "I'll see you off tomorrow."

I stand and follow her to the door. "Thank you for coming by and getting me familiar with your home."

She turns and runs her hand down my face, "My home is wherever you are my dear." I jump forward and wrap my arms around her neck. She drops her head down into my shoulder and takes a deep inhale of my smell. "I just got you back, and now I'm losing you again."

When I pull away I see tears in her eyes. I place my hands on both sides of her face and try to comfort her by saying, "I'm coming back. It'll be okay."

She wipes the tears from her eyes as she turns to Allister who stands and walks over to us. "Make sure you keep in contact with her the entire time. If anything goes wrong, you send those Mori Noki in after her. I don't care how you get it done, my girl is coming back to me."

Allister wraps his arms around her and pulls her into his chest. His black hair shielding both their faces from my sight. I step into them and wrap my arms around them both. Allister takes one arm from my mother and wraps it around me. "I'll make sure our girl comes back. I will rip that mountain apart if I must."

My mother nods into us before gliding away. She sighs heavily, "I'll see you both in the morning."

"Goodnight," we both say as she makes her way out our door.

I stare at the door from which my mother just left. The mother I vowed to hate, but has somehow wormed her way into my heart. I don't know if I'll ever fully forgive her, but this is a good start.

Allister's voice pulls me from my thoughts, "So, I was thinking."

I turn to him and cut him off, "A horrible idea really."

A salacious grin cracks Allister's face. I know he remembers the first time I used those words, while he was teaching me how to control water, the first time he really opened up to me.

He cracks back, "Smartass. I was thinking we could spend your last night here in my family's secret room. I'll leave our door open so Cedar can come sleep in here like usual."

I glance at the room around me. The room which has become home. I did offer to move to his family's room though, so I shrug, "Sure let's go."

Allister smiles and playfully picks me up with one arm behind my knees and one behind my back. I giggle as he lifts me and places a quick kiss on my cheek. "You're the best mate in the world. Never forget it."

I bring my hand to my chest and exaggeratedly squeal, "Me?"

He drops me on my feet before turning around and closing the door, "Don't let it get to your head."

I giggle as we make our way to the room. When we're standing in front of the door, Allister picks me up again. I squeak out, "What are you doing?"

He stares down at me with pinched eyebrows. "Isn't this what humans do after they get married? Carry the woman over the threshold?"

I cross my arms and try to sound serious as I ask, "I thought you didn't know anything about human ways? And we're not married."

"Semantics." Allister chuckles out as he opens the door, vines and bricks fall away. He strides into the room, the moonlight above guiding our way until the door closes and the sconces around us light on their own.

Allister chucks me on the bed. The dust covering the sheets flies around me causing me to violently sneeze. Allister stands over the bed giggling as I melt into the soft bed. I sit up and glare at him. "For that, you get to air out these sheets."

He shrugs. "Fair enough."

I undress while Allister takes the bedding and heads outside to shake it out. I need to get this dust off of me. As I yank my shirt over my head I sneeze again. I grumble in Allister's head, *Dumb playful male.*

When I'm undressed Allister walks in without looking my way. He silently makes the bed and pulls off his boots before lying down in it. I strut around the other side of the bed and crawl in. His eyes never leave the ceiling, like he's purposely not looking at me.

I crawl across the wide bed until I'm sitting naked on my knees by Allister. I clear my throat, but Allister just lies there staring at the ceiling. I groan, throwing my body over his chest. "What's wrong with you?"

Finally, his gaze leaves the ceiling to lock with mine. His eyes don't leave my face though, they stay stuck on my eyes. "Dumb playful male?"

I scoff and wrap my hands on either side of his face. "Yes. I was sneezing up a storm in here."

His eyes narrow. "It's not like I did it on purpose."

Sighing, I throw my leg over his hips, straddling him. I lay my chest down on his, making sure to push my chest out. If all he wants to do is stare at my face I'm going to make sure he has to stare at the rest of me. My finger trails down his chest. "Do you *really* want to sit here and have a silly fight the night before I leave?"

Allister's eyes widen as he takes in my body, and I can feel him harden underneath me. A feline smile quirks my lips and crinkles my eyes at the sensation. I rock my body on his and a tiny growl rumbles his chest.

Allister raises his nose in the air and stares at the ceiling again. He huffs out, "Maybe I do."

I lean forward and begin trailing kisses down his neck. Pulling away, I say, "That's too bad." I wriggle my hand between us. My arm is on top of his hard length as I explore the apex of my thighs. I moan into Allister's neck at the sensation.

Allister's face drops, and I draw back to stare into his eyes. He sharply asks, "What are you doing?"

I chuckle and shrug as a dip a finger inside me, causing me to throw my head back, and I growl, "You've teased me two days in a row now. Somebody has to do something about it."

Allister grabs my shoulders, and before I know it, he's spun me on my back and climbed on top of me. He grabs my hand, which is still between us, and gently tugs it away from me. I cock my head at him, feigning confusion.

I coo, "I thought you wanted to fight?"

Allister pulls his shirt off, then slowly makes his way down my length. When he's between my legs he says, "Well, I wouldn't want you forgetting what it's like being with your mate while you're gone."

Then his tongue is on me.

I throw my head back and moan at the sensation. He's so adept at pleasing me. I guess it's an advantage he can listen in on my thoughts. The moment I think I want him to do something, he automatically does it.

He pumps his fingers in and out of me. I run my hand down my body and drag my fingers through his hair before grabbing a hold of it. I scream as I unravel around him. Peering down, I see him smiling as he feels me tighten around his fingers.

Allister pulls off his black pants before prowling over me. His long hair tickles my nipples and suddenly, I want control. I push on his shoulder and roll him over so I'm straddling him. A growl releases from him as I rub myself up and down him.

I try to seductively slither, my way backward. I sit my butt against Allister's legs while he crosses his arms behind his head and stares down at me with darkened eyes. I smirk at him as I lean down and take his length in my mouth.

He groans and his whole body shakes at my movements. I move my head up and down his velvety length. His moans get louder and more desperate. He throws his arm to his sides and digs his fists into the sheets underneath him.

Just as I feel him start to unravel, I jerk away. "Not yet."

I crawl back up his body and slide his thick girth inside me. I throw my head back as I move up and down and Allister runs his hands up my body. The smell of sex surrounds us, and in my head, I hear his husky voice. *You are the sexiest thing alive. I can't believe how lucky I am.*

I gaze down at him, and apparently, he was holding himself back because he growls and sits up, trapping one of my nipples in his mouth. He sucks, and I scream, falling apart around him.

When I finish, he pushes me off of him on my hands and knees. I don't know how much more of this I can take. My shaky arms and legs barely hold me up while he crawls behind me. He wraps his arm under my middle and holds me up while he enters me. In my head he growls, *Remember how your mouth was running away with you earlier? This is what you get, kitten.*

I snarkily think back, *I should let my mouth run away with me more often.* A moan escapes me as he pounds into me over and over. I relish in the groaning I hear from behind me. His nails dig into my hips, but I don't care, I want more of him, every inch of him inside me.

The hand on my hips moves up to fist my hair. He yanks my head back, the exquisite pain from him tugging on my hair makes me yip. "You're so tight. You're going to undo me."

He pounds into me and between him wrenching on my hair and him slamming into me I scream as I find another release. Wave after wave of pleasure pulses through me. Allister tries to back away, but I need more. I don't want him to drag himself out of me, so I slam myself back into him. As he finds his own release he groans and leans down on my back.

I can't hold myself up anymore so I flop down on the bed, Allister falling with me. He gently rolls over off of me and pulls my back up against his chest, wrapping his arms around me protectively. He even wraps his leg over the top of mine, trying to touch as much of my skin as possible.

"I'm going to miss you love."

I bring his hand to my mouth and kiss the back of it. "I'm going to miss you, too."

Allister's breathing gets deeper, and I know he's about to fall asleep. I wiggle down, ready to fall asleep myself when I hear him whisper, "I love you, kitten."

"I love you, too, Allister."

Chapter Thirty-Eight

Attina

At dawn, I'm standing in front of the opened castle gates. I have my mother's armor on. The roses in full bloom, which top my shoulders, gleam in the sunlight. I'd almost forgotten how lightweight it is.

I yank my mother's sword, which I have strapped across my hips, out of its sheath. The dark runes glitter in the sunlight, and the rose in bloom at the base of the hilt bites into my hand. I pat my leg, feeling the matching dagger in my boot.

Finally, I readjust the bow, my mother and father carved together, before rechecking the quiver full of arrows on my back. I feel like I'm going to war, and I guess in a way, I am.

I haven't offered the armor or weapons back to my mother because honestly, I need them more than she does. Allister strides out of the barn, over to where I stand, in his hand he leads a fully saddled Raven. Her blood red body and black mane sparkle in the sun.

Instead of racing over to them, I stand and watch Raven walk. I want to see if there's any pain still in her back end. I could always take Mylo if she hurts, and I honestly don't want to have the conversation we need to have if she goes on this journey.

Raven must notice me judging her walking because she rips her face out of Allister's hands and trots over to me. "See, I'm fine. I'm going."

Mylo pokes his head out of the barn. I give him a look. He drops his head as he turns and walks back into the barn. By his actions I'd guess he already tried to get Raven to stay and she refused.

My gaze drifts back to Raven's gray eyes. "Are you sure you should be going? You literally *just* fully healed yesterday. Are you sure you can handle this journey?"

Raven glares at me. I know she's pissed at me. I get it. I would be too, but I'm really only concerned for her well-being.

Raven almost growls, "Kalven already okayed me to go."

I make a mental note to give him a talking to when I get back.

"Besides, we've done this entire journey together. We're finishing it together. No matter what."

And by the tone of her voice I know she means, even if I'm pissed at you.

Allister, who was obviously giving Raven and me a moment, slowly makes his way over to us. He grabs me by the waist and pats Raven's face. "You guys ready?"

I glance up at him. If I didn't know him so well I would think he didn't care. His stone face shows no emotion, but I know he's breaking apart inside. Living in Shadow Mountain his entire life he learned how to turn off his emotions, which comes off cold and unloving. But in my heart, I know how much he'll miss me and how worried he'll be until I'm in his arms again. I ask, "The Mori Noki will follow this evening right?"

Allister circles Raven, checking her saddle, as he answers, "Yes, the Mori Noki will be there if you need them." He lifts his eyes and locks them on me as he continues, "If you need help *do not* hesitate to let me know. They're there as a backup for your safety. *Use them.*"

I give him a curt nod and leather creaks as he goes back to inspecting my saddle. Behind me, I hear Ava scream, "Attina!" I turn to see the Mori Noki, my mother, Ned and Kalven, walking down the castle steps.

"For fuck's sake," Raven whispers at my side.

I elbow her before opening my arms and letting Ava slam into a bone crunching hug. After a second, she pulls away. She pins me to the spot with her serious stare, "We're all leaving tonight. We want to give you enough time in case we're spotted by someone, hopefully they won't think we're with you."

I drag her into my arms and lock eyes with each Mori Noki behind her. My voice breaks as I say, "Thank you for risking your lives for me."

Ava takes a step back and she and the rest of the Mori Noki pound their hands to their chests and bow. When they're standing straight again they all shout, "Anything for our queen!"

It's like they all practiced this beforehand. I start to laugh, but Oberon cuts me short as he says, "And our friend."

Tears fill my eyes as I run forward and envelope everyone in my arms. In the little time I've known them, these people have become my friends. I feel blessed to know they will have my back on this insane mission.

I turn to Kalven.

He bows."I'll keep experimenting my queen." He stands, and I walk up to him, throwing my arms over his neck. We had a rough start, but he's Allister's only family, which means he's my family, too.

Then I go to my mother. Her eyes are wet and red. Yes, they're always red, but now, even the whites of her eyes are crimson, like she's been crying for hours, but is trying to hold it together now.

Her gaze travels up and down my body, taking in her armor and weapons. She smirks and places her hands on the roses on my shoulders. She hiccups out, "You keep all of it. It looks better on you than it ever did on me anyway."

I shuck my quiver forward and dig around in it.

When my hand hits on the one thing which doesn't belong in there, I rip it from its hiding spot. As my mother's eyes land on what I pull out, they instantly fill with tears.

The picture I took from mine and Father's house balances in my hand. The one with Father behind my mother and me cradled in her arms.

"I think this should stay with you."

Her hands shakily inch forward. This is the only picture she has of a happier time. When she had her child and her mate in her life—maybe one of the last times.

She brings the frame to her chest and embraces it like she's embracing Father.

I lunge forward and wrap my arms around her. Instantly, she's sobbing. She wraps her arms around me, and if I didn't have this armor on I bet she'd crack my ribs from the violence of her hug.

"I just got you back, and now you have to leave again."

I chuckle and grab her by the shoulders. Pushing her away, I admonish, "You were the one to decide when I left, silly."

She lifts her hand and swats the air in front of her. "You know what I mean."

I nod and drag her in for one last hug, the smell of apples hits me again. "Yes, I do."

Then I sidestep so I'm standing in front of Ned. Before I can say anything, Ned points his finger in my face and croaks, "I'm not going to cry. You're going to be fine."

I smirk and exaggeratedly place my hands behind my back. I nod. "Yes, I will, because you taught me how to take care of myself."

Behind me, Allister shouts, "Hey! I helped with that!"

Ned points his finger at Allister. "You just distracted her!"

I turn to see Allister's face, and I'm not surprised to see a huge shit-eating grin plastered across it. He shrugs his shoulder. "Yeah, you're right." Then he lifts his hand in a questioning gesture. "What can I say? I'm adorable. It's not my fault she hasn't been able to keep her eyes off of me since the day we met."

I hiss at him and shoot him an obscene gesture which only serves to make him wiggle his eyebrows suggestively.

I decide ignoring him is best so I turn back to Ned. Taking a stride forward, I drag him into a hug and lay my head down on his shoulder. "I love you, Ned. Thank you for everything."

When I step back, I see tears streaming down his face. He shouts, "I said I wasn't going to cry!" But his voice is softer when he says, "I love you, too, kid."

I turn to Allister and think, *I love you.*

He slips forward into me. His eyes are serious and in my head I hear, *Come back to me.*

I grab his forearms and lock my eyes on his, "You know I will. I'll be in contact as much as I can. If there's a problem, I'll let you know."

Allister nods, but I see something glisten in his eyes. I stand on my toes and place a soft kiss on his lips. Our mouths move over each other. His tongue runs along my lips. I open my mouth, his tongue claiming me. It's a more passionate kiss than I'd like my mother or Ned to see, but I understand why he needs this.

I tear away and stare into his eyes as I say one last time, "I love you, Allister."

He stares down at me. Whatever I saw glistening in his eyes is now gone, but his lips are downturned and his brow is tight, the anguish already written on his features. His voice cracks as he whispers, "I love you, Attina." I'm turning to Raven when I hear his voice pleading in my head, *Please come back to me.*

I turn back to him and throw my arms back over his neck. He leans down and wraps his arms around me, picking me up as he hugs me back. My voice is choked as I say, "Always, love." He sets me down, and I can't bring myself to even peek up at him, I know if I did I'd turn into a crying mess in a ball on the ground.

I walk over to Raven, a sniffle breaking free. My voice is husky as I croak out, "You want to say goodbye to Mylo?"

She shakes her head. "No, I already said goodbye."

I turn and begin heading out the gate. I'd really rather get on Raven away from everyone. I haven't been wearing my armor or getting on horses with a sword for awhile so I'd much rather embarrassingly fumble up on top of Raven in private.

I notice Raven takes a stride, then stops and turns to everyone who came to say goodbye to us. She pins her gaze on Allister and Ned who are now standing side by side. "Keep each other and Mylo safe."She almost grits her teeth as she says it, like she's warring within herself, struggling to keep the last missing piece from making her heart whole.

Her eyes narrow as they land on my mother. She somehow yells and snarls at the same time, "I hope you die, Titania." Then she raises her nose into the air and passes by her. "Thank you for everything, Kalven." But as she passes the Mori Noki, she spits, "As for the rest of you, I don't know you so I won't waste the breath."

All the Mori Noki bend at the waist and chortle at her response. I shake my head and hiss, "Was that really necessary?"

Raven keeps walking with her nose held high in the air. It's a wonder she doesn't walk into a wall the way she's acting. Behind us, I hear Derek, "I love that horse!"

I put my head in my hand and follow Raven out of the castle's exterior walls. I say to Allister in his mind, *I'm surrounded by idiots.*

He immediately answers, *Idiots who adore you.*

Heat rises to my cheeks as I walk to Raven's side. When we leave the castle walls I crawl on Raven. I'm proud of myself when it only takes me two tries to get on Raven's back.

Chapter Thirty-Nine

Attina

Raven doesn't say a word for hours. The tension hanging over us is palpable, and I've taken about enough I can take of it. I wiggle in my seat, hoping it will get Raven talking, but it doesn't.

I decide I need to just clear the air. I lean to the side to try to catch Raven's eye, but she stares a little too hard straight ahead. I say, "Raven, we need to talk." She doesn't answer so I push on, "I know you hate me right now—"

She cuts me off, "I don't hate you. I just don't like you right now. You hurt me."

I lean down and pat her neck, running my fingers through her mane, untangling the small knots as I go. I plead, "Raven. You must know I never meant to hurt you. I know we talked about killing her, but I couldn't."

Her head snaps to the right, and I lean so she can see the sincerity of my words in my eyes. But she obviously ignores it when she snarls, "When did you go soft?"

Then out of nowhere a branch is slapping me in the face. I drop my jaw open in shock. How did I not see it coming? "You did that on purpose!"

Raven shrugs her shoulder, smirking. "Maybe I did, maybe I didn't."

I glare at her, and she cuts her gaze away from my fiery stare. "You do remember she was brainwashed when she attacked us."

Raven hops her back end in the air, knocking me forward. "You mean *murdered* our fathers? You can't leave out the part where she killed them. You can't just pretend it didn't happen."

I grab onto her neck to keep myself from falling over her shoulder onto the ground under her feet. I screech, "Shit!" before I right myself and scoff. "Yes, Raven, you're right. She murdered our fathers. I won't pretend it didn't happen, but you also can't pretend she was in control of her own actions. You saw her, how crazed she was. You can't tell me the person we see now is the same person from back then."

I swing my leg backward to scramble off of her, but she must be thinking the same thing, because she slams on the breaks at the same time. The momentum of her abrupt stop throws me forward. I try to hang onto the saddle, but the added weight of my armor and weapons drags me to the ground.

I'm able to call to the earth so the dirt beneath me feels like a puffy cloud on a bright airy day and only my pride is hurt. I throw my head up and glare at Raven. "Are you quite done kicking my ass?"

She turns her body to me and drops her face down to mine. I throw my arms around her baby doll head and she lifts me up off of the ground, "I didn't do that one on purpose."

When I'm on my feet, I throw my hands in the air. "Ah ha! So you *did* mean to drag me through that branch!"

She chuckles. I figure it's a good sign, so I jump forward and wrap my arms back around her face. "I'm sorry I hurt your feelings. I would never hurt you on purpose. I drag her head up, forcing her to look at me. I take a deep breath, then confess, "I made her suffer if it helps. I burned the skin off of her hand and almost burned her alive. All she wanted was a hug, and I almost burned her alive."

Raven snarls, "She deserves it."

I let go of her face and shrug. "Maybe. But put yourself in her shoes for a second. You wake up to your mate and mount dead and you know you did it. Your daughter, the daughter you haven't seen since she was a baby is gone, and you have no memory of what happened. How would you feel?"

Raven drops her head, her voice low as she says, "Yes, I suppose you're right." I move to hug her again when she swings her head up and almost knocks me in the face. "But I don't have to forgive her if I don't want to. I'll never forgive her."

When she finishes, I step forward and pat her on the neck, then drag myself back in the creaking saddle. I pick up the reins and answer, "No Raven. You don't ever have to forgive her. I would never ask you to forgive someone you didn't want to. I just wanted you to know why I'm allowing her in my life."

She silently walks off, obviously in thought. We're quiet for a bit before she breaks the silence, "If she hurts you I'll murder her."

My voice is cold when I answer. "You'll have to get in line."

By the time night rolls around, my body is drained. After falling off of Raven and getting smacked in the face I'm pretty damn sore.

Raven is curled up on the ground, and I have my bedroll spread out next to her. I hated to start a fire, worried it would give our enemies our location, but there wasn't much of a choice. With the snow peppering the ground around us, we needed the warmth. I just hope the trees above us keep the smoke in.

We've come across a few Solis on our journey, but I was able to feel them on the air before we were close enough for them to notice us. After I noticed the first Solis we traveled with a protective wall of air around us. I reinforce that wall of air as I move my back into Raven, the heat radiating off of her comforts me. I need to have a conversation before I drift off to sleep though.

I need to figure out how to get into my own subconscious. I close my eyes and think of Kaida. I imagine her in my mind. Her red color, her long sharp claws, how she was so excited to be in her new form.

The more I imagine her, the clearer her form becomes, but I'm still in the real world. Every time I've met Kaida it wasn't under my control, it's been times where I lost control and passed out. There must be a way for me to reach her. Shortly my body gets heavy, and I decide I'll just have to go to sleep and try again tomorrow.

When I open my eyes though, Kaida towers over me. Her head high, searching the horizon. I take in the world around me. Every time I've been in my subconscious, it's just been a black void. Now it's so much more.

I take in the forest around me, birds fill the sky, and I can hear a creek trickling somewhere in the distance. There's plenty of room for Kaida to spread her wings and fly.

What appears to be a crow caws before flying right next to Kaida's mouth. She slices her head toward it and opens her maw, snapping it shut on the bird.

I wince and shout, "Kaida!"

As she exaggeratedly chews on the tiny bird she lies down in front of me. I stride forward and instantly remember I was stuck in one spot prior to this, unable to move my legs. Now, I can stride up to her and pat her snout.

Kaida blows through her nostrils and the force of her breath flings my hair back. "Hi, Attina! What are you doing here?"

I scan the area around us. "I needed to speak with you." I gesture to encompass the paradise around us. "When did this happen?"

She blinks at me like the answer should be obvious. We stand in silence for a second, "Your powers have grown and with them your subconscious flourishes. The more they mature the better suited your subconscious is for me. You didn't think I'd be in that foggy black nothingness forever did you?"

I gaze at the ground and kick the dirt under my feet, "Maybe." Then I have a thought, I point my finger at her and my tone is sharp when I ask, "Hey, you used to be a bird, do you really think you should be eating them?" I point to the sky where birds still fly.

She tilts her head and makes a movement like she's shrugging her shoulders. "Those birds wouldn't leave me alone. They've been dive bombing me for days. Besides I'm a dragon now, not some lowly bird. A girl's gotta eat."

I guess she's right.

I walk over to her shoulder and place my hand on her hard scales. They glitter in the sunlight and feel like soft, over-polished metal, but somehow also fleshy. I wish my Anima could be outside my body like Allister's is. How frightening would it be for Kaida to soar the skies with me on her back?

I start when Kaida asks, "So what did you want to talk about?"

I tiptoe back so I can look into her aquamarine eyes, her eyes matching my own, "I'm going to take on my grandfather." She cocks her head, and I realize she probably has no idea who I'm talking about. I say, "The reason you had that snake chasing after you and devoured you."

She yanks her head back and a snarl rips from her throat. I realize how scary she would be for anyone but me. She can't hurt me. If I die, she dies, we are one.

"I might need your help to defeat him. I might need to use all my power to defeat him. I was wondering if you could help or warn me somehow when I'm about to drain myself? We almost died the last time I did that."

She pushes her nose forward, almost knocking me over. "I'll figure out something."

I nod and lace my arms behind my back. "Well, that's all I wanted to ask. I probably won't wake up for awhile—"

Kaida lifts her head excitedly. "Do you want to go for a ride?"

I jump and throw my arms up in that air. "Yes! More than anything!"

She curls her tail around her body, and I climb up it. Her scales are sharp so I have to be careful, but as soon as I'm on her tail she brings it up to her back, and I crawl off onto her back.

I grab on tightly to the pointed scales trailing down her neck and back as she brings her wings out wide. The skin covering her wings looks soft and translucent. How could something seemingly so fragile be so powerful?

She flaps her wings and lets out a loud growl as we take off. The birds around us spook and scatter and my stomach drops at the height. A squeak squeezes out of my lungs as she soars across the sky.

⸻ ◄O► ⸻

It takes us a day and a half to get to the backside of Shadow Mountain, but we eventually make it. We find the creek mother was talking about. It's not a tiny creek, but not any bigger than the one Raven and I jumped over to run away from that first werewolf all those months ago.

I lean forward and pat Raven on the neck. "Hey, you think you can do this?"

Her head twists behind her. "We've done it before."

I turn my gaze to her haunch where a big chunk of muscle is still missing. It will never grow back and she'll probably never be as strong as she once was. I spin back to Raven's face, "I remember, but last time you didn't have a chunk of muscle missing."

Raven pivots in place and starts walking in the opposite direction. She snaps, "I can do it."

I lean down as she turns back toward the creek in front of us. The water runs over rocks in big white peaks. I bet it's freezing, and with how fast it's moving, if we fall in we'll get swept down steam. "We can find another way around."

Raven doesn't answer though. Instead, she darts forward. I shoot my hands out to hang on to the saddle horn as she takes off at full speed for the creek. At first, her strides are shortened beneath me, but after a few moments, she smoothes out and her speed picks up. I'm surprised to feel her running as fast as she did prior to her injury. Again, at the last possible second she jumps and soars over the creek.

I happily yell as we soar through the air and throw my arms out. Then, in the next second Raven's feet hit the ground. But as soon as she takes a stride forward, I know something's wrong.

Chapter Forty

Attina

I immediately jump out of the saddle. She stumbles forward, and it's obvious she can't put any weight on her back leg.

"Raven!" I shout as I yank her head in to my arms and try to stop her from moving. She throws her head forward, knocking me backwards and away from her.

"It's just a cramp. Let me walk it out." I'm not sure I believe her though. I can hear the pain clear in her voice.

I walk by her side. As the minutes tick by, her leg isn't getting better. Every grunt of pain she makes is like a dagger to my heart. I can't stand seeing her hurt. I would take the pain on myself if it meant she felt better.

I make her walk in circles both ways to try to get the kink out, and eventually it works. She starts putting a little weight on it, then a little more. She grunts and finally puts all her weight back on her foot.

I walk her around for a little while longer before I plop on the ground, exhaustion overcoming me.

Raven continues walking, but shouts over to me, "You okay, kid?"

I bring my knees up and rest my head on them. "I'm fine. I'm just overwhelmed with everything, and you scared the ever loving shit out of me. Let's never do that again."

Then right next to my head I hear her say, "You're being a big baby." I jump and accidently bonk her in the mouth with my head.

She rips her head back and yelps out, "Ouch!"

I rub the back of my head. Luckily, I somehow didn't knock my head open, but man, it felt like I did. "Sorry."

I scan around us. We're in a small open patch next to the river. It's as good a place as any. "I know it's only midday, but can we stop for the night? I need a break."

Raven, who's continued her walking calls over her shoulder, "Sure, just get this damn saddle off of me. I'm more than willing to put off sitting in a stall, unable to help, while you deal with your miserable grandfather."

———◦◦◦———

The next morning we're on the road early. We walk through the forest for a while, but haven't found the cave. My mind races. What if we missed it? What if we went the wrong way?

Raven's voice cuts through my thoughts, "Kid, your anxiety is radiating off of you. Why don't I get your mind off of things? How are you and Allister?"

I peer down at the back of her head. "We're good—how are you and Mylo?"

Her body tenses almost imperceptibly. If I didn't know this horse like the back of my hand, I might have missed it. "We're—uh good. I guess."

I lean to the side. "You haven't even acknowledged him yet. Have you?"

She bounces her head. "We're talking about you here not me!"

I drop the reins and lean down on the saddle horn, breathing in Raven's comforting smell. "Hey, if my relationship is open for discussion, so is yours."

She shrieks, "I don't have one!"

I'm taken aback by her statement. I sit back up. "What do you mean *you don't have one*? You found your mate."

Her head droops as she answers. "Yes, a mate who can't talk. How am I supposed to be mated to a mute?"

I chuckle. "Raven, that horse worships the ground you walk on. He has since day one."

She stops in her tracks and turns her head to me. Her voice waivers as she asks, "You think so?"

I smack the side of her neck playfully. "You silly mare. Yes!"

She drops her front end forward, and I have to lean *way* back in the saddle and hold onto the cantle to stay in place. Raven grunts as she stretches then crawls back onto all fours and shakes her whole body. As a kid, I would call these horsequakes because I get shook like I was in a violent earthquake.

"How am I supposed to know he likes me? I thought mates could talk to each other through their minds, but he doesn't know how to talk, so he can't tell me anything, and I haven't pushed it."

Was I this dense about Allister?

I sigh. "He never leaves your side. He would murder anyone, including me, to protect you. He adores you. I can't believe you don't see it."

She hurriedly spits out, "Well, I haven't been doing anything but eating and sleeping since..." But her voice trails off as I notice a dark hole up ahead.

I throw my hand up and point at it. "Raven, look up there! Do you think that could be it?"

Her gaze flies to where I'm pointing, and she takes off at a trot. Obviously, she's feeling better than yesterday. Thank the gods. I have to move some branches and duck under them, but when the cave comes into view, I know we made it to the right place.

When we make it over to the dark hole of a cave, I'm surprised we didn't see it sooner. This thing is massive. Kaida could fit through the mouth of it kind of massive. And radiating off of it is an evil, oppressive sort of energy.

Raven takes a stride back and pins her ears. She must feel it, too. She stutters, "Ar—are we really going to go in there?"

I don't want to, but I know we have to. Once we go in that mountain I don't see myself coming out. The only way I see me defeating Henrik is if I somehow manage to kill him after he lands a killing blow on me. But it has to be done. I will die if it means all of Arealea is safe from Henrik's evil reign. I jump down and pat her neck, "Yes, we have to."

Her gray eyes lock on mine. "Girl, I don't know—"

I know she's going to say I don't know if we can do this. I also feel the weight of our job, how impossible this is, but one of us has to be strong here. "Nope. We can do this, Raven." I walk to her front, grab her face in my hands, and emphasize, "*We can do this.*"

Her eyes narrow. "How exactly do you plan on going into that scary place and getting us *both* out alive?"

I let go of her head and twist around to face the cave. "With one foot in front of the other. We will figure it out as we go."

I hear her release a heavy sigh behind me. I know she's scared. I'm scared, too. But only one of us gets to break down at a time. Right now it's her turn.

She begins pacing behind me as I start my work. The entire cave has fallen in on itself so much so that boulders jut out the mouth of the cave. Raising my hand I begin to heft the first gigantic boulder out of the way before I realize how much work clearing the hole will be if I haul out every single boulder.

Instead, I focus on crushing the boulders with my powers. The rocks move and shake before falling to the ground in a heap. It takes so much longer than I thought it would to clear out what must be three quarters of the cave. I have to first crush each stone and then when it's smashed into a thousand little pieces I move the ruble out of the cave. I do this over and over, and then, shore up the sides and ceiling to make sure it won't collapse back down on us. It's taxing.

I take a seat on the ground in the cave. Sweat drips down my face. I don't like how exhausted this makes me. What if Henrik doesn't go for my explanation? What if I have to fight him today after I've been so worn out?

Raven's head hangs low, and she stares up at the ceiling like it's made of sticks and could collapse at any moment. "Are you sure this won't all cave in again?"

I twist my head to her. "Don't trust my handiwork?"

She pins her ears and snarls back. "You haven't had your powers all that long. Forgive me if I don't have a ton of trust in them yet."

I flop back on the dirt ground, the smell of mildew hitting me, and fling my arms above my head. "You're forgiven. I think we should stay here tonight. I'm too worn out to face Henrik tonight. Hopefully there won't be much more of the cave left to clear in the morning, and I can face him with more energy than I have now."

Her eyes dart up to the ceiling. "Don't snap at me, but will this hold while you're asleep?"

I wave at her. "Yeah, yeah. It'll hold up for years. I shored the walls with earth. My powers aren't holding anything up anymore. We're fine for the night. No one should even think to search here so we should be safe."

She stands up straight, her head now held high, and strides over to me. "Okay, let's stay here tonight. I'd rather you be fresh when you meet that bastard anyway." Then, suddenly, she's standing above me. "Hey, I can't get this off myself."

I giggle and grab the stirrup, pulling myself on my feet. I don't even have the energy to tack the saddle up correctly; I just uncinch her and lift it off of her onto the ground. Normally, I would hang up each piece of the saddle so nothing drags in the dirt before I took it off and lay the saddle pad on top of it to dry, but I can't bring myself to do even such a simple task.

I lie back down and roll over. I yawn as I say, "Goodnight, Raven."

⸻◆⸻

I open my eyes to darkness. I sit up and stretch my arm in the air, waiting for my eyes to adjust to the dark. Since my Awakening, my vision has gotten better. If I was a human I wouldn't be able to see in the pitch blackness of the cave at all, but now I can at least see outlines of shapes. I search around me. Where's Raven? I hold my hand out and call to my fire. In my palm a small fireball flashes to life.

No Raven.

I shout, "Raven! Where are you?"

There's no answer, so I get up and race down the cave.

"Raven! Raven!"

I get about halfway back out of the cave when I hear horse hooves running toward me. Is that Raven or someone else? I stand in my fighting stance, with my hands in fists in front of my face, and wait for the animal to show itself.

Raven yells, "Kid! It's me! I'm okay!"

She slides on her back end to keep from running into me, and I growl, "Where were you! I was worried sick!"

Raven shakes her head. "I'm sorry. You were sleeping, and I didn't want to wake you. I was thirsty when I woke up. I just went to get some water from the creek."

I throw my hands in the air. "From the creek? Are you insane! Anyone could have seen you!" Then my emotions crash around me. I go from pissed off one second, to utter relief the next. I race forward and throw my hands around her neck. "Someone could have found you and taken you from me. Don't scare me like that again."

Raven wraps her neck around me. "It's okay, kid. I won't leave you again until we get into the mountain. I'm sorry I thought I could make it back before you woke up. I should have waited for you to wake up. I won't do it again."

Tears flood my eyes as I think of what would have happened if someone would have found Raven. They probably would've just taken her into Shadow Mountain, but from what Allister told me there are some depraved Fae who live in this mountain. What if they just killed her on the spot for sport? She could have been taken from me forever.

Then Allister's voice breaks into my head. *Did you find her?*

I jump from the sudden intrusion before relaxing into myself. *Yes, how did you know?*

Raven notices my reaction. "Is it Allister?"

I nod to her as he answers. *I've been listening in. You really should be guarding your thoughts better than you have.*

Not from my mate when I'm away.

He chuckles in my head. *Nice dig at me while still sounding sweet.*

I play innocent. *I don't know what you're talking about. I'm a delight.*

I hear chuckling and then he's gone. He still doesn't realize I've been practicing keeping people out of my mind since he taught me before he left on his journey. I'm perfectly capable of keeping prying ears out of my head while still allowing him access.

I hurriedly inform him, *We're going into the mountain today. I love you.*

I love you, too, kitten. Our friends are in position. If you need anything, yell at me, and I'll get them to you.

Wow, warrior Allister is poking out. *Yes, sir.*

Allister growls in my head, *Save that kind of talk for the bedroom.*

I send him a picture of me rolling my eyes and he sends me back a picture of him pushing me up against a wall. I shake my head and block him out for a second before I get totally lost in the moment.

I work half the day, moving rocks and dirt out of my way, before finding a door. Carved flames crawl up the wood. Kalven told me of this door. It's the same door he escaped through prior to king Rufus' death.

I turn around and wrap my arms around Raven's neck. I inhale her smell, the smell of home, and then I pull back. "Are you ready?"

Her gray eyes lock on mine, her eyebrows pinch, and she nods to me in answer.

I turn back to the door. As I place my hand on the doorknob I say in my mind to Allister, *I'll love you forever.*

He immediately answers, *Forever and a day, love.*

I turn the knob into a dark empty hallway and a wave of negative energy washes over me causing me to physically shiver. My stomach plummets, how am I ever going to survive this?

I take a stride through the door with Raven hot on my heels. Her presence calms me until a voice booms from the room in front of me.

"Who dares try to sneak up on the Fae King?"

Then a ball of fire speeds down the hallway, heading straight for us.

Chapter Forty-One

James

I'm packing a small bag. I left the Eastern Fae's dungeon with only the clothes on my back and since arriving here I haven't received many more clothes. I change back and forth between holey tunics and pants. There aren't many luxuries here unless you're royal, a personal guard to a royal, or a slayer.

Being Tala's brother doesn't automatically make me a slayer. I have to work for it like every other Fae here. Until then, I have to toil, scrap, and scratch, to make it to the top ranks alongside my sister.

As I'm buttoning my meager bag closed, Tala walks in. Her short black hair bobs around her chin. "Hey, you ready to leave tonight?"

I sit down on my bed and pat the bag next to me. "About as ready as I'll ever be."

Inside though, I'm a ball of nerves. It feels like snakes are swirling around inside me vibrating from anxiety. I'm excited to take on Allister, to kill him. To make him pay for what he took from me. There's not a doubt in my mind that I'll make him suffer.

What I'm anxious about is Attina.

How will she react when she sees me? Will she be happy? Will she hate me?

Tala walks over and sits on the bed next to me. The bed squeaks as her weight settles on it. I'm not sure how the shot springs could make any noise at this point, but they find a way. She reaches over and grabs my hand, "It's going to be okay."

I turn my gaze to hers. "You don't know Attina," I say matter-of-factly.

She answers, "I'll get to know my sister in law."

My heart swells with the idea, Attina will soon be my wife. Henrik wants *me* as his grandson.

I can't wait.

Chapter Forty-Two

Attina

I throw up a wall of air as the fire barrels toward us, but I feel the fire burning through my wall almost as quickly as I build it. I try wrapping water through my wall of air to staunch the fire. The water fizzes as the fire evaporates it. I kneel down and bring my hands up, forcing a wall of earth up to block us. The earth holds. Then the whooshing noise of the fire slamming against my wall stops, as the heat of the fire dissipates.

I had planned for this.

I knew the door was once a back exit to the throne room and there was a real chance Henrik would be in the throne room when I opened it. I tug on the dropping feeling in my gut and as I lift my hand a ball of fire illuminates the area around Raven and me. As I stand the fireball grows along with the heat radiating off of it. When the ball of fire grows to the size of my head I drop the wall of earth I built and fling the fire back in Henrik's direction.

I hear a grunt and then the booming voice calls out, "Titania? Is that you?" Then the outline of a massive man fills the entrance of the hallway.

This must be Henrik.

The bastard who took my family from me.

Who's hated me since I was born.

And hunted me down like I was a rat in the chicken feed.

I don't answer him. I just stride down the darkened hallway with Raven on my heel.

Henrik narrows his eyes as I walk out of the darkness. We've been in the murky dark so long, the light from the sconces doting around the vast room burns my eyes. I blink rapidly until the pain dissipates, and I can finally take in the man in front of me. His nostrils flare and his red eyes blaze as they drift down my form and he takes in the horse behind me. His red knee length tunic and pants sparkle in the light. The fabric pulls tight over his arms as he crosses them in front of him. He towers over me and his sour, angry face is more than a little intimidating.

I steel my back as he growls, "Attina?"

Behind him, Talon screeches. I lean around my grandfather's wall of a body and see Talon perched on the back of a massive black throne. His ochre eyes lock on mine, and I shoot him a glare like I would an escaped prisoner who wasn't secretly on our side.

I turn my gaze back to Henrik. "Henrik, I presume?"

He cocks his head like he's inspecting a particularly annoying bug before he decides if he wants to smash it. He snarls, "So you're my half-breed granddaughter who's caused so many irritations."

I stride past him with my shoulders back and my head held high, like I own every inch of this place. I bring my hand up and flick my hair behind my shoulder. "If you would have simply left me alone we wouldn't be in this predicament." I peek over my shoulder at him making sure to shoot him a glare for good measure and continue. "You're the one who had to kick the hornets' nest."

He chuckles behind me. "Hornet's nest? You think awfully highly of yourself."

I ignore his snide remark as I spin and take in the room around me. I take in the dark, marble floors which lead up to smoky quartz walls. The walls have small veins of gold cracking through them, giving the ominous room a little sparkle.

Close to the back of the room on a raised dais sit two thrones. I stand in the middle of the room as I inspect the thrones in front of me. The one with Talon perched on it is obviously Henrik's throne. The charred bones making up the throne screams Henrik. It's twice as monstrously giant as the throne next to it. I say throne, but it's not much more than a wooden chair with a woman sitting in it.

This must be Allister's mother, Kenda.

I tilt my head and move into her line of sight, but her eyes are vacant, like she off in some other world behind her eyes. She's not much more than a shell, her cheeks are sucked in and her dark hair is dull and lifeless.

I notice Henrik prowling behind me. I peer over at Raven, where I left her by the door, and announce, "I don't know who you think you're sneaking up on, but it's not me."

Henrik stops moving as I twist on my heel. His arms lace behind his back and he shakes his head. "Damn, you're a mouthy one." He strides over and towers over me. He leans his face down until our noses almost touch, when he opens his mouth the small of fire and ash hits me. "You're not the one in control here, no matter how strong you *think* you are, I am stronger." Then he cocks his head and asks the question I've been waiting for. "Why did you break into my palace? Did you come to murder me?"

I think, *Yes*, but don't say anything.

I cross my arms in front of my chest and jut my hips out like a sassy errant teenager. My stomach's in knots and a cold sweat has broken out over my body. But I need to keep this charade up. Make him think I have the same bravado he does, like I know I'm more powerful than those around me, give us some common arrogant ground.

I answer, "I came to hear your side of the story. I don't believe you of all people ever found me, a child, a threat." A carefully placed dig at him. I break eye contact with him, turning my back like I don't perceive him as a threat, and make my way over to Raven. As I walk, I talk over my shoulder. "I wanted to know what you want from me. Through my travels I heard of an old back entrance to your throne room. I figured the best way to show you my good faith was to show you the weakness in your stone mountain."

I place my hand on Raven's neck and turn around. I jump when Henrik's face is inches from mine. He followed me across the room, and I didn't hear him? I really need to have my defenses up more. I feel the air around me, trying to detect any other movement, but luckily find none.

He growls, "Or you used the secret entrance to try to assassinate me." I scoff and roll my eyes, but his hand shoots up faster than I can react to and snatches my chin. "Did your human father not teach you any manners? Roll your eyes again, and I will pluck them out of your head and roll them back at you."

I sharply inhale which seems to be the correct response because a serpentine smile cracks across his features and he releases me.

Then he continues, "Although, you actually seem to realize how I could crush you if it pleased me."

I quietly nod in answer. I really do know he could crush me if he so wished. I would put up one hell of a fight and maybe one on one I could kill him, but this is his world. His palace. I know I can't take on him and all of his men. I'm not crazy.

His gaze travels up and down my body, assessing me. "Other than your strange eyes, you look exactly like your mother when she was younger."

I drop my eyes to the ground trying to appear submissive as I answer, "So I've been told."

Henrik places his hand back under my chin and brings my gaze up to his. "I want you to be my heir."

My eyes bulge in utter shock I don't have to fake. Is he serious? He's been trying to murder me this entire time and now he's saying he wants me to be his heir? He must be toying with me.

I cock my head. "I don't want to seem unappreciative, but you've been trying to kill me since before my Awakening. I find that hard to believe."

Henrik turns around and walks over to his throne. He sits down, forcing me to follow him to get an answer. Raven trails behind me as we stand at the base of the dais. Henrik steeples his hands under his chin, stares down at me. "That was one of the few mistakes I've made in my life. I should have been trying to return you to your rightful home, not trying to eliminate you."

"And my mother?" falls out of my mouth before I can bite my tongue.

Henrik's eyes narrow, and I can almost see smoke coming out of his nostrils. "Your mother was a traitor. She was dealt with."

My eyes drift to Talon. It sounds like Henrik thinks my mother is dead. I wonder why he kept that bit of information from Henrik.

I nod like I understand what he's saying. "And my mate?"

Henrik shoots up and dives down the dais at me. I feel his hand on the air around me as it shoots forward and wraps around my throat. I could have stopped him before he grabbed hold of me, but I'd like to keep some of my powers under wraps if at all possible. Blocking him would have raised too many red flags.

His nostrils flare and he snarls inches from my face, "You will have no mate." My stomach drops as his nose travels down my arm and he sniffs my skin, then locks eyes with me again, "You even smell like that bastard."

I gulp. I didn't realize I would smell like him. I figured after a few days on the road I would stink to high heaven.

Henrik releases my neck, and I reach a hand up and rub where he just grabbed. I know I'll have a bruise tomorrow, if I make it to tomorrow. He passes me and makes his way for the throne room doors. He yanks one back, sticks his head out, and I hear sharp voices as he chastises whoever's on the other side of the door.

When he turns back to me he places his hands behind his back. He doesn't say a word until he's sitting back on his throne. Then he says, "I already have a suitable grandson for you. He will be here shortly."

Wonderful. Just what I need, *another* man trying to lay claim to me.

"And if I refuse to marry your suitor and become your heir? What then?" I ask because I'm genuinely curious. He seems to have this whole thing all planned out. What if I were to ruin his plans?

His gaze leaves me and trails over Raven's shaking body and a feline grin crawls up his face. He leans back and lets out a loud sigh like I've finally asked him the correct question to unlock some mystery only he's privy to. "Then I will kill everything you've come to love. I'll start with that beast and then I will go find your mate and anyone else you love so I can torture him in front of you."

I gulp and shift my weight back and forth. I know he's serious, and I can tell by his voice he would enjoy torturing and murdering everyone I hold dear.

Henrik lifts his hand and gestures toward Raven. "Until then, why don't we send the beast to the stables?"

Behind me Raven snorts. I pat her neck. "I'd rather her stay with me. She's a Fae horse, she won't be any trouble I promise."

He snarls, "She's an animal, she belongs with the other beasts."

Raven begins shaking next to me. She doesn't seem to realize either she's coming with me, or we're breaking out of here and figuring out a different plan.

I think to Allister, *Be on guard.*

Be safe, he immediately answers. Just hearing his voice gives me the courage to fight Henrik on this one.

My voice comes out petulant as I argue, "I've come here to see your side of the story. I've agreed to leave my mate for this future. Allowing my Fae companion to stay with me is the least you can do. This is a strange new place, and I'm much more likely to call this home with my friend by my side."

He's silent for much too long. It takes everything in me to stand tall. His eyes bore into me, and I fight the instinct to shrink away. Finally he answers, "I suppose your horse—" He pauses waiting for a name.

I quickly spit out, "Raven."

"I suppose Raven won't be too much of an issue." His eyes dart to Raven in emphasis as he adds, "And if she is—she will be *dealt* with."

I hear Raven's breath pick up beside me under his scrutinizing stare.

His gaze slices back to mine. "And you *will* be married to my grandson. Sooner rather than later."

Grandson? I open my mouth to say something, but I'm cut off by the throne room doors slamming open behind me. "Attina!" reaches my ears and my stomach drops. My shoulders ratchet up to my ears, and I stop breathing.

I'd know that voice anywhere.

James.

Chapter Forty-Three

Attina

It's like I'm stuck in the ice now coating my veins. Everything shifts around me, but I can't seem to move. Henrik seriously wants me to marry James? I try to figure out his thinking, but keep coming up blank.

Then James is beside me, on the ground kneeling in front of Henrik. I notice next to him stands a woman I've never seen before. I wonder if this is the sister who broke him out of prison.

I flick my eyes to her and see her lift her lip and show her canines as she glares at me. Wow. I'm not sure what I did to make this girl hate me, but she definitely hates me.

Henrik clears his throat and my gaze is brought back to him. "Granddaughter, this is your future husband." James stands and quickly takes my hand in his. His eyes are filled with tears as he croaks out, "Attina, you're here. You're actually here! I didn't want to believe it when the messenger came to get me; but it's really you!"

I yank my hand out of his and walk up to the bottom of the dais. I grunt, "Grandfather, isn't there anyone else I could marry?" I throw my hand back and point at James. "I refuse to marry this abusive, deranged fool."

James clenches his jaw in anger and his sister growls next to him, as fire flashes in Henrik's red eyes. His skin turns beet red and he flings a fireball in my direction as he shoots to his feet.

I easily sidestep the fireball, but James cries out as it brushes along his legs.

Henrik yells, "You *will* marry this werewolf. You *will* produce an heir with it. And there will be no further discussion."

I notice how he calls James an 'it'. I cross my arms over my chest and cock my head. "You want me to marry *it?* Why would you want your heir to marry something you don't even consider a person?"

He flings another fireball my way. This time I have to dive out of the way to get out of the line of fire. But I again hear James scream. I guess he wasn't fast enough or smart enough to move. A wicked smile curves my lips as a terribly wonderful idea hits me. I can get two things accomplished if I continue pissing Henrik off just enough to keep him throwing fireballs at me.

"You've obviously been around that bastard step-son of mine too long. You're just as arrogantly stupid as him and you're the spitting image of him when you cock your head. You weren't born here, so I'll give you the benefit of the doubt, but I suggest you knock off the attitude. If not, I'll have to show you your place."

I scoff and exaggeratedly roll my eyes as I take a few strides so I'm standing in front of James again.

A growl cracks through the room and as I thought, Henrik throws another fireball at me. I wonder if he realizes how his temper leaves him open for manipulation. James screams, "Attina!" as I throw up a wall of wind around me. The fire glides off of me and flows right into James.

James grunts and whimpers in pain. I sidestep and admire my handiwork. James' clothes are filled with holes and the skin poking out is blistered and oozing blood. I know Henrik could turn him to ash in a split second, but he must have been holding back since he was aiming at me, his heir. I allow a wicked grin to crawl up my face as I take in the damage.

To our right James' sister gasps. She must have finally noticed my reaction. She shoots to her feet and yells "Sire!" as she places a fisted hand to her chest and bows at the waist.

She stays in that position until Henrik answers in an annoyed tone, "Yes, Tala?" So her name is Tala. Well at least now I have a name for this woman who obviously hated me from the moment she laid eyes on me.

Her hand goes out and she points a finger at me. "She's doing this on purpose. She's angering you on purpose to burn my brother!"

Henrik's gaze travels to me. His eyes rake over me, taking in the wicked grin I've left on my face. A matching grin crawls up his features as he sits back in his throne and cups his chin.

"I was worried you'd be soft like your parents, but it seems you're more like me than I once thought." He points his chin to James. "I knew you two had a history, but he made it seem like a happy history. He said Allister separated you two."

I can't help the words which fall out of my mouth next. "*My mate* did no such thing. Whatever was between James and me died the moment he slapped me. *Before* I realized who Allister was to me."

Henrik growls, but doesn't throw a fireball this time. His voice is sharp as he snarls, "Allister is nothing to you. You will see that soon enough. You will produce an heir with this were-wolf. A more powerful creature than Arealea's ever seen will be created by your union." I notice he completely glazes over the, James slapped me, part.

That's fine I won't be here long enough to participate in any kind of marriage. Besides, even if there's some strange twist of fate, and I'm stuck here, there's no way I would ever sleep with him again.

Henrik breaks my thoughts. "And if you refuse to perform your duties, I will have someone hold you down. I do not require your consent to obtain an heir out of you."

I have to physically stop myself from crossing my legs. My chest hollows out. James would probably be fine with that. Then, as if on cue, I feel his hand on my back.

"Attina, I forgive you for hurting me. Why don't we go to bed? I'm sure you're tired from your journey."

I whirl around and snatch onto his hand. I clamp down on it as hard as I can, feeling the bones crack under my Fae strength.

James' face falls, he closes his eyes, and clenches his jaw against the pain.

I snap, "You don't need a hand to produce an heir. Touch me without my permission again and you'll lose your hands." Then I chuck his hand back to him. He clutches it to his chest and whimpers.

Behind me, Henrik bursts out in a booming laugh. I twist around and see his head thrown back against the throne as he chortles. It takes him a second, but he finally drops his gaze to mine as he clutches his chest and takes in a few calming breaths.

He lifts his hand to his eyes and wipes away what must have been a tear. "You're a feisty one." His gaze shifts from me to James and back again. "How did you get him to follow you so loyally? I've never met a mutt so broken to the bit as this one is to you."

He then stands and makes his way to my side. He throws his arm over my shoulders like we're old friends. Like he didn't completely ruin my life. I have to stop myself from shrinking away from him.

"Why don't we get you situated in one of the royal rooms? You two can get reacquainted after the wedding."

I turn my head and growl at James who now has his hand cradled in Tala's. I peek back over at Raven and motion with my head for her to follow us. She hesitates, but follows.

As I pass the thrones, I take in Allister's mother. She's more of a shell than a Fae at this point. Is this what happens when you lose your mate? Instantly, my chest hollows out. Allister must have watched her go from his vibrant loving mother, to this ghost. It must have been so traumatizing to watch your mother die inside before your eyes; little by little, day after day, and not being able to do anything about it.

No wonder he clung to my mother so tightly.

⸻◆○◆⸻

It's a little difficult getting Raven up the stairs to our room, but she manages. Being a Fae animal she's more graceful and can easily take directions, but it was still a challenge.

I step inside the huge room Henrik brings me to and turn around.

Inside is bigger and more elegant than I ever could have guessed. The walls are a dark smoky quartz with gold veins scattered throughout like the rest of the mountain. The four poster bed in the middle of the room is covered in a black glittery blanket and when I drag my hand across the buttery silk fabric, it takes everything in me to not leap into the bed. In one corner is a matching black tub. I call it a tub, but honestly it's more of a pool. Lavender tickles my nose.

Henrik's voice flits to me from where he stands by the door, "All you have to do is think you want the water in the tub hotter or colder and it will obey. Its magic spelled only for the rooms for our special guests. In the closet you will find whatever clothes you should need. There are gowns or tunics and pants, whichever you prefer. You will also have someone outside your door at all times in case you should need anything at any time of the day.

I twist around and narrow my eyes at him, "It feels like you had this room waiting for me."

He leans against the door frame, but I can barely tell he's doing it because his body fills so much of the opening. "I had plans to go rescue you in motion prior to you showing up here."

"To rescue me?" I don't expect him to answer me, so I just shrug and continue, "Why provide me with all this finery? Allister said he wasn't allowed a room with the royals."

He crosses his arms over his chest and leans his head against the door frame. "I want you to see both sides of the story. Not just what my enemies have filled your head with. I need an heir. I realize that now. Centuries from now when I'm old and frail I will need someone to take my place. Fae follow power, and your child will be the most powerful Fae in all of Arealea, I'll have another chance to mold the perfect heir to follow in my footsteps."

If he thinks I'd ever allow him anywhere near my child he has another thing coming. I don't dare say anything though, I've angered him enough today, so instead I nod and walk over to the one door in the room and open it. He was right. It's full of clothes. Beautiful ball gowns in all colors of the rainbow fill one side of the walk-in closet and tunics and pants are folded and tucked away neatly on shelves on the other side.

When I walk back out Henrik has his hand on the half closed door and his eyes are narrowed on me. "You should really forget Allister. He's not who you think he is. You'll see, blood is the only thing you can count on."

———————◆○◆———————

The next morning I wake up with the dawn. I turn over and peek at where Raven sleeps peacefully at the side of my bed. I had the Fae stationed outside my room bring up a mattress for her. I unsaddled her and she crawled right on top of the soft mattress and passed out before I was able to get in pajamas and crawl into bed myself.

I smile at the vision of her peacefully sleeping. I know if she wasn't with me she wouldn't be sleeping this well. It does my heart good seeing her so content even in such a hostile environment. I roll back on my back and try to contact Allister.

Hey, love. Checking in. I wait and wait, but he doesn't answer. My stomach drops. I try to not let everything Henrik said yesterday get to me, but right after Henrik told me he wasn't who I thought he was he doesn't answer? From our mate bond I can tell he's not with the Eastern Fae anymore. Where is he going?

There's probably a perfectly rational explanation for whatever he's doing.

I decide I need to get up and start moving, get my mind off of him. If I don't focus on something I know the questions will eat me up. I throw my legs over the side of the bed which wakes Raven immediately. She shoots up and flings her head around, taking in her surroundings like she woke up on a different plant.

I chuckle. "Hey, you okay?"

Her eyes lock on me before she lets out a long, jaw popping, yawn. Then she lies back on her side and stretches her legs out. I hear the cracking of her joints as she stands up and bows down, stretching out her back.

"I'm okay. How did you sleep, kid?"

I stand up, stretching my arms above my head. "I don't know if I could have a bad night's sleep in that bed. I stride over to the walk-in closet and call over my shoulder, "You ready to see what this place is all about today?"

I change into a red tunic and black pants. I throw on my old comfortable boots as her voice flits into me. "Why do you want to check this place out? Don't we have a mission to complete?"

"We do. But whether you like it or not it will take time and we have to play nice until the right moment."

I hear her snort. "I don't like this. He's being too rational. I don't remember him from when I was a child, but I know he wasn't this reasonable. He's hiding something."

I think back to Allister and my blood runs cold. What if he's right. What if everything Allister and me went through together was just some calculated game?

I walk back out into the bedrooms and lock my eyes on Raven. "We'll we're just going to figure out what's going on for ourselves."

Chapter Forty-Four

Attina

Raven and I slowly make our way back to the throne room. Yesterday, it was like a ghost town here. I didn't see any Fae apart for the woman left outside of my room. Today, I pass Fae along the way. I wonder if they were all hiding yesterday because Henrik was walking around.

My eyes land on a particularly skinny Fae. Her skeletal form sucks up to the side of the wall, like she's trying desperately to have her body turn to water so she can melt into it. She clutches bedding to her chest and her dull brown hair falls around her sunken cheeks as she drops her head and her lifeless blue eyes advert to the floor. I open my mouth to say something, but I close it immediately. What could I say? I assume the people here already know who I am. Why should they trust me? Why would any of my words be comforting?

As we walk I notice more Fae meandering about. They're all underfed and their stained, holey clothes show me how they've been treated. I scoff and shake my head. Who would let their own people starve and suffer like this?

Henrik, that's who.

When I make it to the throne room doors I'm stopped by two guards swathed in golden armor. The guard to the right stomps forward and lifts his hand to stop me. His voice comes out surprisingly high as he says, "No one is allowed in the throne room."

I narrow my eyes at him. "You know who I am, don't you?"

The man drops his hand and steps back to his position by the door. He shakes his head and answers, "Orders are orders."

"Listen here—" I let the silence fill and wait for him to tell me his name.

He eventually relents, "Agar."

"Agar," I repeat, then I lift my hand and produce a ball of fire similar to what Henrik was throwing at me yesterday. "You have two options. First, you let me in and we all move on with our day. Second—" My eyes drift down his golden armor. "—I melt that armor off of you. I've heard gold is an extremely soft metal. I'd like to see if my fire can melt it. *But,* it'll melt to your skin and who knows how painful that would be."

Agar's hand flies to the throne room door and he pulls back on the handle. The heavy door creaks as it opens. As I walk toward the door I hear Agar whisper, almost too low for me to hear, "Bitch."

I snap my head to him and plaster a shit eating grin on my face as I toss the fireball at him. He screams and jumps away as his hands scramble to put out the fire catching on his chest plate.

I enter the room with Raven on my tail. I search the space as we walk, but I don't see Henrik. His throne is empty; the room around us is silent. The only person I can see in the room besides us is Kenda, who quietly sits on her meager throne. If I didn't know any better I'd think she was a statue from her lack of movement. I can't even see her chest rising and falling, like she's a sad, broken doll. I walk up to the dais, meaning to climb it and touch her, maybe bring her out of whatever spell she's under. Then, I notice the dark bruise wrapping around her eye. It wasn't there yesterday. Henrik must have done that to her.

"I thought I told those imbecile guards I wanted to be alone." Henrik's voice reverberates through the room, stopping me in my tracks. Henrik stalks around the backside of the dais, nostrils flared, before climbing it and sitting in his throne. His eyes dance from my face to Kenda's. "So, you've met Allister's mother."

If I wasn't staring at her face when Henrik's words left his lips I would have missed it. But as soon as his words break the silence, Kenda's eyes spark to life. The life I see there doesn't last long, only a second or two, just enough time for her eyes to flick to me and then back to staring off into the distance. So, is she really in there? She's not some lifeless husk then? The mention of her son must have brought her out of her reverie. I wonder if this lifeless appearance is some sort of self-preservation act?

"I wanted to check her eye." I glower at him, but he ignores me.

He waves his hand dismissively. "Ignore her. I do." Obviously, that's a lie. He couldn't have been ignoring her when he slapped her across the face. Anger and sorrow well in my chest. No wonder he and James are so chummy. They have the same outlook on dealing with women. Then the fire in his eyes flares to life and he adds on, "What are you doing here half-breed?"

I grit my teeth and fire rolls under my skin. I know my exposed arms are turning pink, but I don't care. "My name is Attina—not half-breed."

Henrik cocks his head and his eyes travel up and down my arms as he takes in the red hue now coating me. "Interesting. You're either powerful enough or smart enough to thwart my every attempt at killing you, but you still let your emotions give you away?" He pauses then adds, "You must be more powerful than I thought."

I stifle a growl. "What would you like me to do today? How can I assist you?" I have to at least pretend to be interested in being his heir and taking over his throne one day.

Henrik chuckles. "Well, I guess you're not completely stupid." He cups his chin in his hand while he thinks.

A caw breaks through the silence and Talon flies through the room. He lands on Henrik's shoulder, and I'm shocked when Henrik is able to easily hold his body weight. He is *not* a light bird. I doubt I could hold him, but here Henrik sits like he's holding up a feather.

He ruffles his black and white speckled feathers as he speaks, "Tala closed off the passage the half-breed came through for good. She also wanted me to ask if the half-breed could go practice with the soldiers today." His head is over Henrik's so he can't see when Talon shoots me a worried look.

Henrik slowly nods. "What a good idea." His eyes bore into me. "You'll practice with the soldiers today. Being the heir to the throne, you need to learn to protect yourself the correct way. Talon will show you the way."

Immediately, Talon takes flight like he can't get out of this room fast enough. I dip my head and spin on my heel to follow his red tail feathers, but behind me Henrik clears his throat, stopping me. I clench my hands as I turn back around. The doors behind me creak open. I hear the thump of wings beating out of the room, and I wish I was following Talon instead of locking eyes with Henrik again.

"I've seen your fire power, and I'm assuming you have the power to control earth since you cleared the old passage. Are there any other powers I should know about?"

That you should know about? No. I'd rather he didn't know about either of those, but I didn't really have a choice in disclosing those. There's no way I'm going to show him any of my other powers unless absolutely necessary.

So I answer, "Those are the only ones I know about."

His brow pinches. "Hmm. That'll be all," he says, dismissing me.

I turn and hurry as fast as I can after Talon without running. Raven shoves her head into my back, her warmth calming my nerves.

Talon waited for us outside the throne room doors. As we stride out, I shoot a wink at Agar who now has a small indentation in the middle of his chest, where I melt his armor a little. I guess gold really is an extremely soft metal. Seems dumb to make armor out of something so malleable.

Talon peeks over his shoulder at me before diving into a dark alcove. He lands with a thunk, and I follow him. Raven hangs back so her body shields us.

He whispers, "Why is Allister on his way?"

I take in a sharp breath. I've been trying to ignore the pull I have with him. Ignore the fact that I know he's getting closer. This wasn't part of the plan. I try to reach him again, *Allister?*

But there's no answer. Just a blank nothingness.

I clear my throat and admit, "I don't know."

"Henrik told me to go make sure he gets in safely. Him being a traitor has been drilled into every Fae's head here. He wants me to make sure he isn't attacked when he returns."

I don't bother hiding the shock in my voice when I ask, "He's returning?"

Talon flares out his wings, and I can hear the frustration plain in his voice when he snaps, "That's what I'm asking you!"

I throw my hands up in the air and exasperatedly confess, "I can't reach him. He's blocked me."

Talon ruffles his feathers and furrows his brow. "What? You're joking. This is all some sick joke between the two of you. Right?"

I simply shake my head.

"Fuck!" he yells, but it comes out as more of a screech. He swivels his head back and forth like he's waiting for someone to come looking for who made the noise. Then he takes a waddles toward me and lowers his head conspiratorially. He whispers, "What if he comes back and tells Henrik everything?"

I growl, "He won't."

Because he wouldn't. He couldn't. We're a team. He's a part of my family. He wouldn't betray us like that. My stomach drops—would he?

"Fine. I also wanted to tell you to be careful with Tala. She's only a werewolf, but she didn't fill Allister's position as top slayer on looks alone. She's beat every Fae here *without* magic." He pauses. "She also wants to kill you. Don't let your guard down." He then flaps his wings and takes off.

I race after him. Thoughts pour through my head. Why would she want to kill me? I only attacked her brother a little. He's probably fine by now. Seems a tad excessive to want to kill me for singeing him. He more than deserved it. And what the hell is going on with Allister? Why would he cut me off like this? I bring my hand to my hollowed chest as I run, trying to physically hold my hurt heart together.

Talon soars down floors and floors of stairs before he caws and flies back the way we came. I stop in my tracks as I take in the open dirt area around me. In front of me is sparring ring after sparring ring. Some Fae fight hand to hand, some fight with powers and weapons. The Fae here all appear to be fed well, but there's still something off about them. They move more groggily than they should and their powers seem somehow diminished. The earth is sluggish under the earth wielder's guidance and the water being summoned simply flops around.

From the smell in the air we must be a floor above where they keep the horses and livestock. I'm glad Raven's with me instead of in whatever hell hole those poor animals are kept in. I turn to see Raven carefully making her way down the stairs.

"Hey, half-breed!" reaches my ears, and I turn around to see who dares call me by that name.

Tala strides over to me from across the room. Her lithe, athletic body bunches as she glides across the floor. I didn't notice before, but her narrowed eyes are the same iridescent brown as James'. Anger radiates off of her a permanent teeth showing snarl on her face. No, not anger—hatred. Her short black hair brushes the sides of her chin and she lowers her head like a dog who's been beaten by their master one too many times and is now going in for the kill.

I cross my arms over my chest and tap my foot. "Can I help you?"

James runs up from behind her and throws his arms out to block me. He screeches, "Tala stop! You can't do this."

Her eyes narrow on him. "I can, and I will."

James surprises me when he lifts his fists. "Then you'll have to fight me."

Out of the corner of my eye, I notice Fae stop what they're doing and are making their way over to us to watch the show. James and Tala obviously don't notice them though as the two of them begin bickering like brothers and sisters do. I idly wonder how she got away when the Fae murdered their entire village. James thought his whole family had died that night. Was she here this entire time?

Then, all of a sudden, it feels like I dove head first into an iced over lake—Allister's here. I can feel him. He's just outside the mountain.

I have to stop myself from running to him. He's blocking me for a reason. Either it's for my own good or he's betraying us all. Either way I need to stay away from him for as long as possible. So instead, I walk up behind James and place a hand on his shoulder.

He drops his hands and twists around to face me. I coo, "It's okay, James. You don't have to get between us. This needs to happen one way or another. Best to get it over with now." Turning to Tala I raise my fists. "So, are we gonna fight or what?"

Around us, Fae cheer, "Fight!"

Chapter Forty-Five

Allister

I 've dreaded this day since I was sent out on my secret mission to kill the half-breed.

But the day has finally come.

I stride through Shadow Mountain's doors with my head held high, like the hero come home that I am.

Chapter Forty-Six

Attina

Tala snarls, her now pointed teeth on display, and runs at me.

She raises her fists and swings at me faster than I have time to react. She connects with my chin, throwing me back. Talon wasn't lying when he told me not to underestimate her. She's tough.

There's a sensation of liquid dripping down my chin as the metal tang of blood coats my tongue. I wrench my hands up and block her next attack. I have to keep moving backwards to prevent her from overcoming me. I throw up a small wall of earth. She stumbles over it, catching herself before falling to her knees.

A scream wrenches from her throat as claws form at the end of her furry hands.

James shouts, "Tala, stop!"

She ignores his plea and slices at me with her claws. The crowd cheers around us. I jump backward, but all it seems to do is incite some primal chase response out of her. Her lips quirk up in a grin and she charges at me like a wolf who's cornered their next meal.

I throw up wall after wall of earth, but even with everything Oberon taught me, she simply runs right through them, turning them to dust. I gather my power. This would be a lot easier if I was able to use all of my powers. But I told Henrik I could only wield fire and earth. I need to stick with those two. I gather the earth beneath and in front of me. I build layer upon layer until I have a solid wall ten feet deep. As Tala gallops at me thick, coarse, brown hair billows up her arm and a shit eating grin full of elongated teeth cracks up her face.

I wait for her to get so close she can't slam on the breaks. She'll have to run smack into my wall. Hopefully she'll be running so fast she'll knock herself out and we can be done with this.

I steel my nerves as she barrels down on me. A few more strides, and she'll be on me.

I hear James shout, "Attina!"

I throw up my wall of earth and am almost knocked back from the impact of her body slamming into it. I don't even have a second to relax though as a werewolf comes barreling through, breaking it, leaving a cavernous hole in the ground. The animal flies at me with its teeth bared and claws aimed for my throat.

I stumble backward and the werewolf lands with its paws on either side of my head. A loud growl bellows from its chest as drool drips down its elongated canines. The Fae around us chant, "End her," over and over, but I ignore them.

I cock my head to the side. "Wow, Tala. Not a pretty look on you." She brings her maw down, snapping by my throat. I press my hand against her chest just as I feel a canine graze my throat. As her tooth punctures my throat, the warm liquid trailing down my neck as I unleash my fire on her.

Her fur lights to life. The smell of burning fur fills the air. Fire spreads from her chest, crawling all the way up her body. The fire sputters with green as her fur burns from her skin. She rears back and a howl breaks from her muzzle. A loud, "Wow," and some mumbling breaks out in the Fae around us.

Almost instantly she turns back into a human, but now she's naked. She rears over backwards and falls to the floor, dragging herself into a ball. Her skin is red with burns, and blisters cover her once pristine body. Where she once had short brown hair framing her face—now she's bald.

I hear James' pained scream as he races over to her. "Tala, no!"

He lifts her shaking body into his arms. She whimpers as he drags her to him. I was burned as badly as her when I was a child. I didn't yet have a healthy respect for fire. I was goofing around by our campfire, even though Father had told me time and time again it was unsafe. I fell into the fire and got burned all the way up my arm, even singed some of my hair.

By the next day, blisters had formed and started popping. Father had to clean them daily to prevent an infection. I remember the pain that shot through my arm every time Father touched me.

She must be in excruciating pain.

James's gaze cuts to mine, his jaw tight with anger. "What the fuck were you thinking Attina!"

There's some muttering from the crowd as everyone starts dispersing. The show is obviously over. I lock my eyes on James, cross my arms over my chest, and jut my hip out. A cold drop of blood trails down my neck where Tala bit me. I tap my foot on the ground in annoyance. I would feel bad for her if she hadn't tried to murder me in disguise of teaching me how to fight. This was never about helping me, or even about settling up things for some offense I laid on James.

No. This was an attempt on my life.

A thought hits me.

"I was thinking she was making an attempt on my life. The future *heir's* life." As I emphasize the word *heir*, James' eyes go wide in realization. "I was brought down here on the guise that she wanted to help me learn to fight. To protect myself. Not for a fight to the death. Had she succeeded she would have killed the future heir." I throw my hand out toward Tala's naked trembling body, balled in his arms. "What do you think Henrik would have done to her if she'd killed me? Trust me, this is much less gruesome than what he'd have done."

James prowls toward me and by his flaring nostrils and the malice radiating off of him, I know if his arms weren't holding Tala he would be trying to slap me right now. Memories flash through my mind. Us in Sanctuary, me in a ball on the ground, the feeling of fire radiating along my jaw from where he slapped me. I don't let him see how he affects me though. Instead, I lift my chin and steel my back.

Then a croaked, "Wait," breaks the silence.

James and I both stare down at Tala's form in his arms. She lifts a shaking arm and places it on his chest. Her voice wavers as she continues, "This is a mercy compared to what Henrik would have done."

James stutters, "I...I...I—"

I cut him off, "Shut up, and get her wounds cleaned before infection sets in."

James iridescent brown eyes lock on mine, and he silently nods as he pulls her body close to his chest and walking off with her.

From behind me, I hear, "See, I told you she was soft." My blood runs cold, and my stomach drops as my chest hollows out.

I know that voice.

It's the voice which brings light to every darkened day.

The voice that brings balance to my world.

The voice which has whispered sweet nothings under silk sheets in the darkness of lovers.

"Allister."

I spin on my heel to find Allister standing next to Henrik. Henrik has a knowing smirk plastered on his face. I can almost hear him say I told you so. A feline smile curls up Allister's lips as his velvety voice drawls, "Hello, kitten."

Instantly Raven's head is pushing against my back, grounding me. I need her more than she knows right now. The walls feel like they're closing in on me. The room feels like someone threw a log on the fire and there's a roaring blaze flickering to life at my side making me break out in sweat. Even my skin feels too small. I push a thought toward him. *Allister?* But I am met with nothing but silence.

Did he really fool me so entirely?

I never knew who James was until after I gave myself to him.

Is Allister just as bad as James?

No, he's worse.

He fooled me.

He manipulated my heart.

I turn my back to them as tears well in my eyes. Not tears for Allister, but tears for what we could have been. I never put Raven's saddle on this morning because I didn't figure I would be riding her, but I guess I was wrong. I run my hand down her neck, dragging my fingers through her soft mane, grounding myself. When I get to her shoulder I grab a chunk of her mane in my hand and swing my leg up and over her back.

I lean down and whisper so only Raven can hear me, "Get me out of here, girl."

There's only one way out of this hell and it's up the stairs and past Henrik and Allister. I drop my head and furrow my brow, determined to get past these bastards. I kick up Raven and like always she takes care of me. She has to jump up the flight of stairs to reach the top and it's a little sketchy taking the stairs so quickly, at one point she almost falls down, but she comes through for me and gets us there. I don't give Henrik or Allister a second look as we run past.

But before we can make it down the hall and away from them I hear a crack and a wall of ice appears out of thin air, blocking our path.

I seethe. "Let us by." Then I continue staring straight ahead.

I huff as I wait for him to let us pass, but he doesn't.

Instead, I feel a callused hand touch my knee. "Aren't you happy to see your mate?"

His voice makes me stiffen. Raven teeth snap together as she tries to bite Allister. Good girl.

Plastering a feline smile on my face, I slice my head down toward Allister and his beautiful face almost breaks me. Almost. He wants to play games? Hell, I can play them, too. Holding on to Raven's mane with one hand, I lean down and raise my other hand to Allister's face. Gently I stroke his cheek as I cup it—holding his face there, and I run my other hand down my leg, to where my dagger hides.

I suggestively whisper, "I'm so glad you're here. You have no idea how much my body has missed yours."

His eyes widen, and his jaw goes slack. Jerking out my dagger, I drive it into his back for his betrayal. But I can't bring myself to kill him, so I aim for his shoulder instead of his heart. I want to stab him in the heart for breaking mine, but I can't.

He screams and wrenches himself away from me. I rip the dagger back out of him and a chunk of his flesh comes with it. His hand shoots to the back of his shoulder as he drops down into a sobbing ball. In the throes of pain, he loses his grip on his powers, and the ice wall drops in front of us, leaving our way open.

I gaze down at the bloodied dagger in my hands and giggle as I lean down and wipe it on his back. It leaves a wet, glittering trail, and I growl at him. "Don't be such a bitch. It'll regrow. But if you *ever* try to touch me again I'll do this to your favorite appendage between your legs. Try regrowing that."

My gaze drifts up to Henrik whose mouth is dropped open in an awed expression. I face forward and kick Raven in the sides making her shoot forward and take off back to our room.

I lie flat on Raven and cling onto my friend's neck all the way to our room. She's surprisingly quiet on the way there. I assumed she'd say something snarky like I told you so. But she must know I can't handle her criticism right now. She ended up liking him too. Hell everyone did. We all trusted him.

When we make it to our room I slide off of Raven, but don't even try to catch myself. I let myself collapse to the ground in a ball and fall apart. I wail and scream and pound the floor. This can't be happening. This isn't real. I feel like my heart is being ripped from my chest. My heart can't hurt this bad and still keep beating right?

Raven silently hangs her head by my curled up body. Never leaving my side. Never telling me I'm being dramatic. Simply standing there, being present with me. Being the friend I need as my world, my very being, breaks and crumbles into a million pieces.

Chapter Forty-Seven

Attina

I'm awoken by a knock on my door.

I search my surroundings. At first I'm not sure where I am. It takes me a second for everything to come rushing back. I'm on the ground in my room, in Shadow Mountain. I'm on my side with Raven lying next to me, her head wrapped over the top of me. My cheeks are stiff from dried tears and my eyes are so puffy they're hard to open. I'm in the same clothes from yesterday; I didn't even have it in me to change before I fell apart.

As soon as my latest memories hit me, my chest hallows out. Allister showed up. He showed up to my fight with Tala. Standing by Henrik's side. Was this all planned? Was what we had ever real? Simply a means to an end. My chest tightens as I start to panic. How can this be real? How could he trick me so thoroughly? What am I going to do now? He was such a big part of my plan. What if he tells Henrik everything? The Eastern Fae put their faith in me, and I failed them.

I gasp for air that won't come and the world beings shaking around me. Raven's bleary eyes rapidly open and close like she's waking up from a deep dream. She gingerly stands, but wobbles from the earth moving under her. Small rocks break from the ceiling showering us.

"Hey, kid. Calm down." Then her face is right back in front of mine. "Remember what we talked about all those months ago? Breathe. It's okay, kid. You can do this. *We* can do this."

I do as she instructs and take deep breaths in and out over and over until my emotions calm. The earth finally stops moving and my resolve hardens along with the mountain around us.

This changes nothing.

I will still overthrow Henrik. If Allister tells Henrik our plans I will just have to be a better shit talker than him. I can do this. I have Raven and everyone back home. My friends are outside waiting for me to signal them. I'm not alone. I won't let a man take my destiny from me.

I am the rightful heir to Henrik's throne.

I overtook the Eastern Fae throne. It might rightfully be Allister's, but he vetoed his birthright when he betrayed us all. I will take over both thrones and lead the people of Arealea to peace.

I take in a deep breath and release it. Raven nudges me with her head, "Hey, you okay, kid?"

I shake my head as I climb to my feet. I wrap my arms around her head and whisper into her elongated ear, "I'm definitely not okay, but we can do this. We will take over both thrones and bring peace to this world, even if it's just the two of us."

Her eyes are steely when I step away from her. Her voice is hard and confident when she says, "We can do this." Then I remember someone knocked on our door, so I walk over to it and place my hand on the door knob. When I open the door, I'm not ready for what faces me.

Allister's form fills the door.

I staunch a gasp by holding my breath. His purple eyes lock on mine, and I see the man I used to know there. It's enough to knock the wind right out of me. But I don't let it. His chiseled jaw clenches as he takes me in. I push out my chest and raise my chin. Allister's eyes drift down to my chest, and a growl leaves his lips.

I lean down and jerk out my dagger. I'm surprised my hand doesn't shake when I point it at him. Taking a deep breath, I dive past him out of the confines of my room. As he turns to me, I notice a bandage poke out of his tunic. He winces, and I smile inside a little. Good, he deserves to hurt after what he's done. He moves to follow me, but Raven shoves by him so she's between us.

He shouts, "Attina!"

I let Raven pass me, and I narrow my eyes and cross my arms over my chest. I snarl out, "What could you *possibly* have to say to me, Allister?" Raven touches her head against my arm, comforting me with her presence.

Allister opens and closes his mouth like a fish unceremoniously yanked from a lake. He takes in a sharp breath as his eyes drift down to my stomach and back up to search mine for something. I stand my ground though. I notice he lifts his hand slightly before bringing it back to his side and clenching his hand. Then his shoulders droop and he hangs his head. "Henrik would like to speak with you. He sent me to fetch you."

I repeat, "To *fetch* me. Like I'm someone's property—wonderful." He opens his mouth to say something else, but I turn away from him, walk past Raven, and continue my way down to the throne room. I can feel him following us. I try not to care, not to feel comforted by his presence, but I can't help myself. My body doesn't want to listen to my broken heart. He's still my mate and my body doesn't understand how deeply he's betrayed us.

When I reach the throne room door, Agar and the other guard slowly drag open the doors before I can stop and demand them to. They bow as I pass, but I can just make out them glaring up at me through the slit of their helmets.

Then, I hear Allister, "Glare at the future heir again and your head and neck will find themselves separated." My heart jumps at his threat. He's still protecting me. But I squash my thoughts before they have a chance to give me hope.

When I make it to the base of the dais I stop and look up at my grandfather and his wife. He's decked out in a blood red, glittering tunic. Allister stops in front of his mother and kneels in front of them. He bangs a fisted hand against his chest. I roll my eyes and glance over to Allister's mother. She is decked out in a matching outfit to Henrik.

I notice both of them are wearing their crowns today. Their crowns are the same sort of crowns you would see in any fairytale book. But instead of points there are flames. At the tips of the crown are egg sized rubies and citrine gems trailing down the sides of each flame. The light glistens off of each stone, making them almost sparkle. I'm entranced by their crowns.

Henrik's deep voice booms, "Now you see only blood can be trusted. I told you your mate was not trustworthy, but I can tell you didn't take the news well."

The throne room doors open again and James is prodded inside. I can hear he's arguing with the guards, "But I need to take care of my sister. Henrik can wait right?" he almost pleads.

For a split second, I almost feel bad. Him watching Tala and me fighting couldn't have been an easy sight for him. He just got his sister back and he's still in love with me—crazy, overprotective, controlling, obsessive love. But then I remember he's an asshole, and the feeling quickly vanishes.

The doors clank close in James' face. He stands there and stares at the door for a second, his shoulders drooping, before he turns around. As he turns, he seems to drag on a mask of confidence. He lifts his head and pulls at the bottom of his green and brown tunic, straightening it. But no matter how much he tugs at it, it still has wrinkles from where he must have been sitting by Tala's bedside.

He meanders over to where Allister, Raven, and I are. It takes him so long to get to us, Henrik actually growls with annoyance. James stops so I'm between him and Allister. He doesn't even look at me though, making me wonder why he chose to stand by me. I must be his least favorite person. Is he afraid of Allister? He must have forgotten I'm the one who's hurt him the most, Allister only punched him. James's hand grazes mine as he copies Allister and kneels in front of Henrik.

Raven and I are the only ones left standing. A burst of pride blossoms in my chest. I refuse to bow to Henrik on principle alone, but Raven doesn't have to do that. She doesn't have to place the same target on her back for refusing to bow, to show submission. She could submit, but instead she stands proudly by my shoulder, her head held high.

Henrik narrows his eyes at us and cocks his head, like he's assessing, deciding if fighting about this is worth it or not. He seems to come to some sort of conclusion as he glances to Allister and James. He declares, "You two may stand." He searches each of our faces for a moment too long. He's either assessing us or he's trying to prove he's in charge here, I can't tell which.

When he's done staring he sighs, almost as if he's disappointed. I want to groan. Why would he call us down just to play these stupid games? I give in and ask, "You called for us?"

His red eyes shoot up to my aquamarine ones. I know the cold, threatening stare he's giving me right now has made grown Fae soil themselves, but I refuse to show any fear. I straighten my frame and wait.

The air grows thick in the room. "I had hoped to marry you two today." His eyes drift back and forth between James and me. "But you look like shit. I won't have a member of my family, half-breed or not, appear anything, but perfect in front of my court."

He pauses like I should thank him so I do. I bring my arm up and bow at the waist with a flourish. "Thank you, Grandfather. How can I ever repay you?"

Before I can stand back up though, Henrik stands in front of me with a knife, he pulled out of somewhere, pressed against my neck.

In my mind I hear from the little part I keep open for Allister, I hear him roar, *Never take your eyes off of your enemy!* I gasp, but train my eyes on Henrik's.

His red eyes drill into mine and his nostrils flare as he snarls, "You will learn your place or I will filet you alive. I won't make the same mistake I did with your mother. I'm giving you liberties I don't extend to anyone, but family. Don't take them for granted."

What liberties? Allowing me to not bow to him? Woohoo, big deal.

He drags his knife down my throat. He slides it soft enough it won't slice my throat wide open, but sharp enough it leaves a nice gash. He turns away from me and stalks up the dais. He throws his hand in the air dismissively and calls over his shoulder, "You *will* be married tomorrow. Make sure you're presentable." When he sits back on the throne, he places his fisted hand on his chin and glances between Allister and me. "After she's married Allister you won't get to touch her again. You might want to get whatever you can in before tomorrow."

My mouth drops. Did he just insinuate Allister should *take* me one last time while he can? What the actual fuck!

I move my mouth to say something, but Allister cuts me off. He throws his fisted hand to his chest and yells, "Thank you, sire," before turning and grabbing my forearm.

I shout, but my screams are cut off by Henrik's booming voice, "Oh Attina, knock it off. Give my top slayer one more night of fun."

I slice my head toward where Henrik sits on the throne. My body heating up, my skin turning red. I bring up my hand, intending to summon a fireball, but Allister yanks my arm one more time, and I hear, *Knock it off, you're gonna get killed.*

I tug on my arm, but his rock hard grip drags me along. I retort, *Like you'd care, liar.*

We make it to the throne room doors and he chances a glance back at me. His drooping eyes almost appear sad for a split second, but then they're back to being cold. The doors open and he yanks me out with Raven following.

As the doors are closing I can just make out James' sad, confused voice, "Why would you send Attina with him?"

Then Henrik's voice carries down the hall. "Shut up, boy. It's none of your concern. You're marrying her tomorrow—" He says more, but his voice trails off as Allister drags me up the stairs.

When the three of us make it to mine and Raven's room, Allister all but chucks me inside. I stand there with my back turned toward him, rubbing the arm he dragged me here with.

I hear Raven's hooves clop against the floor and the door slams behind me.

Before I can turn around strong, solid arms wrap around me from behind. His wonderful smell coats me, calming me. I place my hands on his arms and lean my head back against his comforting shoulder, losing myself for a second in his reassuring warmth and strength.

Chapter Forty-Eight

Attina

I shake myself out of whatever spell I've fallen under and bring my arm forward as I take all my strength and slam my elbow into Allister's stomach behind me. His breath leaves his chest in a whoosh and he lets out a groan, releasing me as he bends over in pain. I turn around and stare down at him. My heart crumbles for a split second, but I remind myself he's a liar. He's not the Allister I fell in love with.

Allister grunts. "Attina. I'm sorry. I had to."

I push his shoulder and he exaggeratedly falls to the ground. I roll my eyes at his attempt at being playful. Towering over him, I roar, "You don't get to touch me anymore, remember?"

His drooping saddened eyes lock on mine and they almost melt me. They travel down to my stomach and back to my face.

He almost yelps as he says, "You have to understand why I came back. You didn't give me a choice. You think I wanted to leave our people?"

I shake my finger at him. "Oh, no, you don't get to blame this on me. You lied! You were working for him the whole time! How could you! I thought you were different." I lift my hand to my rose necklace and rub it as I walk over to where Raven glares at Allister. I drag my hand down her neck, the action soothing me more than her. "You may leave us now."

Allister stares at me through lowered brows as he stands and stalks over to me. His voice is low, conspiratorial, as he says, "You know I can't leave. Henrik expects me to take you one last time. If I'm seen outside of this room he'll suspect my loyalty."

I cross my arms and point my nose in the indignantly. "It's not my problem what Henrik does to you." I gesture toward the door. "Please leave or I'll have to kick you out."

A sexy, knowing smile trails up his features. His eyes brighten, almost sparkle. "I'd like to see you try. But in your condition I don't see that as being a very good idea."

I ignore him and stride over to the door, grabbing the door-knob and pulling on it. The door only opens a crack before Allister's palm slams against it, closing it. His hands end up on either side of me, trapping me.

He too loudly tsks and growls, "You aren't going to get away from me that easily. I get one last night with you. I intend on having you until you're married off. Even if that means taking you in front of the entire court."

I whirl around, glaring at him with my lip raised in a snarl. I open my mouth to yell at him, when I hear him in my head.

You really don't understand do you? His eyes search mine, and it's only then that I see the confusion in them.

What the hell is going on, Allister? I'm so confused. He's acting so strangely.

Is this all a show to get in my pants? Who am I kidding?

He's so much stronger than me and we're mates. My powers don't work on him. If he was really following Henrik, he would have taken me by now, and there's not much I could do about it.

He answers, *There's someone listening. Just go with it.* I want to ask more, but he yells, "Now get over to the bed like a good girl."

My body sags, and my toes curl at being ordered around. Something close to shock registers on Allister's features at my reaction. His brows furrow, and his breathing stops entirely for a second as he wiggles his hand in a *your turn* gesture.

I open and close my mouth. Suddenly, when I'm put on the spot, I have nothing to say. Then I finally answer, "I'll chop off whatever appendage you try to touch me with."

"Promise?" he answers as he gently guides me away from the door and over to the bed.

I sit down on the plush comforter, and he squats in front of me. I pin my gaze on him and think, *Okay, now explain yourself.*

He reaches up and gently strokes my knee. I slap it away and glare down at him. He sighs as I hear him in my mind. *I had to figure out a way to come protect you two.*

I throw my hands in the air in aggravation. He agreed to this plan. It's not like we just took off in the middle of the night without his knowledge. I think, *Raven and I are perfectly capable of taking care of ourselves. You're not making sense. I thought we decided you would stay with the Eastern Fae and protect them until I signaled you. Instead you leave them, block me from talking to you, and show up here. Now you're best buddies with Henrik again. What did you have to give him to make him trust you so quickly? What did you have to sacrifice?*

Allister stands and stares down at me with an intensity I haven't seen since I died in his arms. My chest tightens under his gaze. This can't be good.

Make no mistake, kitten. I would burn the world if it meant saving the only reasons for my existence.

His answer still doesn't make sense. He says reasons? I know he loves Raven, but I doubt she's a reason for his existence. *What did you give up, Allister? And reasons? As in multiple? You're not making any sense.*

Allister crouches back down and places his hand on either side of my face. His eyes bore into me, and I can hear his breath coming out in hard huffs. What has got this man so riled up?

Attina. You're carrying our child.

My stomach bottoms out. Without thinking, I wrap my arms around my stomach. What? No. That's not possible. How? I mean, we weren't particularly careful, but there's no way I could be pregnant *and* in the enemy's lair.

I blurt out the first think that comes to mind. "I thought it was rare for Fae to carry children. How..." I trail off.

His eyes dart back and for the between Raven and I. *Are you sure you want to have this conversation in front of Raven? We could have it here.*

I snap. "Whatever you say to Raven you can say to me. I have no secrets from her."

He shakes his head. "Luckily, your little sentry left after our performance. I told you it might be different for you. You're half human, and humans reproduce like rabbits."

He slowly hoists himself to the bed next to me like I'm some wild, spooky horse who could run off at any moment.

Wait. There's an idea. I could run away.

I could go back to the Eastern Fae, wait to have the baby, and then come back. Deal with Henrik then.

I scoff at my absurdity. It's not like I could run off if I wanted to. I'd never make it out of here alive. I knew there was no leaving this place once I got inside.

Now I'm stuck.

I sigh and cover my face. Tears welling in my eyes. I'm not upset I'm carrying our child. I'm upset I'm in this terrible place about to put both our lives in incredible danger. Then something hits me.

I twist my head toward Allister. "Does Henrik know? Why did you cut me off and just show up here?"

Allister leans in and wraps his arms around me with one hand on my stomach, as he leans his head against my shoulder.. He nuzzles his face in my hair and whispers, "He doesn't seem to, but I wouldn't put it past him. He's always seemed omniscient when it came to the goings on within the mountain." He shrugs.

"Maybe he's keeping his knowledge secret until tomorrow at your wedding. And as to why I cut you off? You would have told me to stick to the plan. I couldn't stick to the plan when I found out."

I scoff and turn to argue with him, but Allister drags me back on the bed. He pulls me into the nook between his arm and chest. I allow him. I need the comfort right now. I need him to hold me tight and tell me everything is going to be okay—even if it's not.

"How did you know I was pregnant?"

He tugs me in tighter. "I didn't at first. I could tell something was different about you through our bond. Something felt... extra. That's the only way I can describe it."

I throw my hands up in frustration. "And you just assumed I was pregnant? How could you know? There's no way I'm far along enough to be certain."

"I assumed something was extremely wrong with you. But when I saw you earlier, when I really looked into your eyes—I knew. Something in me clicked. You're carrying our child."

I rub my belly. Could he be right?

We lie there for a second before I hear Raven's hooves clop against the floor. She stops at our feet and stares down at us. I sit up. Allister follows me, but groans the whole way. Her mouth opens and closes in shock. It takes her a minute to get her words out and her gaze shifts back and forth between Allister and me, but eventually she does.

"She's really pregnant?"

Allister solemnly drops his gaze and nods, like he's a kid who lost their favorite toy.

I reel back away from him. "I didn't realize how upset you were. If you don't want us, say so now."

I know I'm being irrational. I know it's upsetting. I'm here in this horrible place with our child, hell I was upset, but I need him to be the strong one. The one who thinks everything will work out.

He turns and wraps his arms around me. I half-heartedly fight him for a second before melting into him. As Allister holds me, Raven cuts in. Her voice is deep and harsh as she says, "What did you give up to get in Henrik's good graces again Allister? How far did you go to come back here?"

Allister pulls away from me, sits up, and dejectedly stares at the ground at his feet. My chest hallows out. This is not going to be good. What could he have given up?

"The Eastern Fae throne," comes out of his mouth, and I have to lean forward and hold my mouth to keep from throwing up right there on the spot.

"You *what!*" Raven and I shout simultaneously.

Allister shoots to his feet and begins pacing back and forth. His voice is almost panicked as he argues, "You have to understand how terrified I was when I realized it wasn't just your mind I heard the last time we spoke. I couldn't just leave you here to be fed to the wolves. Not when you're pregnant. Not with our baby." He stops moving, and his body slumps. "I told him I took over the Eastern Fae throne for him. It was my birth right and it's also my right to give the title away to someone stronger than me. I explained to him how I was always on his side. I guided you to where you are now and served him the Eastern Fae throne on a silver platter."

Raven lifts her back leg and swings it out and around at him. Allister is barely able to dive out of the way. There's no way she did more than scratch him. Then she yells, "What were you thinking! Mylo's still there! What if Henrik demolishes that castle! How could you!"

He brings his fingers up to his luscious lips and shushes her. "You have to be quiet."

Man I wish I was that finger. I shake myself. What's wrong with me? I just attacked him for betraying me, and now I'm thinking of him doing dirty things to me with his lips? My hand flies to my forehead. "What about our plan? You're not there to bring our forces."

He throws his hands over his head. "Stop. Listen. One thing at a time." He shoots a glare over at Raven, "You should know by now, I would never leave Mylo in danger." Then he seems to have some sort of epiphany, because his eyes grow wide and he leans away from us as he waves his hands back and forth. "On that point, you both should have believed in me. I can't believe you actually thought I tricked you this entire time! You even attacked me!" He points to where I cut a chuck of flesh out of the back of his shoulder.

He stares me down, waiting for a response. I should feel bad about what I did, but I don't. He stopped communicating with me. He blocked me, not the other way around. I shrug and simply state, "You could have prevented all this by communicating Allister."

I watch as the wind is blown out of him. His whole body slumps. His voice is quiet when he responds, "You're right. I'm sorry." His eyes travel between Raven and myself as he reiterates, "I'm sorry to both of you."

I smile at him, but Raven only lifts her head in the air. Always the tough one. She's almost staring at the ceiling when she orders, "Fine. Then communicate what the new plan is."

"Where to begin—" Allister starts as he paces the ground in front of Raven, who is now lying on her bed, and me. He cups his chin and explains, "I didn't leave everyone at the castle. They're here." He lifts his hand to stop the questions he obviously can tell want to spill from us. "Please let me finish. It will be easier if I can just get through everything."

I silently nod and Raven lies down on her side like he's yet to say anything.

"I brought everyone with us." He glances down at Raven. "Including Mylo." Her ears prick up, but she doesn't react beyond that. I swear she's bound and determined to act like she doesn't care about him, but I bet she'll be the one to fall the hardest out of all of us. "I left them half a day's ride away from here. I have Ava and some others creating a hidden barrier like you can do. I was able to reach Ned. He's the new commander of Sanctuary."

"So, Demarco was going to back out of our deal?" I ask, unsurprised by this turn of events.

"Sounds like it. Ned didn't have a problem dispatching the backstabber though. Now everything's in position for you to take on Henrik." It probably wasn't hard for Ned to physically slay Demarco, but what about emotionally? They've been friends for so long. It must have taken a heavy toll on him.

I rub my stomach and stare at the ground. I was nervous about taking on my grandfather before, now I'm terrified. I was willing to lose my life in pursuit of peace. I find I'm a lot less willing to lose my life when it means I would lose my child's as well.

Allister walks forward and lifts my chin. "Hey, did you hear me? Your army is almost ready."

I yank my chin out of his hand and whimper. "My untrained army, and half an army at that. The humans aren't here. The prophecy can't be fulfilled without them. I might have wanted to take on Henrik before, but now? What do we do, Allister?"

He sighs as he sits down on the bed next to me, but it's Raven who shocks me when she flings herself up onto her feet and brings her head inches from mine. She barks, "You don't get to die this time. I knew that's what you were thinking. I just didn't want to believe it! You came here to sacrifice your life for everyone around you. Well guess what, the easy option just got taken from you. Now you have to live through this the hard way, like the rest of us."

Allister's jaw drops and he whines, "You were going to sacrifice yourself? What about me? What about your people?"

I slice my gaze to him and snap, "It crossed my mind. Did you think this was going to be a walk in the park? That no one would get hurt?"

He drops his head, but skims over what I said. "We have to deal with tomorrow first. You're marrying James."

I wave my hand in the air. "Who cares. Once we overthrow Henrik it won't matter if he says we're married or not."

Allister stands and turns toward me. The eyes he pins me with scare me, they're so full of worry and anger, I've never seen this look on his face before. "No Attina. He's decided to marry you through a blood vow. It's how the first Fae married each other. It's such an archaic tradition no one uses it anymore. There's no breaking it or acting like it didn't happen. Henrik will mingle your blood. Your lives will be tied together forever. If he bleeds, you will bleed. When he dies, you will die. I've never seen it done with someone who wasn't Fae, but the Fae even share powers after a blood vow marriage. You'll be one being afterward, and I don't know how it would affect our girl."

His eyes travel down to my stomach, and I wrap my arms around myself protectively. The earth begins to shake around us. I swear I used to have such good control over my powers, but in the few days I've been here I've lost control over them. My emotions have been all over the place and with them, my powers.

Allister drags my face to his. His eyes bore into me. "Breathe." He breathes with me, taking exaggeratedly deep breaths in and out. I copy him and within a few seconds the ground around us stops rumbling.

With my calm comes an idea. "Then, we'll just have to make sure James *can't* get married tomorrow."

Chapter Forty-Nine

Allister

As I lie awake, I take in the sounds of Attina and Raven's gentle snoring. I tug Attina tighter into my chest and she groans a little. The sound's surprisingly sexy. I rub my hand up and down her back, but try to think of things like infected wounds, or my mother, to calm my arousal. Attina's arm inches over my stomach, and I suck in a breath.

This woman still has no idea what she does to me. How she twists me up.

She simply has to move and my whole world zeros in on her. I know allowing Henrik to think I gave him my kingdom was a hard pill for them to swallow, but it had to be done. I couldn't stay away from them.

Not when I realized Attina was carrying our baby.

She was feeding off of Attina's nerves. I could see her thoughts, her fear, and it broke me. I immediately woke up Oberon and started preparations to move everyone to the outskirts of Shadow Mountain. I was only a day ahead of everyone so they should be out there hiding, continuing their training, while they wait for my word.

Attina said we'll just have to make sure James *can't* get married tomorrow. But I don't think she realizes how tricky her proposition is. Henrik obviously knows about my powers. If he suspects I hurt James or prevented him from marrying Attina tomorrow he'll find out the truth.

He'll realize we're standing against him.

Attina presses her body closer against me and moans in her sleep like even asleep her body realizes her mate is next to her, and it wants a release. I groan and ever so slowly slide out of bed. I can't think straight with Attina this close. I need to go for a walk.

I get out of bed, making sure not to accidently trip over Raven in the dark and gently tug the door open. It squeaks. I immediately pause and spin my head around to check on my girls. I sigh in relief when I see them both move on their beds, but not wake. There's only one place in the mountain I can go to clear my mind.

When I make it all the way down to the stables I crinkle my nose. I don't remember it smelling so pungent. This used to be a small haven for me. I walk down an aisle with stalls on both sides. Peeking over at the sleeping horses, I'm sad to see they're standing in an inch of their own filth. I stride around, noticing all the other animals are in worse conditions.

When I round the final corner, where the feed shed is, I see a slight male Fae snoring on top of a stack of hay.

"Boy!" I boom, anger coating my words.

He startles awake so hard he falls off of the hay pile with a thud. He grabs up a pitch fork and points it at me as I see realization flooding over him and he drops it, letting it clank to the ground. As I take in his sandy hair and gray eyes, I'm shocked. It's the boy I saw the last time I was here. The one who was protecting his brother from me. He's much too young to be out here by himself all night.

He leans away from me, obviously too scared to run, but not wanting to stay either. I kneel down on the ground so he's not so intimidated. I soften my voice and coo, "Hey, do you remember me?"

Obviously my tactic works because he stands back up straight and lifts his chin in an almost defiant way. "Everyone knows you, Allister."

I turn my head toward the livestock around us and then back to the boy, "What happened here? No one's taking care of the livestock anymore?"

He drops his head and kicks the floor in front of him as his meek voice comes out, "Everyone's too weak to work. I'm the only one left."

Shock washes over me. "What do you mean everyone's too weak?"

He sighs, getting back in his makeshift bed. He sits and stares down at me like he's holding court. "There isn't enough food to go around." Meaning Henrik is refusing to feed his people worse than before I left. "I'm working as hard as I can—"

I cut him off, he doesn't need to apologize. "It's too much work for one Fae. You're doing wonderfully for being on your own. I'll get you some help."

He bounces in his seat. "Really?"

His happiness breaks my heart. He's a child, he should be worried about being a kid, not if he can get some help doing work men should be doing. I stand up and reach my hand over to his head. I'm happy to find he doesn't flinch away from me when I scrub my hand through his hair. I chuckle out, "Yeah. We'll figure something out."

He jumps up and wraps his arms around my midsection. Against my belly button he says, "Everyone says how scary you are, but you're not so bad." He pulls away and looks up expectantly at me.

I puff my chest out like I'm filled with pride. He doesn't need to know it's not just a show. "I'm glad I have your approval."

He laughs a high pitched laugh only a kid could make and then wriggles away from me. He jumps back into his bed, and I can almost see a physical weight lifted off his shoulders.

He falls back to sleep faster than I ever thought possible for anyone. Must be a kid thing. I quietly snigger as I turn around and make my way back up to my mate. Well, this hasn't helped me figure out anything.

Oh, well.

Then I hear a coo and a flap of wings behind me. I turn to see Hazel perched on a stall wall. I rear back and cock my head. "How in the hell?"

She ruffles her feathers. "I have my ways, boy." Boy? Damn, I thought I had grown on her. I guess not. "Do you have a solution for tomorrow?"

My eyes widen, and I silently shake my head. It always shocks me how she knows everything.

"You need to put a false memory in James's head. Make him take on someone stronger than him in front of Henrik."

I sit there and let her words settle over me. Then I finally get her meaning. "You want me to force him into a fight with me." She nods, her sharp beak glistening in the soft light given off by the few sconces around the room.

"Take him down."

Chapter Fifty

Attina

Waking up in Allister's arms again is a welcome peace I hadn't realized how much I'd missed. I'm not sure what time it is since there's no window in my room, but honestly, I don't care. I'd stay like this all day, listening to his snores, wrapped in his warmth. I wiggle back close against his body when I hear a knock on our door.

Allister shoots awake and pulls my dagger out from under my pillow where I always keep it when it's not in my boot. In a flash he has it raised and is searching the room for threats with me pulled tight against him. I snicker and pat his leg.

Glancing up at his chiseled jaw in the dim light of the room I say, "Always the warrior."

He nuzzles his head down into where my shoulder and neck meet and playfully growls, "Your warrior."

I worm away from him and giggle. "You can put the knife down now. It was only a knock on the door."

He doesn't drop the dagger down though. He takes the blanket and wraps it around his waist. He took his shirt off before bed last night so with the blanket wrapped around him he looks like he could be naked.

He then leans down and lifts the sheet he left me up to my throat, covering my nightgown. I give him a questioning look as realization of what he's doing floods me. In my mind I say, *You were supposed to take me one last time.*

A grunt escapes his lips as he stands up straight. I can almost physically see him pull on the mask he wears here. Straightening his back and loosening his shoulders as his face falls into a mask of indifference. Briskly he strides over to the door, pulling it wide so whoever is there can see the room behind him.

Leaning against the door, he snarls, "This better be good. We were in the middle of something."

In front of Allister I see the Fae who was ordered to stand at my room door in case I should need anything. Her frail form almost sways as she stands in front of Allister. No, not sways, shakes. Is she really that scared of him? I clear my throat and carefully wriggle out of bed, making sure to keep my sheet up and covering my clothes. I have to keep up our charade.

I raise my chin and, like the queen I will be, march over to place myself between my citizen and the thing that scares them, even if it's Allister.

When I make it to the door, I shoot Allister a withering glare, making sure this Fae woman sees it. She begins shaking harder, obviously waiting for me to be as evil as my grandfather. I push Allister in the chest hard enough to make him stumble back. His voice is dark and laced with lust when he groans, "Where was this aggression last night princess?"

I throw my hand out toward the door. "You may leave. You've fulfilled the king's wishes."

His eyes roam up and down my body, taking in my form in a claiming stare. "You're not married yet. You're mine until you're married off to that dog." He then turns around and makes his way back to my bed, lounging on it like it was his own.

I shout over my shoulder, "We'll see about that," as I turn back to the Fae woman at the door.

Her eyes drift up to mine slowly, and then they dive back down to the floor. The shaking calms a little as she whimpers. "Henrik would like to see you alone."

Allister calls from the door, "Alone? He doesn't want to see my beautiful face?"

I turn and growl, "No one wants to see that mess."

The smile that crosses his face is predatory as he whispers, "Don't say things your mouth can't pay for *princess*."

I physically shutter, making sure the woman next to me sees it. I turn back to her and softly lay my hand on her arm. The bone protruding under her skin is cold against my hand. But she doesn't jerk away or shake worse, so I decide to try my luck.

I place my other hand on her shoulder. "Give me a few minutes to get dressed. I'll be right back."

She nods, but it's so quick and minute I almost miss it. "Please hurry. Henrik doesn't like to wait." I know by her voice she means he will take it out on her.

"What's your name?" I ask.

She whispers, "Leta."

"I will be quick. Henrik knew I would be indisposed, it was his proclamation I would be so. He will *not* take my tardiness out on you, Leta." I place my hand under her chin and drag her gaze to mine. Striking black eyes meet mine. I almost gasp at their beauty. "As heir to the throne I will protect you and my people."

She almost sags at my words. Her chin wavers and her eyes fill with tears as she nods. I take a step back and gently close the door. Spinning around, I lean my back against the chilly wooden door and let out a sigh.

Across from me, Allister's eyes light up, and I hear him in my mind. *You did spectacular! Look at you go!*

I shoot him a scathing glare and think, *I shouldn't have to play these stupid games to protect these people. No one deserves to be this scared or this malnourished. The soldiers are even losing weight. How does he plan on taking over the world with such an army?*

Allister stands and walks over to me, letting the blanket fall to the ground. He pulls me from the door and takes me in his arms. I rest my head against his chest and take in a deep breath of him. The smell of a forest just after it rains fills me with an added strength I hadn't realized I needed after seeing someone so broken and scared.

Don't underestimate him or his soldiers. They may be underfed now, but they will fight to the death for their king. He has them so brainwashed they see him as almost a god. Soldiers willing to lay down their lives for a higher being are much more powerful and resilient than you realize.

I lift my head to peer up into his eyes. *If that's true, how will our untrained soldiers have any chance at defeating them?*

He pulls me away from him and stares down at me, determination and confidence clear in his eyes. *Don't underestimate your mother either. She's one helluva teacher.* He then wraps me in another hug. My shoulders and ribs creek as he presses down on me almost too tightly. I grunt, making him release me. A glimmer of mischief flashes in his eye just before he turns and walks over to my closet and says out loud this time, "So what are we going to dress you in for your meeting?"

I think, *You're not worried about me going there alone? What if he marries me off right now?*

Allister turns and his face is solemn. *He won't. He wants the whole of his people to see you married off.* His eyes flash down to my stomach, and I wrap my arms around myself protectively. *I'm not sure what he wants, but I will be here,* he points to his head, *if you need me.*

Allister helps get me ready in a brown dress with green crawling pinstripe vines up it and a pair of matching soft silk shoes. I'm not a fan of dresses, but Allister insists Henrik will appreciate the lack of utility in it. I complained enough about not being able to hide a weapon in it that Allister ripped another dress to fashion a garter strong enough to tie my dagger to my thigh.

As I saunter into the throne room I brush my hand against my dagger, the motion reassuring me. In all honesty, what is a dagger going to do against the most powerful Fae alive? Not much. But it sure makes me feel better all the same. When the doors close behind us, Leta bows and backs into the corner of the room before kneeling on the floor like a well-trained dog heeding its master's call. Anger wells in my chest.

Henrik sits perched on his throne with Allister's mother slumped next to him in her meager throne. His eyes drift over to Leta, but his gaze cuts back to me when I announce, "You called for me?"

My heart skips when an evil smile cracks his features and he stands. As he prowls over to me the overwhelming presence of him hits me. His power radiating off of him. I almost cower and call for Allister, but just like my mate does, I again drag on my mask of indifference.

When Henrik stands in front of me he cocks his head and chuckles to himself. He shakes his head, brings his hands behind his back and whirls around, walking to the other side of the room. I follow the clear invitation.

He calls over his shoulder. "You will be married today. I know you're not excited, but it's for the good of our people."

I want to snap. I want to scream. Hell, I want to stab this man in the back with the dagger made by someone he killed, but I just silently follow instead of sign my own execution.

So instead, I simply ask, "How's it good for our people?" I'm genuinely interested in how he's justifying this.

He peeks back over his shoulder as he pushes on the rock wall of the mountain, or what I thought was the mountain. A set of hidden doors open out onto a black stone balcony.

The view is breathtaking.

I walk to the railing and the rock warms my palms. It's such a shocking sensation from being in the chilly mountain. I realize how much I miss the warmth of the sun on my skin, how the breeze feels blowing through my hair again. Shadow Mountain towers over the trees below us. I can just make out how the leaves on the tops of the trees dance in the wind. A flock of brown birds fly up out of the treetops, obviously spooked by something I can't see. I absentmindedly wonder if our people are down there and they spooked the birds and wonder if Ned and the humans have arrived yet.

Henrik clears his throat and for a second I freeze and panic, I wonder if I let my block slip, but his words prove I didn't. "You really aren't suited for this life. Your father—" He says the word like he's tasted something rotten on his tongue. "—probably had you living out in some hovel digging in the mud."

I slice my gaze toward him, feeling my powers itching to release from me. The ground rumbles off in the distance and it's all I can do to take deep breaths and calm myself. Once I've calmed down, I politely say, "I grew up in a town full of humans. We all lived in small houses."

He scoffs. "Just like your mother. She always wanted mercy for those animals."

I'm taken aback. I'd figured once she found her human mate she changed her ways of hating humans, but maybe she hadn't hated them all along. Could she have really advocated for us? Maybe that's why her mate turned out to be a human, to change these hateful ways.

I deflect with, "You were going to tell me why I must marry James?"

He grips the balcony so hard I hear the stone crack beneath his talon-like fingers. "If you would like to one day rule, you must do this. To prove your loyalty."

I decide to be frank. "How in the world does this prove my loyalty and what do you get out of this?"

"This proves you will do anything for this kingdom. You do not fully grasp everything that will be yours if you succeed."

But I do fully grasp what will be mine. I ignore the 'if I succeed' part. I play the part of granddaughter who wants this, who wants to be queen of everything and act like my greed blinds me. Obediently, I wait for him to continue.

"Your union will produce the most powerful offspring this world has ever seen." He glances at me for a second, and I see the crazy gleam in his eyes people have told me about. I instinctively take a step away from him.

But I realize a second too late it was a show of weakness. I try to play it off like I wanted to move back to the balcony and get a better look at the horizon, but as I turn away I see a shit eating grin crawl over his face. I want to punch his smile off his face, but instead I grab onto the railing and squeeze all my anger out.

The railing groans under the pressure, and as he takes a stalks forward, I hear Henrik barely whisper, "Interesting." He yanks my shoulder back.

My eyes shoot up to his crimson ones. This close, I can almost see the fire dancing inside them. I stare into those eyes. But as I stare I notice those aren't flames dancing in them. Three snakes move and sway in his eyes.

His hydra.

But how is that possible? I've never seen anything like this. Have I simply never noticed it in others? I feel the sudden urge to inspect my eyes in a mirror.

Henrik pulls me out of my reverie when he stomps forward into my space and places a palm on my belly. "But first, we have to get rid of this abomination."

Chapter Fifty-One

Attina

Abomination?

I cock my head in confusion. "What?"

He loudly cackles. "Oh don't tell me you didn't know! This is priceless! You're carrying my great grandchild. I would assume it's your mates?" His tone suggests I've had relations with all the men in Arealea.

I scoff in offense. "Of course, it is!" Then I turn and hit the railing next to us, pretending to be angry. "That bastard! He tricked me and now this?"

He gently places his hand on my shoulder attempting to portray the loving grandfather any granddaughter would want. His voice is cold and I smell fire as he says, "You don't have to worry. I will take care of it. I know he was doing my bidding, but this is *not* the way I wanted things done. Allister will pay for what he's done in due time."

I want to say, yeah you wanted him to kill me and be done with it, but I bite my tongue and leave the words unspoken. Instead, I look up to Henrik with sad, scared eyes. "You'll take care of it?"

His face softens. "Yes, my child. I will fix it prior to your wedding. If we don't handle this, the ceremony won't work."

I sniffle and bite my cheek until I bleed, causing tears to well in my eyes. It takes all the acting skills I can muster, but I gaze up at him and I pray I can school my face into a showing he's my savior for doing me this favor. He leans down and wraps me in a tight hug. But instead of being comforting, it's cold and stiff.

Leta guides me back to my room when Henrik, and I are done talking. I'm glad she stayed while we talked. Relieved I don't have to remember where my room is. My mind is going in a million different directions. This is all going too fast. What are we going to do? I know the first thing I have to do though.

Allister?

His sensual voice fills my head. *Yes, my love?*

Our room now!

Now Allister's voice is panicked when he answers, *What happened?*

I simply answer, *He knows.*

I'm not halfway up the stairs when I hear a voice I've known my whole life call to me, "Attina!" I try to ignore him, but he calls to me again and this time, even Leta stops.

I groan and spin around. "What, James?"

He races to my side and goes to grab my hand before his hands stop midair and he takes a jumps back, obviously remembering my perchance to violence. His voice is panicked and his jaw is tight as he asks, "Did you know?"

"Know what?" I ask completely confused. Does he already know about our baby? I doubt it.

"Know what Allister tried to do?"

I scoff and pinch the bridge of my nose. I don't have time for these games. I twist around and motion for Leta to continue up the stairs. "James, I don't have time for this little spat between the two of you. I have to get ready for our wedding. Please leave me be."

I'm surprised when he takes a prowls away from me and turns to go back down the stairs. I follow Leta and my breath catches when I hear James say, "You're right. It makes no difference anyway. As soon as I'm king, the Fae will be executed for his crimes against us."

I stop in my tracks and turn to watch James trek down the stairs back to whatever hole he crawled out of. I glare at his back, if he thinks I'll ever let him lay a finger on Allister, no matter what happens, he has another thing coming.

I follow Leta until we get to my door which she holds open for me. I absentmindedly say, "Thank you," as I walk forward.

She stops me in my tracks as she drops her head and whispers, "I'm sorry."

I twist to her and cock my head as I answer, "Sorry for what?"

She takes a deep breath, almost seeming to muster up all her courage and peeks up at me. Her eyes are full of sorrow as she whimpers, "I'm sorry for all you've been through and all you're going to go through."

My heart drops.

This woman has been through so much, and yet here she is apologizing for things she didn't do and had no hand in doing. I'm already teetering on going crazy so tears flood my eyes, and I dive at Leta. She stumbles away, but I wrap my arms around her and fall apart with my head shoved against her shoulder. As she awkwardly rubs my back, I whimper out, "Thank you."

I'm nudged in the back by something soft. "Hey, kid. Why don't you come inside?"

Raven's voice sobers me, and I realize what I just did. I attacked this poor woman, forced her into an embrace she obviously didn't want, and fell apart in front of her. Not a good way to show how strong I am. To show I'm capable of being a leader.

I stagger backwards and stutter, "I-I'm so sorry. I shouldn't have—"

But she places a hand on my shoulder, cutting me off. She chuckles. "It's okay. I'm just glad someone here has a heart."

I nod, but all of a sudden, my mouth starts watering and my stomach heaves. I quickly spit out, "Thank you," as I run into my room and shut the door behind me. Raven opens her mouth to say something, but I raise my finger to tell her to hold on as I race over to the tub and hurl my guts up. I sit there and place my head against the tub, letting the metal cool my sweaty forehead.

Behind me I hear the door open, but my stomach rolls again and before I can turn to see who it is, I'm retching again. A warm, reassuring hand rubs my back in circles. "Shh. It's okay, I'm here."

When the nausea passes, I turn and glare at the beautiful man by my side. I growl, "You did this to me."

He stands with his hands raised like he's trying to calm a raging dragon and maybe he is, I mean my anima is a dragon. He walks backwards away from me. "You mean *we* did this."

I stand and turn around, crossing my arms across my chest and jutting out my hip, trying to push every inch of sass I have in me into this conversation. "Nope, it's all your fault. Why am I even puking? I can't be very far along."

His eyes trail up and down my body and his face softens, "Stress can make you sick too, and you have an abundance of that in this shit hole. But you're beautiful, you know that? You're glowing."

I clumsily uncross my arms and rub the back of my neck, "No, that's just the sweat from puking."

He strides into my space. My skin heats as he places his hands on my hips and drops his forehead to mine. Then he whispers, "No, you're just you. You're breathtaking."

I open my mouth to answer, but Raven cuts me off with a gagging noise and cries, "Okay, that's enough you two. If you've forgotten, I'm in the same room as you."

Allister turns his head to Raven and winks at her, "Then leave and let mommy and daddy do adult things."

I snigger until Raven walks over to the door and starts banging her head against it. I wriggle out of Allister's arms, invocating an annoyed grunt from him, and walk over to her to pat her on the neck. "Hey, you're gonna make someone come see what all the ruckus is about." Then she turns her head into me and surprises me by saying, "I just want to go home."

My shoulders sag. I know what she means. I want to go home, too, back to the Eastern Fae. Back to a simpler time when all of this was just in the future, and we could be happy in the moment. I wrap my arms around her head and place mine on top of hers. "I know girl. I do, too."

Then Allister's arms are wrapping around me and over Raven's head, "All this will be over and we'll be home soon guys. I promise."

As his words, all this will be over, sink in I feel like a bucket of cold water has been thrown over me. I gasp and yank my body back, pushing him away. He grabs for me, but I knock his hand away and begin pacing the floor, a cold sweat breaking out over my skin, nausea rolls over me again, but this time I'm able to hold it back.

Allister's voice is laced with concern as he says, "What's wrong? Did something else happen?"

I glower at him and snap, "Did you really think I called you up here for a little puking party? I'm not *that* dramatic. I said Henrik knows, remember?"

Allister lifts his hands. "Well, you *are* pregnant."

I growl at him and he takes a step back, his eyes going wide like he finally realizes the gravity of what's going on.

"What did he say?"

I huff and plop on the edge of the bed. "Henrik wants to *handle* our little problem. He said the ceremony won't work if I'm carrying your child."

He shouts, "Fuck!"

I bury my face in my hands and start to cry. My body shakes so hard I feel my back muscles spasm in response to the heaving being wracked against them. I cry out, "What do we do?"

Allister runs over to me, kneeling in front of me. He rubs my knee, letting me know he's there, before pulling me down into his lap. "Shh, it's going to be okay. You'll be all right. Give me a second to figure this out."

I wail in his arms while he rocks me back and forth.

Then I'm awakened by a soft voice, "Hey, wake up little kitten." I shoot up and hit my head on something as I search my surroundings.

It takes me a second to again remember I'm in Shadow Mountain. I hear Allister groan next to me and see his eyes are slammed shut and his hand cups his chin. I realize I was sleeping in his lap and his chin is the thing I hit my head on. I clamber out of his lap and onto my knees in front of him.

Placing my hands on either side of his face, I screech, "Are you okay?"

He pulls his hand away from his chin, and I sigh when I realize he's not bleeding.

He winces when I touch his chin, but opens one eye. "Kitten *does* have claws."

I throw myself back and almost topple over in a laughing fit. "I can't believe you remembered that from when we first met."

He rubs his chin and stands, holding his hand out to me. I take it and he pulls me up against his body. My mouth goes dry and my gut twists in need. He smirks and runs his hand down to the small of my back, pulling me against him. His voice is husky when he says, "How could I ever forget our first meeting? It's burned into my brain like a blinding beacon of light and hope."

My knees literally go weak, and I wobble a little at his words. How can this brute of a man be so eloquent? It's just not fair.

I push away from him, needing the space to clear my head. I walk over to where Raven lies and run my hand down her neck, the motion grounding me. I call over my shoulder, "So did you come up with a plan?" I can't believe he sat there on the floor with me in his lap sleeping. He must have been so uncomfortable, but he sat there for the gods know how long. What time even is it? My stomach drops, and I spin around. "When's the wedding?"

Allister simply smiles at me. "Now."

⚬

Allister said he had it all handled, but wouldn't tell me how he handled it. I walk into the throne room in a gown Allister found in my closet—a wedding gown. How long had Henrik been planning this?

The dress I wear is form fitting and flows all the way down to the floor. Most of it is see through, everything except where it covers the necessary bits is tightly woven floral lace. I wonder why he picked floral? A long train follows me, making walking in this thing a challenge. The top is cut in a V down between my boobs and my arms are through straps which hang around my forearms, just tight enough to make it constricting.

The only thing holding me together is Allister by my side and Raven at my back. I hear Allister in my mind. *You look stunning. A queen waiting for her king.*

My king is already by my side.

I hear a growl inside my head and then Allister says, *Just wait until I maul you.*

I answer, *Promises.* I try to hide the scoff and fail miserably; thank goodness no one is watching us. Henrik and Allister's mother sit on their thrones peering down at James who seems to be arguing with them. Why the hell would Henrik let him argue? Tala stands next to her brother with her arms wrapped around his forearm, her teeth not out in a snarl for once. She seems to be pleading him to stop, but of course, James doesn't listen to reason.

Even the voice inside my head comes off panicked as I plead, *You still have a plan right?*

Allister simply answers, *Always, my love.* Then he breaks off to go take a position by his mother at the base of the dais. His mother's eyes drift to him and then over to me. When they land on me, I see a spark of something. Is that pity? Her face stiffens like she doesn't want to see what's about to happen next.

"He's out to get me! He'll undermine my authority!" James screeches like an errant toddler who isn't getting to play with his favorite toy. I notice he's back in his fancy green and brown tunic and his sister matches him again. Raven nudges my back before she walks over to the back corner of the room.

Henrik, who's also back in his fancy attire with his beautiful crown placed perfectly atop his head, booms, "Enough!"

James and Tala both jump at his abruptness as I walk up behind James and stop.

Henrik stands and throws his arms out like an excited grandpa, "My child! You look absolutely mesmerizing."Funny, I thought I looked like the harlot he thought me to be, with how low and see through this dress is.

I smile sweetly up at him as he places his hand on the middle of my back and guides me behind the dais. He calls over his shoulder, "Give Attina and her grandpa a second to talk, we'll be right back to get things started."

No.

As if on cue, the throne room doors open and people start filing in. I turn to look at Allister as I begin to panic. Allister barely nods and gives me a smile like nothing's wrong in the world and he's happy for me. No, this can't be happening Allister had a plan.

He promised this would all work out.

You promised, I snarl into his mind, and I lift my hand calling a fireball into my palm as Henrik turns his back to me and opens the balcony doors.

Trust me, I hear Allister answer, and I glance behind me at him. From where we stand the dais blocks the rest of the room from watching, all except James. His mouth is dropped open, eyes wide in panic. I glare over at him, willing him to keep his damn mouth shut, but I doubt it'll make much of a difference.

Henrik chats as he opens the hidden doors to the balcony, "Just one little talk with my granddaughter and we will—"

Then the doors burst open and a wild wind blows my hair back. Henrik stomps back and bumps into me. I let him take the brunt of whatever is coming through the door. I stretch around Henrik's massive form to see who or what burst through those doors, but I'm not ready for what meets my eyes.

Her voice comes out in a growl as she says, "Hello, Father."

Chapter Fifty-Two

Attina

The room behind us gasps, and I stumble back as I take in my mother's body blocking our way to the throne room. She stands like a warrior queen with her hands on her hips and her chin lifted into the sky.

She takes in her father and then her gaze drops to me standing behind him. She lifts her hands in the air and yells, "Baby!" before she tries to push past Henrik. He shoves out his meaty arm to block her path. I gulp back my worry for her safety. He drove her crazy and sent her to kill me and my family. How's he going to react to her showing up out of the blue?

He grabs her forearm and lowers his head. His nostrils flare and he grits his teeth as he whispers just loud enough for me and my mother to hear. "What the fuck are you doing here? I thought you were dead."

She pats him on the shoulder and grabs his arm with her other hand. Digging her nails into his hand she physically pulls it away from me. Her voice on the other hand is loud and chipper as she strides over to me and places her arm over my shoulder. "Nope! Sorry, Father, not dead. You made me crazy and sent me out to kill my entire family, but I'm still alive." She scoffs and gazes down at my dress, "You couldn't even get my baby her own dress? You reused the one you planned for me? It was hideous then, and it's hideous now. She's not some prized cow you're trying to sell, Father."

Everyone, Henrik's entire court, mumbles behind us. Henrik growls lowly. "Keep your voice down."

My mother lifts her hand to her opened mouth as she peers around behind us. "Oh, no. I've interrupted something haven't I? Oh and spilled your dirty laundry!" She twirls around and grabs my hand, dragging me away from the balcony, pulling the comforting smell of apples to me. She seems so confident and composed, but I feel her hand shaking in fear. How this woman is putting on such a good show, when she's obviously frightened, out of her mind is beyond me. "I heard you were trying to regain favor with your people prior to taking over the rest of Arealea, but I didn't believe it." She walks me over to Allister and deposits me next to him, as she continues to make her way around the dais.

People gawk and whisper when they take her in. Some even shout traitor, but she ignores them completely, like this is her show and no one is going to stop her from being the main event.

She makes her way over to James and stops, looking him up and down. She doesn't even say a word to him, she just cocks her hand back and punches him square in the face. He falls backwards into Tala's arms, his hand goes to his nose and blood streams through his fingers. I bring my hand to my face to try and hide my chuckle, but fail miserably. People around me gape in my direction.

My mother makes her way past James and Tala, who snarls at her with semi-elongated canines, and back around to her father. He stands there in shock with his mouth hanging open in shock. She stands on tip toes so she's nose to nose with him. "You know, if you want your people to back you, you should try feeding them something more than moldy bread."

Henrik grabs her by the throat and she screams as his hands turn red. He snarls, "I had hoped this wedding would help my cause, but you've seen to it that this day is ruined. I wonder why?"

His gaze drifts to me, but my mother uses the opportunity to attack. An arc of lightning darts into the room, hitting Henrik on the arm. He shouts in agony and stumbles back as a torrential rain begins pouring. My mother dives out of the room and rolls onto the balcony.

Henrik blindly throws a fireball at her, but it fizzles out once it hits the rain my mother summoned. She dives over the railing, and I panic. I go to run over to her, but Allister grabs my hand, stopping me. *She's fine.*

I take my place back next to Allister before Henrik can see I've moved. When he turns toward the room he's holding the arm my mother hit with lightning. The skin on it is black and misshapen. He stands up straight, straightens his crown and screams, "Everyone, out!" Then he glares across the room, his eyes landing on James, Tala, Allister, and myself. "Everyone except you four."

Everyone in the room files out leaving the six of us—alone.

Henrik stomps over to the dais and James, Tala, Allister, and I move so we're standing in front of him. Allister, Tala, and James kneel and drop their heads. Henrik's gaze travels over us and sticks on me. He lifts the arm my mother burned and points at me. Now I can see he's already healed. Even for a Fae, his healing is remarkably accelerated. It really shows how much power resides inside him.

"You!" he shouts.

I wrap my hands behind my back and lock my fingers together. I shake my body a little. I want him to think I'm scared of him. I mean I am scared of him, but with Allister by my side, I'm having a hard time showing my fear. "Yes?"

"What the hell was your mother doing here? You two were acting pretty chummy back there. And what a convenient time for her to show up, just when I was about to get rid of that abomination Allister put inside you."

James shoots to his feet and shouts, "What!" His head swivels between Henrik, Allister, and my stomach.

Henrik and I ignore his outburst, and I answer his question, "You do realize you sent that woman to kill me and my family right? Do you really think I would be crazy enough to befriend the woman who murdered my entire family? She took everything from me. I watched as my father, the man who raised me, and my mount were brutally murdered on the night of my Awakening. I tried to kill her then, but I obviously failed."

"Then why didn't you attack her just now?" Henrik throws his hands in the air before slamming them back down on the arms of his throne.

I shout back, pretending I'm shocked he could think I would befriend my mother, "I was in shock! The last time I saw her she murdered everyone I love. Then she just strides in here like we're best friends? And you were just trying to 'get rid of' my child."

His eyes narrow and his face reddens as he roars, "I told you this ceremony won't work with that thing inside you!"

I ball my fists. "That thing is your great grandchild! I agreed to marry James to save everyone I love. I did not agree to this." I was trying act scared, but I can't pretend with this.

Suddenly, Allister's voice is in my head. *What are you doing?*

Henrik pinches the bridge of his nose, but his voice lowers and softens as he says, "You're not thinking clearly. Allister betrayed you." He points to my stomach. "That thing will betray you, too." Then he stands and walks out to the balcony. He's out there for a second before he strides back in with a gray goblet in his hand.

What's that? I ask Allister. But I'm met with silence. This can't be good.

Henrik makes it back to his throne and sits down with the goblet in his lap. "This will purify your body. We will take care of that thing today and then—"

James interrupts him. "What thing?"

I sigh. Why did I never realize how dense this boy is? I would say man, but he's not a man he's a boy.

Allister stands and roars, "I told you she was *mine*. The baby inside her is also *mine*."

"You attacked my sister last night and now this?"

I pinch my brows. What? Allister was with me all night. I ask, "He did *what*?" I hear Raven's footsteps behind me, always by my side when I need support.

James throws his hand out toward Allister. "He tried to attack Tala last night.

Henrik howls, "Guess my granddaughter wasn't enough for you, eh, Allister?"

Tala's face scrunches, and her voice is worried when she says, "No, he didn't, James."

In my head Allister says, *I told you I had this handled.* Out loud he chuckles, "The dog went crazy, I'm telling you, it's time to put him down."

James unclenches his jaw, throws his head back, and a guttural scream rips from him as brown coarse hair sprouts up and down his arms. He charges at Allister, knocking me down in the process. I wrap my arms around my stomach as my butt hits the ground. Raven moves to try to block my fall, but she doesn't make it to me in time as I'm flung back, and I hit my head against the rock floor. Allister's worried gaze lands on me, his mask slips and for a split second he bites his lip and worry coats his features. While he's distracted with me, James throws a punch and connects with Allister's nose. I hear the crunch of it breaking.

Allister's thrown backwards sliding against the marble floor and James transforms into his massive wolf form. His elongated canines drip with saliva as he stalks around his prey. Allister brings his hand up to his nose, and I hear the bones crunch again as he repositions the bones. James snaps his jaws as Allister slowly stands with his back to him.

I almost shriek, but catch myself as James flies through the air at Allister. But Allister lifts a hand and James is stopped midair. He drops to the ground and curls in a ball, screeching in pain. His body wracks back and forth from the excruciating pain Allister is putting his mind through. He's forced into changing back to a human

Allister chuckles. "Someone should have put you down a long time ago dog. I am more than happy to step up and do the dirty work no one else has."

Then a scream comes from where Tala stands, and before I know it, she's transformed into a werewolf identical to James's, but bigger. I have to lift my head to fully take in her huge form. The ground almost shakes at each pawfall.

She runs straight at my mate, jaws open, teeth bared. He drops his hand and bounds out of the way a second before her gaping maw devours him. He rolls toward the throne room door and she chases like a dog after its favorite toy. She leaps past her brother who climbs to his feet. His gaze shifts to me, then down to my stomach, and I can see the sadness behind his iridescent brown eyes.

Another snarl rips from his lungs as he changes back into his werewolf form and runs after his sister. Allister gets Tala under his power seconds before James slams into him. He's thrown into the wall behind him and the werewolves go in for the kill.

If I was playing the part, I wouldn't care they're about to kill the man who betrayed me. But I can't. I raise my hands and pull on my fire. Fireballs form in both of my hands, and I scream as I throw them at James and Tala.

My fireballs hit their marks and singe the werewolves' backs. They howl in pain and slice their heads around to face their attacker. I call more fire and wait for their assault. Tala snarls and snaps her jaw as she takes off after me.

Behind her, I see Allister trying to drag himself to his feet and panic flashes through James's eyes. He takes off after his sister and jumps on her back, knocking her to the ground. They go rolling across the room and slam into the wall.

Behind me Henrik screams, "Enough!" His voice is so loud, it makes the room shake around us. I'm surprised with the violent vibrations this mountain is doing, that none of the rocks have broken loose yet.

Everyone stops where they stand. I drop my hands and let my fire peter out. Allister shakes his head, and James and Tala who are now panting, transform back into their human form, are naked. My cheeks flush. It's not like I haven't seen James naked, but I've never seen another girl naked in my entire life. I'm surprised to find her form, the curves of her body and the softness of her skin, pleasing. My eyes linger, but when I hear Allister's voice in my head, *You like that too, huh?* I twist back to where Henrik still sits with that damn goblet in his lap.

You almost died and that's the first thing you have to say? I hardly think this is the time. I snap at Allister.

His sultry voice breaks in, *It's always the time kitten.* My cheeks heat and my core pools. I shift back and forth uncomfortably while everyone else returns to stand by me in front of the dais.

When James makes it back to my side, I see a slice running down his face from his forehead, over his eye, to his chin. He squints as blood drips onto his chest and the floor beneath him.

When did you do that? I ask because I never saw Allister draw out a knife, but here James stands bloodied.

I can almost hear the smirk in his voice when he answers, *You always forget I'm not just some pretty face.*

I start to answer, but Henrik pulls my attention back to him. "While that was entertaining the four of you have managed to somehow ruin this entire day. How are we going to explain the groom's injury to the rest of the court?" Henrik's stare lands on me and he holds my stare for a second. "I have a feeling this was all some plan to get out of marrying James, but I know you wouldn't do that because you understand the consequences." His gaze then shifts over to where Raven stands behind me.

I move so I'm further in front of her. "I *will* marry him, but drinking your potion wasn't part of the deal." I point with my chin to his goblet.

He roars, "You will drink it or you and everyone you love will die." Allister, James, and Raven take in sharp breaths. Tala, on the other hand, just bends over and tries to catch her breath. It must be exhausting transforming into their wolf forms.

I glide toward him and negotiate, "I will drink the potion *if* you agree to leave the humans alone. Let them live their lives in hiding—"

I don't even get to finish as Henrik cuts me off, "Never! The humans are scum who need to be wiped off the face of Arealea!"

I cock my head. It's almost like he's threatened by them. Why would someone so powerful be threatened by a people who stand no chance at defeating him? "Why do you hate them so much?"

"They are weak. The strong survive and the weak are culled from the herd. There is a reason this mountain doesn't have a prison. *Any* threat to the throne is considered a death threat. Those disgusting beings stole my daughter, my right hand. They attacked my mountain and drew first blood. I intend to make them pay."

Realization hits me like a stack of bricks. He's pissed because my mother ran off with my father. I know he's been evil for most of his life, but is it possible she was the one soft spot in his stone heart?

I shake my head. "If you want me to drink your potion and produce an heir with James, this is my proposal. You spare the ones I love *and* the humans. You agree to those terms, and I will do as you wish."

"You will do as I wish or I will kill you."

I cock my head. "And lose the only chance to get the heir you want? I'm your only grandchild."

"Your mother could have another child." He places his hand on Allister's mother's hand and she flinches. "I could have another child with my queen."

I blatantly scoff. "My mother? Don't make me laugh. And your queen? She appears to be barely keeping herself alive let alone producing an heir. No, this is your one chance."

Chapter Fifty-Three

Attina

Henrik tears his hand away from Allister's mother's hand and throws the goblet to the ground. The goblet clanks against the floor and red liquid splatters on the dark marble floor, and I have to jump back to keep the pooling liquid from staining the hem of my dress.

Henrik's gaze drifts down to the ground and stays there. He huffs as he quietly ponders my ultimatum, grunting to himself every few seconds like he's talking to himself. I shift my weight back and forth and pick at my nails while I quietly wait. The whole room feels like it's charged with electricity, and I wonder if I were to touch Allister if there would be a shock.

Finally, Henrik lifts his head and locks eyes with me. He slowly says, "Let me think it over. I'll send for you in the morning and give you my answer." He lifts his hand and waves us away. "Now, get out of my sight, all of you." Then he puts his elbow on this armrest and places his head on his fist.

Raven pushes her head into my back, making me move my feet. I follow Allister out of the throne room. We pass by the door, and Agar whispers, "The freak finally got what he deserves."

Allister spins and lifts his hand. It's all the motion needed to make Agar jump away from him. Allister tsks, but passes him by.

Behind me, I hear James call to me, "Attina, wait!"

I groan and roll my eyes. I keep walking, but hear his running feet behind me.

Then he screams, "Ouch! Fuck, Raven, you bit me!"

I whirl on my heel and glare at him, making sure to keep my eyes fixed only on his face and not the rest of his naked body. He might be a bastard, but he's always had a nice body. Tala prowls up behind him, completely comfortable in her nakedness, and I have to concentrate on James to not let my eyes drift down her body.

I groan. "What do you want, James?"

His eyes catch on something behind me, and I assume Allister's stopped and is waiting for us to finish our conversation. "Is it true? You're carrying another man's child?"

I scoff and plop my fisted hand on my hip, hoping my annoyance radiates off of me. I simply answer, "Yes."

His mouth drops open and his gaze passes from me to Allister and back again. The hurt is plain in his voice when he says,

"How could you? You're mine and you gave yourself to someone else?" His cut has stopped bleeding, but flecks of dried blood flake off at his words.

I narrow my eyes at him. "I was never yours, James."

An evil smile stretches across his face and he pointedly stares at Allister behind me and almost coos, "You will be after tomorrow." Then he turns and walks in the opposite direction with Tala following. The light glistens off her bald head and I almost feel bad for singeing her as I watch her hips sway while she walks down the hallway.

I jump as Allister's lips brush my ear, and he whispers, "You really do like that don't you?"

I pivot around and he grabs me around the waist, holding me tightly to him. I feel his hardened length against my belly. My cheeks heat, and I almost lose myself in the moment before I remember I'm supposed to hate this man. I shove him away from me and snarl, "Let me go Fae," and I stomp up the stairs to my room.

When I make it to the room, with Raven and Allister in tow, Leta bows and opens the door for me. I thank her and walk over to my closet. I'm trying to undo the zipper on my back when Allister appears behind me, his hand covering mine. I drop my hand and let him help me out of my dress.

He leans forward and kisses my neck as he drags the zipper down. He wraps his arm around my stomach and pulls me back against him as I wiggle out of the dress his hands roam over my naked body, making me throw my head against his shoulder and moan.

"Could you not?" Comes from the room next to us, and I fling myself further into the closet. How could I forget Raven was in the room behind us! I swear this man turns my brain to mush.

Allister chuckles and hands me a fresh gray tunic. I throw it over my head and hang my head in shame as I walk out of the closet. "Sorry, Raven," I whisper.

She shakes her head. "It's fine, I didn't see anything. I just have to chop my ears off now." Allister chuckles behind me, and I elbow him in the stomach, making him grunt. "We need to talk about what just happened."

I nod and move over to the bed. Sitting down, I cross my legs under me and Raven moves to her bed and lies down. I flick my gaze to Allister. "Where are the humans?"

He pinches his brows and his eyes almost glaze over. After a couple of seconds he answers, "Ned says they should be here by sunrise. Why?"

I nod and sigh. His words take a weight off of my shoulders. I gaze back and forth between the two of them. The two people who have stayed by my side through everything, who will be by my side until the very end. "We need to end this tomorrow."

Allister walks over, sits down, and drops his arm over my shoulder. He pulls me against him. "You're right. We got lucky today. He already suspects something's off. We won't have another chance tomorrow." His other hand moves to my stomach and he rubs my stomach in small circles.

I gaze up at him, suddenly worried. "You know I was just playing the game earlier right? I'd never do anything to harm our child."

He leans down and places his forehead against mine. "Yes, I know. Henrik will never agree to your terms you know."

I smile and lean forward, planting a soft kiss on his lips, "I'm counting on it."

Allister brings his arms around me and drags me into a bone crunching hug. "I'm going to go get us all some food. I know neither of you have eaten much and we'll need all our strength for tomorrow. Then we need to discuss everything that's changed today."

Raven and I share a look as he leaves the room. I stand and walk over to where she lies on her bed and lie down against her side like I used to do when we were traveling to Sanctuary. She nudges me with her soft muzzle. "Hey, kid, you okay?"

I lean my head back against her, staring up at the dark rock ceiling and sigh. "Everything is moving too fast. I feel like it was just yesterday when we were camping with Father and all this started."

Raven wraps her neck around me and puts her head in my lap. "I know what you mean. We've been on the run ever since." She sniffles. "I miss them every single day. Do you think it ever gets easier?"

I roll my head against her back. "Yes, and no. I think some days will eventually be easier than others, but I think it will always be hard. I don't think you ever really lose someone though, I think they're still watching over us, like they always did." She nods, and I pet her head as a tear rolls down her face.

Allister throws back the door and happily shouts, "I'm back!" His face drops as he takes us in. He quickly drops down to the ground with the food in his arms and kneels in front of us. His voice is coated with worry when he says, "Are you guys okay? What happened?"

I shift to look at the food he has cradled in the fabric of his black tunic. Moldy bread and rotting fruit—like usual. My face falls. I was hoping he would be able to find something a little more filling. I glance up at him and shrug, "We were just talking about Father and Oak. How everything's going too fast."

He wraps his arm over my shoulder and drags me to his side. "It'll all be over soon enough and then we can rest until our girl comes, if that's what you want."

I rub my head into his chest and nod. "Raven and I will cuddle until our baby comes."

He shakes me once. "Hey, what about me? I don't get any of those cuddles?"

I rub my head back and forth into his chest. "No. Someone has to run our kingdom."

He chuckles. "Okay fine. But until then you need to eat. And I'm having hay brought up for Raven."

Raven almost sounds in awe when she says, "Thank you."

After we're done with chewing around the spoiled parts I'm back lying against Raven and feel her take a deep breath. I pat her haunches where the werewolf attacked her. I don't want her part of what's going to go down tomorrow. I stare at Allister, "I need to get her out of here."

Raven's head slices to me and she roars, "No!"

I peer over at her. "This is not up for discussion. You will not be in that room tomorrow. I need you somewhere safe—"

Allister interrupts my thought. "We have to get her out tonight then. I can sneak her out."'

Raven whines, "Attina! I don't want to leave your side."

I turn and place my hand over her heart. "I don't want you to either, but it would kill me if something happened to you. I need you to go and find my mother." Raven opens her mouth, but I cut her off. "This is not up for discussion. I can't be worried about you while I face Henrik. I know you hate her, but she will protect you. You have to do this for me. If you love me you will trust me and go."

She drops her head and slowly nods, acquiescing.

A silence falls over us, but Allister breaks it. "We also have to talk about Kalven's experiments."

I cut my gaze over to him and cock my head. "I thought he got nowhere with my blood?"

Allister leans back on his hands. "That's not necessarily true. While you were traveling here I helped him capture a couple more Solis. He infused your blood with theirs, but the only difference was they seemed to calm down, like they'd been given a sedative."

I snap, "Okay—so how does that help us? I can't infuse my blood with every Solis in Arealea so they can all take a nap." I don't understand why we're even talking about this. If it's not something that can help us, why waste our breath? Based on our battle outside the Eastern Fae castle, Henrik can guide these beings into a fight. He could use them along with his werewolves and his soldiers against our people. We know this, so why is he bringing up something that won't help us in the long run?

"Well, your mother became increasingly interested in Kalven's experiments. She visited him daily. She even gave him some of her blood."

I cut him off, "Great. But again, she can't give her blood to all of the Solis so I don't see how that could possibly help."

Allister sits up and reaches forward placing both his hands on either side of my face. "Then stop interrupting me and let me finish."

I pinch my lips together and nod, allowing him to continue.

"Through trial and error, they found her powers can control them."

I cock my head in confusion. It's not like they're immune to any Fae's powers.

He sighs and clarifies, "She can use her power against one Solis and it affects the others."

My mouth drops open, and I glance between Allister and Raven. Raven's mouth is almost to the floor next to mine. "How?"

"We talked about it and the only thing we could come up with is Henrik's experiments with her. His magic can control all of the Solis, right?" I nod. "He used his magic against her for over a decade. Some of it must have absorbed into her."

Now that he says it out loud, it makes sense. "I never put much thought into it, but she killed her mate and you said when a Fae loses their mate it can drive them crazy. Do you think that's why she came out of Henrik's crazed spell? Maybe on some level she went crazy when my father died and it brought her out of the spell Henrik put on her?"

He furrows his brow and stares at the ground in thought for a second. "You know what, I bet you're right."

"Well this will make things easier."

Chapter Fifty-Four

Attina

We stay up late into the night talking about our plans, how things could play out, and how we could counter every possible outcome. By the time we finish talking it's late into the night.

Allister stands and announces, "I better take Raven out of here while I can."

Worry immediately floods me. What if someone sees them leave and tells Henrik? I wrap my arm over Raven's back protectively. "How are you going to get her out of here without being seen?"

Raven nudges me. "Kid, it's okay. I trust your mate."

I jerk back away from her and bring my hand to my chest in mocked shock. Allister and Raven chuckle, but Allister answers my question. "Talon and Hazel will help me."

I'm suddenly annoyed. "Talon's done nothing except sit with Henrik and where's Hazel been this whole time? I thought they were helping, what happened to that?"

"Talon has been in Henrik's ear. Why do you think he's been so level headed? Who do you think convinced him he needed an heir in the first place?"

My mouth drops. "So he's the reason all of this is working?"

Allister nods. "I've also talked to Hazel since I've been here. She'll guide Raven out to Titania. She's helping as much as she can, but if Henrik sees her, he'll kill her. She has to stay hidden."

I quickly saddle Raven before throwing my arms around her neck. I sigh and try to fight back tears. I don't like that she'll be away from me during what's to come. I hate that this is the only way I can protect her. "Tell my mother if she lets anything happen to you—I'll never forgive her."

Raven nods in answer, but I see unshed tears glistening in her eyes. She wraps her head around me and her voice catches as she says, "Be careful, kid. Stay alive." She pulls back and gazes between Allister and amends, "Keep each other alive."

Allister and Raven turn to leave, but an idea hits me. I call, "Hang on one second." I go over to the corner of the room where I left my armor, bow, and sword. I pick them up and bring them to Allister. I hand them to him and lock eyes with Raven, her gray eyes narrowing in confusion, "Please make sure my mother gets these. She can use them more than I can tomorrow. I'll be in that hideous dress. I can't very well put my armor over my dress now can I?" I try to sound playful as I add, "And where in the world would I hide my bow and sword?"

Raven nods, but Allister argues, "Not the sword."

I cock my head up at him. "Why not? I can't use it tomorrow."

He walks over and leans my sword against the bed before coming back. "Yes, you can. I'll carry it. You might need a sword to take on Henrik."

I shrug in answer before I give Raven one last big hug. Tearing away from her, I walk over and perch on the edge of the bed. Then nod to Allister. He returns my nod, and then heads out of the room with Raven, my armor, and bow in tow. As I sit there the gravity of everything happening hits me. What if Raven dies? What if my friends and family die. How could I ever forgive myself?

I break down and sob into the sheets.

I'm still crying when I hear the door open, and I can feel Allister's presence stride into the room. "Hey. You okay, kitten?"

I don't even sit up, I just shake my head into the pillow. The bed next to me drops and he pulls me into his arms, cradling me. I throw my face into his chest and wrap my arm over his shoulder, holding him against me. "What if everyone dies tomorrow? All because of some stupid prophecy we can't know is real. What if I'm really nobody, and Henrik wins in the end?"

Allister pushes against my shoulder, forcing me to look up at him as he says, "Hey. I don't want to hear that kind of talk. For one, you're not nobody. Even if the prophecy isn't real, which I think it is, you're the most powerful Fae I've ever met besides

Henrik. You're Arealea's best shot at defeating someone who would tear this world apart. For two, I'm not going to lie to you, people will die in this war, Attina. It's inevitable."

I yank back away from him, not wanting to hear the truth. I just wanted him to lie to me and tell me everything's going to be okay. Is that too much to ask?

He pulls me back to him, stares into my eyes. "But you and I will deal with it. We will handle the pain of their loss, the feeling of guilt, everything that comes with starting a war for our child and every future child. We will build a better world for them, a safer world."

I drop my head down into his chest. I know he's right, and I hate it. I want the happily ever after the princesses in the stories Father read me as a child got. By the end of every story everything was tied up in a pretty bow, everyone was happy, and good overcame evil. Here, in the real world, the bow is more snarled than I ever could have imagined and good doesn't always overcome evil.

Allister lays me down on the bed and moves to lie next to me, but I haul him on top of me. "If good might not overcome evil, I want one more night with the love of my life."

His eyes widen in shock before narrowing conspiratorially. His voice is thick as he says, "As you wish." His lips crash down on top of mine, his tongue running along my lips.

I open my mouth and let him in. His hand runs from my stomach, under my tunic, up to cup my breast as I wrap my arms around his neck.

His nimble fingers pinch my nipple making me moan into his mouth. The noise seems to release his inner beast, he brings his hand behind my head and laces his fingers through my hair as he grabs onto it and pulls my head back, giving himself access to my neck.

He trails soft kisses down my neck and between the kisses he says, "Have I told you how beautiful you are my queen?"

I groan and wiggle beneath him. He always knows just what to do and say to get this reaction out of me. I'm surprised this time when he says my queen it doesn't worry me. I am his queen. The Eastern Fae are my people. My home. My voice is husky as I say, "Once or twice."

His hand travels down to my pants, undoing the buttons. He hooks his finger over the edge of them achingly slowly. I growl and drag my pants off before ripping my tunic above my head. As I tug it off though, Allister slams his hands down on my arms, pinning me to the bed with my arms tangled in my clothes.

He brings his face down close to mine. "You're ruining my fun."

Then he reaches underneath me and flips me over onto my belly before lifting me up onto my knees. Suddenly, he sheathes himself inside of me. I cry out in pleasure while he rocks back and forth. As he moves, a pressure inside me builds. I move against him looking for a release. He brings his hand under me and massages the apex of my thighs, making me fall apart around him. I scream and buck in pleasure, my legs go weak, and I fall to the mattress.

He moves with me and leans down to whisper in my ear, "You're going to have to do a lot more than that if you want to get me off of you." Like I would ever want that. I wish we could stop time and stay in bed like this, satisfying each other, for the rest of our lives.

He thrusts inside me hard as if in emphasis to his words as I finally free my arms and bring my hand up behind me, wrapping it around his neck. I drag his face down to mine until I can look him in the eyes.

I kiss him and say, "I'll love you for the rest of our lives."

My words are his undoing. He pushes into me one more time as he falls apart around me. He flops on the bed next to me and drags me over so my back is pressed against his chest. We sit there and pant for a second, trying to get our breath back. Allister wiggles his arm under my head, and I turn around and kiss his nose.

Wrinkling his nose, he lets out a breathy laugh.

I reach my hand up to his face and take it in. The angles of his cheeks, the way his black hair sticks to his face from sweat, how his eyes glitter down at me. I could lie here forever. My chest hollows out as I realize this could be the last night we have together.

Well if this is going to be the last night we have together, I want to make it a night the gods will speak of.

I run my hand down his sculpted body and over his length. He grabs my hand. "We should get some sleep. I want you well rested for tomorrow's fight."

I haul myself up on my elbow and trail kisses down his neck like he did to me earlier. "If this is the last night we have together I want to spend it pleasuring you."

He growls as he flips me onto my back. I think he's going to say no, but then I feel his hardened length against my thigh. My eyes shoot open in surprise that he's already ready for round two. "I'd rather pleasure you kitten," he says as he crawls down the length of me, trailing kisses as he goes.

⸻◆⸻

The next morning I'm dressed in my terrible wedding gown again, waiting for Allister to return. After reassuring me the human army finally arrived he went to his quarters to get his fighting leathers and weapon. I'm a little worried Henrik will know what's going on when he sees Allister dressed for a fight, but I'd rather him figure us out early, than have Allister be unprepared. I wanted him to wear his armor instead, knowing the metal would protect him more than simple leathers, but he confessed he left his armor at the Eastern Fae castle. He knew Henrik would recognize it and be suspicious about him giving Henrik the Eastern throne.

The door is thrown open and Allister strides through like he owns the place with his head held high and his chest pushed out. "You ready to meet your destiny?" I take in his form and my breath hitches. He's dressed like the first day I met him. He's in his black fighting leathers which curve every muscle just right. His sword is strapped along his back, but this time, mine sits right beside it. Back then he was on a mission to kill me. A mission my grandfather sent him on, but he's Henrik's top slayer no more.

He's my avenging angel.

My love.

I step forward and lace my hand in his. "Our destiny."

Chapter Fifty-Five

Attina

Allister and I stop outside the dark wooden throne room doors. I take a deep, calming breath and brush my fingers against the dagger tied to my thigh. The fabric covering me is so thin I can feel the coolness of the blade.

Agar sneers at us, through his golden helmet, from his position guarding the throne room doors. His companion chuckles on the other side of the door. Their armor clinks at their movements and their spears wiggle in their delight.

Allister cocks his head and asks the Fae, "What's so funny?"

But Agar answers, "You're going to lose your—" His eyes predatorily travel down my body causing a growl to release from Allister. "—plaything today. We were just talking about how you're finally getting what you deserve."

I twine my fingers through Allister's, the calluses on both of our hands rubbing together. Agar's eyes travel down to our hands and a sneer of disgust crosses his features. Allister peeks down at me before smirking at Agar. "She's still mine for now."

Agar pushes off the wall, lifting his spear like he's thinking about attacking. He shouts, "The heir is not yours!"

I flick my hair back, ignoring his outburst. "Open the doors." I am perfectly capable of opening any door, but he's pissed me off. He needs to be reminded of his place.

Agar falls back into his position and opens the door for us. Just as we pass through them though I hear him mutter, "I can't wait till I can kill that miserable traitor."

I assume he doesn't believe Allister's story about him betraying me. Maybe Agar isn't as stupid as he appears to be? I flick my wrist and a stone lifts from the floor and knocks him between the legs. I hear him groan out and his armor jangles as he bends forward. I bring my hand to my face to try and hide a giggle, picturing what must have happened brings a smile to my face, but there's no hiding my amusement.

As the doors slowly close behind us, Henrik's booming voice breaks the silence of the room. I take in a sharp breath when I find the rest of Shadow Mountain is already waiting for us.

Allister tries to release my hand, but I clamp down on his fingers, *What's the point of hiding it now?*

His eyes travel to me. His brow pinches and his eyes appear almost sad with concern as his gaze travels to my stomach.

I hold my head up high as I drag him along to the base of the dais. Today Henrik and Kenda appear to be in their most regal attire. The crown he wore before sits atop his lifted head and his red and golden tunic is cut to perfectly match the lines of his body. Allister's mother is matched in the same color, but her tunic is loose fitting, like she's lost weight since it was made for her. A sheen of sweat coats her brow and pale skin. If it's possible she looks to be in even worse health since my arrival. Her gaze travels down to us, locking on where Allister and my hands are joined. I notice her eyes run over Allister and then over to me, landing on my stomach, and then her eyes glaze over and she leans her head against the back of her throne.

James and Tala stand on the left side of the room, in front of Henrik. So Allister and I take up the space in front of Kenda. James is in a green and brown tunic which isn't surprising since green is his favorite color, but the thing that is surprising is Tala stands by his side in a matching floor length dress. Her low cut strappy dress caresses each and every one of her curves, making my eyes travel up and down her body, a toothy snarl on her face like usual.

Henrik's voice is coaxing as he says, "I see you two have made up."

I lift my chin and make sure my voice carries throughout the room as I answer, "Even *if* he betrayed me, he is still my mate." Henrik's eyes narrow at Allister, the anger making him shake. The Fae standing on the edge of the room waiting to watch me marry James, gasp in shock. A few murmurs reach my ears, and I turn my head to them for a split second. When I turn back, I see Kenda's eyes locked on me. I slightly incline my head to her before turning back to Henrik. I can almost see the anger burning in his eyes.

He says, "Well, I think—"

But I cut him off; there's more these people need to hear. I ask, "Have you made your decision on if you'll spare the ones I love and the humans if I agree to get rid of mine and Allister's child and marry," I turn my head to James in emphasis, "James instead?"

The room breaks out in cries and the people around the room aren't even trying to hide it now as they break into blatantly loud conversation. Henrik sits there on his throne seething at me. His body shakes and his skin starts bleeding into a red color. His voice cracks on the last syllable as he screeches, "Silence!"

Everyone in the room jumps except me. I was expecting his reaction. He wanted to quietly guide me out of the room so he could feed me the liquid I spy sitting between the two thrones to me yesterday. I figured he didn't want everyone to know he was trying to get rid of a baby out of his granddaughter and her mate. Children are rare with the Fae, I was betting on them being cherished, and I bet right. If Henrik wanted to win his people back, I've all but made it an impossible task.

Now it's his move.

He huffs in his throne for longer than necessary before he opens his mouth. "You." The word comes out accusatory like I had single handedly ruined everything, and maybe I have.

I squeeze Allister's hand a second before a fireball is barreling down at us. I hear James shout, "Attina! No!"

At the last second, I throw up a wall of rock, but almost as soon as the wall is up, it melts from the fierce heat bombarding it. I release Allister's hand and raise both of mine. I call to the earth to rebuild that wall faster than it can melt. Then I send water up through the rocks to cool them. But the heat bearing down on us is too fierce. It sears my skin making me hiss from the pain. I wrap a protective wall of air around Allister and me until Henrik relents.

When the fire falls away I drop my earth wall to see Henrik glaring at me. Beside me I see James has transformed. His teeth are bared and his hackles are up, but his jaw is tight and his head swivels back and forth between Henrik and me, like he's not sure who to be infuriated at—me for making such a scene, or Henrik for attacking me. The fact that he's not sure who to be mad at shows me how far he's fallen from the boy I knew growing up.

I force my fear down and ground out a chuckle as I say, "Well, the groom turned into a furry monster, I guess that means there's no wedding today either. Should we try for tomorrow?"

Henrik stands, and I instinctively slide away from him. I instantly hate myself for it. Again, I'm showing weakness. Allister pulls me back forward, and up against his body. I let his warmth and strength wash over me. In my head I hear, *There's no stopping now.*

Henrik calmly saunters down the dais, his hooded eyes shifting between James, the room, me, and Allister. Tala growls and bares her teeth at me. Well at least I know where she stands, even though I saved her from Henrik's wrath in our fight. I don't know why I ever expected her to change.

Henrik stops in front of me, and I have to crane my neck to peer up at him, the smell of fire radiates from him. I can hear the anger in every syllable coming out of his mouth as he bellows, "Everyone, out!"

Around us Fae silently file out of the room. I can feel everyone's fear for the man in front of me thick on the air—and it angers me. How he could make these people live in such terror for so long is unimaginable to me.

To Allister, I think, *This isn't going well. Get everyone out of here and get our army here.*

He squeezes my hand. *You can do this.* Then out loud, he says, "I love you," as he turns and runs into the mass of people leaving the room.

Henrik grunts and throws a fireball after him, but he just ends up hitting an innocent man. Thankfully he's too skinny for the clothes he's wearing and the fire only burns a hole through his clothing instead of burning through his skin.

While I wish I could have my mate by my side during this battle, I'd rather he leave and take care of the one's I can't. I know he'll return, he always returns.

I steel my back and stand up straight against the hulking Fae towering over me. He growls down at me, but his voice almost comes out sad as he says, "You could have had it all."

I furrow my brows in confusion at his change. One minute he wanted to kill me, the next he sounds sad? What the hell is this about?

He throws his hands in the air gesticulating as he reiterates, "You're my granddaughter Attina Drake. You could have had everything. You could have been the next on the throne. Rule these people. Rule all of Arealea by my side."

Well there's no going back now. I throw up a wall of air between us, before I tell him the news that will cause a war. "I will rule over all of Arealea, not you. I already rule the Eastern Fae. *I* took that throne, not Allister. It's his by right, but I overtook it so." I mock wince, "*technically* it's ours—not his to give away. Also, I'm not a Drak. My father's last name was Lukas. I am Attina Lukas and you will bend to my rule or you will die by my hand."

Henrik opens his mouth to, I think, speak, but instead fire shoots from his mouth. The fire hits my wall of air and bounces back at him, but I know my wall won't hold long and instead of waiting I roll out of the way. When I'm out of the way, Tala pounces on me, her lacey dress crawling up her thighs.

I throw my hand up and my fist connects with her jaw, causing a growl to rip from her chest.

Henrik calls from across the room, "Tala, I order you to end her."

She stands as an evil smile cracks her features and her eyes darken. In one breath she's a human standing on two feet and in the next she's covered in fur and on all fours on the ground. Her long nails tap on the floor as she stalks over to me.

I crawl backward, trying to get enough room to stand and get away from this massive wolf. But before I can get my feet under me Tala's flying through the air. My hand goes in the air and rocks form around my body, shielding me.

But she never lands. Instead I hear growling and snapping.

I peek around the stones blocking my view and gasp as I watch James's wolf has knocked her to the ground and is riding the back of Tala's. He grabs onto her neck with his teeth. But, although he's bigger than her in human form, Tala dwarfs him in wolf form. She grunts and snaps before groaning and standing up. James jumps off of her and puts his body between Tala and me.

Henrik must be watching because as I stick my head over the stones, a fireball passes by my head. I duck under my protection and yell, "You're always having someone else do your dirty work for you. With Allister's father and now me. Who else has blood on their hands because of you?"

I pull on my fire and lob it in his direction as I quickly crawl out of my stone protection and race at him. Snarls and snaps come from my left, but I can't give them my attention. I need to keep my eyes trained on the evil in front of me. Henrik grins as he barrages me with fireball after fireball. I throw up my wall of air and force water into it, so I have a swirling bubble around me, putting out all the flames being thrown at me.

I've kept my water and air powers hidden. I didn't want him to think I was a threat to him, but now? Now, there's no turning back. I bring my hand up and a chuck of stone is ripped from the ground and with a loud thunk, it hits Henrik, but it barely knocks him back at all.

I skid to a stop in front of him. "Are you sure you want to do this grandfather? It's not too late. This doesn't have to happen." But as soon as my words leave my mouth Agar comes barreling in and shouts, "We're under attack! There's an army outside our walls!"

Henrik's eyes glance at him for a second, and then they narrow and land back on me. He growls, "So this is the plan? You come here and trick me into taking you under my wing with the intention of overthrowing *my* kingdom?"

Well, I tried.

I throw a fireball toward Agar. It hits his armor and melts it. He howls in fear and pain. From the moment I saw that golden armor I didn't understand it. Gold is so malleable—so breakable.

Then from the door Allister runs in astride Cedar. Cedar roars as he races at Agar and Allister pulls his sword over his head before slicing it down and sheathing it inside Agar's chest. Agar's face goes ashen white as blood spurts out of his chest and trails down his body.

I smile up at Allister, but the pride for having such a capable and loyal mate fades as Henrik's voice breaks the moment. "No wonder you want to take over everything. You're the female version of me."

I take a stumble back and glare up at him. "I am *nothing* like you."

"Your mate just murdered someone in front of you and you smile? You're definitely *my* granddaughter." He stalks forward, but I'm thrown for such a loop I don't notice. "At your age, I reveled in death and destruction, too."

My mind goes back to when my mother was in the cells at home. How I feasted on her pain, how it filled me with so much pleasure to see her in pain. Then, when I made Commander Demarco grovel on the floor to me. How I felt so powerful. Even Hazel talked about me needing to be checked when it came to my wicked nature.

I fall to my knees lost in my thoughts, everything around me goes hazy, and I bring my hands to either side of my head, holding it, trying to hold it together. I bend down and rock back and forth.

I can't be like him.

I can't be a monster.

From somewhere in the distance, I hear Allister shout something, but I'm so far lost in my own thoughts, I can't hear what he's saying. His voice gets louder, and I finally peer over at him, the haze in my head making my vision blurry.

Allister races over to me with his sword held in the air. He's screaming Henrik's name. Why would he do that? I turn my head to where Henrik was standing and throw myself back when I realize he's almost on top of me. He pulls a dagger out from somewhere behind him, and I throw my hand up trying to block the inevitable.

This is how I die, on my knees in front of Henrik.

Weak.

I watch my scared face reflected in the blade of the dagger as it slices down at my head. Closing my eyes, I grit my teeth waiting for the death blow to come.

Chapter Fifty-Six

Attina

"M om!" Allister shouts.

I open my eyes and tears instantly fill my eyes as I take in the scene in front of me. Allister's mother stumbles into my lap, a dagger protruding through her chest. Blood pours down her glittering red tunic and her crown is nowhere to be found.

Allister screams as he and Cedar race toward us. Allister swings his sword down at Henrik who jumps backward and dodges the blow. James and Tala's head snap up at the commotion, instantly their fight's forgotten and they sprint over to where Allister is pursuing Henrik.

I bring my hand up to Kenda's ashen face and whimper out, "Why would you sacrifice yourself?"

She lifts her shaky, skinny hands and caresses my face. "You are my son's mate. You carry his child. Your life has more meaning than mine."

I drop my forehead to hers. "All he's wanted is a relationship with you. This whole time. All he's wanted is you."

Her voice is weaker and catches as she answers, "He has you now. You take care of each other. Lead this world into a time of peace." Then she goes limp in my arms.

I lay my head down and scream.

The room violently shakes around me as I throw my head back and a shriek wrenches from my throat. Boulders shake from the mountain above us and slam to the ground.

Allister screams into my mind, *Attina! Get it together!*

He pulls me out of my reverie. He's right. I drop my head up to see Tala knock Allister off of Cedar against the mountain wall with a heavy swipe of her huge paw, and a gnarly snarl on her face. He's thrown against the hidden doors to the balcony and skids across the balcony, his back slamming into the handrail. Cedar doesn't hesitate. He jumps forward and slams into Tala, their bodies are a blur of fur and claws as they go rolling to the left.

I scream, "Allister!" as I stand and race over to the fray. I push air behind me to propel me faster forward, but I can tell I won't be fast enough. James is already on top of Allister, pinning him down. He hovers over Allister and snarls, the sound vibrating through my chest. Henrik stands to the side sneering down at the scene in front of him. I'll never make it. Even if I do make it, Henrik will stop me.

There's only one thing to do.

I stop and throw both of my hands forward, pushing all the air I can at James. He lifts his head toward me as soon as the air leaves my hands, like he can sense the attack. He must be more sensitive to things in his wolf form, but it doesn't save him.

My air hits him broadside, knocking him sideways. He hits the railing and the force of my attack throws him over the ledge. I watch as his panicked paws flail in the air, looking to find purchase on anything, but finding nothing to grab hold of.

I race over to the balcony and as I move I hear Tala scream to my left, "James!" I turn to see her race over toward the balcony, but Cedar isn't done with her. He bites down on her back haunch and rips her back to him. Her claws drag down the stone floor causing a loud, deafening screech to fill the room. She jumps up and turns around snapping as she transforms back to her naked body. She throws her body over Cedar, and I hear a cry rip from him just as I lose sight of them.

As I make it to the balcony, Allister is lifting his hands to block a fireball coming toward his face. I throw up a shield in front of Allister and slide behind it myself.

I hear Tala screech from inside the throne room. "He's dying!"

I know it was a *long* fall, but he's a werewolf. The fall could have broken something, but he shouldn't be dying, just out of the fight. Allister brings his own powers out and brings water up to add to my already weakening shield. I risk a quick glance over the balcony and my eyes widen at what I find.

Tala was right.

My stomach drops, and I have the sudden urge to regurgitate the moldy food I had last night.

Below I can just make out James's fur covered form, but smaller bodies crawl all over him. Not regular bodies, Solis. The Solis Henrik must have called to when he heard an army was attacking. They rip and tear at his flesh turning the snow around them red. I throw my hand out and shoot fire at them, but it's no use, my fire peters out before its heat reaches any of the Solis attacking him.

One Solis with half a body drags itself over top of James's limp body. I can barely make out it digging its teeth into his neck and blood flying through the air as it rips a chuck of flesh out of his jugular. He transforms and shrinks back into his naked human form. Blood flies around and rains down on top of him, staining his skin.

I yell, "James!" His gaze goes from almost glazed over to meeting mine. He mouths, I love you, before his head lulls to the side.

Tala and James must be connected somehow because as soon as he closes his eyes for the final time, Tala roars. I hear a loud snap and then silence.

Out of nowhere Henrik's fire ceases.

I furrow my brows and turn to Allister who is still staring at Henrik with more hatred than I've ever seen anyone exude. A second later a massive brown wolf stalks onto the balcony. Henrik's lips slowly quirk up into a smug smile.

She doesn't give us a chance to attack her. Her lips curl into a chest vibrating growl, saliva drips down from her canines to the ground. She rears back before pouncing at us. I bring my hands up to try to block her, but Allister's body smacks into my hand as he meets her in the air.

I scream "No!" at the top of my lungs. I can do nothing but watch him and a werewolf slam into each other. Their tangled bodies flying over the railing, following James down the mountain. I stand up and slam my body against the hand railing. I'm helpless to watch them tumble down the rock mountain. When they hit the ground snow flurries fly up around them. They both lie still and from this high up I can't tell if their chests are moving or not.

I know Allister won't be able to hear my voice so I shout into his mind, *Allister! Are you okay?*

He grunts into my head and my body almost topples to the ground in relief. "He's alive?" Henrik says behind me. I twist around and push myself back against the railing, trying to get as far away from him as possible. He turns away with his hands laced behind his back and walks back into the throne room.

My jaw drops. I'm flabbergasted. One moment he's trying to kill me and the next he casually walks away?

Over his shoulder, he calls, "You're lucky he survived. Fae go crazy when their mates die."

I call to Allister, *You good?*

He answers, *A little banged up, but I've had worse. Tala's waking up. Got to go.*

I hurriedly add, *Stay alive.* Then I follow Henrik back into the throne room.

When my eyes adjust back to the darkness of the room Henrik is circling the dais, walking over toward where Allister's mother fell. "She was a perfect example of how Fae go mad after their mates die."

I scan the room for Cedar. I find him in the corner stumbling up to his feet, shaking his head. The loud crack must have been Tala slamming his head to the ground. She must have knocked him out. Cedar shakes his head and locks his purple eyes on me. "You okay, mate?"

I answer, "Yes, please go help Allister."

Cedar dips his head before racing past me and diving over the balcony after Allister. I feel better knowing he'll be with my mate, protecting him.

Behind me I hear a hoot and then Hazel's voice. "And why didn't you go crazy when your mate died?" I don't bother to whirl around; the threat is Henrik in front of me. I feel Hazel's wings flapping through the air and then she's on the ground next to me.

Henrik's eyes lock on Hazel, but he doesn't even seem surprised to see her. "You can't break what's already broken."

Then I feel another set of wings flapping through the air toward me. Talon lands on the ground on my other side and finally Henrik's mouth drops and surprise lights his eyes. "You?"

Talon nods and readjusts his wings. "You've kept me on a leash long enough." He leans forward to peek at Hazel, but as we all watch his movement fire flies through the air at us, slamming into Hazel. Air rushes out of her lungs as she's hit in the chest with the fireball and she's thrown backwards into the wall behind her. The feathers on her chest are either missing completely or charred. Her puckered skin is exposed and bloodied. Her chest is still and her eyes are shut.

I race over to her, and Talon screams, "Hazel!" Then he's in the air flying at Henrik. He throws fireball after fireball in the air at Talon, but he ducks and dives, dodging Henrik's assault. He makes it to Henrik and flings his legs forward, dragging them down Henrik's face and leaving red, bloody streaks as Henrik lifts his hand and slams it into Talon's body, sending him soaring across the room and he slams his head into the wall.

I hope he's only unconscious as I gently place my hand on Hazel's side, wiggling her body trying to wake her. She's unresponsive for a second before she grunts. I don't have the time to check and see if she's all right, she's alive and that's all that matters right now. I stand and face Henrik again. Face the final threat.

Henrik is now huffing where he stands staring at me. His voice is cold and calculated as he yells to me, "You come here, I take you under my wing, and this is how you repay me?"

I cock my head, but don't answer him. He's not looking for an answer. His breathing becomes more labored and his muscles start bulging.

"You turned *everyone* against me. Even Talon!" His skin blazes red, but instead of his fire coming to the surface, scales start sprouting along his skin.

I keep my eyes locked on him as I stalk sideways, trying to make my way to Talon. I'm not sure what's about to happen, but I know it isn't good. I call to Kaida as I move. *Kaida you in there?* I'm honestly not sure if this will even work. Will she answer? Will she drag me into my own subconscious leaving us vulnerable and probably dead?

I let out a breath as she answers inside my head. *I'm here.*

I ask, *Can you see what's going on?*

Get out!

Fuck. How bad can this be? *What's happening?*

He's turning into his Anima!

I want to ask so many questions, but as Henrik's face darkens and turns lizard-like I know I don't have the time. I scoop up Talon and race back over to Hazel. They're so heavy it's hard to carry both of them simultaneously, but I don't have a choice. I notice Cedars' paws scrape down the mountain, slowing his descent.

I glance back at Henrik as I race out onto the balcony. His dark body is growing bigger and bigger and a second head sprouts out of his neck, but not his head—a lizard's head. Red light peeks out between his scales as he breathes. His arms and legs lengthen and turn to claws.

I call back to Kaida, *What do I do?' I'm trapped.*

Kaida shrieks, *I'll help as much as I can.*

I'm confused at her answer, but I can't ask what she means. My voice catches as I stare at Henrik's changing form. He has to bend his head as he continues to grow. Another head pops out of the other side of his neck, blood flying everywhere. Sharp dagger-like canines protrude out of his elongated mouth and his ears lengthen into sharper points.

I think, *Kaida! I could use some help here!*

Henrik's growing body fills the room now. The stones above him begin groaning from the pressure his form's putting on them. I know it won't be long until he topples the mountain completely. If that happens I'm bound to be squished by falling rocks. I shift Hazel and Talon in my arms, their heavy bodies are already putting a strain on my arms.

After what feels like ages, I finally hear Kaida in my mind. *You need to jump.*

I scoff. *Very funny.*

Her voice is hard when she answers, *I'm serious. If you die, I die. Now jump!*

My stomach drops. She can't be serious. *I can't fly. We'll die.* A loud crack breaks my thoughts. I glance up to see the three heads of Henrik's hydra burst out of the top of the mountain. Boulders bigger than the Eastern Fae castle begin falling. One the size of Raven topples over the ledge Henrik's body has created, plummeting straight for me.

Kaida shouts, *Jump!*

I only have a split second to make a decision.

I decide I'd rather fall to my death than be squished under a boulder so I pitch my body over the handrail of the balcony.

Chapter Fifty-Seven

Attina

I close my eyes as I plummet toward the ground below me. The scream ripping from my lungs is silenced by the wind rushing past me and slicing at my face and arms.

This is it.

I'm going to die.

One last time, I tell Allister, *I love you.*

My vision flashes to his like it did the first time we met, and I see myself falling from the top of Shadow Mountain. Nothing but a tiny speck drifting down to the ground. I think I hear him roar, "No!" But there's no way I could hear him from all the way up here.

My vision shifts back to my own, and I search the battle ground below me. Directly under me James's torn bloodied limp body lies. The Solis have all given up on him and are out finding new prey.

Allister slices his sword down across Tala's face. She shrieks before pulling her lip back in a snarl and pouncing on him. Every Solis in Arealea and Henrik's made werewolves flood the area along with Henrik's soldiers. There are more werewolves than I ever could have imagined, where did he keep those things?

Kaida's voice breaks my thoughts, *Hang on.*

What does she mean hang on? Hang on for what?

But just as the thought leaves my head the skin covering my shoulder blade rips open. I writhe in pain, bending into a fetal position, I grind my teeth and try to grit through the pain, but I fail as a scream is wrenched from my lungs. It takes everything in me to keep my hold on Hazel and Talon.

It feels like my bones are being pulled from my body. The wind slices by parts of my body which were just inside me. The icy sensation does nothing to help with the pain rushing through every inch of me.

Out of nowhere a flap sounds behind me and my descent slows down.

What the—?

I crane my neck around and whimper when I see what's behind me—Kaida's wings flare out behind me, catching the air and slowing my descent. The crimson scales glisten in the sunlight.

Um, Kaida?

She yells, *Move your shoulders! Flap your wings!*

I do as she says and move my shoulders up and down, the wings mimic my movement and our descent slows until I'm in the air flapping my wings and hanging in place.

I need some guidance here. I'm worried any second I could mess something up and fall to my death. *What do I do now?*

She chuckles like I'm stupid for not already knowing this, but I've never had wings. How would I know what to do? *Point your body the direction you'd like to go and flap your wings.*

I swing my legs out behind me and face myself toward where I can see Allister and Tala fighting. The current of the wind pushes and pulls me off course, and I almost slam into a tree. I'm able to bank my shoulder into the trunk and land on a tree branch. I take the opportunity to perch Hazel and Talon in the frozen tree before I dive back into the air. I quickly find I can manipulate the wind around my wings and direct my movement while I glide on the air.

Flying is exhilarating. Why did no one tell me I could do this?

I soar down into the fray. Cutting above clashing swords and warriors screaming in pain. I wince when I see one of our men run his sword through another Fae, his guts fall to the ground with a loud thud. I turn my body and slice through the air toward where Allister and Tala still fight. He backs away from her with his sword held in front of him, blocking the swipes of her big paw. Ice shards fly up from the ground, aiming for her chest, but she nimbly ducks and dives out of the way. She rolls past soldiers and is lost in the fray.

I glide over Allister's head, pulling my sword from the place he's kept it on his back. The steel warms my hands as Allister's head swings up to see who took my sword. A smile breaks across his face, his shoulders sag, and tears wet his eyes as I drift down to the ground, slipping in the slick snow beneath my feet.

He shouts, "You're alive!" Then he pulls back, and his eyes lock on my wings. His features twist in confusion. "How in the—"

But I miss the rest of his words as I see a blur of brown fur jump up behind him, and I don't even think as I push him aside. I run my hand up my sword, lighting it on fire, and thrust my sword toward her. The sword sizzles as it pierces Tala's wolves flesh and the smell of burning hair tickles my nose. Blood runs down my sword, warming my hand. My slick hand slams into the base of my cross guard.

Allister spins around and takes on two Fae who must have come to Tala's aid. His sword slices through the air and the men scream as metal meets metal.

Tala's wolf's mouth opens and closes as she looks down to see my sword rammed through her chest. Tala changes back to her human form as she sputters blood in my face. Her hands go up to my sword and I rip my sword out of her chest, she falls to her knees in front of me. Her eyes lock on mine and she whispers something I can't hear. I bend down and place my ear by her mouth.

I barely make out, "Henrik will kill you and everyone you love, half-breed."

I jerk back away from her, but am grabbed by clawed hands. I hear pounding on the ground as a bellow breaks the cries of battle. There's a thud behind me and the clawed hand drags down my arm as it falls to the floor. I turn to see a Solis in a heap on the ground and Raven's gray eyes staring back at me.

Without thinking, I throw my arm over her, the wing pulling on my shoulder at the movement. I gaze up to my mother sitting astride her. Her armor sparkles in the sunlight and my bow is strapped along her back. A sword is in her hand dripping blood.

I wink at her. "Thank you." I ask, "Where's Ned and the Mori Noki?"

She turns her head and points to her left. When I look to where she's pointing I can see Ned, atop a snarling Cedar, and the Mori Noki surrounding the humans, as Solis and were-wolves inch in around them.

I turn back to my mother as I feel Allister's back slam against mine. His panicked voice reaches my ears. "There's too many."

"What are we going to do?" I ask no one in particular.

Above me, my mother smirks as she lifts her hand into the sky. I tilt my head to see what she's doing. Thunder rolls as dark clouds crawl across the sky. Lightning sparks and crawls over the clouds before flying down into my mother's awaiting hand.

I scream, but it's drowned out by the noise of the lightning crackling through my mother. She brings her other hand out and points at a Solis close to us. One moment the Solis is on top of one of our Fae soldiers' shield and the next it's flopped over on its side and seizing on the ground. I'd almost forgotten Allister said she could attack all the Solis at once. Thank the gods for that mercy.

Then I hear cheers break out around us as all the other Solis fall to the ground and seize around us. Humans race forward and begin cutting off the heads of every Solis around them, leaving the Fae and few werewolves left to be taken on by our Fae troops.

I feel the warmth of Allister's hand as he pivots me around. His purple eyes drift over my wings. "What happened?"

I open my mouth to answer him, but a boom cracks in the distance. I turn around to face Shadow Mountain just in time to see it crash to the ground. This entire time Henrik has been shifting and growing until his body became too heavy for the mountain to hold his weight.

My mother's eyes lock on mine. "Are you ready for this?"

I cock to the side in question as her red eyes shift into an elongated pupil. Then she grunts as blue bat-like wings appear under her arms. She throws me my bow and her armor, before jumping off of Raven as her body morphs into a scaled beast. Her mouth lengthens and shifts to a scaled snout and her teeth extend past her lips.

Raven shifts sideways into my side. I can hear her breathing picking up as she watches my mother transform into a teal dragon. Whereas Kaida has four legs and a set of wings sprouting from her back, my mother is more humanoid. She stands on her now bent legs and her arms have turned into wings which attach to her side.

I scoff at her. "You know you could have told me we could transform. I almost died jumping off that balcony!"

She shrugs and when she opens her mouth I'm surprised to hear her voice is the same, just a little huskier. "It didn't come up."

I throw my hands up in exacerbation. "Well how do you do it? Do I only have wings?" How did my family hide this gift for centuries? How has no one found out about this until now?

Her face sags. "Probably. Henrik being the oldest is the biggest. When I first started shifting I could only summon wings like you. The total shift will come with time."

Henrik in his hydra form lifts a leg out of the mountain and crawls out onto the battlefield. Fae and humans scream as his foot comes down on top of them, squishing them. I howl, "We don't have time!"

Without an answer she turns around and flaps her arms until her feet hover off of the ground. I move to follow her, but Allister grabs me by the forearm. "Let me come with you."

I turn to him and raise my hand to his cheek. "You need to stay here and lead our people. Let me handle this family drama." I hand my armor and bow to him before I flap my wings, lifting me off of the ground. I turn my head back and forth gazing between him and Raven, "Keep each other safe."

Then I turn and shoot off into the air toward my grandfather. Toward the end of his reign of terror.

In my head, I hear, *Come back to me, kitten.*

I will. I promise.

I peek back just in time to see Allister drag my armor over his head, hop on Raven, and race over to where the Mori Noki are cutting down the enemy. Ava, who now sits atop Mylo, whirls dirt and dust around a werewolf, confusing it while Hudson races around it faster than my eyes can follow and cuts it with his sword. My chest swells at the sight of everyone fighting together.

I face forward and take in what I'm about to face. The red hydra screams as it sees me and my mother flying at it. I try to yell to my mother, but my voice is swallowed up by the wind. I pound my wings with all my might until I make it to her. "How do we kill him?"

Her scaled eyes narrow. "We have to rip out his heart."

Chapter Fifty-Eight

Attina

"Rip out his heart?" I parrot.

She simply nods in answer.

I stare down at my sword and maneuver so I can rip the dagger out from under my dress. Well I'm guessing I'm going to need these. I don't know any other way we can get to his heart.

He throws his head down and fire pours from his mouth, shooting directly for us.

"Mom!"

She dives out of the way just in time. I duck under the flame, but Henrik follows my movement. My mother turns around and flies back the way we came. I plunge down away from the rain of fire to follow my mother out of range.

Hovering in place, I ask her, "What do we do?"

"If we get too close, he'll burn us alive. But we have to get close to him somehow."

Henrik takes another step forward and another, killing everything in his path. My mother and I fly away from him, but as I peek down, I see where he's going, and my stomach drops. "He's walking over to Allister and Ned. He's going to kill everyone we love."

My mother growls as her eyes drift down to my sword. A nostalgic smile creeps up her face and crinkles her eyes. "I'm glad Silas gave that to you."

This really isn't the time to be having a moment, but I can help it. I lift my sword and have to choke back tears at the mention of my father's name. I lock eyes with hers. "He never stopped loving you. Ever."

She nods and darts off toward Henrik. "Take your shot when you can."

Her words give me an idea, I shout after her, "Hey, stop! I'll be right back." She turns back to me and furrows her brows. I take off back the way we came. She calls something to me, but I'm too far away to hear whatever it is.

I shoot down to the ground and land by Allister's side. He has my bow string pulled back, but I snatch it out of his hands before he can release the arrow. Then, I glide over to where Oberon is taking on a werewolf. I yank him back and away from the fight, his lip lifts in a snarl before his eyes widen when he realizes who snatched him back.

Without a word, Liam blinds the werewolf while Lincoln uses his powers to rip a tree from its roots and slams it into the creature. Derek comes out of nowhere and slams his shoulder into the beast, crushing its chest.

Oberon places both hands on my shoulder and stares down at me. "What's wrong, my queen?"

"Did you have those metal arrows made for me?" He crinkles his brows and nods as he opens his mouth. I cut him off, "Where are they?"

He simply points at Ava as he races off somewhere behind me. I duck under flying swords before crashing down to meet their intended target as I race over to her.

I shout, "Ava!"

She spins around on Mylo's back and when she takes in the wings poking out behind my body her face lights up. Her lips curl into a lopsided grin and her eyes almost sparkle as she yells, "Attina! You look beautiful! I want wings!"

Even with our impending doom and all this death and destruction going on around us, she gets me to laugh. I chuckle out, "Maybe we'll make you a pair when this is all over." She bounces up and down in the saddle clapping her hands. I never thought someone so positive could exist in this world, but here she is cheering me on at every turn.

"Do you have those metal arrows?" I hurriedly ask. I have to get back and help Mother.

She kicks Mylo forward, leans down, and plucks an arrow out of Hudson's quiver behind her. "Here you go. Do you need more?"

I should only need one, but I'd rather be safe than sorry so I answer, "Just one more." She repeats the motion and then I have two arrows in my hand.

She adds, "They've also been dipped in Chalcanthite so be careful." I fight back a gasp as I remember the substance one of Allister's men rubbed over his sword. The sword he ran through Allister with. It's the reason I almost lost him, the reason I realized who he was to me. Chalcanthite rips your powers and healing abilities away from you, basically leaving you human. I glance up to where Henrik is still stalking toward us and grin. This is perfect. Maybe we don't have to physically rip his heart out, just keep it from healing itself.

I flap my wings until I'm level with Ava and throw my arm around her. I pull her into a tight hug and whisper into her ear, "Thank you for being the best friend I've ever had," as I take off into the air.

I push a gust of wind behind me to shoot me faster over to where my mother still hovers just outside of Henrik's fires reach. "Where have you been?" she scolds.

I hand her my sword, the sword which used to be hers. "I'm going to distract him. I need you to cut a hole to his heart." He's so big I don't think even these metal arrows will penetrate his flesh enough to pierce his heart.

My mother doesn't even question me, she simply nods, turns, and takes off toward Henrik. I fly after her, but instead of following her; I shoot up to Henrik's muzzle. He stops his advance long enough to blow fire at me. I dig down inside me and yank up a boulder, throwing it at him. It disintegrates in the fire, but stops its advance. I shoot sideways, taking a page out of Allister's book I call to the water in the ground and trees around us. The water bends to my will and forms into hardened shards of ice.

Henrik notices my mother and swats at her like an annoying fly who just keeps pestering him. I fling the shards of ice at him. They hit their mark, embedding in one of his faces, one even punctures his eye. His three heads roar as the affected head bends down to his shortened hand so he can clear the ice from his eye.

His other heads snake over to either side of me. One breathes fire at me, and I shoot up into the air just in time to keep from getting singed only to fly straight into the mouth of the other head. My shoulder grazes against one of his teeth and a searing pain blooms along with the wet, sticky feeling of blood running down it.

The jaw snaps down over me, his breath is hot, humid, and smells like ash. I grab onto his tongue as he tries to swallow me. Bringing my sword up, I chop down onto his jaw. In one swift motion, I cut off the bottom half of the head's jaw. The dripping, sucking noise of flesh being cut penetrates my ears in a sweet harmony.

The head wails in pain and flings itself back while I fall out into the open air. I shrug my shoulders, making my wings flair out. It sounds like cloth on the wind as my wings hold the air and catch me. I remember from stories read to me as a child if you cut off a head of the hydra, two more will sprout from its neck. So, instead of going after the head with no jaw, I turn my attention to the last two heads.

The one I blinded with icicles recovers from my attack and lifts its head. It still has a thick icicle protruding from its left eye. The ice is so stuck in there, the lid can barely close around it. I fly at it trying to get its attention when I notice out of the corner of my eye the other head locks its gaze on my mother, who by now, has made it to Henrik's chest.

The lizard-like head flies down at her. I barely have enough time to drop down and land on top of it, knocking it out of the way. I grab a hold of my dagger and stab it into the top of its head. A sick squelching noise reaches my ears as my dagger melts into flesh. Henrik flings the head back and forth, and it takes everything in me to hold on to the dagger as I'm thrown around like a ragdoll.

The hydra wiggles as it flings around. The head with the one eye flies around my head, attacking, but never hitting me. It seems to be having a problem finding me with only one eye. And the head I cut the lower jaw off of simply hangs in the air like it's not sure what to do now that half of his teeth are missing.

We move away from the fray, off through the forest, away from everyone I love. Finally, from the beast's chest, my mother yells, "Okay, your turn, baby!"

I release my dagger and let the head swing me far away from the body. But the head chases me. I dip and dodge out of its way, but it's relentless. I even bump into the other, half-blinded head a few times.

I need some help. There's no way this thing is going to let me get far enough away from it to shoot an arrow into its heart.

I call down to my mother, who's still hovering close to the hydra's chest, "I need some help! Can you distract it?"

"I'm on it!" Then soars up and slams her body into the bottom of the head I shoved the dagger in. Well, that's one way to distract it. It turns its heads to lock its eyes on her. She beckons him after her and takes off the way we came. Henrik looks back and forth between my mother and me, but decides my mother deserves his wrath more than I do.

I drag my bow over my neck and nock a metal arrow. They wrapped the tip of the arrow in cloth like we talked about, so I grab the tip and yank on my fire to light it. As Henrik turns to follow his daughter, I position myself so I can see the open slice my mother cut running down the hydra's chest. I can already make out the skin stitching itself back together.

It's now or never.

I release a breath and let go of the bow string. The arrow flies through the air toward Henrik's hydra form. Before the arrow can hit its mark though, I yank out the second metal arrow, light it, and shoot it.

The first arrow hits with a thunk right in Henrik's chest. The three heads slice over to where I hover in the air. The three sets of eyes, minus the one with the icicle still in it, narrow in on me, and a world shaking growl rips from the beast's lungs. But, just as the howl ratchets up, my second arrow hits its mark.

The growl stops completely.

The hydra's eyes go slack before they glaze over. Three necks fall to its chest as the beast crashes to the ground in a lump. Trees burst into splinters as he crushes everything beneath him.

Far off, I can hear our people's cheers of joy. They must've been able to see the beast crash to the ground. Before my eyes, the hydra slowly disappears and transforms back into Henrik. I lock eyes with my mother. She nods to me, and then flies down to where Henrik fell. I gaze over to the battlefield where smoke drifts up into the clouds and where the smell of blood and death lingers. I know we lost people, and I know it's selfish, but I send up a silent prayer that my friends and family made it out alive.

I shake my head and dive down to the ground where my mother, still in her scaled form, stands over Henrik's still body.

I walk over to her and lift my arm; the motion makes my wing sound like a cloth flapping in the wind. I wrap my arm around her shoulders. She breathes deeply as she stares down at him. I don't even know what to say. Should I be consoling her? She hated her father though. Maybe I should be congratulating her?

I decide to simply ask, "Do you want to take his body back?"

She silently shakes her head, her brown hair swings around her shoulders. "Just leave him here. He can be alone like he's made everyone feel his entire life." I can tell she wants to say more, but she closes her mouth and her shoulders sag.

I bring her into my side and playfully shake her. "Hey, at least we stayed with our family's tradition. Family killing family for the throne."

She scoffs and lifts her hand to cover her face. "That's not supposed to be a good thing."

I slide in front of her, blocking Henrik from her view. "We're going to change that."

She shakes her head and pulls me into a hug. "No, baby. *You're* going to change it."

I push her away so I can stare into her eyes. "Are you leaving?"

She drags me back into her arms and her voice cracks as she shouts, "No! I just got you back. I'm not going anywhere. Never again."

My shoulders sag and tears prickle my eyes. I hadn't realized how much I wanted her to say no. How much I want her in my life. To laugh with her, to cry with her, to finally get to know her.

I wipe the tears from my eyes as I step out of her grasp. I reach my hand down and take hers in mine. "Are you ready to go back? See Ned?"

Her gaze turns conspiratorial. "You noticed that, did you?"

I rub her back. "You deserve someone by your side too. You've been through hell and he's a good man. I approve."

She laughs as she smacks me on the arm. "I didn't know I needed your approval."

Lifting my chin in the air I indignantly say, "I *am* your queen now. Of course, you need my approval."

Chapter Fifty-Nine

Attina

When our feet touch back down on the blood-soaked battlefield a mass of people come running at us. Some are cheering, some are crying. Mother almost instantly changes back to her normal form and without thinking about it, my wings disappear. I really need to figure out how this whole transforming thing works.

Ned runs up to us. I notice the skin around his unburned eye is green and purple from an already forming bruise. He must have been hit hard. He picks my mother up, spinning her around.

Ava jumps off of Mylo, runs over and buries her head in my shoulder. She looks completely flawless, like she wasn't just on a battlefield seconds ago. Then, I hear a loud roar and see Cedar pushing past the rest of the Mori Noki circling us, until he's right by my side.

He rubs his massive head against my hip and simply says, "Mate."

When Ava releases me, I place my hand on Cedar's head and pat him. "You know people are going to start thinking mate is all you can say." I'm glad he's here though; if he's alive it means Allister is still alive.

I stand up on my tippy toes and scan behind the crowd, searching for Allister. Then from behind me, on the other side of the crowd, a sultry voice booms, "Move aside!"

The Fae in front of him part and bow as he strides over to me on Raven with his chin lifted, like a bloodied warrior home from the battlefield coming to claim his prize. He has a cut over his left eyebrow and the blood has dripped down into his face, but otherwise, he seems unscathed. Raven tries to walk to me like a regal stead, but by the time they're halfway to me I can almost feel the anxiety radiating off of her.

She trots over to where I stand and slams her face into my chest. I let out a grunt as the weight of her head slams into me, knocking the air out of my chest. Hands wrap around my hips and suddenly I'm being twisted around into Allister's awaiting arms. His rainstorm smell floods my senses as he plunges his face into my neck and takes a deep breath before he lifts me off of the ground and spins me around.

Everyone around us chants, "Queen Attina!"

From in the air I can see where Hazel and Talon perch side by side on a branch, and I feel like a weight has been lifted off my shoulders. I was worried about them since I left them unconscious in the tree. I also notice Mylo sneaking up behind Raven who appears to have a rare smile plastered across his muzzle.

Somehow we did it.

We defeated Henrik.

We saved Arealea.

But as Allister brings me back down I notice the Fae far off in the distance. Henrik's soldiers and citizens. I'm glad they made it out before the mountain crashed to the ground. Some search the grounds for their fallen companions; some simply sit on the ground with their head between their legs. Leta paces in the distance.

I need to do something about this.

I drag Allister down into a swift kiss before I stride over to Raven and mount her. I gaze out over my people, taking in the blood and dirt caking their faces. I call out, "Everyone, Henrik's soldiers included, listen to me now."

All of our people stop everything they're doing, but I'm surprised to find even Henrik's Fae stop and turn to me. I turn Raven around and she picks her way through dead bodies scattered on the ground so I'm smack dab in the middle of the battlefield.

When everyone has walked or limps their way over to me I gaze out over everyone around me. "You are all one people now, humans and Fae alike." I turn my gaze to the crumpled mountain to my side. "People of Shadow Mountain! Your home has been destroyed by my grandfather. You will always have a home with the Eastern Fae *or* you can stay here and rebuild your home. Humans!" I notice some people perk their heads up, and I direct my words toward them. "You will no longer be persecuted. You can leave Sanctuary and live your lives out under the sun. We will forever be one people."

Allister comes up and places his hand on my leg as Ned sidles up next to him. "Your Commander, Ned, will work with us to get everyone relocated. We won't let our people be without a home. We will send Fae soldiers out to kill off the rest of the Solis so humans never again have to be afraid."

When he's finished his thought I gesture to my mother. "If you need *anything* to relocate your family please let my mother, Titania, know." As I gaze down at her, her features soften, her chest swells and something akin to pride flashes in her eyes.

I bend forward and pat Raven on the side of the neck. "You ready to go home, girl?"

Mylo walks up beside us and rubs his face against hers. "More than ready, kid."

I lean over and wrap my hand under Allister's chin, pulling his face toward mine. When our lips touch electricity sparks between us, just like the first time we ever kissed, hopefully like all the times to come, for the rest of our lives.

Surprisingly, none of the Fae from Shadow Mountain decided to stay and rebuild, even the surviving soldiers. I wonder if there were just too many terrible memories in that place. Maybe a new home will be good for them. A fresh start.

Since the Fae from Shadow Mountain would be coming with us I sent my mother with Ned to help the humans set up new towns. The Mori Noki left from the battlefield to clear Arealea of the Solis scourge, when they returned to the Eastern Fae; I made them and Ned the heads of our war council. Ned dropped his title of Commander. He lives in the castle now, allowing the humans to settle down where they wished.

We looked for Kenda and James's bodies, but we couldn't find anyone under the crumbled wreckage of Shadow Mountain. After Henrik wrenched it apart, it was left as more of a hill than a mountain. Sometimes I still think of them, How Kenda sacrificed herself for her son's mate. She knew the pain of losing a mate and was willing to sacrifice her life to keep her son from feeling the devastation she felt for so many years.

But I think of James more than I care to admit. I gaze out on the trees around my castle and think of our days hunting in the trees around Daruk. When things were simpler, back when we were simply two best friends, out in the woods. Some days I miss him. Other days I remember how unhinged he could be.

But Father and Oak still get me the hardest. I miss the sound of their laughs, the way Father could just give me one look, and I'd know I'd messed up. The deep throaty chuckle floating to my ears when I did something silly and the calming tone of his voice when he read me to sleep at night. I miss the way Oak just got me.

Some days he understood me better than I did myself. He always knew just the right thing to do or say to cheer me up when I needed it. I know Raven misses them as much, if not more than I do. We're blessed to have each other. I don't know what I would do without that snarky and ornery mare. I'd be lost without her.

Nine months after the battle, I gave birth to a beautiful baby girl. She has Allister's black hair, but my aquamarine eyes. She is the most gorgeous, precious thing in all of Arealea. We named her Kenda, after Allister's mother because without her, none of us would be here today.

Today, Allister and I are having our mating ceremony. We decided we would take a page out of Henrik's book and pay homage to the old ways by performing the blood ritual Henrik was going to perform on James and me.

Allister wanted to just have it between us, but Kalven put his foot down. He advised we invite everyone from all of Arealea to watch the ceremony to bring Arealea's king and queen together as one forever.

At one point in our relationship, I worried about Allister outliving me since I'm half human. With this ceremony, I won't have to worry about that ever again. Allister immediately agreed, to him it was just another reason to show off his mate and our baby girl.

I, on the other hand, had to be coerced into it. I finally acquiesced, but on the condition we have a ceremony like our human ones. Kalven loved the idea. He said it was the perfect way to merge humans and Fae together.

I stand at the end of an aisle with Fae and humans commingling and crowded together on either side. I'm in a dress my mother made me. I found out my mother is truly talented with a thread and needle.

All the tunics we found in the tree Allister and I stayed at were made by her hand. She made me a dress with a tight bodice and flowing bottom. Lace is laid over the shimmery white fabric with roses in full bloom strewn throughout the lace. It's absolutely gorgeous and everything I ever fantasized about as a human girl growing up dreaming of her future wedding.

Ned has his arm laced through mine. Traditionally the father should walk the bride down the aisle, but with my father gone, I figured who better to be my father figure than the man who was by my side through it all when my father couldn't be. He gazes forward to my mother, now his wife, who has taken up a seat in the front row to watch her daughter and the man she raised bond themselves together for eternity.

I pull on his arm, grabbing his attention. "I never got a chance to tell you, I'm sorry about Demarco."

His bright green eyes pierce me with their sudden sadness, but in a split second he plasters a happy smile on his face. "Don't be. He was a good friend at one time, but he stopped being that person as soon as he became the Commander of Sanctuary. I had to choose between him, someone who wasn't inherently good anymore, or you." He leans in, and I can hear happiness coating his words as he says, "And I think I made the right choice."

I smile up at him, tears brimming my eyes. I told myself I wouldn't cry today, but who am I kidding? I'm a crybaby. I face back forward and concentrate on not falling on my face in front of all these people.

I gaze down the aisle to where Ava stands in a purple dress the same color as Allister's eyes with Kenda in her arms and Raven by her side. I still get anxiety when she's in anyone else's arms. I'm told this feeling will go away, but I still struggle with it daily. I don't think it will ever get easier for Raven though, who even now has her muzzle touching Kenda's chubby leg.

Next to her stands Kalven, who will hold the ceremony. Cedar stands with his head held high like the royalty he is, and next to him—

Next to him stands the most stunningly gorgeous man I've ever laid eyes on. He stands with his chin held high and his chest out in pride. His father's armor glistens in the sun and his onyx tunic underneath it hugs every one of his substantial muscles.

I chuckle as I watch him flex those muscles with his eyes locked on me; a show just for me. His angular jaw clenches as he breaks his gaze from mine just long enough to take in my gown. When his eyes meet back with mine, they're mischievous and sparkling. Then I hear, *I can't wait to rip that off of you later.*

Don't you dare! I squeak back.

We stroll down the aisle toward my family. Orange and red fall leaves sprinkle down on the wind from the trees around the castle. My eyes stay locked on Allister while all of our people, human and Fae from all of Arealea, stare and whisper around me. I can only make out a few words. Some say, "She's beautiful" or "So handsome." I try to quell the jealousy stirring in my stomach.

When we make it to the end of the aisle I turn and hug Ned. "Thank you for everything Ned." He nods and moves to sit with my mother, but I grab his arm and turn him back to me. "I mean it. I couldn't have done this without you, dad." He pulls back and rubs the back of his neck as tears fill his eyes. Then he drags me into a rib crushing hug and whispers to me, "You're the daughter I always prayed for." He quickly pulls away, wipes his eyes, and sits by my mother who wraps her arm over his shoulder and drags his head to her sparkly aquamarine dress, an homage to her mate.

I then turn to Ava and place a soft kiss on her cheek, "Thank you for being the best friend I could have ever asked for."

She bounces on her feet, making Kenda giggle, and cheerily smiles. She cocks her head to the side. "I figured you liked me when you asked me to hold your little one. You never let anyone hold her." Raven clears her throat next to her, and Ava amends, "Okay, anyone but Raven."

I giggle because it's true. Raven rarely leaves Kenda's side so if I need to leave the room while she's sleeping Raven will watch over her. In all fairness she's usually sleeping against Raven's side.

I place my head on Raven's and breathe in her scent. She's always smelled like home. My companion. My confidant. My trusty steed. I never would have gotten here today without her help. What do I even say to her? How can I convey how precious she is to me in just a few simple words? I open my eyes in shock when she simply says, "I know." Like she could read my mind or feel what I feel.

I rub her cheek, and then I turn around to my mate. His eyes drag down my frame, and I stand a little straighter at his hungry stare. I feel silly for being jealous earlier at the girls around us pining after him. Of course, they all want him. He's magnificent. But he's mine. His eyes are only for me. I know everyone can tell how thoroughly and completely this Fae loves me.

I reach out and lace my hand behind his neck and tug him in for a kiss. Kalven clucks disapprovingly at me, he told us not to kiss until the ceremony was done, but I don't care. I am queen, I will do as I wish.

When I step back in position, Kalven begins the ceremony. Ancient words are recited. I try to copy Kalven as best I can, but I don't know the language so it ends up being mostly mumbling on my part. Then Kalven pulls out the dagger Ned gave me back in Sanctuary. I stop, my eyes bulging, and turn to Ned and my mother, who both shrug. I turn back to Allister, but my mind races.

I ask Allister, *How did they find it? I lost my dagger when we defeated Henrik.* I hadn't noticed at the time, but when I put my dagger away, before I got my bow, it had fallen to the ground. We searched for it, but couldn't find it. I thought it was lost forever.

His eyes glint with mischief, *I've wanted to tell you! Remember when they went on their honeymoon?* I roll my eyes; of course, I remember. Mother helped me with Kenda a mere two weeks before she and Ned ran off on a honeymoon. I was *not* ready for them to leave. *They didn't go on a honeymoon; they went to find your dagger!*

Kalven clears his throat, interrupting our conversation. "Now, if the king and queen would pay attention to the ceremony and not whatever conversation they're secretly having, we could conclude this and head on over to the celebrations.

My cheeks heat until I feel burning all the way up to my ears. I mouth *sorry* to Kalven who just shakes his head, making Allister snicker.

In my head, I hear, *You look so beautiful when you're embarrassed.*

I hiss, *Shh. You're going to get us in trouble again!*

I hear his throaty chuckle in my head, then he says, *Kitten, we're king and queen now. We can do whatever we want.*

I turn to Kalven and pretend like I don't hear Allister. Kalven holds out his hand. I place mine in his before he drags my dagger deeply along my palm. I hiss at the skin splitting sensation. He grabs a wooden bowl from behind him and fills the bowl with the blood spilling from my hand. When he releases me, Ava hands me a cloth to staunch the bleeding.

He repeats with Allister.

The table behind him is full of mixed herbs, some dried, some fresh, and some boiled into a tea. He mixes these herbs with our blood and turns back to us, handing me the bowl.

I bring the bowl to my lips and take a swig of the metal tanged concoction. I fight a gag as I hand the bowl to Allister.

I taunt him, *It tastes so good. You'll love it.*

As Allister brings the bowl up to his lips I have to fight back a laugh. When he brings the bowl down I see the disgust written on his face, and I blow out a laugh. His eyes narrow at me as he hands the bowl back to Kalven.

Kalven wraps his hand around both of our writs and lifts them in the air. "The mating ceremony is complete! Your king and queen are now one! Meet for the first time, Allister and Attina Leon!"

Everyone around us cheers, but I'm confused. I don't feel any different.

That is until Kalven releases our wrists, and I touch Allister. In a flash, everything that he feels, everything that makes him who he is floods into me. When his purple eyes meet mine I'm flooded with the feeling of adoration, love, and need. I throw myself at him as the cheering around us ratchets up. His hands travel down my body, and I jump into his awaiting arms like I knew he would be there to catch me, like I could feel his body moving.

Our kiss deepens, and I moan against his lips. As his need grows so does mine until all I can feel is him. I whimper into his mind, *Take me somewhere, anywhere. I need you now.*

Without another word he turns with me in his arms toward his family's secret room. I dive my head down into his neck and begin trailing kisses down it. Behind us, I hear Kalven say to the crowd, "This is normal for such a ceremony. Now while they have their party let's have ours!"

More cheers erupt, but I barely hear them over the need I have to take this man and make him mine over and over. "Raven, watch Kenda."

She screeches, "Have fun."

I knew she would hear me even above all the shouting and cheering around us. But when Allister pulls back and his eyes lock on mine, I can almost see our future together. The years we will spend side by side. The love we will share and my heart about bursts from happiness.

And it's then that I know—

I am home.

Epilogue

Three years later

I lie on the ground, rubbing my necklace, under the tree which used to be my mother's hiding place. Above me Allister and Kenda climb the tree, her giggles flit down to me forcing a smile to grow on my face.

In the distance, Raven, Mylo, and Cedar sunbathe. They've become inseparable since Kenda's birth. I've never seen more protective nannies in my life. Talon and Hazel disappeared shortly after we took down Henrik, and I haven't seen them since. I'm not terribly surprised; it's in Hazel's nature to disappear, and Talon was never terribly friendly.

Like I promised the tree when we left for the Eastern Fae, we're visiting. We've been coming here monthly as a little family getaway from the trials of ruling an entire nation. Allister and

I decided after this trip we would begin bringing in trusted advisors, some Fae, some human, to help us run Arealea.

It's too much for only a handful of people, and with Kenda growing; Allister and I want to begin her training. She might be a princess, but I still want her to learn how to defend herself. If I start from an early age, it will become second nature to her. I hope she will never have to use the skills we'll instill in her, but I'd rather her not need them than not have them.

That night, Kenda sleeps between Allister and me in the tree house. Allister whispers, "You can't tell me I snore as loud as she does."

I scoff. "You know she had to get it from somewhere and it definitely wasn't me." He reaches his hand over Kenda and waits for me to place mine in his.

When I do, he says, "There's nowhere in all of Arealea I'd rather be than in this tree house, in this bed. You two are my world. I want you to know that through the good times and the bad, I will always cherish you my love."

I squeeze his hand as my eyes tear up. I have to swallow past the knot in my throat. "Both of you are everything I never knew I needed."

Then a flash of happiness hits my brain, but it doesn't feel the same way Allister's happiness feels. There's something different about it, something I can't put my finger on. I gaze down at Kenda.

Since our mating ceremony, Allister's and my powers have slowly merged. Now I can hear everyone's thoughts around me. It's become a challenge to deal with the barrage of constant noise, but with Allister and Ned by my side, I've been able to control the ability. Allister on the other hand *still* can't seem to conquer fire.

I sit up as slowly as I can and gaze into Kenda's face, but she's sleeping. Then, all of a sudden, my stomach grumbles, and I burp up a fireball.

Allister's eyes widen before they drift down to my stomach. He dives over Kenda, his lips crashing on mine.

Kenda sits up and rubs her eye. "Why did you do that daddy?" Her little voice is heavy with sleep.

Allister's face is now in mine. His hands cradle either side of my face, and his voice has a hint of pride in it. "Because your mommy has made me the happiest man in the world."

She shrugs and turns on her side. "Oh, okay." She's grown accustomed to how Allister just blurts out how much he loves us. It's second nature to her now.

Allister's eyes stay on mine as he elaborates. "You're going to be a big sister."

She immediately sits up and hurriedly asks, "Really?"

He nods while she jumps up and starts bouncing on the bed, screaming in joy. Allister tackles me in a fit of happy laughter.

I never thought my life would turn out the way it did. I was happy simply being a human, but now I couldn't imagine my life any other way.

Other books by Caitlin Denman

She Awakens series:

She Awakens

She Rises

She Conquers

She Reigns

About the Author

Caitlin lives and grew up in Southern California with her family and her three horses, three dogs, and a cat. She graduated from Cal Poly Pomona with a bachelor's in agribusiness. Besides writing, she loves training and competing on horses. She has competed in barrel racing, breakaway roping, team roping, and mounted shooting. She has owned and ridden horses since she was twelve-years-old.

Caitlin would love to connect with each and every person who loves her books. You can find her on social media or email her at:

- Facebook: https://www.facebook.com/groups/caitlin-srideordie
- Instagram:https://www.instagram.com/caitlindenman-books
- caitlindenmanbooks@gmail.com

Acknowledgments

First off I would like to thank my fans. Without your support I couldn't keep doing what I love.

Next, I would like to thank my parents. They've been through this entire journey with me, through the tears and meltdowns, to a finished series. They are my biggest fans and I can't tell you enough how much I appreciate and love you.

Thank you Nana and Barby. I don't know what I would have done without your editing skills. You guys caught so many silly mistakes and I appreciate all your help. You both pushed me to be a reader which is why I'm an author today. I love you guys so much.

Thank you Paul Smith for being my Allister and my first, and most brutal, BETA reader. Without you Allister would have never come to life and this series wouldn't have been finished. You pushed me to finish these books even when I felt like I'd never find the end. You read every single word I wrote and, without remorse, edited them. You made sure I took breaks and didn't get too overwhelmed. I love you.

Thank you Belle Manuel for editing this monster of a book and for being such a great friend. I will forever appreciate how much insight you've given me through this journey and our live author chats have really expanded my horizons. And for letting me bounce ideas off of you and talking me off the ledge a time or two.

Thank you to my sissy, Laura Trujillo, for being my PA and keeping me in line. I would be lost without you. You're there for me when I need you and I don't know what I'd do without you.

Finally, thank you to every single person who helped bring this book to life!